LAST WOLF at EAGLE WELL

LAST WOLF

at
EAGLE WELL

Robert C. Mowry

New York

LAST WOLF at EAGLE WELL

© 2017 Robert C. Mowry.

This is a work of fiction. Names, characters, businesses, places, events, and incidents are either the products of the author's imagination or used in a fictitious manner. Any resemblance to actual persons, living or dead, or actual events is purely coincidental.

Published in New York, New York, by Morgan James Publishing. Morgan James and The Entrepreneurial Publisher are trademarks of Morgan James, LLC. www.MorganJamesPublishing.com

The Morgan James Speakers Group can bring authors to your live event. For more information or to book an event visit The Morgan James Speakers Group at www.TheMorganJamesSpeakersGroup.com.

Shelfie

A **free** eBook edition is available with the purchase of this print book.

CLEARLY PRINT YOUR NAME ABOVE IN UPPER CASE

Instructions to claim your free eBook edition:
1. Download the Shelfie app for Android or iOS
2. Write your name in **UPPER CASE** above
3. Use the Shelfie app to submit a photo
4. Download your eBook to any device

ISBN 978-1-63047-943-5 paperback
ISBN 978-1-63047-944-2 eBook
Library of Congress Control Number:
2016900415

Cover Design by:
Rachel Lopez
www.r2cdesign.com

Interior Design by:
Bonnie Bushman
The Whole Caboodle Graphic Design

In an effort to support local communities and raise awareness and funds, Morgan James Publishing donates a percentage of all book sales for the life of each book to Habitat for Humanity Peninsula and Greater Williamsburg.

Get involved today, visit
www.MorganJamesBuilds.com

Habitat for Humanity®
Peninsula and
Greater Williamsburg
Building Partner

≫— CHAPTER 1 —≪

Almost dark enough... Another ten minutes and it'll be too dark to see the smoke, yet not dark enough to see the flames from afar... Of course, who's to see them anyway?

The tow trailer's been switched from the truck to the ATV... Gas can's on the trailer... Rifle's in the scabbard... Gloves... Toss those gloves under the truck's fuel tank... Already hid that ladder and all the other stuff back at the well. Hope no one knew he had those things with him... With luck, this site won't be found until the coyotes, buzzards, and wolves have their way with whatever's left of the body... Got to get out of here without being seen... Close call getting in here... Don't want that again... Got all the dried grass and brush pulled away... Surely don't want to start a forest fire...

Well, here goes. The match scratched across the grit and flashed to life. Seconds later it was tossed to the ground, on top of the trail of gasoline leading to the government pickup truck. Whoosh! The gasoline-soaked truck was instantly engulfed in flames. In mere minutes, the flash of flames subsided substantially, without setting any of the surrounding grass or brush on fire.

That's it… This will burn down now without spreading.

The starter on the ATV whirred, and the engine came to life. With the throttle twisted open and its wheels spitting sand, the ATV—trailer in tow—sped out the rarely-used, remote two-track road.

Rusty Redtail's boot heels tapped on the saltillo tile as he walked across the second-floor hallway. He hesitated just outside the office door. He'd been on the job for nearly six months now, and it seemed he'd done nothing important so far to earn the respect of his boss, or even be noticed. Graduating near the top of his class with both law and criminal justice degrees from UNM last year, he'd fulfilled one of his longtime dreams when he was hired on at the Albuquerque FBI office. However, he now felt his hiring wasn't so much for any of his knowledge, skills, or intellect, but for diversity reasons. Putting a Native American on the staff made his boss look good, insightful, and politically correct.

Rusty then stepped in front of the open doorway. As he reached up to knock, Special Agent Harland Carter looked up from his computer.

"Come in, Redtail. Here, sit down," he said, motioning to a row of chairs across the front of his desk. "I'm giving you an opportunity, Redtail. Yes sir, this could be a feather in your cap. Ahh… hope that didn't offend you."

Rusty gave no response as he sat in the first chair in the row.

"I'm putting you in charge of this murder case," Special Agent Carter said, nodding to an open file on his desk.

"Murder case? In charge?" Rusty asked, leaning slightly forward. "How is that federal?"

"Yeah, it's ours. It's a… Well, you're the natural one to do it. Yes sir, it's got your name all over it. BLM Ranger found burned to a crisp. Shot first, so it seems. Down near some forsaken crossroads called Datil

Well, believe it or not. San Agustin County it says here. Near Mag…
Magdalena? That out near your old reservation?"

"Only about three or four hours away," Rusty said. "Closer to
here, really."

"Oh well, lots going on in this, what they call a city here, this
forsaken Albuquerque thing, and, well, figure there can't be but a
handful of people out there in those mountains who could have done
this crime. Just go out there and solve this," Special Agent Carter said.
"See Liz before you go. Have her find you a room out there—unless
you want to take a tent, if that's more your style. Ahh… just kidding.
Whatever, just don't spend a lot of money, with the way things are now,
you know. Of course, I don't know what you'd spend much money on
out in that desolate land.

"You're to meet up with the BLM's own guy on this out at the
local sheriff's office in that Magdalena place. Nine in the morning,"
Agent Carter continued. "The dead ranger's truck is still out there,
somewhere. Process the area. Have the truck sent in here. We'll go over
what's left of it. Body, what little there was left of it, is already at some
funeral home in Socorro. We've got some sort of an autopsy and all of
that covered there. All that stuff's in this file here," he said, handing
Rusty a folder. "You're in charge of this. Don't let that cactus cop or
hick sheriff waste your time. Use them for what you can, but always
remember, you're in charge.

"Keep me informed," Agent Carter said after a few seconds of
silence. "Surely cell phones work out there, somewhere. Any questions?"

"A vehicle. I'll need one of the SUVs," Rusty said.

"Guess so. Bring it back clean, undamaged. Remember, those
are mostly for looks. No four-wheel drive. They're a hefty price tag,
though. Don't go hitting some moose, or whatever's out there, with it.
Just get this done, Redtail. Solving this quickly would look good for
you—me too."

Rusty Redtail stood alongside BLM Ranger Chub Murry and San Agustin County Sheriff Wesley Cutter as they surveyed the burned-out truck carcass and the scene around it.

"What all's been done since you found this?" Rusty asked.

"Just what we had to," Chub said. "Got the body out, what there was left of it, you know. What hadn't burned, coyotes or wolves or some critter took care of most else but the bones. Ain't right for any man to be treated like this, even if he was dead first—especially Jimmy. We were nearly like family. Worked together a long time."

"Couldn't get an ambulance in here," Sheriff Cutter said. "Had to haul him out on the back of one of those utility ATVs. Put all we could find in a body bag, so we did."

"Shot in the head, the file says. That happen here?" Rusty asked.

"Ahh—assume so," Sheriff Cutter said. "Guess that's your job to find out. I know how you federal boys are, but I've got some ideas, if you want to stoop so low as to ask some lowly local sheriff his opinion."

"You know this area—the people. What do you think?" Rusty asked Sheriff Cutter.

"Got two families hereabouts who've been feudin' ever since the early cattle drive days. All kinds of old rumors about things they did to each other and anyone else who got in their way. Cattle rustling, fence cutting, even worse. Since I've been here, nearly twenty years now, there's been dogs killed, cattle missing, flat tires, and so on. Each always blames the other. Ain't had any real trouble with any of the young Calderone kids, but that Duke Atwood is one wild hombre, for sure. Had him locked up again last weekend. Bar fight. Broke some tourist's arm."

"An Atwood in a bar fight?" Chub said. "Thought that whole clan was a bunch of strict Mormons. What's Duke doing in a bar?"

"You know how it is, sometimes," Sheriff Cutter continued. "None of that holy teaching seemed to catch with Duke. Few years back, Duke did six months up in the state pen in Los Lunas for stealing some fella's pickup truck and stripping the fancy wheels, tires, and some other stuff off it. All that said, though, I'd still put my money on the Calderones being behind this. More their style."

"Never had any trouble with the Calderones, Sheriff," Chub said. "I was a part of the investigation into the Atwood's guide service and those illegal hunts they supposedly set up a few years back. That was all inside stuff, though. Some family members and church leaders from up in Utah stretched the law some, well, quite a bit, I'd say."

"Yeah, I'd say killin' comes easy for any of them," Sheriff Cutter replied.

"Killing an elk without a proper license on one's own ranch is a lot different than killing a BLM Ranger," Chub said. "Both the Calderones and Atwoods pay their grazing fees like clockwork. Never heard either one squabble about anything except that the other always had the best grass or better wells or something like that. Never knew either one to have a spat with anyone else, just with each other."

"I've read some old stuff around the office," the sheriff said. "Never any convictions, but stories go way back. Back to when old Fernando Calderone showed up here from Old Mexico with about fifty head of mixed-breed cattle all with a road-brand burned in with a running iron. Story was that there was blood spilled by his guns down yonder, and he picked here to hide out from the Mexican federales. He did have a good-sized poke of money with him, though. Never said where it came from, that I can tell."

"Any strangers around here lately?" Rusty asked.

"Always strangers," Sheriff Cutter answered. "This is kind of a back way from northern New Mexico and Texas over to Phoenix and around there. A lot of people who don't want to run with all those trucks and the like on the interstates cut through here. Those White Mountains over in Arizona draw thousands of vacationers each year. Hunters in the fall too.

Campers all summer. You say you grew up over around Cloudcroft, you know lots of people want to get up to seven or eight thousand feet and cool off when the valley temperatures are triple digits. As a rule, most folks passing through here aren't looking for trouble—usually trying to find peace and relaxation."

Rusty walked over to the truck. He looked inside. The cloth and plastic of the interior were burned or melted away, and only rusted, charred metal remained. Rusty studied things in silence for several minutes.

"He wasn't shot here," he then said. "Not in his truck anyway."

"Now how in the world can you look at this burned skeleton of a truck and determine that?" the sheriff asked. "You have a vision or something?"

"Ranger Hanson was shot in the head, right? Went clear through. In the left side and out the right. If he was in his truck with the windows down, the glass wouldn't be all over the inside floor. If it broke in the fire, it would be inside the doors. If he had the windows up, the driver's side would be shattered and be inside, as it is. However, the bullet would have gone out through the passenger's side and blown the glass outside. There's a full window's worth of glass inside over there too. I'd say someone smashed both windows in from the outside with a rock or hammer or something like that. No, Jimmy Hanson wasn't sitting in his truck, and most likely nowhere near here, when he was killed.

"Give me half an hour to take pictures and make some notes," Rusty continued. "Then we can get this thing out of here. Hard to get a wrecker in, a big one anyway. Might have to use a chain or tow strap."

"That's one of the odd things," Chub said. "When Jimmy left the office the other day, he had an extension ladder up over the headache rack. Curious, I walked over to his truck and looked into the bed. He had a length of chain, twenty-five feet at least, and a shovel and pry bar in there. I didn't think too much about it. Jimmy was a real history nut. He was always chasing after some old lost treasure or the like.

"The thing is, though," Chub continued, "when I found his truck, none of those things were with it."

"Any sign of his wallet, a briefcase, or computer?" Rusty asked.

"He never carried a briefcase," Chub said. "Kept his papers in a manila folder. No sign of that, but the fire surely burned it up. Couldn't find any sign of a wallet. Things were such a mess, though. His laptop melted down to a glob of crisp plastic. Who would want to steal a ladder and other work tools and leave a laptop?"

"Wasn't a robbery," Rusty said. "A robber would take what he wanted and run. Whoever did this took the time to move this truck for who knows how many miles, and with great effort. Must have been a second person, or at least a towed vehicle or something. This is a lot more than a robbery. Too much planning and way too much cover-up."

"I've seen enough," Sheriff Cutter said. "High Plains Garage has a winch truck on a one-ton four-by-four. I'll have Hector get this out of here."

"Get it out to the paved road, then on a flatbed and up to our lab in Albuquerque, Sheriff," Rusty said. "Tell this Hector guy I'll be by to pay the bill in a few days. Where's his shop?"

"High Plains Garage, Hector Gonzalez. Off South Second Street in Magdalena. You can't miss it," Sheriff Cutter replied.

"All right, Sheriff. I'll probably see you tomorrow," Rusty said. "Maybe you can take me out to meet these Calderones and Atwoods you talked about. Any other possible suspects you think of too. You know the locals will talk to you a whole lot more than to a stranger like me. I'd appreciate your help."

"Need me anymore, Agent Redtail?" Chub asked.

"Rusty. Call me Rusty. Yeah, I want to see Hanson's widow. You know her, right?"

"Sure," Chub said. "We were all friends."

"This has to be tough on her. A five-year-old son, the file says. Still, I need to see her as soon as possible. Can't rule out that she might be in danger. Don't push her, but see when you can set up a meeting. If she'd be more comfortable, you're welcome to join me. That's probably best, really."

"I'll uh… I'll go stop by when I get back to Socorro," Chub said.

"I'm staying at the Trails End Lodge in Magdalena. Room 202," Rusty said. "Here's my card. Let me know when we can meet with Sally Hanson. As I said, I'll be here half an hour or so, then go back to the hotel. Call me anytime. I don't have to tell you how limited the phone service is out here, so leave a message."

"Yeah, I'll go see Sally, little Jimmy too," Chub said. "She'll want to get to the bottom of this. She'll help you, I'm sure."

"OK, Chief," Sheriff Cutter said to Rusty. "I'm out of here. See you around."

Minutes later, alone at the scene of the burned truck, Rusty sat on a boulder and pondered what lay ahead of him. Why the fire? It didn't totally destroy the body—the arsonist had to know that would be so. He hadn't seen the body yet, wasn't sure he wanted to, but it was easily identifiable—had been so already by local dental records. The truck was easily identifiable as a federal government vehicle. Whoever did this surely knew this would bring a major investigation. There had to be something mighty important to do this, and do it up so drastically.

This obviously wasn't the original crime scene. Maybe the perpetrator wanted to point this toward someone else rather than just hide the truck. It was hard to pinpoint the exact time of Jimmy's death. He'd been missing five days before the truck was found. It had rained hard twice during that time, destroying any other tracks and markings around the scene.

He'd probably been killed sometime the day he first went missing. But what if he wasn't? What if he'd been held to get information before being killed? What was he up to anyway? Was he acting alone? Was this job related or personal? Was everything totally legal, or was Ranger Hanson into something shady? From what little Rusty had in the file about Jimmy Hanson, he appeared to be an exemplary employee and good family man. However, things like gold and old treasure were known to derail many good men.

Rusty thought about the two families Sheriff Cutter brought up as probable suspects. They seemed to confine any hostilities to each other. Even young Duke Atwood's antics didn't indicate cold-blooded murder. If the Calderone clan fled Mexico, that was a hundred twenty years ago, four generations at least. Still, the local sheriff wasn't to be ignored. Sometimes gut feelings had warrant. If Ranger Hanson had gotten in the middle of something between these two families…

Rusty took pictures until his battery ran down, then he walked to his Suburban and slowly drove out of the canyon on the seldom-used old ranch road. Why here? Why Ranger Hanson? Where was his ladder and other things? Out here on a remote ranch, using a shovel, pry bar, even a length of chain would be common. But a ladder?

Maybe Sally Hanson would have some answers. That wasn't going to be an easy interview. He'd never done anything like that before.

Three hours later, driving into the small town of Magdalena and pulling into his hotel parking lot, Rusty's mind was still rolling around these questions, along with many others—with no answers.

A short time later, he sat in the café attached to the Trails End Lodge. After he'd ordered his dinner, and, as he sat sipping iced tea and reading the day's Albuquerque paper, the hotel and café owner came over to his table.

"Señor, I'm told you are here to investigate this thing with Ranger Hanson. FBI, I am told. I am pleased you are here. Manny Rodriguez," he said, extending his hand. "My wife and I own this place. Been in my family since Mr. Frederick Wolf left town."

"I'm glad you have this here. Guess I'll be making this my home for a while. I'm Rusty Redtail. Yeah, I'm with the FBI. You knew Jimmy Hanson, did you?"

"Oh sure. He was often in here," Manny said. "We had many long talks. Things of the old days. Things my father and grandfather talked about. He was very interested in tales of events of the past."

"Anything special lately?" Rusty asked.

"He told me last week, the last time he was in here, he said he was onto something. Said he'd soon have a surprise to tell me about."

"Before that, the last month or so, was he talking or asking about anything special?" asked Rusty.

"Well, he was always interested in that old 1897 robbery and murder. Many have been taken in over that. Jimmy, he was very infatuated, I think the word would be, with the life of old Señor Maxwell Wolf."

"Maxwell Wolf?"

"Sí. Señor Wolf, he owned much of this town back then, the end of the 1800s. In fact, he built the hotel, this whole block of buildings here too. This here, where we sit now, this was the bank. Next door was the saloon, next to that was the mercantile."

"This was the bank? That was back in the cattle drive days, right?" Rusty asked.

"Sí, Magdalena, she was the biggest cattle shipping point in all of the country. Maxwell Wolf, he owned the bank, the hotel, the mercantile, the cattle holding pens. He had dealings with the railroad too. He had his hand in everything that happened here—most of the business things anyway. Very wealthy, most powerful man, so was Maxwell Wolf."

"Any family left around here?"

"No. His son, Frederick, he left in 1955. That is when my father purchased all of this. Now it is mine—mine and my missus. Strange thing that was. I was a wee child. There was lots of talk. Mr. Wolf, he said he planned to go to Arizona. No one ever saw him again. Some say…"

Manny stopped talking and seemed to be in deep thought. After a moment, Rusty asked him a question. "Something suspicious about his leaving?"

"Seemed to be so—maybe. That was right after the sheriff, Señor Bucky Tuttle, also disappeared. The sheriff, he was always chasing after the Eagle Well, so the old folks said. Those gold coins from that '97 thing too. All of that, he sought after.

"The sheriff, he and Fredrick Wolf were friends, somewhat," Manny continued. "They hunted and such together. Some say the sheriff did that to gain information from Frederick. The way they both disappeared—it wasn't natural. I was a wee child, but heard all the stories told by many. That was the talk for much time after that. Every day did someone talk about what happened to the sheriff and did Frederick Wolf have any part in any of it. Some thought they took the money and ran off together, that the sheriff was alive and well—maybe down in Mexico."

"This '97 thing you mentioned, can you tell me what that is?" Rusty asked.

Manny looked around the café. It was filling up. "That, señor, will take some time. I see we are getting busy now, and I must help in the kitchen. If you come back when we are slow, some afternoon, perhaps, I will tell you all I know and have heard—anything that might help in any way catch who did this awful thing to Jimmy."

"I'm sure I'll be here often, for a while," Rusty said. "Maybe tomorrow. I might have to go down to Socorro in the morning, but maybe in the afternoon."

Manny nodded as he rose. "Señor Rusty, watch your back. Only that Jimmy had watched his more. I fear there is more trouble to come."

⤜— CHAPTER 2 —⤛

Agent Rusty Redtail went to his room, turned on the news, then pulled off his boots and stretched out on the bed. Minutes later, his cell phone rang.

"Rusty? It's Chub. Sally Hanson said she'd like to see us about nine in the morning. Is that OK?"

"That's good. I'll see you a little before that. Hey, thanks for setting this up."

"Sure. See you then."

"Nice to meet you, Agent Redtail," Sally said, extending her hand to him when Chub introduced them. "Please, come sit down." She led the way into the family room and sat in a chair that had two others opposite it where Rusty and Chub then sat.

"Please call me Rusty. I'm sorry we have to meet under these circumstances. I'll do all I can to solve this and, well, you might be able to help. I'm not here to pry or anything like that."

"Oh, I know that," Sally said. "Of course I want to help, any way I can."

"You have someone to be with you?" Rusty asked. "You should have someone here with you."

"I have family coming in from Texas. Should be here by noon," Sally said. "That will help some. Please, find who did this. I'm not a vindictive person, but, for my son…"

Rusty nodded slowly. He took a deep breath. "Anything you can think of that might point me in the right direction?" he asked. "Anything strange around here? Strangers at the house or following you or like that?"

Sally slowly shook her head. "Jimmy never said anything about being threatened or being in any danger. In fact, lately he seemed extra excited. He was always chasing after some old thing and said several times lately he was getting close to something big. He, like I said, was excited."

"And you haven't noticed anything unusual around here?" Rusty asked.

"No," Sally said. "Surely you don't think… Am I in danger?"

"I don't know," Rusty said. "I hope not. Be extra careful, though. I don't want to alarm you. You have enough on your mind now, but please be extra careful until we get this solved."

"Yes, of course," Sally said, a worried look replacing her sad one.

"Jimmy kept a journal, I'm told," Rusty said.

"Yes. Every night he wrote in it. He enjoyed that."

"Anything written in there that's unusual, something different?" Rusty asked.

"I haven't looked at it—I never did."

"Could we look now?"

"Actually, Agent Redtail—Rusty, I'll lend that to you if you promise to return it. I want to someday pass it, all of those things really, on to our son, when he's old enough to appreciate such things. See, Jimmy also has several folders full of notes and outlines. He wanted to someday write a book about Maxwell Wolf. Oh… there was something. About a week ago, Jimmy did say that he was changing his opinion of Mr. Wolf—the whole Wolf family, really. I don't know what he meant. Maxwell Wolf always seemed to be somewhat of a hero to him. Maybe he wrote something down."

Sally rose and went into another room, then returned several moments later with a file box. "Here's the last two journals. The book notes too, and I don't know what some of these folders contain. This should be everything for the last several years."

"I'll get this back to you after I get through it. May I copy anything that might be of interest?" Rusty asked.

"Oh sure. Whatever you need," Sally said. "If I think of anything after my mind clears some, I'll let you or Chub know."

The three moved toward the door. As Rusty was about three steps from reaching it, he felt something tug at his pant leg. He stopped and looked down at a little boy who had a tight grip on it.

"Mister. Hey, mister. You gonna find who hurt my daddy?"

"Ah… I'm surely going to try. You must be Jimmy, right?" Rusty knelt down to be face to face with the little boy. "I'm going to do everything I can to catch this bad guy."

"Then can my daddy come back home? Mommy needs him real bad."

Rusty slowly straightened up and stared down at the child. Sally stepped over and took Jimmy's hand. "Come now," she said. "Mr. Rusty has to get started looking."

Rusty looked at Sally. He nodded slightly. "I'll do all I can. I promise you. Everything I can."

≫———≪

Rusty got back to his room shortly before noon. He took in the box of Jimmy's journals and other notes. He picked up the current journal, then walked over to the café and sat at a window table.

Manny came out of the kitchen and over to him. "Señor Rusty, you talk to Sally Hanson?"

"Yeah," Rusty said. "I've got Jimmy's journals and a bunch of notes he had. Guess he planned to write a book about Maxwell Wolf and other history around here."

"We talked many times," Manny said. "The preacher man, Buddy Bell, he and Jimmy, they talk much too. Señor Buddy, he knows mucho history. Sí, even more than me, I think."

"Buddy Bell? Where do I find him?" asked Rusty.

"Be in here soon. Every day—most anyway—he is here for lunch. There, see, that is him now," Manny said, looking out a window into the parking lot. "I will introduce you."

A graying and balding man with a large, droopy mustache came through the door. Manny motioned for him to come to the table where he stood talking to Rusty. "Come, meet Agent Rusty Redtail, the FBI man working on the Jimmy Hanson case."

"Heard you were in town. I'm Buddy Bell," the man said, extending his hand. "Preacher over at that little community church up the hill. Just call me Buddy. I don't cotton to any of those religious titles."

"Call me Rusty. Manny here tells me you and Jimmy were both local history buffs."

"There's so much history around here. The good, bad, and ugly," Buddy said. "Whatever you're looking for, it happened here."

"Sit down, please," Rusty said, motioning to a chair across the table. Buddy pulled back the chair, started to sit, then pulled it back some more to be able to get his rather large belly behind the table.

"Oh, the kitchen," Manny said, looking that way. "I must go help Rosanna. Later then." He turned to walk away.

"The special, Manny," Buddy said. "Iced tea."

"Make that two," Rusty said.

"Sí, two specials, two teas," Manny said as he rapidly walked to the kitchen.

"So, you and Jimmy talked a lot about the history here," Rusty said. "He seemed to be very interested in Maxwell Wolf and something that happened back around the turn of the last century."

"Yeah. The murder of Franz Frick," Buddy said. "The cattle buyer from Chicago. The whereabouts of all his money too."

"I have Jimmy's journals, his book notes also. Anything I should look for?" Rusty asked. "You know what could have gotten him crossways with anyone out here?"

"I've racked my brain," Buddy said. "Can't think of a thing. Sometimes we'd go out on Saturdays trying to track down some old thing that had gotten abandoned and forgotten."

"Anything recently?" asked Rusty.

"Well, yeah. The old Eagle Well, maybe. We thought we found it a while back. It's strange, but what we found looked as if someone tried to make things look as if it was an old abandoned well. But there was no signs of an actual hole where there should have been one. We pulled back the big rocks and that old corrugated metal that looked as if it covered an abandoned hole. But there was no hole there. Never had been. It was all staged."

"Any chance it somehow filled in?" asked Rusty.

"Layers of rocks and such. No, there'd never been a hole dug there," Buddy said. "Seems someone set all that up to look like that was where the phantom Eagle Well was located."

"Any idea why?"

"Not really. It was kinda spooky," Buddy said.

"When do you think that was set up?"

"Long time ago. The old wooden windmill tower laying there was mostly rotted away. Must have been laying there for fifty years, maybe even a hundred or more. You know how long stuff lasts out here in this dry climate."

"Anybody else know about this?" Rusty asked.

"Sheriff Cutter. Wesley's a good friend. He and Dee are members of my church. Church wouldn't survive without their generous support."

"Did he go out there with you to that site?"

"Yeah. When we told him about it, he wanted to go see it. I don't think I told anyone else. Don't know about Jimmy or Wesley, who they may have told."

"What's the story on this Eagle Well anyway?" Rusty asked.

"Story? Many stories," Buddy answered. "Kind of local lore or whatever. Supposed to be a well out there that old Maxwell Wolf used to hide money in. Through the years the stories have grown, you know how that happens. Old stories go that Maxwell used that well as his private bank—an underground vault, I guess."

"Was it supposed to be a real well? A water-producing well?" Rusty asked.

"I think it was believed to have produced water at one time," Buddy said. "It may have just been during those real wet years back in the early 1890s. A lot of shallow wells were dug then that soon went dry when the climate changed back to its normal dry."

"So, no one but this Maxwell Wolf knew where this Eagle Well was?" Rusty said. "Not even back in the day?"

"I'm not sure it really exists. Lonny Calderone leases most of the old Wolf land now. The Cutters own the deeded land. That's Wesley and Dee's ranch now. Both claim there's no well out there that they don't know about. Of course, it might be very well hidden. Then too, if no one's been around it for a hundred years, one could walk right by it and not know it was there. That's big country. Lots of canyons and rock outcrops. Lonny didn't know about the fake well site we found on his ranch, and there's even that old tower laying there. Oh yeah, we did talk to him about that. I forgot about that."

"Where'd the name come from?" Rusty asked.

"Again, lots of stories," Buddy said. "Some say there was a nest of eagles in the windmill tower every year. That wasn't all that uncommon. Others—well, some say it was because it hid gold eagles—coins. Some even say they were part of the missing hundred thousand dollars of gold eagle coins stolen by whoever murdered Franz Frick."

"A hundred thousand dollars? Back in 1897?" Rusty said. "That was never found?"

"All newly minted coins. They never showed up," Buddy said. "Well, some believe Sheriff Bucky Tuttle found them and then took off back in '55."

"So, Sheriff Tuttle's disappearance might have been tied to this 1897 deal?" Rusty asked.

"Draw your own conclusion. Everyone else has."

"What happened to Maxwell Wolf?"

"Closed the bank in the '29 crash," Buddy answered. "Wasn't a lot of cattle business left here by then. Nothing much was selling anyway. He died suddenly about six months later. His wife and young son, Frederick, took over what was still in operation—the hotel, saloon, and such."

"I'm told there's none of the Wolf family left around here," Rusty said.

"None living anywhere that anyone around here knows of. Frederick was the last, well, guess he had a little daughter. He up and sold everything real quick like right after the sheriff went missing. Went to Arizona, he told everyone. No one ever heard from him again. His wife had family here, and even they never heard from her again—so they always said."

"Any of her family left?" asked Rusty.

"No. All died or moved away. Wouldn't know where to find any of them. I do think Frederick's wife's mother was the last to leave, and she went to somewhere in Texas, if my memory serves me right."

Neither man said anything as their food was served. After eating about half his burrito, Rusty stopped and asked a question. "When did you and Jimmy discover this well thing?"

"Two months ago—mid-July."

Rusty ate some more of his food, then stopped and spoke again. "The last day Jimmy was seen, Chub saw an extension ladder on top of his truck and a chain, some tools, and other things in the truck bed. Any idea what he was doing with that?"

"No," Buddy said, shaking his head. "He did say he might soon have a surprise for me. Of course, he'd told me that several times before. Jimmy was an extremely optimistic guy. I always figured it was a good thing he had that steady government paycheck to support his rainbow-chasing hobbies."

"You were with Jimmy when you fellas discovered that fake well, as you call it," Rusty said. "Any reason you weren't with him last week?"

"Thought about that. Even asked him if I could join him."

"What did he say?"

"He got a serious look, then said that it was best he did this alone. He said something about maybe some danger, and that he needed to do this during the week, like it was official business. That didn't make any sense then—still doesn't."

Rusty and Buddy finished eating in silence. Manny came out with a pitcher of tea and refilled their glasses.

"Señor Rusty, where do you begin?" Manny asked.

"Jimmy's journals and notes. I'll start in early July and come forward. Maybe he made notes of something that will help. He didn't tell Sally anything, though she indicated they didn't talk much about all his history-chasing adventures."

"Sally is sort of a town girl," Manny said. "She'd come out here sometimes, but you could tell she'd rather be in Albuquerque shopping than looking at elk and turkeys."

"When can you get away and go with me out to where that well thing is?" Rusty asked Buddy.

"Go out there? Out to that fake well? Oh... I'm awfully busy. Meetings, helping the old people, you know. I'll have to let you know on that."

"OK, sure," Rusty said. "Maybe Sheriff Cutter will want to go with me."

"That would be good," Buddy said, "though he's awfully busy with his bulls, you know."

"Bulls?" Rusty replied.

"Oh yeah," Buddy said. "He raises some of the best rodeo bulls in these parts. He's the top bull breeder in New Mexico, really. That's mostly a Texas thing I think."

"I'll see if he wants to take me out there," Rusty said. "Bulls or no bulls, he is the sheriff here."

"Yeah," Buddy said. "I'd like to go but ... Oh well, to tell you the truth, I'm not really wanting to go out in the wilderness until this killer is found. I shouldn't be fearful, but I'll admit it, I am."

"I understand," Rusty said.

"Well, I have to get back to the church," Buddy said. "Always something to do."

"Sure. I want to get into all this stuff of Jimmy's," Rusty said. "Might see you here tomorrow then?"

"Like I said, most every day."

Both men rose to leave. When they neared the register, Sheriff Cutter walked in the door.

"Just talking about you, Wesley," Buddy said. "Agent Redtail here wants to go out to that fake well thing we took you to. Thought you'd want to take him."

"Nothing there," the sheriff said. "Someone's joke. They knew for years people would try to make something of it. Laughing in their grave every time someone finds it and thinks they've found that phony Eagle Well. You want to go—I'll take you, when I have time. Figured you'd go up on a mountain and do some dance around a bonfire, beat on a drum, and conjure up some spirit that would tell you what happened to Jimmy. You being of that breed."

Rusty didn't respond. Buddy cut in. "Ah, Wesley. That wasn't necessary. This isn't the time for glib words."

"Just having some fun with the chief here," Sheriff Cutter replied. "You can take it, right Mr. FBI man?"

"You agreed to take me out to the Atwoods and Calderones. That's more important than that well thing," Rusty said to the sheriff, ignoring his question. "Tomorrow work? I'd like to go as soon as possible."

"I could just call and have them all come in here—not at the same time," Sheriff Cutter said. "No need to waste time going out there."

"No, I want to see their settings," Rusty said. "You don't know what you might learn when you're in the other person's comfort area rather than an interrogation room."

"Suit yourself. Tomorrow's fine," the sheriff said. "See you in here about nine then."

"Good," Rusty said. "See you then."

Back in his room minutes later, Rusty started reading Jimmy's latest journal. He started with July first of this year, to see what Jimmy had written about the site he and Buddy had explored. What he'd written matched what Buddy had said. The next month's notes produced nothing of interest other than the fact that Jimmy had visited that site three more times, looking for clues. He was convinced that setup was a decoy but held some clues as to where the real Eagle Well was located.

Then, on September first, Jimmy indicated he thought he had a clue. Something he found at that old wooden-windmill tower told him something. He'd followed his hunch and it led him to an old, now unused ranch road some miles away.

He'd used an old topo map and determined where this abandoned road met an occasionally still-used road. He'd gotten to that spot and started back the abandoned road. He had to cut brush and remove several deadfalls.

A few days later, he was back there again. He was surprised to find fresh ATV tracks on the road he'd cleared, even beyond. He cleared off more of the road and by late afternoon, about the time he was going to quit for the day he'd come upon a dry-wash and off to its side beside a tree and large boulder was an exposed corner of a buried old railroad tie. Some rocks and gravel covered a metal plate laying on the tie frame.

He wrote that he could tell the rocks had been moved recently. He quickly rolled them away, then slid off the plate. There was an old well. His flashlight was nearly dead, but he thought he saw a strongbox down the three-foot-by-three-foot hole, which he estimated to be about twenty feet deep.

He noted that this was where the ATV tracks stopped and turned around. He did likewise and headed out as darkness approached.

That night, he wrote that he had gathered up a ladder and whatever else he thought he'd need, then planned to go back there the next day. What was never said was where he found this newly discovered well or where the road started that led him to it.

As sort of an afterthought, with nothing supporting the statement, Jimmy wrote that his recent suspicions were surely true and he had to radically change his long-held opinion of Maxwell Wolf.

That was the last entry in his journal.

⇒— CHAPTER 3 —⇐

Reading the journal had been the easy part. Rusty looked at the files of notes organized in multiple folders lying in the box Sally Hanson had given him.

He rose from the small, hotel-room desk and walked to the window. Out at the northwest edge of town lingered the remnants of the old cattle holding pens where, for nearly eighty years, grass-fattened cattle from all over southwestern New Mexico and southeastern Arizona had been loaded onto rail cars. When the railroad stopped service in the 1970s, they pulling up the tracks. These pens, though the last ones used in the entire United States, had now been empty for more than forty years.

Rusty grabbed his hat and pulled on his boots—neither one official FBI attire but natural for this reservation-raised Apache and very practical for the climate, terrain, and local culture in rural New Mexico. He walked along the side of the street and across town over to the pens. He climbed up on the old fence and sat on the top rail. He closed his eyes and took a deep breath.

Got myself into this, didn't I, Lord? This is what I wanted, or thought I did. That poor little boy… I've got to solve this—maybe some of that old stuff too. Sort of scary, though. Only a few hundred people in this whole area, and most likely one of them is a cold-blooded killer. Surely do need your wisdom and guidance on this. Your protection too.

After climbing down from the fence and sitting on an old railroad tie that had been leaning against a post for some time, he got to thinking of what things must have been like in days gone by. Rusty closed his eyes and half-dozed off, thinking about what he'd heard about 1897. The cattle coming in… The buyers and peddlers… Maxwell Wolf's empire… The cowboys… The murder and robbery…

The train's pace slowed ever so slightly with each passing mile. The climb from Socorro to Magdalena, a mere twenty-seven miles, rose over seventeen hundred feet. Fortunately, today there was only minimal lightweight freight in any of the cars. However, behind its one passenger car was a long string of empty cattle cars strung out for a hundred yards.

"Almost there," Franz Frick said. "Long, long way from Chicago. Next year I believe the Lakeside Meat Company can send a younger man out here. Yet, as forsaken as this is, I've been told that if one thinks this is the end of the world, they should see where these trails coming in here begin. Personally, I never care to. This is way too far out for me."

"You and I see things differently, my old friend," Abe Stein said. "You come here with chests full of company gold coins and leave with rail cars full of smelly cattle. Me, I come here with containers of JB Stetson hats, Joe Justin boots, and other paraphernalia these cowboys want, then leave with empty containers and chests full of gold coins. What I do here in three months is more than many others with their expensive mercantile stores do in an entire year of sweat and toil. I see Magdalena as a gold mine—you see it as a stinky manure pile."

"You being from Fort Worth, stink is the norm," Franz said. "Now in Chicago—"

"Chicago has nothing over Fort Worth, except wind and snow," Abe said. "A few more railroad lines, maybe, but Fort Worth is the hub of commercial business in Texas, and that makes it one step ahead of Chicago or anywhere else."

"So you say. Keep thinking that," Franz said. "I assume you'll join me in a game of poker tonight? You'll see Chicago prevail at the table, so you will. Remember last year?"

"I remember you cleaned up on that local baron, Maxwell Wolf," Abe said. "He wasn't very happy."

Franz chuckled. "That's the only way one ever gets up on a banker. Beat him at the game table. Other than that, he has his hand in your pocket every time."

"Old Wolf owns about everything out here, so it seems," Abe said. "If there was another hotel to stay in or saloon to eat and drink in, I'd be the first in line to support them. I'd think the Southern Pacific would capitalize on this."

"Probably too seasonal. I'll bet come fall and winter, this is nearly a ghost town," Franz said. "Might as well be a ghost town all year. Nothing but dusty cowboys and a few saloon girls at its busiest. When I leave here in a month or so, I'm going to sit up front and look down these tracks and never, ever look this way again."

"I'm getting mighty hungry," Abe said. "Join me for a steak when we get there? The freight company will put my merchandise in storage until I'm ready to set up shop in a few days."

"I'd like to, but I've got to get my money up to my room, then chain those three strongboxes together and to the bed."

"Why don't you just take it all to the bank and let them do what they're set up to do with money?" Abe asked.

"Banks are what people rob," Franz said. "Nobody goes into a hotel room to rob a hundred thousand dollars in gold. Besides, I do a lot of my business at night, after the boys have had a few drinks or quite a few. I need to be able to get my hands on my money whenever I need it, not when the bank is open."

"A hundred thousand in gold coin, you say?" Abe repeated.

"A dozen San Francisco Mint bags with nearly fifteen pounds each. Some five and ten dollar coins, but mostly twenty-five and fifty dollar pieces. One hundred and sixty-six pounds of shiny, new gold coins, all in three Chicago Safe Company strongboxes with three brand new heavy-duty locks. To get my money, someone would have to know how to open locks, then either carry out a dozen bags of coins or the entire boxes. Safer than any bank, so it is."

"Might be. I'll see you at the tables later then," Abe said. "Magdalena's just ahead. We're slowing down."

"Yeah, later," Franz said. "I can't wait to get more of old Maxwell Wolf's money."

Rusty shook himself awake, got up, then walked back toward the hotel. Getting hungry, he entered the café and sat at a table by the window. Manny Rodriguez saw him and walked out of the kitchen with a glass of tea. He set the tea in front of Rusty, then sat across the table from him.

"You find anything of help in Jimmy's things?" Manny asked.

"Not much. Well, yeah, there's some interesting things there," Rusty said. "Unfortunately, he didn't say where things he'd found are located. I'll have to get out there now and find them as he did. I do have some good clues, though."

"Tomorrow, you are going with Sheriff Cutter?"

"He's going to take me out to the Atwoods and Calderones. He thinks someone in those families is the most likely suspect."

"Sí, the sheriff, he is always wanting to make one of them guilty for whatever wrong goes on here," Manny said. "He has a real bad attitude toward these two families—others too."

"I kinda got that impression. He doesn't think much of me either," Rusty said.

"Somehow he gets elected," Manny said. "I think many of the ranch people see him as an important one of them. He's a big man in this bull thing. Me, I think he's all bull himself."

Rusty responded with a slight smile, then he changed the subject. "This building, you said this was owned by Maxwell Wolf, right?"

"Sí. It has been remodeled many times. Little of the original still shows. As I said before, where we sit now was the bank. Behind us was the Horseshoe Saloon. The hotel was where it is now, of course. It too has been remodeled several times. My father, he bought all of this in 1955 when Frederick Wolf quickly left town. Someday, I hope my daughter will return and take it over. I hope but do not really believe it will happen. Young people today—"

"You said you'd tell me what you know about what happened in 1897. You have time now?" Rusty asked.

"Oh, there are many stories," Manny said. "I have probably heard them all."

"What's generally believed to have happened?"

"The cattle buyer from Chicago, Señor Franz Frick, he played poker in the saloon that night, back then." Manny nodded to the next room over. "Then, he went to his room. The next day he didn't show up anywhere. The sheriff, he and Maxwell Wolf, they went into his room and there he was, dead. Knife still in his heart. All his money was gone."

"Anyone suspected back then?" Rusty asked.

"Sí, many," Manny said. "Mostly those he played poker with that night. He won much. It seems he did so too often and many thought he cheated."

"Who was in the game with him?"

"Several came and went, but the big loser was a peddler, old friend of Franz's, Señor Abe Stein, I believe his name was. He came here many years. Sold hats and boots and such to the cowboys. He never came back after that year, I'm told. Fernando Calderone and Horace Atwood both lost some money, and it's said they were both very upset at Franz. They were here making preparation for their herds that would soon be arriving. Each accused the other of stealing this money and killing Señor Frick. I believe that was the beginning of the bad blood between those families that still exists today."

"How much is believed to have been stolen?"

"Franz had said he had one hundred thousand dollars in gold coins. All fresh from the mint, he had said. That is what is always believed to have been taken."

"That's what someone else told me," Rusty said. "That's a bunch of gold. A lot of weight also."

"Over one hundred and fifty pounds. I forget exactly how much. The strongboxes were opened. The keys to the locks had been taken from Señor Frick's coat pocket. Only the bags of coins were taken."

Rusty took a long sip of his tea, then set it down and remained silent. After a moment, he spoke. "Let me go back into that old saloon room for a moment, all right? I've kinda lost my appetite right now. I'll be back in a little while, then order."

Manny opened the door that had been cut through the old adobe wall between the old bank and the saloon. "Excuse the mess. It is only for storage that we use this now," Manny said.

"No problem," Rusty said. "I just want to spend a little time here. Sort of get a feel for that night, if I can."

The room had an eerie feel to it. The dark, old wooden bar still cut across the room a few feet from the back wall. Cobwebs were strung across the old bottle racks, and the large, bar-back mirror was cracked in several places.

Rusty sat on a large cardboard box marked "napkins" and closed his eyes.

What happened here, Lord? One man who was here that night died and most likely another who was right here did the killing. Does any of this matter now?

Somehow, Jimmy Hanson seemed to believe it did.

"This isn't much fun," Franz Frick said as he pulled the pile of coins and a few bills over to him.

"Why do you say that?" Abe Stein asked. *"You're winning nearly every hand."*

"I wanted to get into the pockets of old Maxwell Wolf," Franz said. *"I want some of that rich old buzzard's money. Where is he anyway?"*

"Working late at the bank, so he said," Abe replied. *"Said he'd maybe join us tomorrow night."*

"Then maybe I'll just call it quits tonight," Franz said.

"Señor," Fernando Calderone said. *"A chance to recover mí dinero. One more hand, por favor."*

"You think you can beat me even if we play ten more hands?" Franz asked. *"Not a chance."*

"Ain't figured how, but you have to be cheating," Horace Atwood said.

"That's a mighty brazen charge. Just might be that I'm a better player than anyone here. Up in Chicago, we play for real stakes, not the pittance laying on this table. This, my friends," Franz spread his hands out over the small pile of bills and coins in front of him, *"is not worth cheating over."*

He then tossed a dollar bill back to each of the other three players left at the table. "Have a bottle on me."

He picked up the rest of the money, tossed back his drink, then rose and slowly walked out of the saloon toward the hotel.

When Rusty pushed back his plate an hour later, Manny again came over to him.

"Maybe tomorrow you will learn something to tell who killed Jimmy," Manny said. "I still can't believe that someone from here would do such an evil thing."

"Hard to figure. I haven't found anyone yet who has anything bad to say about him," Rusty said. "What do you think about it being one of the Calderones or Atwoods as Sheriff Cutter seems to think?"

"Oh … those are old, rough families," Manny said. "They survived through tough times. To survive out here back in the hard days, oftentimes men did things they might not be proud of, but were necessary to do to survive. Today, this is not so much the way. As a child, many times I saw some of the Calderone men at the church during confession time. Not so much today. Times have changed—so have people."

"Duke Atwood—rabble-rouser kid or real bad actor?" Rusty asked.

"Most every family seems to have one who is, as they say, the black sheep," Manny said. "Duke, he puts pleasure ahead of all else. I see no pleasure in killing Jimmy and all else that was done. Me, I don't see Duke doing this. He has always faced up to his mistakes."

"Any ideas on who might have done this?" Rusty asked. "It almost had to be a local."

"So it would seem. Though…" Manny paused, then went on, "I think it is possible there could be some wanted criminal hiding out in that wild country. Lots of game, even cattle, to eat. Wells around too. Be careful when you're out there. You shouldn't go alone."

"Maybe I shouldn't," Rusty said as he rose and started for the register. "Oh, just thinking, what room over in the hotel was Franz Frick killed in?"

"Ahh, Señor, that was such a long time ago." Manny paused. Rusty didn't move, but stared at Manny, who looked down at the floor. "It was room 202, the room you are now in. But, Señor, that was a long time ago."

A short time later, Rusty opened his room door, then entered and flipped on the light. He went to the window and pulled back the curtains. He walked over and sat at the desk, then pulled out one of the folders of Jimmy's notes from the file box. He lay it on the desk in front of him, then looked over at the bed. This, of course, wasn't the same bed Franz Frick was killed in, but it was the room. Rusty closed his eyes, then thought about that night back in 1897.

"Who's there?" Franz Frick called out as he was awakened by the opening of his room door. "Get out of here. You have no business here. I'll yell for the sheriff," he said as he sat up in his bed.

Suddenly, a wooden club smashed across Franz's head, knocking him flat on his back in a dazed condition. Then, a pillow was stuffed across his face. The intruder slid a knife out of its sheath, then thrust it into Franz's heart.

When Franz went limp, the intruder removed his hand from the knife, leaving it protruding from Franz's chest. He then reached into the dead man's coat pocket and removed a ring of keys. In a few seconds, all three strongboxes were opened. The contents of one was quickly removed and taken to a wagon waiting up the back alley behind the hotel. Two more trips to the room, then the wagon started slowly, and quietly, rolling out of town.

⪢— CHAPTER 4 —⪡

Jimmy's stuff giving up any clues?" Sheriff Cutter asked Rusty the next morning in the café as he sat across the table while Rusty finished his breakfast.

"Oh, well I haven't solved anything yet," Rusty said. "I've learned a few things. You hearing anything around the area?"

"Nah. Figure if it wasn't the Calderones or Atwoods, it was some weirdo stranger passing through," Sheriff Cutter said. "Might well never solve this, you know."

"There's a lot of work to do. I haven't hardly begun yet," Rusty said. "From what I hear, there was an incident here in 1897, then one in 1955, with neither one ever being solved. I'm not about to have that happen again. I'll solve this. Jimmy was a federal ranger—a public servant. If I don't solve this in a few weeks, there's liable to be fifty agents in here tearing apart your whole county. You best hope I solve this."

The sheriff didn't respond. Rusty emptied his coffee cup, then rose and picked up the ticket. "Let's go. You can fill me in on all the goods on these two families as we drive."

"Ain't no good. Just a bunch of bad and ugly hombres," Sheriff Cutter said. "Since I know where we're going, I'll drive. Besides, showing up in that ugly black hearse you drive might scare the heck out of these simple ranch folks."

Rusty placed his briefcase on the passenger side floor and climbed into the sheriff's quad-cab pickup. Neither man said anything for the first ten minutes. Rusty observed the changing landscape as they climbed toward the Plains of San Agustin and the VLA, the very large radio telescope disks that spread out all over this high plain.

Breaking over the last rise, Sheriff Cutter started talking. "We'll go see the Atwoods first. I called Andy last night. Said we'd be out this morning. Told him to have Duke there. Said he'd try."

"They have a large place?" Rusty asked.

"One of the largest around," Sheriff Cutter said. "A full hundred sections. Over sixty thousand acres. Mostly BLM lease land, but about five sections actually deeded. Good water too."

"That's big for New Mexico. Sounds like west Texas. What do they raise?" Rusty asked.

"Pretty straightforward beef operation. Red Angus mostly now. Of course, story goes that when old Horace first settled here, it was anything he could cover with his brand. It's said he picked the pastures clean from Utah to here."

"When did he settle here?" Rusty asked.

"Year after all that cattle buyer killing and missing money deal. Real suspicious."

"What's the ranch called?" Rusty asked.

"The Seven Springs."

"That many flowing springs out there?"

"Nah," Sheriff Cutter said. "The old story goes that it was named for old Horace Atwood's seven wives. Could be back then there may have been seven watering holes, if you counted all the flowing springs and some wells mixed in. There's a lot more now, of course."

"They still practicing Mormons?" Rusty asked.

"Yeah. No seven wives, though," Sheriff Cutter said. "They're still always running off to the temple up in Salt Lake, down in Mesa, or, I hear, there's a new one now over in the Safford Valley. Don't make sense to me. Running all around like that when you got a ranch to run."

"About as bad as running off to rodeos all over ten states or more," Rusty said.

"Hey, that's my business. That's what I do," the sheriff said.

"From what I've observed," Rusty said, "some of those Mormon groups are well organized and self-supporting. Could be the Atwoods sell a lot of their cattle inside their own belief circle. They'd need to go where those people are, and that would be where the temples are. Could be as much about business as your rodeos."

"You sticking up for them heathens?" Sheriff Cutter asked.

"It's easy to throw a blanket over something without knowing all the details," Rusty said.

"Far as I'm concerned, you can take your blanket back to your reservation."

Off to the north, off by one of the telescope dishes, Rusty spotted a small herd of pronghorns. "Has the drought these last few years hurt the pronghorn and deer herds?"

"Sure has," Sheriff Cutter responded. "Twenty years ago, we'd have passed twenty or thirty of those little goats by now. Sometimes today I can drive all day and not see anything with four legs. Not even a jack rabbit. Seems as if the turkey and javelina are all that are doing really well these days. The elk, there's pockets up in some areas where they're plentiful. Some have migrated down into valleys where they've never been before.

"Then there's all the coyotes and those detestable wolves," Sheriff Cutter continued. "Can you imagine, the do-gooders in the government, the ones you work for, they brought back those killer wolves and turned them loose on our cattle? Bunch of idiots in Washington and even out here who don't know a thing about ranching tell us we need these bloodthirsty beasts roaming amongst us killing our herds. Then the fines they put on killing one of them… And they expect me as a local sheriff to help them? Crazy people. I'm a rancher first. I'm not some wolf cop. Out here we live by the triple S policy. We look out for each other."

"Triple S policy?" Rusty asked.

"Shoot, shovel, and shut up" Sheriff Cutter said. "Look in the back of most any pickup truck out here. There'll be a shovel. That's for burying the dead calves the wolves kill—that's what you'll be told, but really—"

"How many of your calves have been wolf killed?" Rusty asked.

"That doesn't matter. It's always possible it could happen. Things are bad now. This drought has been hard. Then with the game poachers, like the Atwoods, that sure doesn't help. Without wild game, those wolves will really come after our cattle."

"Tell me about the Atwoods and their poaching problems," Rusty said.

"They run a half-baked guide service," Sheriff Cutter said. "Mostly for their extended family and church cronies in Utah. Got wind they weren't being too worried about everyone having the proper licenses and so on. They have a landing strip out there, and small planes come and go all the time. They used to have their own plane, but I don't think they do anymore."

"So they were busted?"

"Well, sort of. All they actually got charged with was that Duke had a cousin, or something, take two elk. The fella claimed one was for his father, who was in a wheelchair in the back of the pickup."

"Big fine?" Rusty asked.

"Well, once the judge heard the story and the fact that the old man was a disabled vet who swore he was right there, just unable to shoot, the judge dropped the case with a warning. Guess the old man did have a license. Him being a war vet and all, well, it still ain't right. They just haven't gotten caught at anything else, that's all."

"Anything else?" Rusty said.

"I've heard stories. I'd say that bunch is feeding half of Salt Lake with our elk meat. I'd bet on it," Sheriff Cutter said.

Neither man said anything for a while as the sheriff drove toward the Arizona border. Passing Datil Well, then nearing Pie Town, he turned north, up a gravel county road. Ten minutes later, they came upon a large rock and timber entranceway with the carved wooden sign announcing the entrance to the Seven Springs Ranch, with owners Andy and Duke Atwood.

The sheriff turned the pickup onto the ranch road.

"They have some pride in this place," Rusty said.

"Arrogance is more like it," Sheriff Cutter said. "They just think they're better than anyone else, that's all."

It took another fifteen minutes to reach the ranch headquarters. As they drove in, Rusty asked a question. "Any other children besides Duke?"

"Bunch of older girls—half-dozen, at least," Sheriff Cutter said. "Duke's the baby and only boy. Those girls are all off in some big city. Bunch of lawyers and doctors and the like. Never see any of them around here. I don't anyway."

They pulled up in front of the main house and parked beside several other pickup trucks.

"Nice place," Rusty said.

"Don't let looks fool you," Sheriff Cutter said as he opened his truck door.

They walked toward the main ranch house, and just as the sheriff reached up to knock on the door, it opened.

"Sheriff Cutter," the middle-aged man said. "Come in."

"Andy, this here fella is that FBI agent I told you about. Like I said, he's investigating the Jimmy Hanson thing. Guess he's also got some questions for you too, Duke. Good to see you're here," the sheriff said to a lanky young man with long hair tied back, his shirttail out and a snuff can in his shirt pocket.

"Ain't had much sleep for a day or two, Sheriff, Mr. FBI man too," Duke said. "Might not be much help. Don't know anything anyway."

"Call me Rusty. Rusty Redtail, out of the Albuquerque office."

"Redtail?" Andy asked as he reached out and shook Rusty's hand. "Apache? Navajo?"

"Mescalero Apache, mostly. A little Mimbreño blood. Grew up out on the rez over by Cloudcroft."

"How'd the likes of you ever end up with the FBI?" asked Andy.

"It's what I always thought I wanted," Rusty said with a shrug. "Time will tell."

"We don't have any coffee around here. We don't—well, Duke does—the rest of us don't drink the stuff," Andy said.

"That's fine. Glass of water would be good, though," Rusty said.

"Kitchen table OK?" Andy asked.

"Best place in the house, usually," Rusty replied.

"Make yourself comfortable then," Andy said, motioning toward the table.

He arrived there a minute later with two glasses of water, then set them in front of his guests. He and Duke then also sat at the table.

Rusty opened his briefcase he'd set on the floor. He took out a legal pad and across the top he wrote the date and the name "Atwood."

"Jimmy Hanson," he then said. "Did either of you know him?"

"Oh sure," Andy said. "Out here you get to know all the law fellas. Sheriff here can tell you how it is."

"He ever been here, to your home?" asked Rusty.

"Couple of times to discuss lease things and so on," Andy said. "They cut our cattle allotment back a couple years ago. We didn't like that, of course."

"Big argument over that?" Rusty asked.

"No—no, I understood, as dry as it is. No one likes to be told they have to cut back on their livelihood, though."

"Couple of years back, you said. Any discussion about that since?" asked Rusty.

"None," Andy said. "It's only gotten drier since. We've had two wells go completely dry, and several others are pumping off nearly every day now. Just talked to a driller last week about drilling some deeper holes. Guess it's come to that."

"Speaking of wells. You know anything about that old Eagle Well people around here talk about?" asked Rusty.

"Story always was that was on Wolf land. Calderones bought up most of those rights back in '55 when Frederick Wolf left the country. Sheriff here bought the house and headquarters area," Andy said.

"You ever see that well?" Rusty asked.

"No, I try real hard to avoid anything to do with those Calderones," Andy said. "Sheriff knows that. There's been bad blood ever since our families both settled here back in 1898."

"Both settled here in 1898? That's a year after all that money went missing, right?" Rusty asked.

"That's what started the trouble," Andy said. "Fernando Calderone accused Granddad Horace of the killing and theft, so granddad accused Fernando back. Me, I think, from what I've learned, it was that boot peddler from Fort Worth who did it and absconded with the money."

"Jimmy ever talk to you about looking for that Eagle Well?" asked Rusty.

"No, we never talked about stuff like that. We talked one day about my family history of settling here, but that was all," Andy said.

"When was the last time you saw Jimmy?" Rusty asked.

"Oh—month or so ago," Andy replied. "Saw him over at the café in Datil."

"You talk to him?" asked Rusty.

"Yeah. He was with Chub, that other BLM fella. Yeah, we talked. Nothing important that I recall."

"How about you, Duke?" Rusty asked. "When did you last see Jimmy?"

"Can't say," Duke replied. "Never paid him much mind. I mean, he was a straight shooter. Married and all. Never saw him in a bar or out at night. I'd pass him out on the road and wave, but that was about all. Now that I think about it, I did see him awhile back over at the Pie Town Café."

"Anyone around here ever talk bad about Jimmy?" Rusty asked.

"Nah. He was Mr. Clean," Andy said. "His truck was found on Calderone land, right? If he was lookin' for that Eagle Well, that's supposed to be out on Calderone land also. I'd say that's who you should be talking to. They may not have killed that old cattle buyer and stole that money, but I'd bet a month's wages they killed that sheriff in the '50s."

"Based on what?" Rusty asked.

"Based on there being Calderones and a lawless bunch at best," Andy answered.

"How's the cattle sales?" Rusty asked.

"Well, we had to sell off more than we wanted to when they cut our allotment," answered Andy. "However, so did a bunch of other guys.

Now we're selling fewer head, but the price is right good. Best I've ever seen. We're doing quite well, really."

"Got a text from my lab this morning," Rusty said. "It looks as if Jimmy wasn't shot close up, and it might have been from a considerable distance. Probably a 45-caliber bullet. Could be something like a 45-70. I figure there's lots of those old ones around, with a few of the new Marlins or Henrys, maybe Sharps too, right? You guys own anything like that?"

"Oh, I've got an old 45-90 my grandpa hunted a few buffalo with. Old Sharps," Andy said. "Hasn't been shot for years, though. Want to check it?"

"No, I'll take your word," Rusty said.

"Don't think you can even buy ammo for that anymore. Have to load your own, I 'spect," Andy said, seeming to reflect on the old gun.

"How about you, Duke?" Rusty asked.

"Ah … well, for guiding elk and … yeah, I have an old Winchester 1886. Of course, that's a 45-70."

"Is it here?" Rusty asked.

"No. It's out at one of the cabins," Duke said. "Haven't shot it since last season, though, honest."

"Well, I might want to examine it later. Can you bring it in here in case I need it?" Rusty asked.

Duke nodded.

"Anybody else have access to that gun?" asked Rusty.

"Oh, I guess one of our hands would. We're pretty open about lettin' the boys borrow what they want," Duke said.

"Without asking?" Rusty said.

"Like I said, we're lax about stuff like that. If someone used my gun, they know to clean it and put it back where they found it. That's just the way it is."

Rusty was silent for a moment, then continued. "Here's my card. Please call me if you learn anything. Anything at all that could help." He finished his glass of water, then rose. "Thanks a lot. Just remember when you're out and about, there's a killer running around here and they might be using a gun that can do the job from hundreds of yards."

"Hadn't really thought about that," Andy said. "Guess I figured this was personal, something against the government. Knowing the way most of us out in these parts think. The fact that we all might be in danger—"

"We'll probably talk again," Rusty said. "Talk to your hands—anyone. You learn anything, call me, please."

"Yeah, for sure," Andy said.

"Stay out of trouble, Duke," Sheriff Cutter said as he rose to leave. "Be more like your old man here. Get yourself a wife and settle down. Just one, though."

Rusty looked at the sheriff, then turned to Andy and slowly shook his head. Andy just nodded. He apparently was used to the sheriff's digs. Andy put his hand on Duke's shoulder, holding him down as Duke glared at the sheriff and tried to rise out of his chair.

"Someday, Sheriff," Duke said. "Someday."

⟫— CHAPTER 5 —⟪

Neither Rusty nor Sheriff Cutter said anything until they were well out on the ranch road.

"Could be lying," the sheriff then said. "That Duke's a snake."

"I don't think so," Rusty said. "I think they told us the truth. At least on what matters, for now."

"Duke even has a 45-70," Sheriff Cutter said. "Despite what you think, there's not all that many around here."

"If he'd used it to kill Jimmy Hanson, why would he have told us about it? He could have buried it out in the mountains somewhere, never to be found. It was bought long before any federal transfer records," Rusty said. "You know any of the hands who work there?"

"They come and go," Sheriff Cutter said. "A few local boys who like to do some cowboy work are there. A couple hang around with Duke. Others are family guys, you know? Andy always runs a criminal check on new hires he doesn't know. There's no real bad actors out there. Only Duke."

The two men were again quiet for a moment, then Rusty asked a question. "How's the rodeo stock business anyway? Bulls, I hear. How many do you have?"

"Too many, sometimes, not enough others," Sheriff Cutter said. "Tough business—tough as those bulls sometimes. It's not like raising sheep, for sure. I keep several dozen in development. Sell a few each year, but mostly haul them around and rent them out to rodeos. Have one coming up this weekend in Cherokee, Oklahoma. Have to leave tomorrow. Be gone until late Monday."

"Guess I'll stay around here through the weekend," Rusty said. "Maybe by then our lab will turn up something on the truck, though there wasn't much left to go on. Don't expect any prints or DNA."

"Maybe when we get out here to the Calderone's ranch somebody will confess and you'll have this all wrapped up today," Sheriff Cutter said.

"Lonny is head of that operation now, right?" Rusty asked. "Any kids?"

"Several teenagers—all girls. One boy—early twenties, I think." Sheriff Cutter said.

"What are their names?"

"Don't know. Never had any trouble with any of them. They sorta stay out on the ranch. I do see the boy out at the cowboy action shoot occasionally, but I've never talked to him."

"Yet you really think one of them could have killed Jimmy Hanson?"

"Gut hunch. The truck was found on their land. They really guard things tightly. I don't see anyone getting that truck in there then getting back out without being seen by one of them."

"If you killed a federal ranger, would you hide the evidence on your own land, knowing that someday it would be found?" Rusty asked.

"Maybe they're not that smart. I don't know."

After a moment of silence, Rusty asked another question. "What about you, Sheriff, you have any kids?"

"No. Just my bulls. Dee has a couple of quarter horses she treats like kids. Way back before we married, she raced around those barrels, back before that became popular and profitable."

"That whole rodeo thing has become big business, hasn't it?" Rusty said.

"Thank goodness. Nothing gives me a rush more than seeing one of my bulls tossing a top rider in less than the eight-count. That's what gets my blood flowing."

"So you root against the rider while most everyone else is for him?" Rusty asked.

"Of course. The better my bulls do, the more they're worth. More money in my pocket."

"I never thought about that," Rusty said. "I never thought about the business end of rodeo, other than the contestant winnings."

"Last year I had two ranked high enough to be at the National Rodeo Finals in Las Vegas," Sheriff Cutter said. "This year, it looks as if I could have four. Maybe more than that at the PBR—Professional Bull Riders Association—finals."

"That sounds awfully good," Rusty said. "I watch a little of that on TV. I'll have to make sure to watch more this year. What's your ranch or cattle company name?"

"Trails End Cattle Company. Our ranch is out toward Dusty. It's about twelve miles to the entry road."

"That road goes south, off by Poverty Creek, then on to Winston and Chloride, right?" Rusty asked.

"Yeah. You ever been down there?"

"Been through that lower part going over to Beaver Head. Came in from Elephant Butte Lake, though."

"Not much between Winston and Highway 60 up here," Sheriff Cutter said. "Our spread goes west, all the way to Highway 12, south of the plains. Actually, we butt up against the Rancho Vaca on the northwest line."

"Rancho Vaca?"

"Where we're going, the Calderone's ranch. We share a fence line, that's all. I don't use any of that western land. They'd like to lease it, but there's no way I'd give them a blade of grass or drop of water."

"If it would bring in some money, and you don't use it—"

"Never happen," the sheriff cut Rusty off. "Our land was owned by the Wolf family until we bought it. None of the Wolfs would ever deal with those greasers, and neither will I. We didn't move here full time until 1995. Before that, we'd come out here several times a year until I sold out my business—all but a couple of wells that I kept. Good producers."

"So, what's your personal beef with the Calderones?"

"Just don't like their type," Sheriff Cutter said.

"You mean where their ancestors came here from?"

"They ought to go back. Be a better country if they all went back home."

"Seems to me they've been in this country around here a lot longer than you have. Doesn't that count for something?"

"Not in my book," Sheriff Cutter said.

"That's quite a book you have. You write me off because I'm Apache. You don't like the Atwoods because they're Mormons. You think the Calderones should go back to Mexico. I'll bet more than one person around here wishes you'd go back to Texas. A lot of my people still wish all whites would go back to wherever they came from. Those elk and turkeys out there probably wish even my people had never come here. Where does this stop?"

"This should all be part of Texas," Sheriff Cutter said. "Then Texas should pull out of this stinking government we have now and clean out all the scum polluting the right way of life."

"The right way? Your way, you mean," Rusty said.

"Yeah, like I said, the right way."

"You know, Sheriff, if Jimmy Hanson wasn't a white boy who came here from Texas, and he was either a Catholic or Mormon, I'd have you on the top of my suspect list."

"Yeah, probably so. But Jimmy was one of the good guys—Texas born. He belonged here. It's someone who doesn't belong here who killed him, I'm telling you."

Neither man spoke for quite a few minutes. Once back out on the pavement, Sheriff Cutter turned back east. Rusty started talking again. "I've been told that both Horace Atwood and Fernando Calderone were in the saloon playing poker with Franz Frick the night he was killed."

"That's the way the story goes," the sheriff said. "Then, shortly thereafter, they each brought in their herds. They both went back home, then were back in the spring and bought their ranches. The Calderone's was much smaller, as was their herd. It wasn't until they got a hold of the Wolf lease land that they became a major player in the ranching business around here. They were small players up until then. The Atwoods—they were always big dogs. All that Mormon money. Or that stolen cattle buyer's money."

"Any chance they were in on the murder and theft together?" Rusty asked.

"Doubt it. They never got along."

"But what if that's why? They both knew what the other was capable of, what they'd already done. Each didn't trust the other that they wouldn't do something that evil against them?" Rusty asked.

"Still doubt it," Sheriff Cutter said. "Myself, I figure it was old man Calderone. The Atwoods, well as I've said, lots of money from Utah. Figure they wanted a foothold here near the railhead."

"I saw a copy of the original purchase deeds for both ranches in one of Jimmy's files. The Calderones paid for their ranch in Spanish money. Neither party had any gold coins," Rusty said.

"They'd hardly show up with bags full of 1897 fresh-minted gold eagles," Sheriff Cutter said. "I'd say, those are either down in Mexico or up in Utah."

"So you're not like Andy and think it was that peddler from Fort Worth?" Rusty asked. "He could have spent a coin now and then over there and never have aroused any suspicion."

"How'd he get the money out of here? Where'd he hide it?"

"Maybe he had an accomplice," Rusty replied. "He had several months from the time of the murder until he left town. How did anyone get the money out of here?"

"You think too much. Forget all that old stuff."

"Maybe I should, but Jimmy was really deep into that, and it might well have something to do with his murder. Maybe you should forget all your old stuff," Rusty said.

"That's different," Sheriff Cutter said. "The Atwoods and Calderones ain't dead yet."

"Neither are those old cases," Rusty said. "What if Jimmy turned up something connected to that 1897 deal? What if he found that well and some of the coins? What if the sheriff in 1955 did the same? What if that got him killed—Jimmy too."

"That tells me I don't want to ever find what they found," the sheriff said. "You go ahead and look for that if you want to. I just want to hang someone for murder. None of that other stuff matters. It's all in your imagination. You let that control your thinking and your mind will get twisted, like a man after gold in the hot sun."

"Maybe it's all that peyote I smoke. The firewater I drink too. Maybe all the horse meat—"

"Sense of humor, somewhat," Sheriff Cutter said. "That doesn't fit the FBI profile, does it?"

"Makes me almost human, huh?" Rusty said.

Sheriff Cutter didn't respond. Both men were silent for quite a while. Reaching Datil Well, the sheriff turned south, down State Highway 12. A few miles out the road, Rusty asked a question. "So, what do the Calderones raise on their ranch?"

"Like most around here, beef cattle," Sheriff Cutter said. "Nothing special. Just red Herefords, those hornless, polled ones, mostly. I have seen some Corriente longhorns out on their range, but they must sell them in Mexico. I never see them at the auction up here."

A few more miles down the road, the sheriff turned back east on a county road. In another ten minutes, they came to a ranch road with a simple wooden sign announcing the entrance to the Rancho Vaca.

"Rankles me to even drive back in here," Sheriff Cutter said.

"Don't then. I'll come back myself, now that I know where they're located," Rusty said.

"Here now," Sheriff Cutter said. "Besides, I owe old Lonny some money for repairing some fence one of my bulls knocked down last winter."

"Last winter?" Rusty asked.

"Yeah. Haven't seen him since. Kind of gone out of my way to avoid him. Time I pay up now, though."

In about five minutes, the sheriff drove into the meadow containing the ranch headquarters.

"Someone's over by that shed with the open door," Rusty said as he pointed toward a weathered, board-and-batten building with its sliding door pushed off to one side.

"That's Lonny," the sheriff said. "Don't see the young ones. Guess they're in school."

He pulled his truck over by the building where Lonny now stood watching them. Both Rusty and the sheriff then got out. Lonny Calderone walked toward them.

"Sheriff," Lonny said, "it's been awhile."

"Haven't seen you in town, or anywhere," Sheriff Cutter said. "That fence. I haven't looked at it. I guess you fixed it right. Dee rode out that way once, and she said it looked OK. Three hundred, you said?"

"That'll cover it," Lonny said. "Wasn't all that hard to fix."

Sheriff Cutter handed him three one-hundred-dollar bills. "Sold that bull," he said as he did. "Now, someone else can worry about keeping him inside the fence. Wish he would have bucked as good as he tore up fences. This here's that FBI fella I told you about in my phone message who's investigating Jimmy Hanson's death," Sheriff Cutter said, nodding toward Rusty.

"Rusty Redtail," he said as he extended his hand.

"Lonny Calderone." The two shook hands.

"Nice place here," Rusty said. "It's a lot of work keeping things up, I'm sure."

"It's all I know. Grew up here. My father too. My kids are fourth generation here. Grandfather actually bought this in 1898. Came up from Sonora with only a couple dozen mother cows and a couple of bulls. Had six kids and little else. Grandma, his wife, died two years later. He raised up all those kids by himself. Sort of an outsider, I guess. Got little help from the locals."

"Probably because each of those cows he brought had a different brand run over with an iron," Sheriff Cutter said.

"I wasn't there," Lonny said. "However, there is an old box of records in the house that shows a bill of sale for every cow brought here. How many reales and pesos he paid for each also."

"Where's your kids?" Sheriff Cutter asked.

"Cisco, he is in school in Santa Fe," answered Lonny.

"What kind of school?" Rusty asked.

"To be a priest, Señor Redtail."

"A priest!" Sheriff Cutter said. "Fancy that, a Calderone a priest. At least you won't have to go far to confess all your sins."

Rusty looked at Lonny, closed his eyes, and slightly shook his head. When he opened his eyes, Lonny was smiling.

"Was Cisco here when Jimmy Hanson was killed?" Rusty asked.

"He only left yesterday morning," Lonny said. "The school, it starts tomorrow."

"Convenient," Sheriff Cutter said. "Who else drives an ATV or pickup? Your wife?"

"Very little," Lonny said. "Not around the ranch. Edwina drives to town, rarely so. She has always stayed around the house here. She doesn't even ride a horse."

"Did you know Jimmy Hanson?" Rusty asked.

"Oh yeah. Jimmy was out here often. He liked to talk about old times. He knew more about history here than anyone I know. Why would someone want to kill him? How is his wife—and that little boy? On weekends, sometimes, the little guy would come out here with his daddy. He played with my youngest daughter, though she's much older."

"What was Jimmy talking about lately?" asked Rusty.

"He'd become consumed with finding that well that old stories tell about," Lonny said.

"The Eagle Well," Rusty said.

"Yeah," Lonny said. "The Eagle Well."

"What do you know about it?" Rusty asked.

"As much, or as little, as most anyone else. Jimmy said he found a setting that someone made to look like an abandoned well, but it really wasn't. I don't understand that. It must have been done for some reason many years ago. He said that was on my lease land, old Wolf land, but I've never seen it or heard talk of it by anyone. But then, there's more than one abandoned well around. That's not anything really noticeable."

"I think Jimmy found the real Eagle Well, and that had something to do with his death," Rusty said.

"I haven't been to town to hear much. How was he killed?" Lonny asked.

"Bullet to the head," Rusty said. "From a distance. Probably a 45-caliber. You own anything like that?"

"Well, some years back, over in Springerville, there was a raffle at the sportsman's club. I bought a ticket and won the gun. It's a Marlin. A 444 caliber, so it is. I really rarely use it. Just carry it with me to kill a coyote, or in case of a wolf attack or something. I'd never kill a wolf, though. No, I'd never do that—just scare it away."

"When's the last time it was fired?" Rusty asked.

"Just the other day," Lonny said. "I killed a coyote that was after my chickens."

"Big gun for coyotes," Rusty said.

"Less to bury," Lonny said, then smiled.

"That old wagon over there, over beside the tack building. That boom and old rope rigging, what's the story on that?" asked Rusty.

"Been in the family a long time," Lonny said. "There was a rope ladder that dropped from that crossbar on the boom. I'm told it was Maxwell Wolf's wagon. We used it to clean out the old hand-dug wells. You can carry all your shovels and tools in the wagon, pull right up to the well, and climb down the rope ladder and winch out muck and rocks with a bucket attached to the pulley rope.

"As a teenager, being the smallest male, I climbed down many a well on that," Lonny continued. "Hated doing that as much as anything I ever had to do. I haven't used it for years now. The children, they played on it when they were small. Not so now."

"You have some four-wheelers—ATVs or whatever you call them?" Rusty asked.

"All ranchers do now. It's the common way to get around today. Less work and easier on the body than a horse. Go anywhere. Takes a good road to get around in a pickup, but these little rigs will go about anywhere. Saves a lot of time on road upkeep, fuel too."

"Can I see yours?" asked Rusty.

"In the shed here," Lonny said. "Of course the hands have several others out working now." He then turned and led the way to a well-used side-by-side with a dump bed. "This is mine. The kids, they ride that little one over there," he said, pointing to a small single-seat Honda.

Rusty walked over to Lonny's vehicle and looked at the tires. He noted the tread pattern and the manufacturer. He pulled the gun out of the scabbard. He dropped the lever. It was loaded. He levered out the cartridges, then looked down the barrel. It was freshly cleaned. Rusty reloaded the tube, then levered a round into the chamber, set the hammer, then slid the gun into the scabbard.

"That was a nice prize," Rusty said. "Kill anything with that, so you could. And I don't care how many wolves you kill, as long as I don't know about it."

Lonny sheepishly smiled, but said nothing.

"Scare wolves, you say," Sheriff Cutter said. "What about Jimmy? You shoot to scare him too?"

"Jimmy? Me, shoot at Jimmy?" Lonny said. "Surely you don't think—"

"That 444 would make the same size hole as Jimmy had," Sheriff Cutter said. "He was found on your property. Yeah, Lonny, I'm asking if you shot Jimmy."

"Señor Sheriff, how can you think…"

"You haven't answered my question," the sheriff cut in. "Did you shoot Jimmy Hanson?"

"No! Never would I do such a thing," Lonny shouted. "You never have any trouble with me or any of my children. My Edwina and I cause no one any trouble. We work, we raise our children. We go to church—"

"Yeah, and confess what?" Sheriff Cutter said. "You been in town to confession since Jimmy was killed?"

"No, Señor Sheriff," Lonny said. "Why do you think such of me?"

"So you don't have any problem if I go check the brands on all your cattle?" Sheriff Cutter asked.

"No problem," Lonny said. "You will find none but that which have been born to my own cows. I know my grandfather, maybe even my father… Well, maybe they may not have been so careful about all the calves they brought in for roundup. That is not the way it is today. We obey the laws of God, and of man. We are not the type of people to do this thing to Jimmy Hanson. He was a friend."

"Ever have any disagreement with Jimmy or the BLM in general?" Rusty asked as he looked over the ATV Lonny said was used by the children. He noted two new front tires.

"I was unhappy when they cut my cattle allotment. But, as you see, it is so dry. To run more cattle than what they say would be a bad thing. They know best."

"You know Chub Murry?" asked Rusty.

"Oh yeah," Lonny said. "Señor Chub, he was like a brother to Jimmy. You know, one day they're best of friends, the next they're arguing over the color of the sky. But they were a good team."

"Their fight ever go beyond words?" Rusty asked.

"Oh no. Nothing like that. Just things like what job to do next or even where to eat lunch."

"When will your son be back home?" Sheriff Cutter asked.

"Thanksgiving, for a few days," Lonny said.

"How about a phone number where I can call him?" asked Rusty.

"Sure. He has a cell phone. I'll write the number for you," Lonny said, taking a pencil out of his pocket and taking the pad Rusty handed him. "He might be hard to reach. I believe he will be kept very busy there."

"I understand," Rusty said. "Right now I don't have any reason to call him. Have you seen any strange vehicles around here lately?"

"Oh—maybe," Lonny said. "Last week, one day. Over at the Datil Mercantile. A pickup with Utah plates. Saw that Duke Atwood in the passenger side."

"That's probably not that unusual," Rusty said. "I'm sure the Atwoods have friends and family up there."

"Yeah, but there was a rack full of guns in the back window," Lonny said. "There's no game-animal, rifle-season open now—nothin' but coyotes and the like."

"Maybe they're just scaring wolves and killing coyotes," Rusty said.

Lonny just smiled.

Rusty paused, then spoke again. "I'll be out here looking around. Might have Buddy Bell or the sheriff here with me. I want to see that fake well and try to find the actual murder scene."

"You mean he wasn't killed where they found the truck?" Lonny asked.

"No. That was staged," answered Rusty.

"Why?" Lonny asked.

"If I find that out, I'll probably find out who did it," Rusty said. "That's what I really need to know. Please call me if you learn anything. Oh, be careful out here too. Might still be a killer with a long-range rifle. He killed a federal ranger—probably kill anyone who gets in his way. Stay safe."

"Heck, Agent Redtail, my family hasn't been safe out here since we came here," Lonny said. "Not as long as the Atwoods are still in this county. You don't have to look no further than Duke Atwood if you want to find your killer."

Neither Rusty nor the sheriff said anything until they were back out on the pavement.

"It's one of them," Sheriff Cutter said. "I'd bet on it, sure as I'm here now, we've talked to the killer today—their family anyway. Kinda creepy thinking that one of them would go kill like that and that maybe you and I could be their next target. Figure we, especially you, might be next on their list if we get close to what got Jimmy in trouble."

Rusty was silent for a moment. Then he looked over at the sheriff. "I came out here to solve this. I'm not a local. I've got no score to settle or friend to protect. You pull out of this anytime you want. The only thing that will stop me is solving this—or a bullet."

≫— CHAPTER 6 —≪

Rusty carried the box of Jimmy Hanson's papers into his office in Albuquerque.

"Hey, Rusty," Liz said, "what do you have there?"

"Everything on this side of this box, the last pages marked in this journal too. Can you make me a copy?" Rusty asked. "I want to get the originals back to Sally Hanson."

"Sure. How are you coming along down there?"

"Making headway, I think. Several suspects, nothing tied up yet."

"There's some mail and messages on your desk. Nothing important," Liz said. "Guess you've been checking what I've been e-mailing you."

"Sure, every day, well, usually every night when I get back to the hotel."

"We've tried to keep a lid on things—keeping the TV guys and such away from you," Liz said.

"I appreciate that. I haven't seen any of them down there so far. Here, see if you can turn up anything on this also," Rusty said, handing her a note. "Frederick Wolf. He left the area down there back in 1955.

Sheriff disappeared about the same time. The Wolf family supposedly moved to Arizona. The locals aren't real sure about that. His father was sort of the town leader back in the early cattle drive days."

"I'll get on it," Liz said. "Let you know what I turn up."

"I'm going over to my apartment and check my mail and pay some bills," Rusty said. "I'll be back later.

"Harland's in a meeting now," Liz said. "I'm sure he'll want to talk to you."

"Maybe his meeting will last all day."

"You should be so lucky," Liz said with a smile. "You staying the night up here?"

"No," Rusty said. "No need for that."

Two hours later, back in his office, Rusty's phone buzzed.

"Yes," he answered.

"Rusty, Mr. Carter wants to see you," Liz said.

"Yeah, sure. Thanks."

"Oh, I haven't come up with anything on that Frederick Wolf yet," Liz said. "Haven't had time to start on that, really."

"OK, Liz. It might be a lost cause anyway. Might just be local lore. Things are pretty slow out there. Lots of time to think up all kinds of useless things."

Rusty walked back the hall to Harland Carter's office. The door was open. He stepped in front of it.

"Come in, Redtail," Special Agent Carter said. "Been reading your e-mail reports. Ready to pick up the perp?"

"Not yet," Rusty answered. "Soon, hopefully."

"We'll all look good if that's so," Agent Carter said, staring at Rusty.

"I'm going to need a chopper for a few days," Rusty said, staring back at his boss, looking for his reaction to this request.

"Chopper?" Agent Carter's eyebrows rose.

"Big area out there. They measure things in sections rather than acres. I need to find what Ranger Hanson stumbled onto that got him killed."

"Any idea what you're looking for?" Agent Carter asked. "You sure he stumbled onto something or did he step on the wrong toes?"

"He seemed very amiable with all the locals. He did his job but was liked and respected," Rusty said. "No, he got into something someone didn't want him to. I don't think it was job related."

"Well, give me a few days' notice if you really need that chopper," Agent Carter said, pushing back from his desk.

"I will. Most likely two days next week," Rusty said.

"Anything else?"

"I have Liz working on some things. That's all for now."

"Just get it done, Redtail. Sooner the better," Agent Carter said.

Passing back through Socorro on his way to Magdalena, Rusty stopped to see Chub.

"Hey, Rusty, how's things going?" Chub asked.

"Slow, but I'm making progress. You hearing anything?"

"Lots of questions," Chub said. "Jimmy was well known, and liked, around town."

"Have you seen Sally Hanson?"

"She's in Dallas. Don't expect her back for a week or so,"

"I have Jimmy's journals and notes, that whole box. I made copies of what I wanted too. I really don't want the originals out there in that hotel. Can you keep them here? Give them to her when she returns?"

"Sure," Chub said. "You find anything interesting in any of that?"

"Lots," Rusty said. "I wouldn't know where to begin without what I've learned from Jimmy. He's really helping solve his own murder."

"I'd like to come out and help you, but being shorthanded now without Jimmy, I'm buried here," Chub said. "Maybe one day next week."

"I'd like that," Rusty said.

"Yeah, me too," Chub said. "Be kinda odd being out there without Jimmy, though. We were usually out there together—much of the time anyway."

Rusty got back to Magdalena shortly before dark. Opening his hotel-room door, he found a note from Manny asking him to come to the café. He set down his box of copies of Jimmy's things, along with his briefcase, then closed the door and walked over to the café. It was sparsely occupied at this hour. Manny came out of the kitchen once Rusty sat at a table.

"I was hoping you'd get back tonight," Manny said as he sat across from him. "You learn anything in Albuquerque?"

"Not really. I'm going to get a chopper, probably next week," Rusty said. "Maybe I'll spot something from the air."

"Sheriff Cutter, he's out of town," Manny said. "Duke Atwood was in here this morning. Had some other young fella with him. They argued quite a bit. Duke wasn't happy. I looked when they left. The other man, he drove a blue pickup with Utah plates. I never saw him before."

"That's the second time I've heard about that pickup," Rusty said. "Think I'll go out to the Atwood's tomorrow and see what that's all about. Does Duke come in here often?"

"Rarely," Manny said. "He's usually over at the bar. This was rather unusual."

"Anything else going on?"

"Oh yeah," Manny said. "Some reporter, newspaper he said, he was in here after the lunch rush. He asked a lot of questions. Few made any sense. He wanted to know who was investigating this. I don't think he wanted to be here. Like he was sent here to get a story he had no interest in."

"That's probably a good thing," Rusty said. "I don't need some nosey, curious reporter in my way. Think he'll be back?"

"Not so," Manny said. "I told him all the bad stuff I could think of. 'Spect he went back to the city."

"Where was he from?"

"Think he said where, but I paid no attention. He never even left a card. I should have asked him again when he left. Like I said, I don't think he wanted to be here and much less wants to come back."

"Hope you're right," Rusty said. "Glad I wasn't around."

The next morning, Rusty went out to see Andy Atwood. He stopped at the Datil Store for a cup of coffee. As he toyed with the spoon, he looked up and saw Lonny Calderone over in the grocery section. Rusty waved to him. Then Lonny walked over his way.

"Agent Redtail," he said as he reached Rusty's table.

"Have a seat," Rusty said, motioning to the chair across from him.

"Just came in for a few things over in the store side," Lonny said. "Fancy seeing you here. How's your investigation coming along?"

"Sort of going in circles, it seems," Rusty said. "I'll bring in a chopper next week. Don't be alarmed if you see it flying around."

"Looking for that imaginary Eagle Well site?" Lonny asked.

"It seems Jimmy might have found it," Rusty said. "He said he did anyway."

Lonny was silent for a moment, then looked at Rusty. "Guess maybe it does exist. I never was a believer. Cisco, my son, he often went searching for it. Think he covered every inch of our ranch, but never found it—never told me if he did."

"He and Jimmy Hanson ever go out together?" Rusty asked.

"Not sure. I think I'd discouraged Cisco so much, chastised him for wasting time when he should have been working, that he quit talking to me about it—most everything, really. I think he was still looking, though. He believed that money from the old 1897 robbery was hidden there."

"Put there by whom?" Rusty asked.

"Well, to be a good Calderone," Lonny said, "I'm supposed to say the Atwoods. Cisco once said he'd come to another conclusion. Not sure how, or who. I'm sure he knows more about all of that than I do."

"If you asked him about it, would he tell you what he knows or suspects?"

"Oh maybe—maybe not. You know how young folks are with their parents. Maybe someday I'll become smart to him, again. Right now…" Lonny paused. "Don't get me wrong. I'm very proud of my son. Hard to tell him that now, so it is."

"Maybe I should call him," Rusty said. "I haven't yet. Don't be so hard on yourself. We were all young once."

The two men sat in silence for a moment, then Lonny slid his chair back. "Best get these things home. Edwina is waiting for them to make supper for tonight. If I see you up in that chopper, I'll wave to you."

"Sure. See you again, most likely," Rusty said. "Actually, in a day or so after I'm up in the chopper, I plan to be out on your ranch and nose around those old roads some."

"Make yourself at home," Lonny said. "Nobody'll bother you."

Lonny left and Rusty finished his coffee. After paying the bill, he walked back out to his Suburban. He then pulled back on Highway 60 and headed toward the Seven Springs Ranch.

Rusty pulled up to the ranch headquarters just as Andy Atwood was ready to get into his pickup. He turned and looked at Rusty, then walked toward him when Rusty parked and opened his door.

"You just caught me, Agent Redtail," Andy said. "I was heading for Springerville to an appointment and to get some supplies."

"Springerville?"

"Yeah. From here it's about ten miles closer than Socorro and has a whole lot more ranch-supply places," Andy said. "Most of us out around here do most of our business over there."

"I hadn't thought about it being closer," Rusty said. "I've never spent any time in Arizona."

"Can't tell there from here, really," Andy said. "I always figured those who wanted to split this territory into two, horizontal, east to west strips rather than two boxy areas were right. Better yet, they should have left it all one. We'd have had some clout then, being a much bigger state. We're a victim of the Civil War, you know? Lincoln divided-up New Mexico Territory with a north to south line to split up the two southern sympathizing areas of La Mesilla and Tucson. Thus creating the Territory of Arizona. Now, Washington doesn't know either of us exists, except to tell us how to run things. Sorry bunch of wine-sippin' pansies, so they are. Most have never been out here or done a hard day's work in their pampered lives. That's how I see it anyway."

"I hear you. Our Albuquerque office is proof of that," Rusty said. "I'm sure I'm out here because no one else wanted to get mud on their boots—shoes really. Growing up on the rez I learned a thing or two about how Washington works."

"Probably so. How can I help you?" Andy asked.

"Just a couple of things. I'm getting a chopper in here next week. You might see it around. Don't want you getting alarmed."

"I'll tell Duke. Some of his friends are into that black helicopter stuff. We certainly prepare for disasters—I just don't try to create them, or see them where they aren't."

"Good," Rusty said. "Duke's friends—I've heard several times he's hanging out with another fella in a blue Ford pickup with Utah plates. Anything you know about that?"

"Oh yeah. That's Alec, his cousin. Alec just got back from his mission trip. Went to Argentina, so he did. We kinda thought Alec coming down here and spending time with Duke might be a good influence on my boy."

"Is it working?" Rusty asked.

"Not that I can see. Not much anyway."

There was silence for several seconds, then Andy spoke again. "Hey, I've gotta go, really. Got a doctor's appointment. Don't want to be late."

"Nothing serious, I hope."

"Yeah, me too," Andy said.

With that, Andy turned and walked over to his truck. Rusty started his Suburban, then followed Andy out to the pavement. When Andy went west, Rusty turned back east, then stopped at the first place he could safely pull off the road. He pulled out a plat of the Seven Springs Ranch property he'd gotten from Jimmy Hanson's things. He compared that to the survey map covering this area. Several private roads cut through the Seven Springs Ranch. Rusty pulled back onto the pavement, drove a mile back the road, then turned back north on the first of these roads. He drove very slowly, looking for anywhere someone—Jimmy really— might have cut open an old abandoned road as he had described in his journal.

At lunchtime, Rusty went to the old café at Pie Town. He ordered a bowl of stew and piece of strawberry-rhubarb pie.

When the waitress brought his check, Rusty pointed to the empty pie plate.

"That was good. Hear Jimmy Hanson liked that. His favorite, right?"

"Sure was. You knew Jimmy?" she asked.

"Rusty Redtail," he said, taking out a card and handing it to her. "I'm investigating this case."

"Oh… I just, really, it still doesn't seem real. Jimmy would be in here most every week. He'd bring his little boy out sometimes on weekends. His wife once also. He was always treasure hunting, I guess you'd call it. Looking for lost gold or any old artifact."

"Any trouble with anyone?" Rusty asked.

"Not really. You know, some of these guys out here have a real thing against anything government. Some wouldn't speak to him. That's all I ever saw."

"Duke Atwood?" Rusty asked.

"Oh, Duke's not some hardened criminal. He's just a guy who puts having fun ahead of everything else—even if his fun isn't always legal. He and Jimmy got along. Actually, awhile back I saw Duke and Jimmy sitting at the same table. I could see Jimmy was asking Duke a lot of questions. He had one of his old maps, or something, out on the table. I surely don't think Duke would harm Jimmy, or anyone, really."

After lunch, Rusty spent the rest of the afternoon driving across the seldom used old roads and two-track trails shown on the old survey map. As the sun lowered in the west, he pulled back out onto the pavement and headed toward Magdalena.

By the time he crossed the Plains of San Agustin and just as he started into the first dip in the rolling hills, he looked in the mirror and saw a spectacular sunset behind him. He pulled off at a forest road entrance and sat there admiring the sight.

Thanks, Lord. I needed something to get my mind off this case. These people all seem so out of character for any to be a cold-blooded killer. Yet I believe that among us—even someone I've met, is such a person. I surely need your guidance here.

Being late and almost fully dark when he arrived in Magdalena, Rusty went to the café to eat before going to his room. When he walked in, he immediately saw Sheriff Cutter sitting at a table. He assumed the woman with him was his wife. The sheriff motioned for Rusty to join them.

"Still here, Chief?" Sheriff Cutter asked. "Haven't nailed down our killer yet?"

"Not yet," Rusty said, sliding out of a chair across from the sheriff.

"This is my wife, Dee. We're just getting back from that rodeo over in Oklahoma. Trailer out back is still full of bulls."

"Nice to meet you," Rusty said to Dee when she extended her hand to him.

"Likewise," Dee Cutter said. "Don't pay any mind to my husband's comments and crude remarks. He really doesn't hate everyone. He just likes to build himself up by trying to make others feel inferior. Stand up to him—I do. Being an Indian's got nothing over being a woman in Wesley Cutter's mind. I think he spends too much time around those ornery bulls he raises. He's becoming just like them, sometimes."

"Good thing I'm not raising chickens, or sheep, or the like and becoming like them," the sheriff cut in.

"How did your bulls do?" Rusty asked.

"Eight for ten in the two days. Not bad. I should be getting my invite letter to the Vegas Nationals in a week or so. Can't wait to go to Vegas."

Manny came out of the kitchen with the sheriff and Dee's plates of food. He motioned for the waitress to refill their iced tea glasses. "Señor Redtail's order too, Lisa," Manny said.

"I'll just have a bowl of your posole. Couple of hot corn tortillas too," Rusty said when Lisa arrived at the table.

"Must go to the kitchen," Manny said, stepping away. "Short on help tonight—been so all day."

"So, what's going on?" Sheriff Cutter asked.

"Not a whole lot," Rusty said. "I'm getting a chopper next week to give things a good look from the air. That might help. I've studied Jimmy's notes and journals. Wish he'd have been more detailed on locations. He was very excited, I can tell, but I'm told he'd get that way often. He wrote for his own information, so he left out a lot of detail that would help me now. I don't think he ever intended anyone else to have to make sense of his notes. Have you thought of anything I should look into?"

"I haven't thought about it much at all," Sheriff Cutter said. "I'll take off my rodeo hat and put my sheriff hat back on tomorrow. The vet will be out first thing in the morning before I turn these guys back out to pasture with the others. I'll keep them penned up tonight. Probably be over here by lunchtime."

"Anything you need from Springerville?" Dee asked her husband.

"Just put that check in the bank," he said.

"I'll have to be back here by noon," Dee said. "Ladies' lunch for the church women is here then. In fact, I'm fixin' to bake some cookies yet tonight. We're taking food boxes to those old folks, as we do every month."

Lisa brought Rusty's soup and tortillas.

"Any coffee made?" Rusty asked.

"Hour or so back," Lisa said.

"Oh, that's fresh," Rusty said. "As long as it wasn't yesterday morning's, I'm OK."

Lisa left, then returned with a cup and glass of water.

"Great posole," Rusty said.

"Manny's mother makes it," Lisa replied. "She's past eighty but still insists on doing some things here. I've learned a lot from her."

Sheriff Cutter pushed back his plate, picked up his tea glass, then emptied it. "Good to be home. Love those rodeos, all those big-name riders and such. Love hearing my bulls' names called out over the PA system and all of that. Still, after a few days of that, then a few more days on the road pulling that big trailer and nursing those bundles of fur and bones, my old bed will feel mighty good tonight."

"Yeah," Dee said. "Hearing those coyotes, even a wolf, is a whole lot better than some of that new screaming they call country music these days. I know this makes me sound old, but everybody must be deaf these days."

"I'm with you on that," Rusty agreed. "It's not an age thing. It's having a taste for quality over quantity—sound over noise."

"I get enough noise with somebody's snoring," Dee said.

Sheriff Cutter didn't respond. Dee tossed her napkin on her plate, then pushed it back from the edge of the table.

"Ready?" the sheriff asked Dee. "Still have to get those boys penned up in stalls and you want to bake cookies." Looking at Rusty, he said, "Probably see you tomorrow then, Chief."

"Wesley," Dee said.

"Call me what you want," Rusty said. "Actually I rather like that title. It indicated I'm the boss, that I have authority over you. Yeah, me Chief—you brave. Kemo sabe, maybe? "

Sheriff Cutter rapidly pushed his chair back and stood up. "Let's go," he said to Dee, who looked at Rusty and smiled broadly, then also rose and they walked to the register.

When the Cutters were gone, Manny came back out and sat down. "That Miss Dee, she keeps the sheriff in his place. I think she is the one who makes that business work."

"Probably, and Wesley Cutter's ego makes the sheriff's business work," Rusty said.

"It isn't much to be sheriff of San Agustin County," Manny said. "It's really only a part-time job, as you see. I think that is why the sheriff imagines trouble that is not real. Like with Duke Atwood and Lonny Calderone. He imagines things so in his mind he is doing something important. That is how I see things."

"Dee does seem like a nice lady," Rusty said.

"Everyone likes her. Would that Wesley Cutter should be more like her," Manny said.

"You know what they say about opposites attracting," Rusty said.

Rusty finished eating, then left the café and walked over to his hotel room. He opened the door, stepped in and flipped on the light switch. Something wasn't right. His clothes hanging on the rack were now on the right side. He'd left them pushed to the left. His suitcase was turned around the opposite way from how he'd had it on the stand. The center desk drawer was open slightly. These were not things a cleaning maid would do. Someone had been in his room and had gone through his things. Why? Looking for Jimmy's journals and other papers, most likely.

Good thing I took the originals out of here, and I had my copies with me. I'll ask Manny in the morning who was in town today. Both the Calderones and Atwoods knew I wasn't here.

There was something else. Then it hit him. *That's strange. Awfully strange.*

✦— CHAPTER 7 —✦

The next morning, shortly before seven, Rusty ate breakfast at the café. As he sipped on his second cup of coffee, an elderly man entered, looked around at those seated at the tables, then fixed his eyes on Rusty. He walked over to Rusty's table.

"Reckon you're that FBI fella lookin' into Jimmy Hanson's death."

"Yeah, Rusty Redtail."

"Toby Wilson," the man said, extending his hand out to Rusty. "I'm one of the old-timers hereabouts. Third generation, so's I am. Got any good leads, yet?"

"Oh, I'm working on several things. You have anything I should look into?" Rusty asked as he motioned for Toby to have a seat.

"Wish I did," Toby said. "Downright shame, so it is. They don't come any better than Jimmy Hanson, even if he did work for the government."

"Guess you know about everybody around here," Rusty said. The waitress brought Toby a cup of coffee, then refilled Rusty's.

70

"Bunch of new folks who stay to themselves, mostly. Know all the old ones—the good and the not so good."

"You know all the feuds, the tales of old trouble, I'm sure," Rusty said.

"You mean like the Calderones and Atwoods?" Toby asked. "I'm not sure even they know what started all their huffin' and puffin'. Me, I get along with both of them just fine."

"You don't see either one of them as dangerous killers then?"

"Shoot, no," Toby said. "Oh, I know, if you listen to the sheriff he'll put black hats and strapped-down, hog-legs on all of them. Truth is, he's got nothin' on any of those folks."

"Duke Atwood?"

"Oh, that boy's just feelin' his oats," Toby said. "Wouldn't hurt a stray dog. He's a real burr under old Sheriff Cutter's saddle, though. My guess is old Wesley Cutter was about like Duke Atwood back in the day and that rubs him wrong. Something inside him still wishes he could be wild and free, like Duke, then Miss Dee pulls on his reins."

"That could be," Rusty said. "How well do you know Sheriff Cutter?"

"Well, he tells everyone what he wants them to know. I'm president of the local SASS club. Guess you know about us."

"Single Action Shooting Society—cowboy action shooting," Rusty said. "Yeah, you fellas here are known all over the state. One of the best clubs, I'm told."

"We work at it. Me and old Pete Stock started it way back in the day. Old Pete up and died last year. Falls on me and some of the younger fellas to keep it going now."

"So, does Sheriff Cutter belong?" Rusty asked.

"Yeah, that was what I was fixin' to tell you. Wesley joined up when he moved here. Miss Dee did too. That didn't go too well. She'd shoot with us fellas and whooped old Wesley most every time. After about a year, she stopped coming. Old Sheriff Cutter still gets upset most every shoot. He really can't shoot worth a darn. He hates to get beat, though, especially by Duke Atwood—that young Calderone boy too."

"That be Cisco Calderone?" Rusty asked.

"Yeah. That's his name. Good kid. Quiet, polite. Really stays to himself. Only fella I ever saw him friend up with much was Jimmy Hanson."

"Lonny Calderone belong?" Rusty asked.

"Nah. Too busy ranchin'. Never saw him do anything but work."

"Duke and Cisco ever have any trouble?" Rusty asked.

"Not that I ever saw," Toby said. "Didn't ever see them talkin', not that I can recollect."

"So, what's Sheriff Cutter's club name?"

"Bad Bull," Toby said.

"Not very original, but pretty fitting, the bull part anyway," Rusty said.

"You shouldn't expect much else."

"You said Jimmy and Cisco were friendly. Think they spent any time together away from the matches?" Rusty asked.

"Don't know. I never saw them anywhere."

"What do you know about the Eagle Well tale?"

"Old story. Could be all made up. Used to get mighty lonesome out here in the winter time. Old boys would get to tellin' big windies— stories, tall tales, you know—just to pass the time. Oftentimes they made them up as they went along. Added more each time it was retold. Still, I'd say there really is an Eagle Well of some sort. Not sure it ever produced water. Some say it produced eagles—those gold eagles stolen in 1897. You've heard about that, I'm sure."

"Yeah, sure have," Rusty said. "Any chance there's any truth to the coins being there?"

"Much as anything. That money never turned up, not around here anyway. Some figure old Sheriff Tuttle stumbled onto it in '55 and that's what happened to him. Figure that's possible. I was but a kid in high school back then. Everyone had their own opinion on that. Fred Wolf moving away suddenly always seemed more than a chance thing. Seems no one ever heard from him again. His family used to own this town, so they did."

Toby talked on for several minutes, finished a second cup of coffee, then pushed his chair back and stood up. "Best get back home. The wife, she isn't feeling well. Best see if she needs me. Probably see you around. Come out to the shoot next month, if you can. You need to find me, Manny or Buddy can always track me down."

Toby looked at Rusty before he stepped away. "You be careful out and about, Agent Redtail. Pains me to say it, but there's a brutal killer lurking in our midst. Watch your back."

When Toby left, Manny came over and sat down. "Señor Toby, he is a good man. His missus, she is quite sick. He takes good care of her."

"He seems like the kind of guy you'd want for your friend," Rusty said.

"Sí, he is a good friend," Manny said. "Most who come in here, they are my friends. Some more than others. It is so hard to think that maybe one who comes in here, maybe one of them, is the killer of Jimmy. I hope you solve this quickly. I feel many are looking at their neighbors and others and wondering if they are the killer. This is not good. To be suspicious of our neighbors and friends..."

"Anybody unusual around town yesterday?" Rusty asked.

"No... Don't remember anyone."

"Duke Atwood or Lonny Calderone?"

"Both," Manny said. "Here for lunch."

"They speak?" Rusty asked.

"Saw them say hello. Think that was all."

Rusty thought about asking Manny who might have a key to his room, but he didn't want to worry him. The room key was old style—a real key, not a card. Rusty had looked at the tooth pattern and knew it would be an easy lock to pick. He hadn't locked the deadbolt, and the door had enough clearance that a shim of any kind would probably open the simple latch. Besides, all of this was a waste of time. Rusty was almost sure he knew who'd been in his room.

"Going down to Socorro," Rusty said. "I'm told that's where any of the old newspaper records from here might be, if they exist at all. You know where the Socorro paper's office is located?"

"Sí, on First Street, I think," Manny said. "What do you expect to find there?"

"Anything about the 1897 incident—the '55 too," Rusty said. "Jimmy made references to newspaper stories. I'd like to see them myself. There were no copies in the box his wife gave me."

"I wouldn't expect to find much there," Manny said. "Maxwell Wolf owned the paper here. It passed on to Frederick. Somehow, the records all seemed to have disappeared. My father, he said it was a shame, but they were all destroyed. There might have been some things written in the Socorro paper about these things. Still, you might find much more over in the Springerville paper. Since the main branch of the old Hoof Highway cattle trail started over there, there has always been a stronger tie to that area rather than Socorro."

"Interesting," Rusty said. "Just might have to go over there. Might run into an old-timer hanging around there and get a different perspective than here."

"Sí, stop by the White Mountain Diner," Manny said. "That's a good local hangout. Good food too."

"I'll keep that in mind," Rusty said.

"Toby talk you into joining the club?" Manny asked.

"Well, I might just check it out," Rusty said. "You a member?"

"Sort of. I go a couple times a year. The hotel, the café, who has time? It is fun, though."

"What's your name?" Rusty asked. "Everyone has a club name, right?"

"Sí. I'm Old Beans and Biscuits."

"That fits," Rusty said. "Better than Bad Bull. Well, I'll probably see you tonight. Best get to Socorro."

"I'm Rusty Redtail, FBI agent investigating the death of the BLM agent out at Datil," Rusty said as he handed his card to the receptionist at the *Socorro Voice*. "I'm told you might have some old records of the old *Hoof Herald* from up in Magdalena or you might have some old stories in your own paper about things happening in that area a long time ago."

"Oh... nothing from Magdalena, I'm sure," the young lady said. "I'm told those old records all disappeared with Frederick Wolf, back before my time. I've heard old people talk about all that, though. There's so many mysteries unsolved out in that area."

"Yeah, and now this new one," Rusty said.

"You think Jimmy's death had something to do with some old event?" she asked. "He was always looking into that old stuff."

"You knew Jimmy?" Rusty asked.

"Oh yes," she said. "He and Sally lived up the street from me. That poor little boy. Oh, by the way, I'm Nancy Ward."

"Yeah, Nancy, it's sad for the little fella," Rusty said. "Cute boy." After a moment of silence, Rusty asked a question. "Your records from 1897 and 1955, where do I look?"

"Oh... 1897... No, those were all destroyed back when that old storage building collapsed in that flood in the early '50s," Nancy said. "We lost everything from back before World War II. Now, 1955, that's all on microfiche. Somewhat indexed. Not like today's computer retrieval capacity, but it might save you some time looking through everything. What are you looking for?"

"Anything about the disappearance of Sheriff Bucky Tuttle," Rusty said.

"Oh," Nancy said. "The sheriff the space aliens abducted?"

"Space aliens?"

"An old story back in those times," Nancy said. "You know all that Roswell stuff, right? Well, we had several incidents around here about that same time. I think some people truly believe he was abducted into space."

"You remember any other theories?" Rusty asked.

"Well, only things I've heard. I wasn't even born when that happened."

"Yeah, me either. I just thought, working here and all, maybe you've heard something, that's all."

"Come, follow me," Nancy then said, turning and starting back a hallway. "There's a reader back here. I'll pull the fiche for that time. You can look for yourself."

About half-past eleven, Rusty called Chub. "It's Rusty," he said when Chub answered his phone. "I'm in Socorro, the newspaper office. Looking at archives from '55. You have time for lunch?"

"Always," Chub answered. "That Royal Café, across the street from Walmart. Best in town."

"Noon?" Rusty asked.

"Yeah, I'll be there," Chub said.

In a few minutes, Rusty finished looking at the microfiche, then took the file box back to Nancy. "Thanks for your help. I'll be back after lunch. Maybe I can look at the next two years? I just want to skim through them in case something else shows up."

"Sure. I'll have them out for you," Nancy said.

About thirty minutes later, Rusty and Chub met up at the café. After they ordered their food, Chub started asking questions. "Anything in the old papers?"

"Nothing for 1897. Those archives were all destroyed," Rusty said. "A lot, though, for Sheriff Tuttle in '55."

"Anything you can tie in with Jimmy?" Chub asked.

"Space aliens," Rusty said. "Apparently Sheriff Tuttle was abducted, and Jimmy was killed with a ray gun."

"Yeah, I've heard some of that crap," Chub said. "Anything real?"

"Lots of opinions," Rusty said. "Interesting letters to the editor and so on. Opinions all over the board."

"Anything stand out?" Chub asked.

"Yeah. More than one person pointed the finger at Frederick Wolf—that he was like his father," Rusty said. "That he got away with murder. I assume that meant that old Maxwell Wolf had been accused by some to have been the murderer in 1897."

"Motive?" Chub asked. "Maxwell Wolf seemed to be the richest man in San Agustin County back then."

"It seems so," Rusty said. "Might not have been true, though. He may have been overextended. A lot of small banks were. Business out there back then was very seasonal, with many long months with no money flowing in. But then, on the other side, wealthy people always spark jealousy. Someone's always wanting to take them down. Maxwell Wolf might have been wealthy and honest."

"Or like you said, broke and corrupt."

"Any of that would be hard to prove now," Rusty said. "That's really chasing a rabbit from the case at hand. It seems all this about an Eagle Well started with Maxwell Wolf. He seemed to have an element of mystery about him. Might just be a persona he created to put himself above the lowly locals around at that time."

"That was common back then," Chub said. "The cattle barons, the railroad tycoons, the timber kings, and the like, they often set themselves up in their own universe. Today, as I see it, it's the politicians who act like that."

"Seems that way," Rusty agreed.

The waitress brought their food. They ate in silence for a minute. Then Chub spoke again. "How are you getting along with Sheriff Cutter?"

"He goes out of his way to rub everyone the wrong way," Rusty said. "Must not be anyone else out there who wants to be sheriff."

"Why would anyone want the job?" Chub asked.

"The title. Power. Just to make people squirm when they see you," Rusty said. "To have people call you 'sir.' To wear a badge and openly carry a gun."

"Doesn't interest me," Chub said. "That does fit old Sheriff Wesley Cutter for sure."

They ate in silence for a few minutes again, then Rusty spoke. "Think tomorrow I'll go over to Springerville and see what records they have at the paper there. It seems that's more the business center for most folks out there, rather than here. More ranch oriented, I'm told."

"Probably so," Chub said. "That's where most of the cattle were gathered, then driven over to the railhead at Magdalena. Never spent much time over there myself. Nice area, though. All that White Mountain area is nice. Getting to be a lot of people there now. City people moving up there. Bringing their city ways with them, unfortunately."

After finishing his lunch, Rusty went back to the newspaper office. He skimmed through the next several years of the little weekly paper. Nothing caught his attention until he came across a short article from July 1957. It was about a Mrs. Margareta Houser, local artist in Magdalena, selling her studio and moving to Fort Davis, Texas. She was a native of the Magdalena area and had lived there her entire life, except for the short time she was in art school in

New York City. There was no mention as to why she was moving to Fort Davis. What caught Rusty's attention was that her late husband had been mayor of Magdalena and that her daughter was married to Frederick Wolf, heir to the Maxwell Wolf enterprises in Magdalena.

That seemed to be the last thing written about the Wolf family. Nothing more was found about the disappearance of Sheriff Tuttle either.

Rusty arrived back at Magdalena late that afternoon. He started to take the copies of the news articles to his room, then thought better of it. He left his briefcase containing them, as well as the copies of Jimmy's papers, in his Suburban.

He went to the café to have a glass of iced tea. Sitting at a table by a window, he watched a lizard scurry across the parking lot, chased by a roadrunner. Manny came over and sat across from him.

"Find anything in the paper down there?" Manny asked.

"Maybe," Rusty said. "Space aliens abducted the sheriff back in '55."

"Old story, so that is," Manny said. "I remember hearing that back when all that was still being talked about. Some people really believed that, I think."

"Some people seemed to think Frederick Wolf may have had something to do with that too," Rusty said. "The disappearance of the sheriff, that is."

"My father was one of them," Manny said. "He always said Frederick Wolf was one to watch. He said the whole Wolf family was untrustworthy—downright bad, really. When he bought all this from Frederick, they never met to make the deal. It was all through some attorney. I don't remember who, now. It was as if Frederick didn't want to be seen, or something like that."

"Frederick's mother-in-law, Margareta Houser, what can you tell me about her?" Rusty asked.

"Very nice lady. She would give us little ones candy when she would see us. My mother, she cleaned the Houser home and studio. Mother would know as much as anyone about Mrs. Houser."

"Maybe you could ask her if she knows why Margareta Houser moved to Fort Davis, Texas. There was no mention in the paper of family, or anything else, to connect her to there," Rusty said.

"Mother will be here anytime now," Manny said. "I will have her come and talk with you."

"That would be great."

Rusty and Manny talked on for several minutes, then Manny looked back toward the kitchen. "There is Mother now," Manny said. He rose and walked to the kitchen. He returned in a moment, his mother by his side.

"Señor Rusty, this is my mother, Yolanda Rodriguez. She, as I told you, knew Margareta Houser very well."

"Pleasure to meet you," Rusty said as he rose to greet her. "I understand you still make the posole here. It's as good as I've ever eaten anywhere."

"Gracias, Señor Redtail," Yolanda Rodriguez said. "I hear much good things about you. Por favor, you find who did this to that nice man, Señor Jimmy."

"I plan to," Rusty said as they all sat down. "Manny tells me you knew Mrs. Margareta Houser well."

"Sí. Did her cleaning and such for many years," Yolanda said. "A nice lady, she was."

"She had an art studio here. Did she sell much of her work here?" Rusty asked.

"A few pieces only. Most went to Taos and Santa Fe," Yolanda said. "Those fancy people would sometimes come here and buy her paintings. She made mucho money. Never could I pay what she received for those pictures."

"Did she have family in Fort Davis, Texas?" asked Rusty.

"Well… could be," Yolanda said.

"Could be?" Rusty repeated.

"Sí. Letters. She had a box she kept that was full of letters. When I cleaned one day, I knocked the box over. When I put them back in the box, I noticed they all were from Fort Davis, Texas."

"Was there a name on them?" Rusty asked. "A return address?"

"Sí," Yolanda said. "It was a B. A. Weston, I remember."

"Did that mean anything to you?" Rusty asked.

"Ohh… I thought." Yolanda paused a second. "I thought maybe it was her daughter. Betty Ann Wolf, she was. You know, married to Señor Frederick Wolf. They go to Arizona, so they tell everyone. No one ever hear from them again, never. Just me thinking. Maybe B. A. Weston might be her daughter, Betty Ann Wolf."

"Very interesting. About when would this have been?"

"I was setting up some things for her last Christmas here," Yolanda said. "That would have been 1956. The letters continued to come until she moved. I'd see them in the mail."

"Anything else that seemed strange?" Rusty asked. "Anything else going on?"

"No. Just the letters."

"When she left, did she take any artwork with her?"

"Sí. She had several pictures she would not sell."

"Do you remember what they were?" Rusty asked.

"The old cattle pens, the railyard, or cows on the trail," Yolanda answered. "There was one of this old hotel in the old times, when it was a very fine place. That, she gave to me. It hangs in the lobby now. You have seen that, no?"

"Yeah. I haven't looked closely at it," Rusty said. "I will now. That was a nice gift."

"Sí, very much appreciated," Yolanda said. "The day before she left, she told me to sit in the parlor with her. I believe she wished to tell me something. She started several times to say something, but she always stopped."

"I'll take a closer look at that painting when I go over to the hotel," Rusty said. "I do remember seeing it, though. This was really the place to be, back in the day."

"Finest hotel between Saint Louis and San Francisco, it was written once," Yolanda said. "That story is also framed and on the lobby wall."

"I'll look for that too," Rusty said. "Anything else you can think of connected to Mrs. Houser's leaving?"

"Well, sí, only that when I asked her for an address in Fort Davis, in case I needed to send her something, she told me she wouldn't be at a permanent place for some time. She said that maybe she wouldn't even stay at Fort Davis very long. She said she'd send me a permanent address. But she never did. She just disappeared, like the rest of the Wolf family."

⋙— CHAPTER 8 —⋘

Rusty called Liz the first thing the next morning.

"Hey, Rusty, what's going on?" Liz asked when Rusty greeted her.

"Lots, really. I have some more things for you to work on. In Fort Davis, Texas, check for anything on a Betty Ann Weston. She had a young daughter. This would be back in the late '50s and '60s. Also, anything on a Mrs. Margareta Houser, an artist, out there. A Frederick Weston, or Wolf, too."

"OK, Rusty," Liz said. "Harland has me really backed up. I'm embarrassed, but I haven't even been able to work on that request on Frederick Wolf you gave me. Sorry. This might take a few days."

"Yeah, I understand that," Rusty said. "Do the best you can."

An hour later, Rusty had finished his breakfast and was about to leave the café and go to Springerville when Buddy Bell came in and sat down at his table.

"Thought I'd come in early," Buddy said. "You're never here at lunchtime, it seems. Toby Wilson told me he'd talked with you. Said you might come to next month's shoot."

"Oh, I might," Rusty said. "Guess I was more interested in who all belonged to the club and how they acted."

"That's what Toby said. Good group, really. I'm a real klutz most of the time," Buddy said. "I never win anything. I just do it for the fun."

"I know it's all lead bullets and pistol calibers, right? What do you shoot?" Rusty asked.

"Just 38s. They're cheap. Lots of modern reproduction guns chambered for them too. Only the fellas who are real serious invest in one of the true old guns and calibers."

"Sheriff Cutter, he shoot 38s also?" Rusty asked.

"Yeah. He's got some nice guns, though," Buddy said. "Nice guns don't seem to help him much. He's not a whole lot better shot than I am."

"I heard his wife was better than him," Rusty said.

"Oh yeah, much better. That surely didn't set well with Wesley," Buddy said. "Especially when someone would say that she'd make a better sheriff than him. Fightin' words, those were."

"I'm going to Springerville, to the newspaper office there," Rusty said. "Any other suggestions on where to look for information over there?"

"Not really," Buddy said.

"Manny suggested hanging around the White Mountain Diner. Ever been there?" Rusty asked.

"Oh yeah. A lot of locals do eat there," Buddy said. "That would be as good a place as any to pick up some information."

"I haven't made it out to that fake well site yet. You think any more about going out there with me?"

"Oh… well, to be honest with you, as I said the other day, I'm not too crazy about going out into that back country until you catch that killer. Maybe I've been doing too much thinking."

"I understand," Rusty said. "Well, maybe you can plot it on a map for me anyway."

"Sure. I'll do that. You have a plat of the Rancho Vaca? That's where it's located."

"Yeah, I have a ranch plat," Rusty said. "Next time I see you, OK? By the way, I'm bringing in a chopper next week to fly over this country. Maybe I'll see something from the air. I've covered a lot of country, back and forth across every road I can find."

"Be careful. That chopper will make a tempting target for anyone trying to keep a lid on the fact that they've already killed one federal agent."

Rusty nodded slowly. "Guess you're right. Still hard to figure that anyone out here would do such a thing."

"Could be someone you haven't met. Someone hiding something," Buddy said. "Maybe this has nothing to do with any of Jimmy's treasure hunting and all. Maybe he stumbled onto a drug deal, a pot patch, or something like that. You hear about stuff like that all the time. Could be whoever it was is miles away by now. We're quite a ways from the border, but still, could be illegal smugglers staying off the interstates and such."

"Well, someone had to drive that truck back there, then have a way out," Rusty said. "I think they knew the area well. I'm still leaning towards a local."

"Yeah, you're probably right. I'd much rather it was a stranger, though. Well, if it's dark when you come back from Springerville, watch out for all those elk. You'll probably pass a couple of dozen just grazing along the road's edge."

"That's what I hear. We had them about like that back on the reservation too. Never hit one. Came close a few times—too close."

"Well, gotta go," Buddy said. "One of our older women wants me to stop by. Thinks she has some wild creature in her attic. Probably just a mouse or bat. The joys of being a small-town pastor with a congregation of mostly retired people."

"I'll trade you," Rusty said.

"No—no thanks. I'll stick to catching mice and let you catch the murderer."

Several hours later, Rusty drove around Springerville for some time, getting a feel for the small mountain town. He located the *White Mountain Gazette* office on a side street. He parked, then went inside.

"May I help you?" the receptionist asked.

"I hope so. I'm FBI Agent Rusty Redtail," he said, handing her his card. "I'm investigating the murder of BLM Ranger Jimmy Hanson over by Datil. You've heard about that, right?"

"Oh yes. That man was in here a short while back," she said, "looking for old papers."

"Probably 1897 and 1955, right?" Rusty said as he looked at the badge pinned on the lady's blouse and noticed her name was Sue.

"Ah—I believe that was it," Sue said.

"That's what I'd like to see also," Rusty said. "Maybe some other things as well. Do you keep a file on important people?"

"Well, now we do," Sue said. "I don't know how far back those files go. It's a whole lot easier today. In the old days—"

"Yeah, I'm sure," Rusty said. "Well, I'd like to start with the 1897 papers, if possible."

"Well, those are on microfiche, over in our old morgue building," Sue said. "That will take me awhile to find. What else do you want?"

"Starting with July of 1955. How do you have things cross-referenced?"

"Back in 1955? Not well at all," Sue said. "Think you'll just have to scan each paper. Fortunately, back then the paper was usually small. Little sports or national news then. Mostly local stuff."

"That's what I want," Rusty said. "Actually, I'm looking for some things that took place over in Magdalena, New Mexico."

"Oh yeah, I remember now," Sue said. "That's what that other fella, the one who was killed, that's what he was looking for also,"

"When was he here?"

"Only a few weeks before I learned that he'd been killed," Sue said. "I was shocked when I saw his picture. I hope he got his copies."

"His copies?"

"Yeah, he had a whole bunch of pages he wanted copied," Sue said. "The printer on that old microfiche reader uses that old-style, thermal paper, you know, that roll stuff? Well, we were out of paper when he was here. No one in town sells it. We have to order it over the Internet. Someplace in Los Angeles, I think. Probably comes in from China, like everything else."

"So, Jimmy never got his copies?" Rusty asked.

"Well, I guess he did. He left his address—Socorro, I think. When I got that roll of paper, I made his copies and sent them to him. I hope he got them before... I guess it really doesn't matter now."

"They probably burned in the truck fire," Rusty said. "Any chance you still have his list of what you copied for him?"

"No—I don't think so. That was weeks ago now. Let me check, though. I'm sure I threw it in the waste basket, but the janitor here is so poor at emptying out the trash. He waits until the baskets are plumb full. Give me a minute." She turned and walked into the back room. After several moments, she returned, a smile across her face and a piece of paper in her hand.

"You're in luck," Sue said. "At the very bottom of that trashcan by the fiche reader, there it was. Guess I should thank the janitor for being lazy."

"That's good, great, really," Rusty said. "How many pages are on the list?"

"At least forty. I remember he paid with cash. Didn't want a receipt. I was surprised. I figured this was government business, but it must have been personal."

"Yeah, it sort of was," Rusty said. "Well, can you duplicate this list? That would save me a ton of time looking at all those microfiche."

"I'll have to dig out all of them. That will take several hours at least."

"That will be fine. I'll go look around town for a while. I haven't seen a library. Is there one?"

"Oh yeah. Over on Third Street," Sue said. "There's some local history books there that might interest you."

"Any bookstores where I might buy some local history books?" Rusty asked.

"If you came in from the east, you passed our bookstore—on the north side of the street, about the middle of town."

"Guess I wasn't looking for it," Rusty said. "Thanks. When do you think I should stop back?"

"Well, I'd say about three—maybe sooner."

After Rusty left the newspaper office, he found the White Mountain Diner. He went in and ordered a cup of coffee. He picked up a copy of last week's local paper and glanced through it. He was nearly finished when he sensed someone approaching him from his right. He folded the paper, then looked up at the man now standing by his table.

"Must be your black government vehicle out there," the man in a tan uniform said.

"Yeah. Rusty Redtail, FBI. Investigating the murder of Jimmy Hanson, the BLM Ranger, over in Datil."

"Yeah, too bad about that. Downright shame, so it is. I'm Willy Hays," the man said, stretching out his right hand to Rusty. "Sheriff in these parts."

"Have a seat, please," Rusty said. "I'm having some copies made over at the newspaper office. Heard this was the best place in town for gossip."

"Probably is," Sheriff Hays said. "Bunch of that everywhere, though. You know how small towns are. If there's no news, someone's gonna make up some."

"Unfortunately, what happened to Jimmy Hanson is real news," Rusty said.

"Didn't know him," Sheriff Hays said. "Heard good things after his death, though."

"You lived here all your life?" Rusty asked the sheriff.

"Fourth generation," Sheriff Hays replied.

"You probably know some of the goings on over in New Mexico. Any ideas or stories going around here about who might have done this?" asked Rusty.

"Most of those ranch fellas over yonder come here to trade," the sheriff said. "I know most of them by sight, not all by name. That state line doesn't mean much."

"Any bad actors? Anyone spend much time in your jail?"

"Oh, a few drunk and disorderlies now and again. Bar fights and such. Sometimes just too drunk to drive home. No real crime. No threats or gunplay or the like. Oftentimes, the whole family comes over and loads up with groceries and whatever else they need. No, there's no one I know over there, here either, that I'd be suspicious of."

"I haven't found any real good suspects yet either," Rusty said.

"What's old Sheriff Cutter say?" Sheriff Hays asked. "He's always got something to say about everything. Bet he's trying to pin this on Andy or Duke Atwood, maybe that Mexican fella who's always at odds with Andy."

"Lonny Calderone," Rusty said.

"That's him. Old feud. Not sure these young ones even know why they're supposed to hate each other."

"That's the way I see it," Rusty said. "Of course, I don't know all the details."

"Andy Atwood's a good man," Sheriff Hays said. "Wouldn't hurt a fly."

"What about that poaching thing?"

"Nothing much to it," Sheriff Hays replied. "That was young Duke. He was sorta helping a friend whose father is in a wheelchair. Wrongfully killing an elk doesn't make one a murder suspect."

"Anything odd around here back when Jimmy was killed?" Rusty asked. "That was ten days ago now."

"Well, sort of. Our guy here who works on wells, a driller and such, he was telling me that a few days after that killing, he was going back a ranch road to fix a windmill. Over on that G Bar T Ranch, over on the New Mexico border, seems he came upon a fella in a pickup who seemed to be camping there. Fella grabbed a rifle and sort of held it defensively as Chester drove by. When he came out several hours later, the truck was gone."

"Did he get a plate number or anything?" Rusty asked.

"Partial plate. Oklahoma, so it was. Well, two days later, this fella was picked up over in Flagstaff. Truck was stolen. Fella had escaped from the Cotton County, Oklahoma, jail. Serving a sixty-day sentence for domestic violence. Got drunk and hit his girlfriend, or something like that."

"He's back in Oklahoma now?" Rusty asked.

"Yeah. Be a lot more than sixty days now. Time in the state pen, most likely. Fool thing to do."

"Can you get me a copy of all this from Flagstaff? The contacts in Oklahoma too?" Rusty asked.

"Oh sure. Just finish your coffee, then stop by my office. Over towards Eager, by the school. Can't miss it."

"Yeah. I saw it when I was driving around. No cars there, or I'd have stopped in."

"I'll go get started on that," Sheriff Hays said as he rose to leave. "See you in a bit."

Rusty finished drinking his coffee and reading the paper. The whole time he'd been talking to Sheriff Hays he'd noticed a man at the other end of the diner watching him. Now, the man still stared at Rusty.

Rusty then got up, paid his bill, and went out to the Suburban. He hesitated a few seconds before starting the engine. As he did, this other man rapidly walked out the café door. He looked at Rusty, then got into an older pickup with a very large Rebel flag decal in the back window.

Rusty pulled out of the parking lot, drove west a block, then turned south. Through all of this, he was shadowed by the old pickup. In about a hundred yards, he pulled into a little plaza parking lot and into a parking space. He watched the old pickup park about ten spaces away. Rusty stepped on the gas and sped into the spot beside the old truck's driver's side door.

"Can I help you?" he asked the man, who'd turned his head away from him. Rusty's hand wrapped around his pistol and slid it out of its holster underneath his jacket.

The man turned and stared at Rusty. His reddish face now seemed more flushed than it had in the diner. With his right hand, he swept his long hair back from his face. "You're a Fed. Got no business in these parts. Just go back to Washington and leave us alone out here."

"I've never been to Washington," Rusty said. "Grew up in the mountains of New Mexico. I've got every right to be here. I'm investigating a murder."

"Yeah. That other Fed over in New Mexico," the man in the pickup said, "he shouldn't have been there either."

"Tell you what. I'm on my way over to the sheriff's office," Rusty said. "Why don't we both go over there and talk some more? I've got some questions I want answers to."

"I can save you the time. Back when that boy was taken care of over there, I was in the hospital in Pinetop. The sheriff can vouch for that. Spent three days there. Sorta got into an argument with the wrong end of a knife."

"I've got your license number," Rusty said. "I'm sure the sheriff knows who you are."

"Oh yeah. We go way back. Fact is, he's my cousin." At that, the man turned, started the old truck, then lurched out of his parking space and onto the street.

Rusty then started his Suburban and drove over to the sheriff's office. Inside, Sheriff Hays was at his desk, stuffing an envelope with multiple sheets of paper.

"Met one of your finest a minute ago," Rusty said.

"Oh Lordy no," the sheriff said. "Lester Hays. I saw him in the diner. Suppose he told you he's my cousin?"

"Yeah, after he told me to get out of the area."

"That's Lester. He is a cousin, unfortunately," Sheriff Hays said. "Biggest thorn in my side in the whole county. He's one who's capable of about anything. However, I did verify that he was indeed in the Pinetop hospital when that ranger was killed. Knife about got his liver, what the booze hasn't already destroyed."

"We can't pick our families," Rusty said. "I've got a few out on the reservation I'm not too proud to call kin."

"Glad you, and the voters here, see it that way," the sheriff said. "That Oklahoma fella's name is Travis Evans. I just talked to the sheriff over in Cotton County, Wilson Towner, and he's still got custody of Travis. Said he'd wait to hear from you before he gets him transferred out."

"Good," Rusty said. "I'll call him when I leave here. You folks ever talk about that '55 disappearance of Sheriff Tuttle over in San Agustin County? Any rumors around here?"

"Our sheriff here at the time, Chet Hays, he was my uncle, my dad's brother. He and Bucky were very good friends. Uncle Chet worked that disappearance as much as he could from over here. A lot of people think Bucky found that missing money from the old days and skipped the country. Uncle Chet never believed that. He leaned toward Frederick Wolf knowing about that money, that his father is the one who stole it, and Bucky got too close and Frederick did him in. It sure was strange that Frederick Wolf moved right after that and was never heard from again, not that I know of. Then, others think they were in on something together, Bucky and Frederick. That they both took off for somewhere and lived life high."

"Well, they'd both be dead or really old by now," Rusty said. "Guess it doesn't matter a whole lot these days. Except that Jimmy Hanson was digging into all of that, big time." Rusty paused for a moment, then asked the sheriff a question. "Ever hear about some sort of a phantom well called the Eagle Well?"

"Oh yeah. Sort of like Big Foot," Sheriff Hays said. "About once a year, at least, someone out in these mountains comes in here all excited claiming they've see some godawful creature as big as a moose on two feet or the like. They expect me to drop everything and go chasing after it. Dozens of fellas have spent days looking for that well and the money it's supposed to hold. It doesn't exist. Just a story made up by old Maxwell Wolf."

"To some people, Maxwell Wolf was a community pillar, others see him as a scoundrel," Rusty said.

"Always that way with rich people," Sheriff Hays replied. "He did a lot for Magdalena back in its heyday. Might have done more for Maxwell Wolf, though. I'm sure he stepped on some toes. It seems that a lot of those old barons were more than a little odd. They didn't think, or act, like us common folks."

"Hey, thanks a lot, sheriff," Rusty said. "I'm going over to the library, maybe the bookstore too. Maybe I can find something else on all of this. Probably I'll see you again. You've been a big help. I'll let you know if anything comes up with that Evans fellow over in Oklahoma."

"Anytime. Been watching my back a little closer ever since that shootin'. Hate to think the killer might be out and around here. Maybe even someone I know."

"We'll all sleep better once I solve this," Rusty said. "If this is an anti-government thing, I'm most likely the biggest target, my being federal."

"Probably so," Sheriff Hays said. "Well, if I come up with anything else, I'll let you know. Nice meeting you, Agent Redtail."

"Just call me Rusty, please," he said, then he picked up the envelope, shook the sheriff's hand, and left the office. He drove over to the library and parked in a spot at the north side of the parking lot. He took out the envelope Sheriff Hays had given him, then shuffled through the papers until he found the one with the Oklahoma sheriff's office data. He called the number.

"Cotton County Sheriff's Office. How may I direct your call?"

"This is Rusty Redtail, Albuquerque FBI. I'd like to speak to Sheriff Towner, please."

"Oh—please hold."

It took several minutes, then someone picked up the phone. "This is Sheriff Towner."

"Sheriff, this is Rusty Redtail, Albuquerque FBI. I'm investigating the death of a BLM Ranger in western New Mexico. You've talked with Sheriff Hays across the line in Arizona, I believe. You've heard about this incident, I'm sure."

"Oh, for sure," Sheriff Towner said. "I was expecting your call. You want to talk to my prisoner, right?"

"Yeah, I hear you still have him in your jail, right?"

"Oh yeah. Locked up real tight this time," the sheriff answered. "You can come and take him if you'd like."

"You know him? He a local?" Rusty asked.

"Sort of. Off and on with one of our local gals. I'd say that's off now."

"Got a sheet on him?" Rusty asked.

"Drunk and disorderly. This domestic thing. That's it, really," Sheriff Towner said.

"Your gut feeling: Backed into a corner, would he kill someone to cover for himself?"

"Well... I wouldn't bet against it. He doesn't really seem to be the type though, but he does have a mean streak, when drunk."

"I'd like to come over and interview him. It'll take me all day tomorrow to get near there. How about early the next day?"

"Works for me," Sheriff Towner said. "I'll help you any way I can."

"Good. I'll stay over somewhere around Wichita Falls," Rusty said. "Be up midmorning then."

"I'll have the coffee on," the sheriff said.

Rusty then called Liz in his Albuquerque office.

"Oh, Rusty," Liz said once she recognized his voice. "I knew you'd be calling. I'm sorry, but other cases have me so busy I haven't gotten much done on my Fort Davis search, Frederick Wolf either. I've passed some of that off to Amanda here. Actually, she's from somewhere out that way. She has relatives in Alpine, close by Fort Davis. I'll check with her and see how she's coming. Call me later, OK?"

"Do the best you can," Rusty said. "I'm going to Oklahoma tomorrow to interview a fugitive who was seen over here about the time this happened. In a way, I do hope it was an outsider. A lot of these locals are pointing the finger at each other. They're dragging up stuff that's been buried for a hundred years. Of course, Jimmy was digging up a lot of that himself. Maybe they're right."

"What about the local sheriff?" Liz asked. "Is he any help?"

"Some," Rusty said. "He's more interested in his rodeo bulls. Being sheriff is only a part-time thing down here. I'm over in Arizona now. The sheriff here has been a big help. It seems Springerville is actually the main trade center for that part of New Mexico, for the ranchers anyway. I came over to look at some old newspapers."

"Sounds as if you're chasing some of that old stuff yourself," Liz said. "Nothing better to chase after out there?"

"It's addictive. You know? To solve an unsolved case from the 1800s is challenging. Maybe these old things have a connection to Jimmy," Rusty said. "That chopper set up yet?"

"Yeah. Tuesday and Wednesday. Harland threw a fit when he saw the order. He said he didn't think you were serious."

"Why not?" Rusty said. "He's like the sheriff here. They think I should solve this using some ancient Apache spell or something."

"Any other case he'd have half a dozen agents on it," Liz said. "I've never seen a case, not anything like the murder of a federal ranger, where he only put one man on it."

"That's OK," Rusty said. "I work well alone. I'll get to the bottom, sooner or later. Have to, for Jimmy's little boy at least. Cute kid. Feel bad for him."

"That's a good motivation," Liz said. "Let me know if I can do anything to help. I'll do my best—when I get time."

"Thanks. Yeah, I will need some help next week, if I turn up what I think," Rusty said. "Well, later then."

"Is that a promise?" Liz asked. "When's later—about nine tonight?"

"In your dreams, girl."

Rusty went into the library and found several local history books. He spent several hours reading about the old cattle trail, the Hoof Highway or Beefsteak Trail it was called. He got caught up in reading about some of the events that shaped the trail and its surrounding area. As he finished skimming one book, he realized he was hungry. He looked at the clock: 1:15. He returned the books, then drove over to the White Mountain Diner.

He sat at the counter and ate his lunch without incident. When he finished, he went over to the bookstore to see if they had any local history books that might tell of the Magdalena incidents. He found one on a shelf labeled "Local History" that he'd seen at the library but hadn't had time to go through. He picked up the book, looked at the index, and saw several chapters that looked as if they might contain pertinent information. He looked at the price penciled on the cover: ten dollars. He hung on to that book as he continued to look around. Over on a table, he saw a stack of five books that looked to be the same as the one he'd picked up. He walked over to them, looked at the cover on the top one, then opened it. Thirty-five dollars was the price written there. He compared the two books, saw no difference, then put one back on the stack on the table.

Moments later, Rusty went to the register to pay for his book.

"That'll be ten dollars and eighty cents," the clerk said.

Rusty took out his money clip. "Is this the same book as those on the table?" he asked.

"Yes," the clerk said. "It's a local author. We really push her book. Besides, it's very informative."

"Is this a used book?"

"No, they're all new."

"But this one is ten dollars. Those are thirty-five, right?"

"Yes." There was silence, then the clerk spoke again. "Oh yes. For local people, those who come in the store, we only charge ten. We don't want to overcharge here."

"And those?" Rusty nodded to the books on the table.

"That's what we sell them for over the Internet. You can't expect us to sell to someone in New York for the same as locally, do you?"

"Oh, I guess not," Rusty said. "But ten to thirty-five…"

Rusty left, thinking about some of the Internet purchases he'd made lately. He went back to the newspaper office.

"I have all of that here for you," Sue said, handing Rusty two envelopes. "I've put each of those years in its own envelope. This is everything I copied for that other fella. I hope this helps you."

"Yeah, me too. I don't know what I'm looking for. It could well be there's something here that actually is responsible for getting Jimmy killed. Then, maybe there's no connection," Rusty said as he took out his wallet.

"Just don't let any of it get you killed," Sue said as she handed Rusty a receipt. "Well, anyway, good luck. Come back and see me if you need anything else."

"You've been a big help," Rusty said. "I met your sheriff. He was a big help also."

"Oh, Willy's a good man," Sue said. "We think a lot of him around here."

Rusty then went out to his Suburban. He drove back into New Mexico. Reaching Pie Town, and thinking about a cup of coffee, he pulled into the café parking lot. There was Sheriff Cutter's pickup parked right by the door. Rusty went inside.

"Hey, Chief. Haven't seen you for a couple of days," Sheriff Cutter said. "Thought maybe you'd given up, or gone to some mountaintop to get a vision of something."

"Going to Oklahoma tomorrow," Rusty said. "Got a lead on a jail escapee who was in this area when Jimmy was killed. He was camping out around here. Had a stolen Oklahoma pickup. You see him around?"

"Aah—no. Who told you about that?" Sheriff Cutter asked. "Sounds farfetched to me."

"He was here, for sure," Rusty said. "He admitted that. Right here in your county. He was eventually picked up over in Flagstaff and sent back to Oklahoma. I talked to the sheriff there. Like I said, I'm going over there tomorrow."

Sheriff Cutter sat silently for several minutes, toying with his iced tea glass. After a minute, he spoke. "Sounds like you think I should have known about that."

"I didn't say that," Rusty said. "Nothing like that. I just asked if you knew anything. Thought maybe you could add to what I already know."

"You didn't say how you learned about this," Sheriff Cutter said.

"In a vision, up on a mountaintop," Rusty said, holding back a smile.

"Ahh—guess I had that one coming," the sheriff said, pushing back from the table.

The door opened, and a man came in carrying a box about a foot square. He started toward the sheriff and Rusty.

"Sorry to keep you waiting, Sheriff. My old truck didn't want to start. It takes spells every once in a while," the man said as he set the box on the table, then sat down in an empty chair.

"Haven't been here but a few minutes myself, Shorty," Sheriff Cutter said. "Been talking with the chief here. This is Rusty Redtail. He's one of them fancy FBI fellas. He's looking into what happened to Jimmy Hanson, that BLM Ranger. Shorty here, he loads up my ammo for the cowboy action thing. I don't have the patience, or time, to do that. Melting lead, pouring bullets, measuring powder, sizing brass, swaging it all together—not me. Gladly pay Shorty here.

"Oh, hello. I'm Shorty Walker… Well, Clarence, really but everyone calls me Shorty," the man said, extending his hand to Rusty. "I've never met an FBI man before. Saw that fancy black thing out there. Thought it was a funeral gone lost or something. That must be yours."

"That's the government's, really," Rusty said as he shook Shorty's hand. "Good to meet you. You lived out here a long time?"

"About ten years now," Shorty said. "Me and my Mary Jane moved out here to get away from the city. All the crime and such. Now, with this… a murder right in our area. We never locked our doors before. Now, Mary Jane, she don't like to be alone. I best get back to her."

"Loading ammo for the cowboy shoots, that makes you a few extra dollars, I guess," Rusty said.

"Oh yeah," Shorty said. "I load a lot for hunters and the like too. It all adds up. Cost of things today, it takes all a man can make."

Sheriff Cutter looked at the handwritten bill from Shorty. He took out his wallet and paid the total. "This box here," the sheriff said as he slid a box containing empty shell cases over to Shorty. "I won't need any of these until next month."

"Just let me know when, Sheriff," Shorty said as he rose to leave.

"Tell Mary Jane not to worry," Sheriff Cutter said. "I've got things under control."

"Yeah, knowing the FBI is here will ease her mind, I'm sure," Shorty said as he walked to the door.

Sheriff Cutter pushed back his chair. "Well, Chief. Now that you've put Shorty's wife at ease, have a good trip to Oklahoma. Anything turns up while you're gone, I'm sure I can handle it."

"I'm sure you will," Rusty said. "I'll only be a few days."

"Take your time," the sheriff said as he rose, picking up the box of ammo. "Don't think you'll find anything in Oklahoma. Ain't no mountaintops over there."

"Lots of us Indians, though," Rusty said. "We could have a first-class powwow. Who knows what I'll turn up."

Sheriff Cutter walked out without commenting.

After finishing his coffee, Rusty left also and drove straight to his hotel room. He read some of the old newspaper articles, went to the café, and ate a quick dinner, then returned and started reading more. He was getting sleepy, about ready to quit and turn on the news, when something jarred him awake.

When Franz Frick's body was discovered in this hotel room that morning, there was a knife still buried deep into his heart—a fancy silver-handled knife from Mexico. Engraved on the handle were the bold initials FC.

Fernando Calderone?

>>——— CHAPTER 9 ———<<

Now wide awake, Rusty read the rest of that article on the murder of Franz Frick. He then pulled off his boots and stretched out on the bed. He stared up at the old pressed-tin ceiling and thought about what he'd just read.

Right here in this room… When Franz failed to show for a breakfast meeting with several ranchers and Maxwell Wolf that morning, and didn't answer his door, Sheriff Antonio Ortiz opened the door and discovered Franz with the knife in his heart and the three empty strongboxes chained together and to his bed.

Still thinking on this, Rusty dozed off into a restless sleep.

"What the—" Sheriff Ortiz exclaimed. "Right here under my nose. Murder. Who? Why?"

"Those money boxes are empty," Maxwell Wolf said after walking over to them and looking inside. "He should have put them in my bank. None of this would have happened if he'd only been like everyone else."

"Who would want to do this?" Sheriff Ortiz asked. "Who had a rift with old Franz?"

"A rift? All those gold coins are reason enough," Maxwell Wolf said. "There didn't have to be any trouble between them. However, that knife—'F C' engraved on it. I'm sure I've seen that old cattleman from Mexico, that Fernando Calderone fella, with a knife like that. I'm told he did lose a good sum of money to Franz last night at the tables. Might be a good place to start, if he's not halfway to Mexico by now."

"That knife is suspicious," Sheriff Ortiz said. "Can't figure why anyone who would do this would leave such a high-priced knife behind, especially if it had their initials on it."

"You're right. That doesn't make much sense," Maxwell Wolf said. "Look at that bedding. Blood soaked clear down into that mattress. I'll have to throw all of this out. You catch this guy. I need some of those gold coins to cover my cost on this. Have to pay someone to clean all this up too. Sorry now I didn't get into that game last night and at least win some of his money there."

A short time later, Rusty awoke, the same thoughts still on his mind. He pondered what he'd read earlier. The gold coins contained in twelve bags would have weighed over one hundred fifty pounds. More than one man could carry out in one trip. Had there been more than one person? Or did one man make several trips to carry out the money? Where to? Where was the money taken to? It was never found—unless Sheriff Tuttle found it, or Jimmy, or both. Was any of it still around? Could it really be in some mysterious old well or vault out there somewhere?

Jimmy had taken a ladder with him the day he disappeared. It wasn't in his burned-out truck. Where was it? Down some old hand-dug well? Jimmy must have known he needed a ladder for something. After a long time, and a lot of thought, Rusty finally drifted back off to sleep.

The next day, as he drove toward Oklahoma, Rusty went over each possible suspect in his mind—over and over. For every possibility of guilt, there was a stronger reason why not. He was tired when he reached his motel and, after watching some news, Rusty quickly fell asleep. He awoke the next morning thinking about his upcoming interview with Travis Evans. How easy it would be if he could determine Travis was Jimmy's killer and he'd confess. That was too easy, even for a dream.

Two hours after leaving his northwest Texas motel the next morning, Rusty pulled up to the Cotton County, Oklahoma Sheriff's Office. He parked, picked up his briefcase, then entered the building.

The receptionist smiled at him when he approached her desk. "You must be Agent Redtail," she said.

"Yes. You must be expecting me."

"It's not every day an FBI agent visits us," she said. "I've been here eighteen years, and this is a first for me."

"Well, this will probably be very anticlimactic," Rusty said. "I just want to talk to your prisoner. Is Sheriff Towner in?"

"Right here," came a voice from back the hall. "Come on back."

Rusty looked in the direction of the voice and saw a man standing in the hallway outside an open doorway. Rusty walked back the hall to the sheriff. They shook hands when he reached him.

"Come on in my office here. Have a seat. Make yourself comfortable. How was your trip?" Sheriff Towner asked as he sat in his chair behind his desk and Rusty sat in a chair across the desk from him.

"Oh, the trip was uneventful," Rusty said. "It gave me time to chew over all the information I've gathered so far."

"I've been out in that Gila Wilderness, hunting elk," Sheriff Towner said. "Great country over there. Sure could use some of those mountains around here. Be nice to cool off in July. What brought on this killing anyway? Any idea?"

"Several possibilities. I don't have a prime suspect or motive," Rusty said. "There's several local, suspicious people—I hesitate to call them suspects—but there's a lot of campers and others out through there at any given time. It could be a total stranger. There's always the possibility Jimmy stumbled onto a drug or smuggling situation. I'm going up in a chopper when I get back. Maybe I'll spot something from the air."

"Sounds exciting," Sheriff Towner said. "I've been sheriff here for nearly twelve years. Never had anything like this around here."

"Be thankful," Rusty said. "The folks out there are on edge. They don't know if one of their friends or neighbors has killed a federal agent and gruesomely tried to destroy his body. They fear there could be some psycho lurking around those mountains and canyons, watching them from a distance, looking for his next victim."

"Hadn't thought about that. I never worked in a very rural area. Oh, this is about that way, I guess," Sheriff Towner said. "No mountains or canyons to hide in, though. Old barns, maybe."

"This has aggravated old feuds too," Rusty said. "Neighbors are distrusting neighbors, and old rumors are coming back to life."

"I'll bet," the sheriff said. "I get that here when somebody's dog dies."

"Well," Rusty said. "Why don't I talk to Travis for a while? Has he lawyered up on the charges you have against him?"

"Yeah," Sheriff Towner said. "You'll have to stay away from any of that. He might lawyer up on you too. The bad thing about that is that his lawyer is an hour away. Probably wouldn't even make it here today."

"I'll see," Rusty said as he stood to his feet. "Is he expecting me?"

"No. I didn't say anything. Thought maybe that if he's guilty, you won't be a surprise. He'll be half-expecting someone from over there."

"Maybe he'll jump up and confess, and I can cuff him and take him off to the federal pen in Albuquerque," Rusty said. "Oh, that life should be that easy."

"No resistance from me," Sheriff Towner said as he started back a long hallway. "Travis is the only one in here. You can talk to him through the bars. No one will hear anything."

Rusty followed Sheriff Towner back to the end of the hall, then through a security door and into a room with three barred cells.

"You have a visitor, Travis," the sheriff said, walking up to the only occupied cell.

"You here to get me out?" Travis asked.

"Might take you with me," Rusty said. "I'm—"

"You got a bottle of bourbon for me?"

"No. I'm—"

"Don't care who you are," Travis said, flopping back down on his cot.

"I'm Rusty Redtail, FBI. I'm here to arrest you for murder and take you back to New Mexico."

"What?" Travis quickly sat back up and stared wide-eyed at Rusty. "Murder? What are you talking about?"

"I'd tell you, but since you don't want to talk." Rusty set his briefcase on a small table outside the cell, opened it, then took out a set of handcuffs.

"Hold on there. I don't know nothin' about no murder in New Mexico. You can't pin that on me," Travis said. "Let's talk. Tell me what this is about."

"I'll leave you two alone," Sheriff Towner said. "Just push the buzzer by the door if you want anything. Coffee or water now?"

"I'll take some water," Rusty said. "Water, Travis?"

"Yeah—yeah, OK."

"I'll have Henrietta bring some to you in a minute," the sheriff said as he exited through the door then let it close behind him. Rusty slid the lone chair over to the little table, then sat down. He took out a pad from his case, then a pen from his pocket. He looked at Travis, who sat tapping his fingers on his knees, his eyes blinking often as they danced around the room.

"Who'd you say you were?" Travis asked, now looking at Rusty.

"Rusty Redtail. FBI, Albuquerque office. You know why I'm here."

"No—no I don't," Travis said. "Murder? No. You got the wrong guy."

"Two weeks ago, you were in New Mexico. San Agustin County. By Magdalena and Datil. We know that," Rusty said.

"Yeah, yeah, I went through there," Travis said. "OK, I was fixin' to spend a night or so out there on some ranch. So what?"

"You see a BLM pickup out there?" Rusty asked.

"Oh crap. This is about that? Yeah," Travis said, "I saw one of those trucks. Something wasn't right. I got out of there right quick."

"So, what did you see?" Rusty asked. "What wasn't right?"

Rusty heard footsteps coming back the hallway. He waited until Henrietta brought in two bottles of water. "Thanks," Rusty said, taking the water from her. She turned and started back toward her desk. Rusty handed one bottle to Travis as the door closed and Rusty heard Henrietta walk back out the hallway.

"Water," Travis said. "Dang sure could use something real to drink."

"So, what wasn't right with that pickup?" Rusty again asked.

"That government pickup, see, was towin' a small trailer with a four-wheeler on it—one of them ranch types, you know?" Travis said. "It was late afternoon sometime. Like I said, I was fixin' to spend the night there. I'd pulled off the pavement. Don't know how far I'd driven back this old ranch road—long ways, I think. I wasn't hurtin' nothing. Had me some jerky and half a bottle of bourbon on the tailgate of my, well, the pickup I was driving. Heard this truck coming from on back this road. Didn't think anyone would be back in there. Anyway, I jumped off the tailgate. Fell plumb facedown, so I did. Got into the cab and got ready to leave.

"Like I said," Travis continued after taking a drink of water, "there was this government pickup. The driver saw me and stopped. I didn't want to panic and bring suspicion to myself. Thought I'd just play it cool, you know? Like nothing was wrong. Well, before I knew it, I saw this rifle barrel pointin' out of the driver's window."

"A rifle?" Rusty asked. "You sure?"

"I've looked down the business end of a gun before," Travis said. "Yeah, it was a rifle. Pointing towards me."

"What kind of rifle?" Rusty asked. "Auto? Lever?"

"Ahh… I was pretty wasted, you know? I'd had about half that bottle that afternoon. You look down the hole of a rifle barrel, that about makes a fella lose everything, you know?"

"What did you do?" Rusty asked.

"Hit the key and spun out of there," Travis said. "Lost my bottle and some good jerky, so I did. Must have fallen off the tailgate. Anyway, I stopped over at Datil. That stuff was gone by then. Closed the tailgate, then went on to Arizona."

"What happened in Arizona?" Rusty asked.

"Spent a couple of days there," Travis said. "Got sorta chased out by some work crew or somethin'."

"You have a gun?"

"Well—there was a gun in that truck when—well, when that fella loaned it to me, you know? Well, there wasn't any ammunition. Didn't have money for that. Had to eat and drink, you know?"

"So, back to that government pickup," Rusty said. "What did that fella look like? Big? Small? Pale? Dark? Young? Old?"

"He had a rifle. That about says it all. Like I said, I'd been drinking. Think he was a typical cowboy. Hat, blue chambray shirt—maybe. Seemed about normal size, I'd say. Don't remember him as being real big. His gun was, though. Ain't swearin' to nothin', though."

"Think you could find that place where you saw that pickup?" Rusty asked.

"Well… you get me out of here, I'll sure give it a good try. Can't do it from in here."

"Not today," Rusty said. "Not unless you can come up with more than you have. You talk to anyone about this?"

"Stopped in Show Low at Walmart… No, I didn't talk to anyone," Travis said. "I was keeping things low like, you know?"

"Anything else you can think of?" Rusty asked.

"Bet if I went out there I'd think of something," Travis said. "You should take me over there with you. Bet lots of things would come back to my mind, you know? Nothing like being right there."

"What color was the ATV?" Rusty asked.

"Ahh…"

"I don't think you have anything else to remember, Travis. But I do thank you for what you've told me."

"Who was killed anyway?" Travis asked.

"You—almost. Most certainly if you hadn't gotten out of there when you did. Actually though, it was a BLM Ranger, the guy who should have been driving that truck. You're sure the driver wasn't wearing a tan uniform, right?"

"I'd have noticed that," Travis said. "That would have looked like a cop, and I'd have panicked for sure, even before I saw the gun. Wait a minute. You telling me some killer was driving that truck, and there might have been a body in it?"

"Exactly. Maybe you're being watched over because there's a real purpose for you being alive," Rusty said. "Think about that. God might have his hand on you for some reason."

"That scares me more than looking down that gun," Travis said.

Rusty picked up the handcuffs, held them up, then looked at Travis.

"No—No! You ain't gonna pin killin' some government agent on me," Travis said. "No sir. I didn't do the likes of that."

"Don't figure you did," Rusty said as he dropped the cuffs into his briefcase. He snapped it closed, finished his water, and tossed the empty bottle into a small trashcan, then rose to his feet. "Life doesn't have to be like it is for you, Travis. There's a better life out there, if you want it."

"You sound like some sappy TV preacher. I got a good life."

"I can see that," Rusty said. "Free room. Three meals a day. Even a little window so you can see the sky. Good life, for sure."

Rusty pushed the buzzer and waited for Henrietta. When the door opened, he turned and once more looked at Travis, who sat looking at his feet. "Thanks, Travis," he said, then walked out to Sheriff Towner's office.

"What do you think?" the sheriff asked as Rusty sat back in the chair across from him.

"Messed up kid. No killer, though," Rusty said. "You're stuck with him."

"Yeah, figured that. Not hard to see this happening. His father is in the pen somewhere down in Texas. Looking at something like twenty years or more. Older brother's been in and out all over two states. His mother disappeared when the boys were teens. Don't even know if she's alive. He hasn't reached the point of wanting help yet, though."

"Never give up," Rusty said. "Out on the rez, I've seen the worst of the worst break. Some great examples of radically changed lives out there."

"I'll bet," Sheriff Towner said. "Where'd you grow up?"

"Over by Cloudcroft."

"That's nice country. I'd be for trading Ruidoso for Tulsa any day. Don't think New Mexico would go for that."

"Nor Oklahoma," Rusty said.

"Yeah, just a thought," Sheriff Towner said. "Back to the crime scene now?"

"Think I'll drive over and see some family—old friend too," Rusty said. "That's not much out of the way, and I'd never get all the way to Magdalena tonight anyway. I want to talk to this old friend—old pastor, really. I've known him since I was old enough to remember anything. Wisest man I know. I need a little wisdom about now. My head's all twisted up over this murder. Everybody is pointing in one direction or another. Much of the evidence points all over also. But something in my gut tells me that's all wrong. I should just forget what would be the norm and look for the unexpected. Someone out of the loop, so to speak."

"I know those gut feelings," Sheriff Towner said. "Sometimes they're right, but just as often wrong. I was on the force up in Oklahoma City for twenty-five years, detective for fifteen of it. This here is sorta like semiretirement for me. You've got to follow it all—the evidence, leads, and your gut. Follow it all, Rusty."

"Thanks," Rusty said. "That's what I'm trying to do. Maybe I'll see you again. You never know. I have access to game permits through my family's land. Keep in touch. Maybe someday we can chase down an elk together."

"Now that I might take you up on," Sheriff Towner said. "Of course, I'd have to get my wife to let loose of all that money. That'd be tougher than hunting down an elk."

"You can buy lots of fancy shoes and handbags for elk hunting money," Rusty said.

"Oh, it's not that. We have some grandkids we take care of. Family thing, you know," Sheriff Towner said.

"Sounds important," Rusty said. "More so than hunting elk."

"You get over this way, you stop and see me, Rusty Redtail. Anytime."

Rusty spent the night with his mother in her modest reservation home. They were up into the wee hours of the night talking. After breakfast the next morning, Rusty went over to the little church that he'd grown up attending. An old, familiar blue Chevy pickup was parked in front. He walked up to the front door, opened it, then walked in.

"Pastor Mose—you in here?" he called out. Rusty walked up to the office area off to the side of the platform and knocked on the door. "Pastor Mose. It's Rusty Redtail. You here?"

There was only silence. Rusty walked back outside. He looked around. Then, as he stepped toward his Suburban, he saw someone coming up a trail from way back behind the old cemetery. It was Mose.

Rusty waited for the old man to reach the churchyard. Then Rusty walked over to him. "I'd about given up on seeing you this morning. I didn't think you walked much anymore."

"So very good to see you, my young friend. It is good you come to visit an old man. That is good. An honor to me. Your mother, she tells me you are investigating a murder. That is an important thing. Good thing you do. Come, let's sit at that old table under the ponderosa. My legs—I walk a little bit, then I must sit. This is a place you and I, we have had many a good talk. I remember spending much time here when you were young. When your father died. When your brother went off to war. When your mother was sick. When you went off to school. Many times. Sometimes we said very little—but they were still good talks."

"I miss our times together," Rusty said. "Life is such a whirlwind now. Sometimes I just want to come home and hunt rabbits."

"You are destined for much more than life here doing the mundane. This is the proper life for some—but not for you. To come here to relax, back to one's roots, that is good, for a spell. Those who remain here, they are the followers. You, my boy Rusty, you are one who rises to be a leader. Our people have always had such. It would seem to be so with all types of people. However, I know of ours only."

"I'm searching so hard to solve this murder case, but seem to be the pup chasing its tail. I find possible leads all around, but none go anywhere. I'm doing all I know to do, but getting nowhere. Things that should lead somewhere, don't. I have one person who keeps coming through my mind, but have no good reason to suspect them, just one odd thing."

"Do you have help over there?" Mose asked.

"Some," Rusty said. "The local sheriff, he's—well, he's different. So brazenly opinionated. He's from Texas—guess that explains part of things, but—well, the other BLM Ranger is so busy now, doing two men's work. He can't help much, but he has helped some. A sheriff over across the line in Arizona has helped. All the locals seem to really want to help and catch whoever did this—especially the café owner and a local preacher. There's some old, unsolved things from the past that might well be the cause of this now. It's as if I'm trying to solve three cases—one well over a hundred years old."

"You have to not let this also be added to that unsolved list," Mose said. "This man who was killed, I read where he had a family. They deserve to know who did this. This evil person is a danger to all who they encounter, including you, Rusty Redtail. Stop them, or they will kill again."

"There's two old ranch families who've been at odds since before the last century," Rusty said. "They point the finger at each other and have both helped me some, but I don't see a killer on either side. I'm just coming back from talking to a fella over in Oklahoma who was on the run and in that area at the time, but although he added some good information, he's not the killer."

"You've been busy," Mose said.

"It's easy to get so busy you miss the obvious," Rusty said. "Also, one pushes so hard you forget to take time to bask in solitude and seek help from God's spirit. That's why I had to come see you. I know you'll give me sound counsel."

"The true ways have been forever embedded deep in your spirit from your early youthful years—guiding your soul and mind," Mose said. "I have only been used to reinforce the righteousness that guides you, to reinforce and nurture what your parents planted and you chose to accept. It is the Great Spirit of Almighty God that is important in your guidance, not me. Look to me as a friend, only. Nothing more. Do not elevate me above being one who tried to walk the path laid out before him. Walk your own path, Rusty. Waiver not to the right or left, but stay on your own path. "

"It was so much easier to just blindly follow my heart and soul before I joined the real world I now live in," Rusty said. "When living out here, with my spiritual, righteous family, it was easy to follow the right ways. Now, I'm faced with evilness, godlessness, but what sidetracks me most is plain-old busyness. I get so busy I don't keep my true priorities at the forefront of my mind, my whole life, really."

"You think this only happens to you?" Mose asked. "Two things our spiritual enemy often uses to waylay us. He will try laziness. That works with many. If that works not, then he uses busyness. We must be on guard for both of these traps. Good Godly men—most of those who I've seen fall—first they became overly busy and stopped hearing, or seeking, the voice of the Great Spirit into their own spirit. Then, they followed their soul and flesh into destruction. It has happened to many good men. Too many."

The two men sat in silence for some time. Then Mose spoke again. "This case, as you said, has leads that point you in many directions, with no conclusion. You will get the answer, if you are vigilant, yet patient. I do not believe it will be the obvious. I believe... yes, I believe it will be someone you don't want it to be. You have hints, even now, but it makes no sense. Follow the leads—those physical ones and those on your mind. You will solve this, Rusty Redtail. You will solve this."

"If I don't soon, I'm sure they'll pull me and put someone else on the case," Rusty said. "I'll forever be assigned to a desk."

"No—you will solve this," Mose said. "Push all fears of failure out of your mind. You shall not fail."

The two men sat in silence for a moment. Then, Rusty slowly rose to his feet. "Thank you, Pastor Mose. I needed this time with you—this time here. I must be going now, but I'll see you again."

Rusty clasped Mose's hand. Mose held on tightly. "I think not, my true friend, Rusty Redtail. I think we shall not see each other again, not here. We shall never have a talk such as this again. When we next meet, in our next life, there will be no need to counsel over troubles, there will be none to ponder over."

Rusty held on to Mose's hand for a moment, then let it loose. He stared into Mose's eyes, nodded slowly, then turned and walked away. Reaching his Suburban, he sat in it for a moment, staring over at the old man still sitting at the table. After a moment, he started the engine and drove out of the parking lot.

Three hours later, Rusty sat at the Royal Café in Socorro, having lunch with Chub.

"Learn anything in Oklahoma?" Chub asked.

"Kinda confirmed what I already believed," Rusty said. "So did the sheriff over in Springerville. Well, the fella in Oklahoma did add a few details. He did see some things."

"You narrowing down anything?" Chub asked.

"I believe Jimmy found something, the Eagle Well, or something like that," Rusty said. "Someone, probably a local, had reason to not want something there that Jimmy found to come out into the public. It's probably tied to Sheriff Tuttle in '55, and that's probably tied to that old killing and robbery way back in '97. I'd say it's money, or a cover-up, that got Jimmy killed. But then, that's about what I've felt since the first day I started investigating this."

"Sheriff Cutter really believes it's the Calderones, or maybe the Atwoods," Chub said.

"I can't rule either one out," Rusty said. "However, neither acts guilty. Both appear to be who you'd want for neighbors. Either one could be hiding something, though. Something they want kept hidden forever. Some old family secret that could go back to that 1897 incident."

"Yeah," Chub said. "They appear at odds. That could be a cover. Any chance they were in on all of that together? That that feud has just been a smokescreen all these years? Or maybe one crossed the other?"

"Can't rule something like that out," Rusty said. "Stranger things have happened."

"Sheriff Cutter claims the Atwoods are part of some supersecret Mormon group, and if they did this, you'll never solve it," Chub said.

"Yeah," Rusty said, "and the Calderones are secret agents for the Pope. They stole those old gold coins and sent them to the Vatican. Sheriff Cutter also believes I go up on a mountaintop and chant myself into a spell and have visions and the like. If there was some Mormon Mafia or Pope's Secret Service, the FBI would have a file on them. There's no such file. None on anything like any of that. I think the sheriff gets bored, so he makes up boogeymen to give his mind some satisfaction that his part-time sheriff job is much more important than it really is."

"You're probably right," Chub said.

"He'd like to solve this, so he's going after who he believes to be easy targets," Rusty said. "I'm not finding them so easy, though."

"Yeah," Chub said. "You know, it's real easy to stand back and pick apart someone's religion. I mean, well, I don't understand a whole bunch about Mormonism and Catholicism, but I guess I could pick at what Sheriff Cutter is being taught also."

"How's that?" Rusty asked.

"Well, I shouldn't say anything," Chub said. "I don't want to be like the sheriff. But a year or so back, Buddy talked me into going out to his church to listen to some guy they had coming in to speak and raise money. It was rather weird, as I saw it anyway. He was raising money for some shelter down in Mexico for a bunch of new equipment and the like. He kept saying how giving to this would score us points in heaven. That as we earned our way there, we needed to do things like this or we wouldn't have a spot there. It was like when I was in scouts, earning a merit badge. As if you needed so many of those badges to get into heaven. He never once mentioned God, or Jesus or the Bible, nothing like that. It was all give now and get later. To me, that's just as twisted as all this other stuff the sheriff comes against. Maybe I've said too much."

"How did Sheriff Cutter respond to that?" Rusty asked.

"Wrote a big check. Several thousand dollars," Chub said. "The speaker, he told him that moved him one step closer to a big mansion in heaven. Buddy Bell is a nice guy, but there's just something about him... Well, that's all I better say."

The waitress brought their food. "Better eat up," Rusty said. "We've chewed on poor old Sheriff Cutter long enough."

When Rusty pulled into the hotel parking lot later that afternoon, Manny was coming out of the hotel's lobby door. "Hey, Señor Rusty. Good you are back. You find out anything?"

"Oh, some," Rusty said. "Anything going on here?"

"No—Oh yes," Manny said. "Hector from High Planes Garage was looking for you. He said he forgot to tell you something when you paid the towing bill. He said when I saw you to ask you to stop over."

"Oh well, I might as well do that right now, before I go inside, or I'll not want to leave again," Rusty said.

Rusty drove over to the garage. He walked into the shop area, and when Hector saw him, he motioned for him to come to the office.

"How are you coming along with your investigation, Mr. Rusty?" Hector asked. "You think you have the guilty man in your sights?"

"Not sure, Hector. Ruling out quite a few people, but finding the guilty one is tough."

"For sure," Hector said. "When I towed out that truck, I lifted it up by raising the back end. Then I walked around to make sure there wasn't any loose pieces laying around that needed to be picked up. Stuck in a partially burned bush, I found this piece of paper. It has initials and dates on it. I figure it fell out of the person's pocket when they took out the match or lighter. Maybe it blew off his ATV or something. Anyway, I figure after the fire the wind blew it under the truck, where it got stuck on that bush, what was left of it. That's what I figure. I tossed it into my truck, then forgot about it. When I cleaned my truck yesterday, I found it. It means nothing to me. Maybe you can make something out of it."

Rusty looked at the scrap of paper. Getting prints off of it would be impossible. Hector had handled it, and it had obviously been wet. Still, the dates and initials probably meant something to whoever was there and set the fire—and probably killed Jimmy.

"Might be important, Hector," Rusty said. "Thanks a lot."

"Glad to help," Hector said. "Wish I'd remembered it before."

"I'll let you know if it leads to anything," Rusty said.

Rusty went back to his hotel room and sat down at the little desk. He took out the small piece of paper and looked at it. Though water stained and grease smudged, he made out six sets of initials beside dates. Three were already past, three were in the future.

After drawing a blank for quite some time, Rusty turned on his computer and started playing around on Google. Just as he was about to take a break, the list came alive. There it was, big as life. Still, there could be an explanation for it being there at the truck. It still didn't solve anything—not by itself. Really, it just confused him more. Maybe it wasn't from the killer at all.

>>— CHAPTER 10 —≪

J ust after eight the next morning, Liz called Rusty. "Sorry this has taken so long. Guess you've figured out your case is way down on Harland's priority list."

"I've been busy too," Rusty said. "You haven't held me up at all. I could split myself in several pieces and keep them all busy."

"Well, Amanda came up with some things," Liz said. "You know there's no local paper in Fort Davis. The nearest one is in Alpine. I guess that's only a few miles away. Fortunately, they have an in-depth archive online. Anyway, she found a notice of a Betty Ann Weston joining a woman's club. No mention of a daughter or husband. There's a short clip about the artist Margareta Houser staying at the Limpia Manor Inn. I don't know for how long or where she went. If these women stayed out there, they kept a low profile, at least with things that would show up in the paper. I can't find anything on a Frederick Wolf or Weston out there at all."

"Well, after I'm done with the chopper, I'll probably make a trip out there," Rusty said. "That was all a long time ago, but some old-timer might remember something that would help. It's worth checking out I guess. One more thing, Liz. Can you see if you can find who handled the sale for Frederick Wolf of the bank building, the hotel, and café, and whatever else, back in 1955 when he left Magdalena? The Rodriguez family bought most of that, but the father has passed on, and no one remembers how it was handled. They think they met someone in Socorro. Probably an attorney."

"I'll work on it," Liz said. "That's a long shot, though. Probably all dead—retired anyway. Hey, you be careful out there, Rusty."

"Thanks, Liz."

Not long afterward, Rusty walked over to the café and was eating breakfast when Lonny Calderone came in. Rusty motioned for him to sit at his table.

"Agent Redtail," Lonny said as he sat down. "How are you coming with your investigation?"

"Getting more information every day. I was planning on going out to your ranch to try to find you. You saved me a trip."

"Oh? What can I help you with?" Lonny asked.

"I'm sure you've heard family stories about your grandfather and the 1897 incident," Rusty said.

"Oh, some," Lonny said. "It's not as if we talked about it often."

"Well, the knife that was found stuck in Franz Frick's chest, it appeared to be of Mexican origin and was very ornate with the initials 'FC' engraved on it," Rusty said. "Was that your grandfather's knife?"

"At one time, yes, it was made for him," Lonny said. "Grandfather had been up here the previous year to make arrangements to drive his herd in here and to look for a ranch. He needed to borrow several hundred dollars to put down on the ranch he was buying here before selling his holdings in Mexico. Maxwell Wolf wanted collateral. Grandfather gave him that knife, a very highly decorated saddle, and a very nice concho belt my grandmother often wore. Grandfather was to return by the end of May of the next year and pay off the loan in cash or with cattle. Grandmother got sick. So he was late getting back to the bank. Señor Wolf, he claimed he sold Grandfather's things to a traveling peddler. We had no proof otherwise."

"Then that knife ended up in Franz Frick's heart," Rusty said. "You know whatever happened to that knife?"

"No idea," Lonny said.

"Was your grandfather questioned at the time?"

"Oh sure," Lonny said. "Lots of people thought he was guilty. Being Mexican and speaking very little English, he was an easy target. Why would he kill Franz Frick, take the time to take all the money, but leave the incriminating knife there?"

"Don't know," Rusty said. "That's not logical unless someone wanted to do something so irrational to then use that as a defense."

"Grandfather wouldn't think like that," Lonny said. "He was a simple, straight-up man."

"Was there anything else pointing towards him?"

"Nothing. He paid for his ranch in Mexican money. He sold his compound down there. The cattle he brought, I know not where they came from, but in an old tin box I still have a bill of sale for each one."

"All right, Lonny," Rusty said. "That all makes sense to me. How is your son, Cisco? How is he doing in school?"

"He misses the ranch," Lonny said. "That's all he's ever known. Still, he believes he is called to the priesthood. I cannot argue against that, much as I need him here."

"One more thing about your grandfather," Rusty said. "He was at the table playing cards with Franz Frick the night before the murder, right?"

Lonny nodded his head. "So the story goes."

"Where did he get the money for the game?" Rusty asked.

"I don't know. Grandfather wasn't a rich man, neither was he poor. It was always said that after the game, Horace Atwood accused Mr. Frick of cheating and that he would get even. There was no record of grandfather ever threatening anyone."

"Your girls. They're in high school, right?" Rusty asked.

"We just put them back in public school. Edwina, she tried to homeschool them, but they would not do right. They wanted to do other things, not study."

"So, when did you put them back in school?" Rusty asked.

"Two weeks ago."

"Just after Jimmy was killed?"

"Yeah, the week after, I believe."

"The next week?" Rusty asked.

"Should you even think my girls could do such a vile thing as was done to Señor Hanson, I assure you that is not possible," Lonny said. "They will not even help butcher a cow or wild animal."

"They like to shoot guns?" Rusty asked.

"Oh, they are both very good shots. But they only shoot guns when I am present. They have no guns of their own."

"All your guns locked up?"

"We're a ranch. One does not lock up his guns as in the city."

Rusty's cell phone rang. He took it out and saw that it was Liz. "I'll have to go call this back," he said. "I'll see you soon. Maybe from the air. I'll be up in a chopper the next few days."

Rusty left and went back over to his room. He called Liz back.

"Rusty, you're in luck. The sale of the Wolf property was handled in Socorro. The attorney who handled things was Edgar Swartz. His son, Alfred, now runs things there. I'll text you the phone and address."

"Very good," Rusty said. "Thanks, Liz. I'll see what I can find out there. Hopefully, they have that old file still stored somewhere. Chopper still on schedule?"

"So far. Unless Harland wants it somewhere else, it's yours. Someday I surely do want to take a ride in one of those."

"Only room for two—the pilot and me," Rusty said. "I'll let you know how I make out with Alfred Swartz. Thanks, Liz."

"Remember, Rusty. You're looking for someone who shoots government employees. That chopper would make a great target."

"Yeah, yeah. Remember, someone has been shooting at my people for two hundred years or more now," Rusty said. "Ever since you white people showed up with your guns."

Later that morning, Rusty pulled into the parking lot of the Swartz Law Firm in Socorro. Reaching the receptionist's desk, Rusty introduced himself. The receptionist nodded, then buzzed Alfred Swartz.

"Agent Redtail is here to see you," she said.

She put the phone down. "He's expecting you. First door on the right," she said, pointing to a hallway. "Coffee or water?" she asked.

"Oh, not right now," Rusty said. "Maybe later, thanks."

Rusty started back the hallway. As he did, Alfred Swartz stepped out of his office and stood in front of its door, waiting for Rusty to reach him.

"Come on in," Alfred said after the two men shook hands as they introduced themselves. "Have a seat," he said as he closed the door. "So, you think there's some tie between Frederick Wolf leaving town and the death of Jimmy Hanson?"

"I know it seems to be a stretch, but maybe," Rusty said. "Your father handled that transfer back in 1955, right?"

"Oh yeah. I wasn't born until 1960. Knowing you were coming, and what you were looking for, I had that old file dug out of storage. My father kept everything. This intrigued me, so I rescheduled my appointments for the rest of the morning and started reading this file. I remember something my parents talked about as my father was dying. Something about his biggest regret was being involved in the Wolf case. I didn't think much about it then—not knowing what they were talking about. Father was always supercautious of his reputation—never doing anything questionable. Apparently he believed this case violated his code somehow."

"You've read some of it," Rusty said. "You see anything that's an alarm?"

"All I can really see is that the funds were sent off to a bank in Fort Davis, Texas, to a Frederick Weston's account," Alfred said. "Apparently Wolf changed his name. Then too, there is a notation in father's notes that he really should report something to the authorities. He didn't say what. I wish father would have expounded on this."

"If Frederick Wolf was involved in something questionable... he fled unexpectedly... said he was going to Arizona, but went to Texas... changed his name..." Rusty thought about these things out loud.

"I'm really intrigued now," Alfred said. "Please let me know if this leads to anything."

"Sure will," Rusty said. "This is just getting more complicated all the time."

Rusty left there and went to see Chub.

"What's up, Rusty," Chub asked when he walked in the BLM office. "What brings you to town?"

"Chasing down the attorney who handled the sale of Frederick Wolf's holdings when he left town back in 1955. Talked to the attorney's son, Alfred Swartz," Rusty said. "He had the old file. Now, I think I should go to Fort Davis and dig around out there."

"I know Alfred," Chub said. "You going to Fort Davis tomorrow?"

"Chopper will be in here for the next two days," Rusty said. "Really hope we can find something. That Eagle Well or something. Whatever Jimmy found."

"Sure like to go with you," Chub said. "I hear we have a replacement for Jimmy coming next month. That will help free me up some, after he gets up to speed."

"I've been hoping someone out there would tell you something they saw or heard," Rusty said. "Someone who wouldn't talk to me, my being a stranger."

"Nothing so far," Chub said. "Maybe if I could get out there more, you know, hang around the café or something. Maybe I'll go out to this weekend's cowboy action shoot."

"Might be good. Especially if I'm not around," Rusty said. "The guys might talk more."

"Might be most interesting to see who's not there," Chub said. "Maybe pick up on any rumors floating around. Hope the sheriff isn't there. If he is, that might make everyone clam up."

"I'd appreciate your doing that. Unless I see something from the air I need to follow up on, I'll most likely be in Fort Davis then."

"Supposed to be stormy the rest of the week," Chub said. "Be careful up in that chopper."

"I'm just along for the ride. Couldn't fly that any more than doing so by flapping my arms."

"Spent too much time in one over in Iraq," Chub said. "No fond memories of any of that."

"I understand," Rusty said. "My favorite uncle was shot down in Vietnam in one of those birds. Killed the whole crew."

"My dad was shot down there too. POW for over two years. He made it home, though."

"Easy to get caught up in our own troubles and forget about those who've given it all—or a whole bunch anyway, you know?" Rusty said.

"For sure. Some people never think about anything like that. Maybe they're the lucky, or smart, ones."

"Don't know. Well, I've got to get back out to Magdalena. Want to talk to Sheriff Cutter, if he shows up in town. I want to tell him that we'll be up in the air the next few days and he might get some black helicopter calls. Probably be over some of his land too, since that was all old Wolf land—Maxwell Wolf's."

"Let me know what you find," Chub said.

"Yeah, later, then," Rusty said as he rose and turned to the door.

When Rusty walked out into the parking lot of the BLM office, he spotted a Channel 12 Albuquerque News van pulling into the parking lot. The truck traveled across the lot and parked right beside Rusty's Suburban. A man quickly exited the van's side door and called out to Rusty, who had gotten into his vehicle, started it, and was backing up when the man tapped on his side window.

"Excuse me," he said, smiling broadly. "You Agent Redtail?"

Rusty stopped, lowered the window, looked at the man, then nodded. "Yeah, I'm Rusty Redtail."

"Wally Whiteside, Channel 12. I just have a couple of questions, please?"

"Off camera. Briefly," Rusty said. "I'm quite busy."

"I'm sure you are," Wally said. "Is it true you're the only FBI agent on this case?"

"I'm getting plenty of help from my agency and all the local ones. Ranger Chub Murry here at the BLM is working closely with me. If I need more from the Bureau, I'll ask for it. I have a chopper coming out for a few days. I'm not short on assets at all."

"You going to see Sally Hanson while you're in Socorro today?"

"No. I have nothing concrete that's new, so just calling on her would be meaningless, maybe quite hurtful as she works her way through this. When I have something important, something encouraging, I'll inform her. She doesn't need to be bogged down with investigation details, just the end results."

"Who's your main suspect?"

"No comment on that."

"You have a main suspect?" Wally then asked.

"No comment on that either."

"Sounds like you're chasing rabbits out there. Any chance this will never be solved?"

"Ask me something I can give you an answer to, or let me get back to work," Rusty said.

"I'm told there's lots of tourists traveling through that area, campers, hunters and others. Might it be someone like that?"

"Might be."

"Have you pursued any leads on any of them?"

"Certainly," Rusty said. "I've been to Arizona, Oklahoma, all over."

"Oh… Any chance this was a workplace thing?"

"Workplace thing? Out in the woods? Like a disgruntled elk or a coyote? Cow maybe?"

"You know what I mean. A fellow worker or one of those ranchers leasing land."

"Someone shot Jimmy Hanson, then burned his truck and body trying to cover that up," Rusty said. "Obviously, someone wasn't happy with Jimmy over something. When I find out what, that will lead me to who, and then this will be solved."

"You're holding out on me," Wally said. "There's things you're not telling me."

"Of course."

"If I go out in that forsaken country and dig around, am I likely to learn anything?"

"Sure, lots of things," Rusty said. "Probably nothing about this case, though."

"Not likely, huh?"

"I'm having a tough enough time, and I don't have a camera or recorder. You go out there, the locals will take pictures of you. They've never seen anything like this van before. You'd become the story."

"Yeah… think I'll go back to Albuquerque," Wally said. "Here's my card. Please call me when you get something hot, OK? I'll not hassle you for a story. Nobody in the city much cares about this anyway."

"I appreciate you leaving me to do my job. I will call you when the time is right."

"Thanks, Redtail. Hey, be careful out there. I'd be spooked to death nosing around out in a place like that." Wally then turned and stepped back into the TV van. Rusty restarted the Suburban, then exited the parking lot and headed for Magdalena.

Rusty was sitting at a table in the café talking with Buddy when Sheriff Cutter walked in. He saw them and came over to their table. "What's up, Chief?" he asked. "Haven't seen you around for a spell."

"Just stopped in to have a buffalo burger. I can't get Manny to put horse on the menu. Guess this will have to do."

"Ain't no buffalo burger here," Sheriff Cutter said. "Good old angus beef, so it is."

"Could have fooled me. Tastes like every other burger I had growing up," Rusty said. "I thought we ate buffalo, or horse, or dog, or whatever kind of roadkill we found over on the reservation. Beef, huh? That's awfully white of me, don't you think? Me eating beef."

"Yeah, whatever," Sheriff Cutter said. "When are you going to arrest old Lonny? Or Duke?"

"When are you going to get me some evidence proving either one did this?" Rusty asked.

"That's what you're out here for."

"What? Make up evidence? I'm looking for the truth, wherever that takes me. I'll turn over every rock until I find it."

"What about that boy in Oklahoma?" Sheriff Cutter asked. "You said that back then he was hiding out around here."

"Just a screwed-up kid in the wrong place with someone else's pickup. Not a killer. He did see something, though."

"Oh, what was that?" the sheriff asked.

"He saw the BLM truck towing a trailer with an ATV on it. He got scared and took off for Arizona."

"What kind of an ATV?"

"He doesn't know," Rusty said. "I'd say he was rather drunk, and very scared."

"You believe him?"

"No reason for him to make something like that up," Rusty answered. "He placed himself in the area. Why would he do that if he wasn't?"

"He was in a stolen pickup, drunk, on the run… Probably a friend of Duke Atwood's," Sheriff Cutter said.

"I'll be up in a chopper the next several days," Rusty said. "You might get some calls. Probably be over some of your land. That west side that abuts the Rancho Vaca."

"Ain't nothing out there," Sheriff Cutter said. "My bulls rarely even go there."

"Maybe that's why I should. Maybe Jimmy did. He was somewhere odd. I find wherever that was, things might fall into place."

"Knock yourself out. Look around all you want. I'd do it from the air, though. Just in case one of those unruly critters of mine does decide to wander over that way. Can't imagine what you'd do if eighteen hundred pounds of fire-breathing muscle and bones came charging at you."

"Shoot it," Rusty said.

"And then pay me ten times what it's worth," Sheriff Cutter said.

"Try and collect from the federal government," Rusty said. "Your animal attacks one of its agents. Tell me how that lawsuit turns out. Not to mention the ten years of tax audits to follow."

"Maybe I'll pen up my bulls until you're done playing around out there," Sheriff Cutter said.

"Good idea. Besides, they're probably too tough to make good hamburger. Probably taste more like horse."

"What are you laughing at?" Sheriff Cutter said to Buddy. "Maybe Sunday you should preach about eating unclean animals or whatever it is we're not supposed to do. Give a copy of the sermon to Geronimo here."

"Maybe I should," Buddy said. "However, when I was up in Montreal, I ate horse meat. Mighty tasty."

The sheriff shook his head, then got up and started walking away. "Ain't even hungry anymore. You two ruined my lunch."

Rusty and Buddy watched him leave the café. "He'll get over it," Buddy said. "So, you went to Oklahoma?"

"Yeah, that kid was hiding out there by Datil somewhere," Rusty replied. "I don't think he realizes how close he came to getting himself killed for being a witness to something. I think he saw the killer driving the truck with Jimmy's body somewhere in it. I just wish I knew where he was at the time."

"Where do you think he was?"

"Somewhere on the Rancho Vaca, I think," Rusty said.

"You ruling out the Atwoods, then?" Buddy asked.

"Not completely. We don't know who was in the truck or whose ATV it was. If you were doing something criminal, you might not do it on your own land. Might do it where you want to point to someone else."

"Makes sense," Buddy said. "I still have a hard time believing any of those folks did this."

"So do I. Someone did it, though."

"I still want it to be a stranger," Buddy said. "Any chance someone is living out there without any of us knowing it?"

"Big country," Rusty said. "Thousands of acres that don't see a man for years at a time. Much of it is now owned by out-of-state owners who never set foot on it and only ranch it a minimum to make things legally tax deductible. They might have a hand or two to keep up the water and fences, that's all. Could be someone working on one of those ranches. I'm going to have to widen my loop and start working on that if nothing turns up with what I've been working on so far. Yeah, there's lots of places for a man to hide. Water, game, cattle even. Guess a man could survive indefinitely."

"That's kinda spooky," Buddy said.

"I'm hoping I can come up with some things from the air. I still think Jimmy found something he shouldn't have. I believe that's what I have to find also," Rusty said.

"You still think there might really be an Eagle Well?" Buddy asked.

"Something like that," Rusty said. "Where's Jimmy's ladder? Those other tools and things? Probably at the murder site. He had a ladder to either go up something or down something. In all of this, I've not heard one word about a treehouse."

"I see what you mean," Buddy said. "So, an old hand-dug well or vault does seem to be the logical thing."

"Seems that way to me," Rusty said.

"Still, some escaped criminal hiding out in some old line cabin or such, living off the land, could have done this. Maybe they found that well or whatever."

"True," Rusty said. "And they could be in Arizona or Colorado by now too."

"I would hate for this to never be solved," Buddy said. "Jimmy deserves better than that."

"I'm trying my best. Somebody out here knows something. I'll probably be in Texas over the weekend—don't know for how long. If you go to the cowboy shoot, please keep your ears open. See if there's anything said about this—there probably will be. Chub will probably be there too. I'd like to know what the general public is saying about this."

"Yeah," Buddy said. "Guys loosen up out there. Probably more so over at the Beefsteak Bar afterwards. Maybe Chub can hang around there some. I know Jack, the owner. I'll ask him to keep his ears open. People tell bartenders a lot of stuff they won't even tell their pastor."

"True. I should stop and meet Jack. Maybe sometime next week," Rusty said.

"Well," Buddy said. "I have to get back up to the church. Old Mrs. Taylor said she'd bring me an apple pie right after lunch. I can taste that now."

"Gotta go too. I've got some of those old newspaper articles to study yet. Think I'll go do that. Have some reports to fill out too. There's always reports."

Rusty was out at the little local landing strip well before the nine a.m. scheduled arrival of the surveillance chopper. Other than several tethered, old single-engine planes, the airstrip was vacant. Rusty parked beside the one enclosed hangar and got out. He reached back in and took out his briefcase containing his camera, binoculars, maps, and a handful of granola bars and a couple of bottles of water. With his other hand he grabbed his Thermos full of coffee. He walked over to a concrete picnic table and sat at one end. He poured half a cup of coffee.

Opening his briefcase, he took out one of the maps. The two primary search areas were about twenty miles apart. However, anywhere in a thirty or forty–mile circle was suspicious. He'd marked out several canyons he wanted to fly over that weren't on either Atwood or Calderone land.

Well off in the distance there was the rumble of thunder. This time of morning this was unusual. The summer monsoon season was over, but it wasn't uncommon to still have some storms now—just not before late afternoon.

Shortly after nine o'clock, Rusty heard the faint drone of the little chopper. Searching the sky, he saw the black speck in the east heading toward him. Five minutes later the little aircraft was on the ground. The pilot jumped out and walked over to Rusty.

Rusty rose and shook the man's hand. "Rusty Redtail. Pleasure to meet you."

"Bo Donaldson," the man said in return. "So, tell me what's up. I filled up in Socorro, knowing there wasn't any fuel available out here."

"The primary search areas are these two ranches," Rusty said, laying out on the table the map that he'd platted in the Seven Springs and Rancho Vaca boundaries. "I've got a lot of other topo maps here also and really want to check out some other locations also."

"Sounds like a plan," Bo said. "What are we looking for?"

"A murder scene. Maybe an old abandoned well or something like that. There's supposed to be something like that out here that might have once contained a lot of stolen coins. There's a fake well location also. I don't know what that's all about. I don't think it's really related to the murder, but I'd like to fly over it anyway."

"Sounds like an exciting case," Bo said.

Thunder rumbled off to the distant southwest again before Rusty could reply.

"Checked the weather radar as I came in. Storms moving this way from Arizona. Should be clear up here, though," Bo said, pointing toward the Atwood's Seven Springs ranch. "At least for now."

"Well, let's go out there first then," Rusty said.

"You ever been up in one of these little birds before?" Bo asked, nodding toward the chopper.

"Not really," Rusty said. "Couple of small, fixed wings, but never a chopper."

"Nothing to it," Bo said. "Noisy—kinda twitchy at times too. Nothing to be afraid of."

"Didn't plan on being afraid," Rusty said.

In minutes they were airborne. They skirted along Highway 60, going west, out past the giant dishes of the radio telescope that spread out across the Plains of San Agustin. Then they climbed up into the Datil Mountains. Crossing one canyon, Rusty looked over and saw about a dozen elk bedded-down amongst the cedar and piñon trees.

"Elk down in that canyon over there," Rusty said, pointing toward them.

"I have friends who put in for elk out in this section every year. They usually draw several tags," Bo said. "They seem to get at least one every year."

"Grew up on elk meet—mule deer too," Rusty said.

"Where was that?" Bo asked.

"Mescalero reservation, by Cloudcroft."

"Oh yeah," Bo said. "Lots of game over there. Nice area."

"Good place to grow up," Rusty said. "That's for sure."

"Give me that first GPS coordinate," Bo requested. "What do you think? Do a pass around the perimeter first?"

"Yeah," Rusty said. "I want to look for any roads that go into the ranch that aren't on any map."

An hour later, they were back at the southeast corner, where they'd started. No unmarked roads had been found.

"What now?" Bo asked.

"Let's circle back around and go up each road to see where each one leads," Rusty answered. "The first one is up north, about half a mile or so."

They spent the next two hours flying over the visible roads, but found nothing of interest.

"I'm getting hungry," Bo said. "That granola bar you gave me didn't do much. There's a restaurant over in Pie Town, right?"

"Yeah," Rusty said. "There's room to put this down in the parking lot or across the road. First, though, let's pass over the main ranch headquarters. There was a road leaving there and going northwest that I saw when I was there. Let's follow it, then we can go eat."

Bo swung up the entrance road and over to the ranch headquarters. As they did, Duke Atwood stepped out of the house onto the front porch and watched them fly over. They'd seen half a dozen hands moving cattle over on the north side of the ranch, but there hadn't been any sign of Andy around the ranch anywhere.

They followed the old two-track road up through canyons and across several small mesas, then back down into a canyon. It ended at an old line shack that still appeared to be used. Bo circled around the area, then pointed to the southwest.

"Storm snuck in on me," he said. "That's bad. Another one's come up from the south. There's a solid spot at the end of this road on the west side of that shack. I say we put down here and wait out these storms. Shouldn't be but an hour—maybe less."

"Whatever you think is best," Rusty said. "I've got several more granola bars to hold you over. You won't starve. It would be nice to get out and stretch."

"I could go north and get out of this mess, but I really need to watch my fuel," Bo said. "I have to get back to Socorro to refuel."

"That old cabin might be interesting," Rusty said. "Who knows what's in there."

Bo put the craft down, then he drove in several stakes and tethered it tightly. "This is probably overkill. I don't think the winds will be that strong," he said. "I just like to be safe."

Rusty watched him, then he turned toward the cabin just as the first big raindrops started pelting the earth. Rusty froze. There in the cabin doorway stood a man, and he didn't look very happy.

≫── CHAPTER 11 ──≪

B o," Rusty said. "Over at the cabin."

"Oh… well, he doesn't have a gun," Bo said.

"Let's walk over there, slow like," Rusty said.

After a few steps, but still thirty- or forty-yards away, Rusty called out to the man in the doorway. "Storm's coming. Looking for shelter."

The man nodded, but made no other gesture. Nearing the cabin, Rusty stopped about five feet from the man, then introduced himself. "I'm Rusty Redtail. This is Bo Donaldson. We're with the FBI. We're out here investigating the death of that BLM Ranger, Jimmy Hanson. Figure you've heard about that."

The man nodded, then spit a stream of tobacco juice at his feet.

"Andy and Duke knew we were going to be flying around here," Rusty said. "Don't figure they told you."

"Duke told me," the man said. "Well, it's gonna rain, for sure. Might as well come on in a spell." He turned and walked into the cabin. Rusty looked at Bo, then followed the man through the door.

The cabin was sparsely furnished but adequate to survive in. Rusty surveyed the spacious single room and was surprised to see a large library of books filling several handmade shelves along one wall.

The man sat on a chair at a rustic table and motioned for Rusty and Bo to join him.

"Looks as if you, or someone, spends a lot of time here," Rusty said as he sat across the table from the man, who'd still not introduced himself.

"I like it here, really," the man said. "Live here, so I do."

"You work for Lonny then," Rusty said.

"Worked for the Atwoods fifty years this winter. Of course, it was Preston Atwood who hired me."

"That's a long time," Rusty said. "Most of a man's life."

"Got outta school early and joined the army. Went to 'Nam. Flew one of them whirlybirds, a whole lot bigger than what you got out there. Got shot down and spent two years in a Charlie-camp. Got out and came home. Couldn't handle being around people. Preston hired me to roam around and mend fences and do odd jobs out here. Been here ever since. Die out here, someday, 'spect I will."

"Man could do worse," Rusty said.

"Yeah, that Ranger Hanson fella, he sure did worse."

"You knew Jimmy?" Rusty asked.

"We talked. Wasn't a bad fella—for a Fed."

"Jimmy was really into history," Rusty said. "Bet you know about everything that's ever happened around here."

"Reckon I do at that. Most all anyway."

"When was the last time you talked to Jimmy?" Rusty asked.

"Month or so back. Probably more."

"Remember what about?" Rusty asked.

"Yeah."

Rusty was silent for a moment. He didn't want to push this man. There was too much information here to upset him. He glanced at Bo, who shrugged his shoulders slightly.

"He was searching for that old Eagle Well," Rusty finally said. "You talk about that?"

"Yeah."

"You ever see that?" Rusty asked. "You know where it is?"

"Good idea. I've never been there. I hardly ever leave this ranch."

"So, it's not on Atwood land?" asked Rusty.

"No one ever thought it was. Except maybe that crazy sheriff. Ain't got the brains of a mad cow, so he don't."

"He sorta has it in for the Atwoods, doesn't he?" Rusty said.

"Them and about everyone else."

"Like the Calderones," Rusty said.

"All Mexicans."

"And Catholics, Mormons, Indians, and probably any minority," Rusty said, hoping that was the right response.

"Appears that way," the man said as he cracked a slight smile.

"Anybody but Texans, I think," Rusty said.

At that, a chuckle came out of the man, who slightly nodded.

"So, did you tell Jimmy where to find the Eagle Well?" Rusty asked.

"Where I figure it is—thereabouts anyway."

"How did you find out where you think the Eagle Well is located?" Rusty continued.

There was a sudden flash of lightning followed in mere seconds by a loud clap of thunder. The man rose and walked back to the door, closed it, then returned to the table.

"My father."

There was silence for a moment while Rusty thought about how to inquire more without being nosey or pushy.

"You learned about the Eagle Well location from your father," Rusty said. "How did he know about it? Who was your father?"

"Bucky Tuttle."

Rusty leaned forward in his chair. "Your father was Sheriff Bucky Tuttle? You're his son?"

"Yeah, Charlie—Charles Tuttle Jr., really."

"Wow," Rusty said. "I'll bet you really do know a lot about things here."

Charlie nodded.

"I've got a bunch of questions I'd like to ask you. Do you mind?" Rusty asked.

"Oh… if I can help, OK. This ain't like all the folks in town. They was always askin' questions for no good reason. I just wanted to be left alone. Didn't want to talk none about them two years."

"I won't push, OK?" Rusty said. "You don't want to answer anything you just say so, OK?"

Charlie nodded slightly.

"So, let's go back to that 1897 killing and robbery. I suspect that figures into what happened to your father. Am I right?" Rusty asked.

"Pa said he found where Old Man Wolf hid the money," Charlie said. "The Eagle Well, Pa said."

"Old Man Wolf? He believed Maxwell Wolf was the murderer and thief?" asked Rusty.

"Pa believed it—he said so," Charlie said. "I know it for sure."

"And that got your father killed, right?" Rusty said.

"Said he was going to set a trap to catch whoever came to get money," Charlie said. "Guess he got caught in his own trap."

"So, who then killed your father?"

"Frederick Wolf. They were friends, but Pa never really trusted him."

"You sure about that?" Rusty asked.

Charlie pushed back from the table, looked Rusty in the eye, then slowly nodded. He was silent for a moment, then started talking. "I was a teenager back then. Pumped gas over at the corner filling station. The day Frederick Wolf left town, they pulled in for a fill-up. Betty Ann was driving. I did the windshield, checked the oil and all. Frederick and Betty Ann were arguing something awful. Their little girl was in the backseat, holding her puppy and crying up a storm."

"You hear what they were arguing about?" Rusty asked.

Charlie slowly nodded. "Yeah. Betty Ann kept yelling that this was all his fault. If he hadn't done what he did they wouldn't have to leave town. She yelled about leaving all that money behind. She didn't know who I was."

"What did Frederick say?" Rusty asked.

"He wasn't saying much. I don't think he could say much. He was all wrapped up in a bandage. Bleeding out through it. Big old blood spot under the left shoulder. Right away I knew it was a gunshot."

No one said anything for a moment, then Rusty spoke. "You figure he tangled with your father out at the Eagle Well?"

"That's what I always figured," Charlie said. "Never had the guts to go lookin' for it. Guess I was afraid of what would be in the well if I found it. I just quit school and joined the army as soon as they'd take me."

Silence again prevailed in the little cabin. Rusty didn't know how much more he wanted to inquire. Thunder again rumbled, much farther away this time. Rusty then asked, "So, where do you think the Eagle Well is?"

Charlie didn't answer for a moment. Then he looked at Rusty. "Not sure I want you to find it. I figure, finding that was what got Jimmy Hanson killed. I don't want the same for you."

"You know about Jimmy's death?" Rusty asked. "You know who did it?"

"Figure so, but you wouldn't believe me, then they might come and get me too," Charlie said. "Guess I ain't ready to die."

Rusty figured it was time to switch the subject. "Enough of that. You've helped a bunch, Charlie. It's been real good talking with you. Fifty years here... my, you've watched all those girls and Duke grow up, right?"

"Raised Duke like a pup," Charlie said with a smile. "When his ma died, me and him got real close. Andy, well, he had a tough time of things. Duke needed a fella to talk to, and, well, I kinda knew what he felt. He's a good boy. The sheriff is out for him, but when times are tough, you can count on Duke Atwood."

"I didn't know Duke's mother died," Rusty said. "When was that?"

"Duke was fifteen. Kinda been mad at the world, and all else, ever since, but I tell you, he's a good fella," Charlie said.

Again there was silence, then Bo finally spoke. "I think it's quit raining. Should I go out and get the bird ready?"

"Yeah," Rusty said. "Go get ready." He turned to Charlie as Bo left. "Here's my card, Charlie. Please let me know if you find out anything or remember something that might help, OK? We don't want anyone else getting killed. Have Andy or Duke call me if you want to talk more, OK?"

"Might get things figured out better in my mind," Charlie said. "I know sometimes my thinkin' is all twisted up. Ain't really thought plumb right since all that back in 'Nam. 'Spect I ain't never been quite right since... since what all they done to me there."

Rusty looked at Charlie, who stared down at his feet. After a few seconds, Rusty heard the chopper start cranking the blades around.

"Gotta go, Charlie," Rusty said. "You've helped a lot. If Jimmy could, he'd say thanks. Maybe sometime we can talk more. Not about any of this bad stuff, about good things. Maybe someday?"

Charlie continued to stare at the floor but nodded slightly. "You be careful out there. Your life ain't worth any more than that of a coyote or a wolf."

Moments later, Rusty climbed into the chopper. Neither he nor Bo said anything until they had been airborne for several minutes. Then Rusty asked, "Still hungry?"

"Hadn't thought about it," Bo said. "That was a lot to think on."

"Sure is," Rusty said. "Really glad he talked as much as he did."

"Looks like storms all around us," Bo said. "I say we work our way around them and get back to Magdalena. I'll go on down to Socorro and fuel up. I'll spend the night there. See you about eight o'clock in the morning?"

"That'll work," Rusty said. "Hope the weather clears up tomorrow—heard it's supposed to. I think we'll find something over there. I know where the truck was burned. I had Buddy Bell locate on a map where a fake well, as they call it, is located. Jimmy wrote that the real Eagle Well was many miles away from there, though."

"So, is that a good place to start, or a place to stay away from?"

"I've gotta see it. Maybe there's a trail or something from there to the real well. Jimmy indicated that something there led him to the real well."

Bo skirted around the several small storms that were drifting across the mountains and high-plains area. Reaching the Magdalena airstrip, he started to put down near Rusty's Suburban.

"Something's on your hood," Bo said, nodding toward Rusty's Suburban.

"That's weird," Rusty said. "There's nothing around here to end up there like that."

"I'm curious," Bo said. "I think I'll check that out with you." He cut off the engine, then when safe, he exited the bubble and joined

Rusty, who stood looking at his car's hood. "What the heck is that?" he asked Rusty.

"A dead redtail hawk," Rusty said. "A mutilated redtail hawk."

"How in the world—"

"It's a message," Rusty said. "Someone is sending me a message."

"That's creepy," Bo said. "Who? Who would do this?"

"It was common knowledge I'd be up with you today. Easy to figure my car would be out here. There's no one around out here most of the time."

"But getting that hawk," Bo said.

"Oh, they're everywhere," Rusty said. "That would be pretty easy."

"So, someone is threatening you with death?"

"Could just be a joke. Wouldn't be the first time someone's played up my name."

"That's no joke. A tail feather maybe. A bloody, torn-up bird—that's a real threat," Bo said. "Don't kid yourself."

Rusty walked over, took the bird by the feet, then removed it from the hood. He took it over to a trashcan beside the picnic table, then dropped it in and closed the lid.

"I'll see you in the morning then," Rusty said.

"I have to think about this," Bo said. "This is a serious threat. We're an easy target up there, you know. Someone could easily be out there where we're going tomorrow and shoot us down. I don't like that."

"Could have done it today, without this warning. This is the work of a coward. I'll not cower to this."

"Guess I'm just a mite fearful," Bo said. "I was shot down over in the first Gulf War. I'll never get over the feeling of helplessness as my bird went out of control and dropped to the ground."

"I understand. You get hurt?"

"Broke both legs. I was close to being taken and tortured or killed. One of my fellow squad members saw me go down. He dropped in and saved us all. I still have nightmares."

"Well, let me know," Rusty said. "I'm going out there, one way or another. If I have to get someone else, that's OK, I understand. I don't want you as my pilot if you're too nervous to fly right."

"Let me sleep on it—try to anyway," Bo said.

Rusty went into the café when he got back into town. Manny saw him come in and quickly walked over to him.

"You were up in the air today, no? Find anything?" Manny asked.

"Not much in the air—not about Jimmy anyway," Rusty said. "Interesting day, though. You know Charlie Tuttle?"

"Charlie Tuttle… Sí, he's rarely seen around town. Not for years," Manny said. "Haven't thought about him in a long time. Back when he was young, before going off to war, he was very popular. You see Charlie?"

"Yeah. Storm came up. We put down by his cabin. You think he's believable or totally crazy?"

"Well…" Manny paused. "Back when Señor Charlie came home from Vietnam, he took spells and acted pretty much loco. He'd see things and, well, I don't know if it was all the war or if it wasn't something he'd gotten hooked on over there, you know?"

"But you don't know today?" Rusty asked.

"No one talks about him anymore. He's sorta forgotten. I think that's what he wants. I was very young when all that went on. I never personally knew him."

"The Atwoods seem to have taken him in," Rusty said. "You think they might have owed his father a favor?"

"Never heard of anything like that. But, as I said, I was so very young."

"He owes the Atwoods a lot," Rusty said. "Could be he'd cover for them. He might even do something illegal for them. Just thinking out loud, Manny. I'm just thinking. If Duke wanted Charlie to do something—"

"Andy was in here for lunch," Manny said.

"Saw Duke out at the ranch house," Rusty said. "There was an old Winchester 1886 leaning against the wall by the door in Charlie's cabin. That's most likely to be a 45-70, most were."

"Never have I heard anything really bad about Charlie," Manny said. "I cannot believe he'd kill Jimmy."

"Someone did," Rusty said.

Rusty was out at the airstrip well before eight the next morning. He sipped coffee and studied his maps. After a while, he looked at his phone. Five after eight and no Bo. He waited another fifteen minutes, then decided to head back to town. He decided against calling Bo. If he was fearful of flying out there, then best he didn't.

Reaching his Suburban, he stopped and looked at the bloodstain on the hood. That told him a lot—mostly that he was getting close. It really confirmed that someone around here, probably someone he'd talked to, was the guilty person, or connected to them. Some little nudge inside told him he probably knew who. Oftentimes gut feelings were totally wrong, though. He still needed to turn over every rock to see what was hiding under it. And there were a lot of rocks in this little community.

Suddenly, he heard the drone of the little chopper. Bo was coming. Rusty stood there beside his car and watched the chopper land on the nearby pad. Bo shut off the engine, then got out and walked over to Rusty.

"Thought maybe you weren't coming," Rusty said.

"I thought the same. Didn't know how I'd explain to my boss that I was afraid, though," Bo said. "I don't think he'd buy a dead bird as a justifiable reason to call off the mission. However, the first sign of any danger out there—"

"Fair enough," Rusty said. "Believe me, I don't want to be shot down any more than you do."

"Let's do it then," Bo said as he turned and started back toward the chopper.

Rusty followed, and in minutes they were airborne. About forty-five minutes later, they were at the coordinate for the northeast corner of the Rancho Vaca.

"Let's do the same as yesterday. Do a perimeter flyover first," Rusty said.

"OK. Head along the north border first?" Bo asked.

"Sure. Drop down a little, if you will," Rusty answered.

Bo said nothing, but reduced altitude slightly, then scooted quickly across the fence line. About half an hour later, they had covered two sides and were at the southwest corner of the ranch. They'd seen nothing of interest or out of place.

"Turn east here," Rusty said. "This borders the sheriff's ranch. He raises rodeo bulls. Let's slow down a little. I expect to see an old road or two crossing this fence line. At one time, Maxwell Wolf controlled all of this. Sheriff Cutter claims he doesn't use this area. He won't lease it to the Calderones, though."

Several miles up the line, Rusty saw what he was expecting. The remnants of an old road from long ago crossed the fence line where it ran through a wide, shallow draw.

"Circle around that road crossing," Rusty said, pointing at the old road.

Bo nodded, then dropped down considerably and hovered around where Rusty pointed.

"There's a latia-and-wire Texas-style gate across that old road," Rusty said. "See the wire tied around that pole? The loop around the top of it too. Looks as if someone still goes through there, for some reason. I doubt if it's the sheriff. If he knew about this, he'd surely have something more substantial to keep those bulls of his contained.

Rusty looked over the road in both directions. "Follow that road over that way," he said, pointing out across Sheriff Cutter's ranch. "I want to see where that goes."

Bo turned the chopper and started in a southwest direction.

"Should reach the highway in another mile or so," Rusty said after about ten minutes.

Suddenly, a plume of dust rose from the road ahead. Rusty saw a pickup truck speed over the road toward the highway.

"Catch up to that," he said, pointing at the pickup. "That's no good, for sure."

In a couple of minutes, just before reaching the paved road, they caught up with the truck.

"Duke Atwood," Rusty said. "Yeah, that's Duke's truck. What's he doing over here on the sheriff's ranch? Drop down so I can see in the truck."

Bo skirted up beside the pickup, only a hundred feet or so off the ground, as the truck sped north up the paved highway. Reaching a long, straight section of road, Bo dropped way down behind the truck, giving Rusty a good view inside.

"Two people in there," Rusty said. "The driver's Duke, all right. Looks like Charlie's old Winchester in the window rack. OK, that's enough of this. Let's go back to where we first saw them."

Bo arched upward then turned back to the old abandoned road. He followed it back to where they'd first seen the pickup. He hovered around the area as Rusty searched the ground. Seeing a somewhat level clearing, Rusty pointed and asked Bo, "Can you put down there?"

"In my sleep," Bo said. "Hold on." A couple of slight bounces, and the craft settled on the slightly sloping ant-infested sand drift. Rusty got out and walked over to an area hidden behind a grove of cedar trees. He stopped and surveyed what lay in front of him.

Bo came up beside him. "What the… What were they doing?"

"Dismantling and destroying this," Rusty said. "Sort of in your face to the sheriff, I'd say. Growing pot right on his ranch. Talk about rubbing something in his nose." Rusty walked over and picked up a flannel shirt that hung on a tree branch. "Saw this hanging in Charlie's cabin yesterday. This, and the gun in the truck, confirms who the second man trying to hide from sight was."

"We could circle out of here and be back at that cabin before they get there," Bo said.

"Yeah," Rusty said. "Trouble is, they might figure on that and not go back there for days. They'd come up with a good story by then. Truth is, right now I don't much care about this stuff. It does cloud anything Charlie told us, though."

"You think Ranger Hanson came upon this? Is this what got him killed?" Bo asked.

"No. If he'd have found this and connected it to Duke, this would have been destroyed long ago. No, Jimmy's death was over much more than a few dozen pot plants."

"Yeah, I guess so," Bo said.

"This has been here a long time," Rusty said. "Old Charlie's probably been growing this stuff somewhere ever since he returned from 'Nam. I doubt Andy would put up with it on his land, so what better place than on the sheriff's own ranch?"

"So, what are you going to do about this?" Bo asked.

"Not much. Oh, someday I'll give the sheriff some jazz about growing pot on his ranch. That might be fun. I'll keep this shirt. I might need to use it as leverage to get Charlie to talk more. I'll take a picture of it hanging here, some other pictures too," Rusty said as he took out his phone. When he was finished, Rusty again spoke. "Well, let's follow this old road back into the Rancho Vaca and see where it goes. There's got to be other trails crossing this old fence line too. Judging from where Buddy Bell plotted that fake well, as they called it, I think this will lead us to that."

In fifteen minutes, they were back to where the road crossed the border fence line. They soon crossed over another fence line with a stick-and-wire gate strung across it. This too had drag marks in the sand and looked to have been used recently. A short distance farther, the trail led through a creosote and mesquite filled canyon, void of any large trees.

"Circle back," Rusty said after they'd gone several hundred yards up the canyon. "Over there, south of the road," Rusty said as Bo laid the chopper over into a tight turn, then went back the way they'd come.

"There," Rusty said, pointing. "See that collapsed, old windmill tower laying there? That's what they call the fake well. There's not really a well there. It was just made to look like it."

"Why?" Bo asked.

"Nobody seems to know for sure," Rusty said. "Might have been to draw people away from the real Eagle Well. It seems Maxwell Wolf did some strange, eccentric things. Maybe it was all a joke. At this time, I doubt if anyone knows, or if it really matters, anymore. See, the road out the other way has been traveled some. Jimmy, Buddy, and the sheriff have been here. Maybe others too."

"Where does that road go?" Bo asked.

"According to the map, over to the Rancho Vaca headquarters, with a cutoff up ahead that goes over to the pavement," Rusty answered. "That's how Jimmy and the others were coming in here. Let's go over there, toward the ranch headquarters, and find that cutoff out to the pavement."

Ten minutes later, the old road made a tight turn and the quality of the road somewhat improved as the cutoff to the highway intersected it. Actually, the road toward the highway and also to the ranch house both appeared to be used some—mostly by ATVs.

"Let's go out toward the road," Rusty said. "Out there a ways is where Jimmy's truck was found."

They flew slowly over the road, passing two wells with old concrete tanks half full of stale-looking water.

"Tanks are low," Rusty said. "Mills are turning. Nothing is coming out the fill pipe. I can see why there's no cattle in this pasture."

A short time later, they came to the spot where Jimmy's truck had been found, hidden behind an outcrop of boulders and cedar trees a short distance off the road.

Rusty pointed to the blackened spot on the barren sand. "That burned-out spot, up against those boulders. That's where they found Jimmy's truck."

"Who found it?" Bo asked.

"Chub Murry, another BLM Ranger who worked with Jimmy."

"How? How did he ever see it back here? Especially from the road?"

"I've wondered that myself," Rusty said. "He said he was driving all the roads slowly, with the windows down. Said he smelled it—a burnt smell. He must have a good nose. Well, I've driven up into here, so let's go back the way we came and take the road over to the ranch headquarters."

Bo flew slowly back to where they'd followed the abandoned road in from Sheriff Cutter's ranch. He then made the northerly turn and followed the road toward the ranch house. Rusty figured it was a good three miles until they'd reach the headquarters.

"Looks as if there's three other roads leaving out of here," Rusty said to Bo. "Pick one, when we get there, and just do what you've been doing."

Three hours later, they'd covered all the currently used roads and another seemingly abandoned one. Rusty had seen nothing of interest.

"I've had enough in this little bouncing bird," Rusty said. "Let's go back out that old road we came in on. I want to look at things going the other way. Then let's get back to the airstrip so I can stretch my legs."

"Yeah," Bo said. "Eat some lunch too."

They flew back to where the old road broke off and went over the fence lines to Sheriff Cutter's ranch. Then they worked their way back to the pot grove, then on toward the highway. Suddenly, Rusty saw something. "Down there," he said, pointing towards the road's edge. "Something flashed. Did you see it?"

"No," Bo said. "What was it?"

"I don't know. Circle back, drop down."

Bo reached the area Rusty had pointed to, then dropped down to only twenty feet or so above the ground. Rusty scoured the area. "There," he said, pointing. "It's a bottle—whisky bottle. Yeah, it still has some in it. That's got to be where Travis Evans lost his bottle off the tailgate of his truck. This was where he was chased by someone in Jimmy's truck. So the truck was back in here somewhere, but ended up over yonder… Jimmy was killed back in here, I'd bet on it."

"Well, there is that pot grove," Bo said.

"No—it's much more, I'm sure," Rusty said. "Somewhere, back in here, is the Eagle Well."

The little chopper bumped several times, then drifted off to the east.

"Storm's moving in fast," Bo said. "We best get out of here."

"Guess so," Rusty said. "I'll cover this from the ground. Jimmy got his truck into wherever. I'll have to do the same. I just need to be in three places at once."

"Can't help you," Bo said. "All I know is, I'm glad to get out of here—in one piece."

"I should come right back here tomorrow," Rusty said. "But—"

Lightning flashed, then thunder shook the chopper as Bo sped east.

≫— CHAPTER 12 —≪

Bo dropped Rusty off at the airstrip, then left for Albuquerque. Rusty then drove to Manny's café in Magdalena. Another storm was passing through. Windblown sheets of rain swept across the parking lot. Now, late in the afternoon, Rusty ordered the lunch he'd not yet had, then read the morning's Albuquerque paper. Manny came over and sat across from him.

"So, what did you see from the air today?" he asked.

"A lot," Rusty said. "I've got several areas to really dig into now. It looks as if it's going to be really wet the next day or so. Might be difficult to get around out there. I think I'll go out to Fort Davis for a couple of days. I know that's old news, but I really believe things there are tied into what got Jimmy in trouble."

"Maybe if Jimmy had known more, he'd not have stumbled onto the wrong thing," Manny said.

Rusty nodded slowly.

"He should not have been doing what he did alone," Manny said. "You should not be out there alone either, Señor Rusty. Buddy, he is fearful. Chub is too busy. The sheriff, he seems to care not if this ever gets solved. He only wants to put Lonny Calderone or Duke Atwood in jail."

"Oh, I think he wants this solved," Rusty said. "He doesn't want a killer out here, keeping people in fear. He's a man who wants to be in charge, though. He's not happy that I'm here. He'd like to be the one solving this, but he doesn't really have the training, or skillset, to do it. Maybe, when I solve this, I can let him take some of the credit."

"Don't even think of that," Manny said. "Just concentrate on solving this."

Rusty pulled into Fort Davis about four the next afternoon. Liz had made him a reservation at the old landmark hotel there, the Limpia Manor Inn. When Rusty walked into the lobby, he instantly noticed a large, old painting of the inn from years ago that hung on the wall behind the counter. As he checked in, he asked about it.

"That's quite a painting," Rusty said to the lady who was checking him in. "'57 Chevy parked in front. Was that done about that time?"

"The artist lived here back then," she said. "I was just a child, but I remember her. She taught art over at the university. Sul Ross State, that is."

"Margareta Houser, right?" Rusty asked.

"Why, yes. It surely was. You know of her?" the clerk asked.

"A little. Do you remember her?"

"Well, as I said, I was very young."

"Certainly you were," Rusty said. "You probably knew her daughter, more likely her granddaughter."

"Who are you?" the lady asked, dropping her pen and taking a step back. "What do you know about her granddaughter?"

"Weston was the name they used out here," Rusty continued. "The man was Frederick. The wife was Betty Ann. The little girl, she'd be about your age. She was Debby."

"Just who are you?" the lady again asked.

"Rusty Redtail, FBI. I'm investigating an incident now that might have ties to back in '55. Something that happened before the, ahh... the Westons came here."

"FBI! After all these years... I promised never to tell. Is Debby in trouble? No, of course not now."

"I don't think so. She was just a little girl back then," Rusty said. "Where is Debby now?"

"We were such close friends. Then, well, she left to go to school at Baylor, and I never heard from her again. I'd heard that she was very sick—that she'd actually died. Her mother moved over there too, to be close to Debby. She was always extremely protective of Debby. She never came back here, either. Come to think of it, I'd heard that she died even before Debby."

"So, what did you promise never to tell?" Rusty asked.

"Oh..."

"That her real name was Wolf," Rusty answered for her. "That they came here from New Mexico. That they were hiding. That her father had done something really bad over there. That Margareta Houser was her grandmother. Anything else?"

"Oh my... Yes. Debby told me all of that. She was very lonely. There weren't many girls our age here back then. When her father died—"

"When did her father die?" Rusty asked.

"Oh, not more than a couple of months after they arrived here. He was very ill. I never saw him out of the house. They moved in just up the street from us."

"So, Frederick died soon after arriving here," Rusty said. "Sick you said?"

"Well, you probably know. He'd been shot. I don't think Debby knew much about how. She missed her old friends, but wasn't allowed to ever contact any of them. They even went back to that area several times, but never talked to anyone."

"Why did they go back?" Rusty asked.

"Oh... She told me the wildest story. I never was sure if there was any truth in it."

"Something like going to an old well at night. Having to go down in the well and bring up gold coins?" Rusty asked.

"Oh my. Is that true? Really? That part anyway?"

"There was more?" Rusty asked.

"Just—"

"Just what?" Rusty asked after a moment of silence. "Just that there was a skeleton at the bottom of that old well?"

At that, the clerk stepped back to a stool and sat down. "That poor girl. That poor girl," she repeated. "Having to climb down in that hole with that skeleton there. My, my..."

"What did they do with the coins?"

"She said her grandmother, Margareta Houser, that she had an art client in Santa Fe who would buy them."

"When was this? Shortly after they arrived here?"

"No. The first time was when her mother got real sick. Then, again, just before Debby left for college. There might have been other times. I'm not sure now. They always seemed to have lots of money. Her mother had some fancy horses that she boarded over at the stable on that ranch up north of town. We used to go up there and ride for hours. Her mother loved those horses. Debby and I, we just liked to ride."

"Anything else you can think of?" asked Rusty.

"Not right now. After all these years... Those were good times. We did have good times. If she hadn't gone off to college..."

"You've been most helpful," Rusty said. "Your name? I haven't asked you your name."

"Hazel McCoy now. It was Dodds before I married."

"I'm most fortunate to have met you, Hazel," Rusty said. "I expected to ask all over Fort Davis and not get half the information you've given me. Anyone else here you think could add anything?"

"No… Well, Debby's mother was always real friendly with Jeb Hite. Figured she'd of married him, except Debby hated him. She said he'd never replace her father."

"Jeb still around?"

"Yeah. Old as dirt now though. He's got him a little old mobile home about a mile up towards the observatory. Behind a red barn. Should be an old blue pickup truck under a carport. Like I said, though, Jeb's mighty old. I don't know how much he'll remember."

"I'll put my things in the room, then go see him," Rusty said. "I'll talk to you later, Hazel. Thanks again, very much."

"Jeb—Jeb Hite?" Rusty asked the man who walked out on the porch with the help of a cane.

"That's me, young fella. What can I do ya for?"

"My name's Rusty. I'm looking into some old things you might know about. I thought maybe you could dig back into your mind and help me."

"Old things? Well, I'm old. Can't remember like I used to. Come on up here, and let's sit a spell. Tell me what you're diggin' up."

Rusty climbed the three steps to the porch, then sat down on an old chair beside the one Jeb now sat on.

"So, Rusty you said, what's on your mind?" Jeb asked. "Ain't been too much excitin' in my life for anyone to want to know about."

"Betty Ann Weston," Rusty said. "Old friend of yours, right?"

Jeb didn't say anything. Rusty could tell he was thinking about Betty Ann. Finally, Jeb spoke. "Should have married her. Darned bratty kid didn't like me."

"Betty Ann still alive?" Rusty asked.

"Oh no. Moved out near that college—for the kid. Always, everything for the kid. Only a few years 'til her heart gave out on her. Died the twenty-first of May, 1972. Only fifty-one years old. Derned shame."

The two men sat in silence for several minutes, then Rusty asked another question. "What about the girl, Debby?"

"About a month before Betty Ann died, she wrote me that the kid had cancer real bad. Female stuff. Said she wasn't expected to live but a few months. I didn't go to Betty Ann's funeral," Jeb said. "Couldn't do that. She was buried all alone. Heard that even her kid wasn't able to be there. That cancer is bad stuff. No one came to the funeral, so they just put her in a hole." Jeb buried his face in his hands for several minutes. After a time, he looked up, then stared out into the mountains. "I've done such to an old dog before. But that ain't no way to end a woman's life—not Betty Ann's anyway. I should have gone. Why didn't I go?"

The two men again sat in silence for a time. Then Rusty spoke. "So, you knew Betty Ann quite well, then? You knew she came here from New Mexico."

Jeb nodded. "Knew all about all of that. In fact, took her over there—twice."

"You took her over to New Mexico?" Rusty asked. "To get money—gold coins?"

"Didn't figure anyone else knew about that."

"Tell me about that. You were at that Eagle Well, right? You helped get the coins out?" Rusty asked.

Jeb didn't respond for a minute, then talked softly and slowly. "Know it wasn't really right. Feared I could go to jail or something.

Those bones down at the bottom… Never asked about them. Had to be something no good, though. Took my ladder. Kid went down the hole. Bags full of gold coins, so there was."

"You take them all?" Rusty asked.

"No. Betty Ann was afraid to sell off too many of those coins at one time. She was afraid to have many in her possession too. She figured they were safer down in that well than anywhere."

"So, there were still coins there the last time you were there?" Rusty asked.

"Lots of coins," Jeb said.

"You think Betty Ann ever went back after the rest of them?"

"I know she didn't."

"So, if both Betty Ann and Debby have died, there might still be some of those coins there yet?"

"I'd bet on it. Well, unless…"

"Unless what?" Rusty asked.

"Betty Ann said her father-in-law was a real scoundrel. Maxwell Wolf, I recollect she called him. Said he had several lady friends—kids too." Jeb paused a moment, then went on. "Betty Ann said there was one of them in Arizona, but she'd been taken care of. I don't know what that meant—never asked. There was a little girl there, but Betty Ann never worried about her." Jeb paused again. He sat silently for several moments. Rusty knew he was reminiscing of those days long gone.

"There was another woman, somewhere," Jeb continued. "Betty Ann never knew where, or her name. She had a son, so Betty Ann was told. Just figuring that would make that young one about seventy or eighty years old now. My, my, how time's gone by. He's probably had offspring, maybe several generations by now." Jeb paused again, then he picked up.

"Betty Ann said that woman had a map to the well. That was always her worst fear. That this woman, or her son, would go find the well and clean it out. Take all that money." Jeb again sat and seemed to be thinking of things far away and long gone. After a moment, he continued talking.

"Derned money was a curse. I think Betty Ann worried herself to death over it. Keeping it a secret and worrying that someone would find it. She worried about someone tracing it back to her every time she sold one of those coins. Worry, worry, worry... That's what put her in that early grave. I told her several times to just forget it. We could have been happy without it. But it was always for the kid that she'd go get money or sell a coin. Figure all that stress caused the kid to die of cancer too. I ain't got nothin', but I'm still alive."

After a few minutes of silence, Rusty thought Jeb was finished talking about this, so he asked a question. "You weren't ever tempted to go over there and get some of those coins for yourself after Betty Ann died?"

"Oh yeah, I gotta confess, I did go lookin' for it," Jeb said. "Couldn't find it. That well is really hidden. Fella can walk right past it. I crawled around out there for three nights, figurin' it wasn't safe to be out there in daylight. Finally gave up. Figured it wasn't to be. My luck, I'd have been the one caught with those stolen coins and gone to jail or something. Born a poor boy— gonna die a poor man."

The two sat silently for a minute, then Jeb spoke again. "Don't figure anyone gonna put an old, bunged-up fella in jail now. Kinda feel better having told someone about all that stuff. Sorta like I cleaned out somethin' way down in my innerds."

"You've been a big help, Jeb," Rusty said. "You have any kin around to help take care of you?"

"No kin. Never married. Got me some good memories, though. Me and Betty Ann."

The next day, after Rusty left Fort Davis and was approaching El Paso, Chub called. "Rusty? Chub here. I knew you were going out to Fort Davis. Just wondering if you turned up anything. I saw Alfred Swartz at breakfast, and he asked if you'd learned anything. I guess his father was involved in the sale of Frederick Wolf's assets."

"Yeah, Alfred's who pointed me to Fort Davis," Rusty said. "I did learn a lot. Frederick died soon after arriving at Fort Davis—gunshot wound. Betty Ann Wolf died way back in 1972. The daughter had terminal cancer when her mother died. No one ever heard from her after that. Betty Ann and the girl had moved near Baylor University. I talked extensively to an old childhood friend of the girl's and an old boyfriend of Betty Ann's. It would appear the Wolf family is all dead. Well, there is another twist. There seems to have been a Maxwell Wolf illegitimate son somewhere. No one knows where, his name, if he ever knew about the Eagle Well or the money, or even who his father was. Seems there was a daughter also, but something happened to her... Well, she'd been 'taken care of,' or something like that was the quote. Might have been more. Naturally, this was all quite secretive."

"Strange things never end in this case," Chub said. "And to think, many people in Magdalena revere Maxwell Wolf as a saint."

"There's more," Rusty said. "I'll be going through Socorro in about four hours. You have time for tea?"

"You bet. Just call me when you get close."

When nearing Socorro, Rusty called Chub. "Be in town in about ten minutes."

"Good," Chub said. "There's a little café over by the post office on the town square. Best sweet tea in town. Coffee's good too. C and G Café. Jimmy and I often stopped there. All the cops too."

"Good donuts, then, right?" Rusty asked.

"The best. Ah—so I'm told," Chub said.

"See you there."

Soon after they hung up, Rusty parked in front of the café. He went in and sat in the booth across from Chub, who seemed nervous as he waited on Rusty.

"So," Chub started, "what else did you learn in Texas?"

"Betty Ann made two trips back to the Eagle Well with her boyfriend and took home lots of gold coins," Rusty answered.

"All of them? There's none left?" Chub asked.

"Old boyfriend says there was still a lot of coins still there when she died. He tried to get some of them, but couldn't find the well."

"Wow," Chub said. "Jimmy was right, then."

"Maybe so," Rusty said. He paused, then continued. "Oh—there's a skeleton in the bottom of the well."

"Yuck. Sheriff Tuttle?"

"That would be my guess. Maybe Sheriff Tuttle stumbled into the Eagle Well. Maybe, like Charlie said, Fredrick Wolf got caught up in some kind of trap the sheriff set and they had a fight that led to each shooting the other. Sheriff Tuttle died there—Frederick Wolf several months later over in Fort Davis. Could be that's about what happened."

"So, you think Jimmy got any money out of there?" Chub asked.

The waitress brought over two glasses of tea and set them down before Rusty could answer.

"Haven't seen you in here for a while, Chub," she said.

"Yeah... You know, Melinda, this was where Jimmy and I spent a lot of time," Chub said.

"They catch who killed him yet?" Melinda asked.

"Working on it," Chub replied.

"If they're chasing around out there in that wilderness, they're wasting their time," Melinda said.

"How so?" asked Chub.

"I know who did it. Saw it all set up," Melinda said.

Both Rusty and Chub straightened up and stared right at her.

"Well, who?" Chub asked.

"Sally," Melinda said.

"Sally? Jimmy's wife?" asked Chub. "No way. Couldn't be."

"Surely was, I'd bet my last dollar on it. The Saturday before he disappeared, Jimmy was in here and Sally came in, spitting fire. They had a real bang-up fight. Oh yeah, real nasty. I never saw anything like that from them, never before. Sure as sugar's sweet, she did it."

"What was it about?" Chub asked.

"Sally had relatives in from Dallas, visiting you know? Well, she wanted Jimmy to take them back to the airport in Albuquerque. He was going off to do his usual thing, chasing some old treasure. She didn't want to drive all the way back from Albuquerque by herself, her and little Jimmy. He said this time he was going to strike it rich, for sure. She said he'd be rich alone if he didn't do what she wanted."

"Did he?" Chub asked.

"Don't think so," Melinda said. "They both left. Sally was still spitting fire. I haven't seen her since. Never saw Jimmy again, either."

"I never saw the likes of that," Chub said. "Sally always seems so pleasant."

"Usually so," Melinda said. "Not that day. Mad enough to kill, so she was. She did it. It's always the wife—or husband."

Melinda turned and walked back to the kitchen. Chub looked at Rusty. "Honest, I've never seen anything like that. It can't be. No way. It just—"

"I need to check it out," Rusty said. "I best go alone. She might be embarrassed about this. With you being a friend, well…"

"Yeah," Chub said. "I don't want to talk to her about this. No, you go see her alone. I've heard too much already."

Rusty and Chub sat silently for several minutes. Neither man had yet touched their tea. Rusty finally picked up his and drank about a third of it, then set it down. He took out his phone, placed it on the table in front of him, then said, "I'll call her and see if she can see me before I leave town."

Chub said nothing.

Rusty took another drink of tea, then looked at Chub, who had the look of worry in his eyes. "It was probably just one of those arguments all married couples have. With company, not wanting to drive home alone, she was stressed. Jimmy had his mind and heart set on exploring the well... Things just blew up. Too bad it was in public."

"It better be, that's all," Chub said. "It can't be anyone like this who did that to Jimmy. Shot him in the head. Burned the body. She couldn't do that. No way."

"Probably not," Rusty said. "Besides, she couldn't have done it alone. She didn't know that area, or how to do what was done to his things and the truck. I don't see it."

"Someone out there could have helped her, I guess," Chub said. "But no, she couldn't have anything to do with this."

"Let me talk to her," Rusty said as he picked up his phone.

Rusty scrolled down through the numbers to Sally's number, then sent the call. On the third ring she answered. "Sally? This is Rusty Redtail. How are you and little Jimmy getting along?"

"Well, all right, mostly," Sally answered. "Thank you for getting Jimmy's books and things back to me."

"Sure, thank you for letting me see them," Rusty said. "Listen, something has come up that I need to talk to you about. It won't take long, but it's important. I'm in Socorro now. Can I stop by for a few minutes?"

"Oh, what's this about?" Sally asked.

"I just need some more information on something," Rusty said. "It won't take long, really."

"Now?" Sally asked. "Well, if you must."

"OK, see you in a few minutes," Rusty said, then hung up and slipped the phone into his pocket. He looked at Chub.

"I'll wait on you here," Chub said. "Let me know, OK?"

"Sure. Hey, this is just speculation," Rusty said. "No hard evidence or the like."

Chub nodded slightly, not looking at Rusty.

A few minutes later, as Rusty neared the Hanson house, he pulled over to the side and stopped. *What do I ask her? How do I approach this? Could she really be a part of this? Help me, Lord. I don't want to make this something it's not, but I need the truth, whatever it is.*

He parked in the driveway, then went to the door and knocked.

"Come in," Sally said when she answered. "Come sit in the dining room. Little Jimmy's up playing in his room."

"How's he doing?" Rusty asked.

"I'm still not sure he understands things completely."

"He's awfully young. Knowing what's real and what's not—" Rusty cut off his thought.

"Yeah. Somehow I have to make sure he never forgets his dad. I have to keep alive the memories that he has." Sally paused for a moment, then asked, "So, how can I help you?"

"It's kinda personal. Tell me, tell me about you and Jimmy arguing at the C and G Café the Saturday before he disappeared."

"Oh..." Sally said, hiding her face in her hands. "Wow... Jimmy and I rarely argued. Never in public. That day..." Sally started crying. "Excuse me," she said as she rose and got a tissue. She returned and took her seat again.

"I was so mad that day," she continued. "My mother had come over from Dallas to spend a few days with us. While here, she informed me that my father was diagnosed with early stage Alzheimer's disease. I was just devastated. My father and I are very close. That Saturday, mother needed to be back at the airport late in the morning. I was so stressed that I didn't want to drive home alone with little Jimmy. Just once—just once, I wanted his father to forgo his own interests and be at my side. I really needed Jimmy. He couldn't see it. I never interfered with his interest. He was such a good husband in so many ways." Sally stopped for a minute, then continued. "I went to the café where he usually had coffee. Well, I guess you know how that went. I'm so embarrassed. Mad at myself too. Mad at Jimmy, even more so. If he'd have come with me, maybe he'd still be here."

After a moment of silence, Sally continued. "He kept telling me this time was different, but he'd said that before. He said this time we'd be rich. He was so excited. Maybe he told the wrong person something. Maybe someone followed him to wherever and killed him and took whatever Jimmy found. Maybe... I just think of so many things, but none of them really matter. Jimmy's gone, forever. Instead of being rich, I'm just a poor widow with a little boy who now has no dad."

Rusty and Sally sat in silence for several moments, then Sally spoke again. "Yeah, we argued that day. I just wish I'd have won that argument."

A short time later, Rusty walked back into the C and G Café and sat back in the booth with Chub.

"Well?" Chub asked. Rusty noticed the ice in Chub's tea had all melted, but the glass was full. He'd never touched it. "It can't be, Rusty," Chub said before Rusty replied. "No way did she do it."

"Yeah, I don't think so," Rusty said. "They just had an argument at a bad time in a bad place. I don't think she had anything to do with what happened. If she did, she's one awfully good actress. She's very convincing. She's had awhile to practice and come up with a good story, though."

"She's not acting," Chub said. "You have to believe her. Boy, for a minute there—"

"Well, I best get back out to Magdalena," Rusty said. "Maybe someone out there has something for me."

"I'm just going to sit here awhile," Chub said. "I'll cover your tea."

"Owe you then," Rusty said. "Talk to you soon. Oh, the cowboy shoot. Anything interesting?"

"Sheriff Cutter was there, so he did most of the talking. No one else offered up anything strange. The usual guys were there. The Calderone boy is off in school, as you know. I didn't get anything out of it. Sorry."

"That was a long shot," Rusty said. "Thanks anyway."

Back in Magdalena, Rusty went to his room. After checking his e-mails and answering the necessary ones, he stretched out on the bed. Looking up at the ceiling, he thought about all the suspects in this case.

So many possible suspects on one hand—yet on the other hand, no really serious ones at all—none with any evidence against them. I've chased leads to Arizona, Oklahoma, Texas, all over here down to Socorro… All I keep coming up with is people who convince me they didn't do it… At least, as far as I can tell. Yeah… That one nagging thought keeps going through my mind. But how or why? Nothing seems to point that way. I don't know if that's you, Lord, telling me something, or me being desperate and my mind is playing games. Anyway, thanks, Lord, for keeping me safe. I still need that and your guidance to solve this, please.

An hour later, Rusty went to the café and sat at a booth by the window. He ordered the daily special. He'd picked up an Albuquerque paper in the hotel lobby and now read it while he nibbled on corn chips with Manny's homemade salsa as he sipped his iced tea.

"It's good you had a safe trip to Texas," Manny said as he brought over Rusty's chunky beef burrito, smothered in green chile. "You learn anything? Things about Margareta Houser or Betty Ann and Frederick Wolf?"

"Quite a bit about all of them," Rusty said. "The Wolfs did change their name to Weston. Frederick died from a gunshot wound soon after arriving there. Betty Ann died back in 1972 after moving out near Baylor University when the daughter went to school there. The daughter had terminal cancer when her mother died. So, the proud Frederick and Betty Ann Wolf lay buried in some strange town not even under their own names. Margareta Houser taught art at Sul Ross for a while. Betty Ann made several trips back here to get gold coins from the Eagle Well. I talked to an old friend who was here with her. He said there were lots of coins still there the last time Betty Ann took some. Might still be there today—might not. Oh, there is a skeleton down in the well too."

"That's a lot of information," Manny said. "You sure about all of that?"

"Yeah, I think so. I met the right people and after so many years, they were willing, maybe even wanting, to talk about what they knew. If only the walls in this old place could talk. Imagine the conversations Maxwell Wolf had when this was the bank. Over in the saloon, what all was discussed there. Yeah, if the walls could talk."

"Oh…" Manny said, suddenly grabbing hold of the table. "Señor Rusty, why did I not think of this before now? Maybe this building can talk. The cellar. There is a small cellar under the bank. A trapdoor in the kitchen leads to it. I saw this when I was a wee child. There is a vault with a large steel door, down in this cellar. My father, he knew of it but was too fearful of what might be in it to ever try to open it. He was told that Frederick Wolf also was too afraid of what might be down in that cellar to ever go there. I believe the vault has been sealed since the time of Maxwell Wolf, many, many years ago. Maybe this building will indeed speak to us, Señor Rusty. Maybe it will tell us much."

⟫— CHAPTER 13 —⟪

Rusty sat stunned. *A vault in this old bank cellar? Locked up from the time of Maxwell Wolf? There must be something in there he didn't want anyone to find.*

"There's a trapdoor in the kitchen?" Rusty asked.

"Sí," Manny said. "I'll have to move the prep table, but that will be easy. We might need a new ladder. The old wood one that is there, sí, I remember it as being wobbly back those many years ago."

"What does the vault, as you call it, look like?" Rusty asked.

"As you see in the old movies," Manny said. "Steel door with a big spoke wheel, I think. Dial lock, as I remember. It is a safe, really, I believe. Built into the wall, maybe?"

"We'll need a lantern or two," Rusty said. "Someone to cut out the lock. Who could do that?"

"Hector, over at the garage," Manny answered. "He is the only one I know in town. What else do we need?"

"The sheriff should be here, I guess," Rusty said.

Manny nodded slowly. "He would feel slighted if we left him out. I have not thought about that vault for many years now. Back

170

in the time when I was but a child, after we bought this, Father used that cellar for storage, as the saloon was still in operation. There was some shelves along the one wall. One day that shelf thing fell away from the wall—we must have put too much weight on it. There, hidden behind it was this vault. Father looked at it for quite some time, then he said to never go near it or to even talk about it. I was young and curious and would have liked to have opened it, but of course never could. I won't sleep tonight, anticipating the opening of that door."

"You want to talk to Hector?" Rusty asked. "You know him better than I do. Once he gives you a time when he can be here, can you also let the sheriff know?"

"Sí, I shall take care of all of that," Manny said. "That will make much smoke. There is no window or any vent down there. All that smoke coming up into my kitchen… I hope I don't have to close the café, but, I will if I must."

"I'll see you later," Rusty said.

Sheriff Cutter stood beside Rusty as Hector scratched the striker, then lit the torch.

"Why would anyone put a vault down in a hole like this?" Sheriff Cutter asked. "Not even any electricity down here. Rickety, old handmade ladder not safe for a kid to climb. What if it breaks? We'll all be stranded down here."

"There's an aluminum ladder right outside," Rusty said. "As far as electricity goes, this was probably put in here before there was such a thing in Magdalena. Be patient, Sheriff. In a few minutes, we'll all find out what old Maxwell was hiding."

"I'd bet either gold or bodies," Hector said as he squeezed the valve and started cutting.

172 | Robert C. Mowry

"Ugh…" Sheriff Cutter said. "Now all this smoke. Enough to kill a fella."

"I'd worry more about that spider crawling up your pant leg than a little smoke," Rusty said.

The sheriff looked down, then swatted a large spider from his leg. "Man could die down here," he said.

"You don't have to be here," Rusty said. "I just thought you'd want to be part of this. To see what's in there."

"Probably just a joke," Sheriff Cutter said. "Probably as empty as a dry pasture. Nothing but spiders in there, I say. Old Maxwell Wolf is probably looking down—or up—and laughing right now at us fools."

No one said anything for several moments. Sparks flew from the torch nozzle as Hector continued cutting out the lock. The smoke soon got thick and rank.

"I've got to get out of here," Sheriff Cutter said. "There better be something good in there," he said as he started climbing the old ladder up out of the small cellar.

Hector kept the torch working a circle around the lock. The smoke thickened.

"Enough," Manny finally said. "Come, let's take a break and let this settle."

The three men climbed up out of the small rock-walled, dirt-floored storage hole in the ground. They went into the dining room and sat down at the table where the sheriff already sat talking to Buddy Bell.

"Well?" Sheriff Cutter asked. "I don't see your hands dripping with gold. Empty, right?"

"About twenty percent left to go," Rusty said. "Needed to clear our lungs. I wonder how they ever got such a heavy thing down in that hole."

"Sí, it must have been put in there before the bank was built," Manny said. "The vault upstairs, here, was straight above that one.

Anyone from out of town robbing the bank, they wouldn't know about the second vault underground. Very good idea. Even the locals, such as my father, he knew nothing about such a safe place before he bought it. Maybe only those who built the bank, they might know. Others? When I took over, the saloon was closed and empty. That became our storage area. We never once went down into the cellar. Guess we almost forgot about it, forever."

"Any records of the bank ever being robbed?" Rusty asked.

"Several times," Buddy said. "Back in 1895 was the first time. You know the outlaw trail passed by out west of here, ending over by Alma. Butch Cassidy and those boys sometimes cowboyed on ranches over there as they hid out and made plans. They didn't seem to ever rob anything very close to where they hid. Most of their heists were in Utah or somewhere else up north. However, the story here is that in July of 1895 they rode up here, driving cattle to the railhead, then rode out with the bank's money. Much of it anyway. That's how the tale goes. This was probably easy pickings for a gang like that."

"Guess they weren't arrested," Sheriff Cutter said.

"Don't think they were even pursued," Buddy said. "I guess this was so easy they came back in 1901, just before they supposedly headed to South America. I figure this was boat fare for them."

"That's a good story," Sheriff Cutter said. "Don't know if I put much stock in it."

"The first time, back in 1895, that was just before Franz Frick arrived that year," Buddy said. "The story goes, that's why he would never put his money in Wolf's bank here."

"Sí," Manny said. "Then there is another story that is told, but I know not if it is true. It was sometime later, one robber returned."

"Yeah," Buddy said. "That is a strange story. In 1921, long after Butch Cassidy and the Sundance Kid were declared dead—actually that had been declared several times—there were rumors that Butch was back in the area. That's when a fella drove in here one day in a fancy Buick automobile. While the town's folks were ogling over the first automobile many had ever seen, this fella went into the bank and helped himself to the bulk of its funds. After he was gone in a cloud of dust, some folks claimed it was the same fella who robbed the bank twice before: Butch Cassidy."

"Who all claimed that?" Sheriff Cutter asked. "That's ridiculous."

"Maxwell Wolf swore up and down it was the same man he'd faced-down twice before," Buddy said. "That carried some weight with others who were reluctant to make that same claim until Maxwell did. Some, those who thought Maxwell Wolf a swindler and anything else you can conjure up, they started a story that Maxwell and this fella in the automobile were in on the heist together. That Maxwell Wolf helped rob his own bank and made up the Butch Cassidy story to throw the law off. They say the fella in the automobile was some friend of Maxwell Wolf's, not Butch Cassidy at all. Like the other two times, no one was ever arrested for this heist."

"Interesting," Sheriff Cutter said. "Hey, you're awfully quiet there, Chief. That smoke get to you?"

"Just thinking," Rusty said.

"Let me guess," the sheriff said. "You're thinking that Butch Cassidy killed Jimmy Hanson."

All at the table chuckled slightly.

"Well," Sheriff Cutter said, "are you going to tell us what's going on in that mind of yours?

"I was listening to the stories," Rusty said. "Good history. I've heard about Butch Cassidy and his gang spending time south of here."

"But that's not what you're thinking about," Sheriff Cutter said. "You're thinking on something."

"Just wondering," Rusty said. "Just wondering why someone with a hidden cellar vault like this here would need to have a well out on a ranch to hide money in."

After a few minutes of silence, Sheriff Cutter spoke. "Maybe this is the Eagle Well right here—this vault in the bank basement. Maybe all that talk by Maxwell Wolf about that well was just to throw everyone off."

"That's one thing I was thinking," Rusty said. "But then, what was Jimmy Hanson killed for?"

"Maybe he ran into a band of Mexican smugglers, some of those cartel guys," Sheriff Cutter said. "Maybe it had nothing to do with some Eagle Well or any other old historical stuff he chased after."

No one said anything for several minutes. Then Hector pushed back from the table. "Well, I best get this done. Lots of work in the shop I need to get to."

"Sí," Manny said. "The smoke, it should be settled some by now. At least our lungs are clear."

"Wish I could stay," Buddy said. "But I've got a meeting over at the church. See you all later."

After ten minutes of cutting, Hector shut off the gas, killing the flame. He picked up his hammer and hit the lock. It fell through into the vault.

"Well," Rusty said, "that should free up the latch system. Who wants to try it?"

Sheriff Cutter stepped up and grabbed the handle. He looked at Rusty, then gave the handle a hard twist. It turned. He tugged on the door. It slowly opened. Manny raised the camping lantern he'd been using to illuminate the small room. The light filled the approximately four-feet-by-six-feet vault area.

"What the—" Sheriff Cutter said. The others stood speechless.

An hour later, Rusty sat alone in Manny's storage room—the old saloon. All the contents from the vault had been brought up here. There were boxes of journals, files of news clippings, a box of letters, and several miscellaneous boxes.

Most intriguing, though, were three items: A very ornate silver-adorned Mexican saddle; a very heavy women's silver concho belt; and a knife that fit the description of the one that killed Franz Frick back in 1897.

The saddle and belt, fitting the description of items spoken of by Lonny Calderone, were apparently never sold, as Maxwell Wolf supposedly claimed. The knife... if this was the knife used to kill Franz and that once belonged to Fernando Calderone—how did Maxwell Wolf get possession of it after the murder? Why were these things in this vault? Surely, Maxwell Wolf had more valuable things than these. It wasn't for their value, though that was substantial, that he kept them in there. What special meaning did they have? Why hadn't he, or his son, gotten rid of them?

Rusty sat pondering all of this for quite some time. Eventually, he slid one of the boxes over to himself and took out a ledger book. Code... Everything needed to identify who and what was in some alpha abbreviations and numeric code.

Rusty laid that book aside, then took out another one. It made no more sense than the first. He closed it and placed this one on top of the first, then reached for the box of letters. He picked up a handful and shuffled through them, looking at the return addresses. All appeared to be other banks, coin collectors, or other possible coin buyers. Written under each address was, again, what appeared to be code. This time, numeric only. Rusty opened one of the envelopes. It was empty. So were all the others he checked. They had been saved for the addresses only and whatever the code had told Maxwell.

Rusty figured this was a list of places where Maxwell Wolf had sold some of the gold eagle coins. He'd sell a few at a time to not arouse any suspicion. Rusty tossed the empty envelopes back into the box, then picked up the folder of news clippings. There were two distinct categories divided by a blank sheet of paper. Though few contained actual newspaper identification data, they all seemed to have the same font and layout, which appeared to prove they were from the *Hoof Herald*, Maxwell's own local Magdalena paper.

The largest section of clippings, by far, were all stories about Maxwell himself or his family. A quick perusal of these showed Maxwell Wolf was enamored with himself. It also showed he once ran nearly everything in town. Even stories of the cattle sales tallies each year always seemed to have his name in them somehow.

Rusty skipped over to the other section of clippings. They were all about the 1897 incident, some written by Maxwell himself. Sheriff Antonio Ortiz was often referenced and quoted. Rusty spent an hour or more, reading these accounts.

He then realized he was hungry, so he went over to the café dining room and sat at a window booth. He'd taken some of the old clippings with him and continued to read as he waited for his lunch to be served.

Since it was well past noon and the lunch crowd had thinned out to only a few tables, Manny came out of the kitchen and over to Rusty. He sat across from him. "What do you think, Señor Rusty? Surely there is something there to help you."

"Lots of interesting things, and lots of questions, but so far, nothing to lead to anyone who'd kill Jimmy," Rusty said. "I can't figure why Maxwell Wolf kept the Calderone family's things. What special meaning did they have to him?"

"Sí," Manny said. "When this is all done, and solved, I shall return them to the Calderones. They are rightfully theirs."

"That would be a good thing, however, your family did buy the building and its contents. Legally, they're yours," Rusty said. "I'm sure the Calderones would appreciate getting their old things back, though. That would sort of vindicate their family—forever clear them from any guilt. This really points to Maxwell Wolf being the culprit in all of that back then. He might have had some accomplices, though. I'll dig deep into all that stuff we found. Who knows what will come up."

"Lonny Calderone will be most grateful," Manny said. "He'll treat me right on my beef price when I buy from him, I know he will."

"Then everyone wins," Rusty said.

"So, you think this proves Maxwell Wolf was guilty of the crime back in 1897?" Manny asked. "You see anything that tells you anything about 1955?"

"Not yet," Rusty said. "You know, it's possible only Maxwell knew about this. Maybe Frederick never knew about the cellar and its vault. Old Maxwell might never have sent anyone down there. Frederick Wolf might not have known anything about his father's guilt. No, that's not possible. He knew, yes, of course he knew. It was when Sheriff Bucky Tuttle found the Eagle Well that Frederick Wolf apparently killed him. He knew about the well and the money, but maybe not about this vault."

"If he had, it would seem that Frederick Wolf would have sold what was valuable, then destroyed everything else," Manny said. "To leave all of this was foolish. Surely he would not have left this had he known about it."

"That's what I think" Rusty said. "However, a lot of strange things seemed to go on in that Wolf family."

"That's how it often is with those who have much wealth and power," Manny said. "Often they are—odd, I believe the word would be."

"These people were more than odd," Rusty said. "They were ruthless, heartless, probably cold killers too."

"The sins of the father passed down to the son," Manny said. "I now wonder what kind of man Maxwell Wolf's father was? Did he pass this down to Maxwell?"

"Interesting thought," Rusty said. "Never saw a thing about anyone farther back the family line. It would be interesting to do a genealogy study on them. No time for that now, though."

The waitress brought Rusty's lunch. "Enjoy," Manny said as he rose to leave for the kitchen. "I must go prepare for tonight. Taco special. We'll be very busy."

Rusty read through some of the clippings as he ate, mostly those from the time of the robbery and murder of Franz Frick in 1897. It seemed half the town was under suspicion for one reason or another. Everyone except Maxwell Wolf—at least in the newspaper stories.

One story in the section of articles on Maxwell Wolf intrigued Rusty. Maxwell had obtained a patent on a wagon set up to work on wells. It had a hinged triangle boom that swung out the back that held a double-line pulley system to feed a rope down into the well. It was a kind of portable winch. From off this boom, about two feet from the rope line, a crossbar held a rope ladder that could go down into the hole. The old wagon he'd seen out at the Calderone ranch was probably the prototype, or a production model, of this.

Rusty finished eating, then went back over to the old saloon area and put the newspaper articles back in their folder. Then he fished through the box of envelopes again. He found one bundle with only three envelopes tied together. He untied the string and looked at the return address. They were all from a Pricilla Miller, Show Low, Arizona. Rusty looked at the date stamps and opened the oldest one, dated November 16, 1923. He read the contents:

My Dearest Maxwell,

How I wish you were here. I know the weather is little different here than back home, but I seem to be chilled all the time. My room at the boarding house is simple, but nice. The other women have treated me well, for the most part, considering my situation. Mother and father still refuse to speak to me, or answer my letters.

Only six months, a little less really, until I shall hold our little one in my arms. How I long for that day. If only you could be a part of all of this. You are a part, of course. I hope it is a boy. I will name him Maxwell if it is.

Thanksgiving will be different. I shall miss my parents and sisters greatly on that day. Christmas will be no better. Maybe you will be able to make at least a brief visit sometime?

I shall not take more of your time, now. I pretend that you are with me always—especially at night. Until you can visit, I am content to see you in my dreams.

Your loving sweetheart,

Pricilla

Rusty sat considering this for some time. It told a lot about Maxwell Wolf, but he didn't see where it mattered much to the case at hand. Rusty then picked up the second letter in that group, dated May 2, 1924.

My Dearest Maxwell,

Yesterday our daughter was born. It wasn't the son I so hoped for, but I see you when I look at her. I have named her Maxine May. Maxine for you. That's as close for a girl as I can come to you. May is for being born on May Day.

I am doing fine, as is little Maxine May. I so wish you were here. Maybe soon? I must go now. She's crying and needs to be fed.

The nurse just brought her to me. I do not like to hear her cry. I want to be the best mother since time began. For our daughter, your daughter.
Your family,
Pricilla and Maxine May

The third letter was dated a month later. Rusty opened it, then slowly read it.

My Dearest Maxwell,

I thank you most graciously for the very generous gift. I know you paid for all the hospital expenses too. Are you sure these funds won't be missed? One thousand dollars is a lot of money, even for one of your standing. Maxine May and I will use it wisely.

I do hope you can come visit us soon and meet your, our, daughter.

On that other thing you mentioned in your letter, Maxine being in your will. This is most generous, when that sad day comes, to set up a part of your estate for Maxine May's future. What you have set up for me is unexpected and unnecessary. Does your son, Frederick, know about this? I assume not. Surely not your wife.

This map to where the money for me is located, that is rather confusing to me. This well, as you call it, this is where those coins you talk of are located? Am I to just go there? How would I retrieve my share? It might be best that at that time Frederick would be instructed to go with me. That all seems so far off that I shall not now concern myself with such details.

Please come and visit as soon as you can.
Your loving family,
Pricilla and Maxine May

So, there was a map to the Eagle Well. Was there any chance it still existed? Maxine May was born in 1924, making her now past ninety. She could still be alive—but where? Under what last name? When Maxwell Wolf suddenly died, she would have been about six. She might remember some things from that time. Did Pricilla get the money from the well? Did she actually go to the well? Any chance little Maxine May did also?

Rusty put those three letters back in their envelopes. He then retied the old string around them. He shuffled through the letter box, looking for more letters from Pricilla Miller. He found none.

Rusty then went through several more of the journals. Nothing made sense. He figured that no matter what type of crooked financial dealings Maxwell Wolf had back then, it had no bearing now on solving Jimmy Hanson's murder—at least none that he could connect right now.

Rusty untied the string wrapped around a small, plain brown shoebox. Inside was a small cardboard card with a lock of blond hair attached to it with a yellowed piece of tape. *Maxine May, age two*, the faded writing read. Lying beside that was a small pair of hand-knitted baby booties, knit from white yarn. An old black-and-white photograph of a little girl was under the booties. *Maxine May, age 2* was written on the back, followed by *July 1, 1926.*

Rusty looked at the little girl for a long time. What kind of life did she have? Did Maxwell Wolf provide well for her back when he was alive? Did her mother get some of those gold coins after he died? Did this little girl, now past ninety years old, still live? If so, could he find her?

Much later, Rusty went to his room, still contemplating all these things. Should he pursue finding Maxine May, or was this just another rabbit to chase and distract him, eating up precious time?

>>———<<

The next morning, Rusty called Liz.

"Hey, Rusty. What's up?" Liz asked.

"Oh, I've got another old event for you to look into. My life would be easier if back a hundred years ago these people wouldn't have been so corrupt and inept and the law would have solved these crimes. This might not be anything—nothing today—but I need you to run down what you can on a Pricilla Miller. She'd have been born about 1900 to 1905, probably. Maybe before that. She was probably born in Magdalena, New Mexico, but by 1923 she was in Show Low, Arizona. She had a daughter, Maxine May Miller. May with a "y" like the month. She was born in Show Low on May 1st, 1924. That's about all I have. With luck, Maxine May is still alive—and cognizant of some old events."

"This does seem to be off the reservation. Oops... That probably wasn't a good analogy," Liz said, trying to hold back a giggle. "Sorry, I didn't mean anything by that."

"Well, I guess it fits, the way that phrase is sometimes used these days," Rusty said. "No offense taken. If this was a reservation out here, it would be a big one. This Wolf family seemed to spread their trouble in a wide loop."

"What am I looking for?" Liz asked.

"Well, Maxine May Miller was Maxwell Wolf's illegitimate daughter. She was apparently in his will. If she's alive, she might know something important—without even being aware of it."

"Oh... OK. I'll do my best," Liz said. "How do you turn up this old stuff anyway?"

"It just comes to me," Rusty said. "I'll talk to you later then. Time to get back on the reservation. Thanks."

"Sorry, Rusty," Liz said. "I didn't mean—"

"I'm used to it," Rusty said, then hung up.

He walked over to the café, where he soon was eating his breakfast slowly, and waited for Manny to have time to come and talk to him. As he finished his third cup of coffee, Manny came over to his table.

"I still smell that awful smoke from the torch yesterday," Manny said. "Did you get any good information?"

"Lots of interesting things," Rusty said. "I'm not too sure if any of it will help solve Jimmy's murder, though."

"That saddle and things," Manny said. "In the old days, these were most fancy. Some collector would pay much to add them to their collection, but they will mean most to the Calderones."

Rusty nodded his agreement. "Is your mother coming in this morning?"

"Sí, she is already here. She is in the kitchen, making tortillas. She should be finished soon. You wish that I should have her come and see you when she is finished."

"I just want to see if she remembers ever hearing about someone from way back. Probably even before she was born," Rusty said.

"If they lived here, she may have heard something," Manny said. "In those times past, the old folks talked a lot. They had no TV, or anything, to occupy their idle time back then. They talked much."

Manny then went back to the kitchen. In only a few minutes, Yolanda Rodriguez slowly walked over to Rusty's table. "Señor Rusty, Manny tells me you want to ask me about someone from days long ago."

"Please, have a seat," Rusty said, motioning for Yolanda to sit across from him. She sat down and looked at Rusty as she nervously folded her hands.

"Way back in 1923, maybe back before that, even before you were born," Rusty said, "maybe your mother or someone talked about this. Pricilla Miller—she moved away in 1923."

"Oh my… Prissy Miller, Cassandra's older sister," Yolanda said. "Cassandra was the baby of the family. She was my age. Prissy, she was the oldest. Much older, it seemed."

"Did Cassandra ever talk about what happened to Prissy?" Rusty asked.

"Oh, sometimes. She wasn't supposed to. The family was very embarrassed. Prissy, she, well, she became with child. Who was the father? No one seemed to know—only Prissy. She went away. Such was the way, back then. The Millers, they never talked about her again—never. That was how it was done in that day. It was a great shame for the whole family."

"So, Prissy never came home?" Rusty asked. "Never brought the baby here?"

"Oh no. That would never happen," Yolanda said. "No, never did Cassandra ever see the baby. A little girl, I remember hearing."

"Yes," Rusty said. "They lived over in Show Low, at least at first."

"Cassandra always wondered who the father was. It had to be someone here in town. I always had my thoughts," Yolanda said. "Just my thoughts."

"Is Cassandra still here?" Rusty asked.

"No—no, she died at least ten years ago," Yolanda answered. "She never again saw her sister or that little girl. That's sad, isn't it, Señor Rusty? Maybe that wasn't right. It's what was done, though, back in those days. Today, it is no shame at all for an unmarried girl to have a child. Such is not the right way either. I know not which is worse, the old ways, or the new. The poor children, in either way."

When Yolanda went back to the kitchen, Rusty went over to the old saloon room again and spent the rest of the morning going through things from the cellar vault. At lunchtime he went over to the café dining area. He ordered a bowl of green-chile stew and an iced tea. Buddy came in and quickly walked over to Rusty's table.

"That must have been some find yesterday," Buddy said. "Wish I could have stuck around all day. The sheriff told me about the saddle and knife. That sort of puts a different light on old Maxwell Wolf than what he portrayed himself to be."

"Yeah," Rusty said. "There's a whole lot more in those boxes."

"Anything help you with Jimmy's murder case?" Buddy asked. "Anything from Frederick Wolf?"

"No. It doesn't appear anyone knew about that vault except Maxwell himself," Rusty answered. "I haven't seen anything put there after Maxwell's death. I think that if Frederick would have known about what was there, he'd have disposed of it all, one way or another. There's some very degrading and incriminating stuff in there."

"Maxwell Wolf must have been a very secretive person," Buddy said. "To have a vault right in the bank and his son not to know of it. Of course, Frederick was only a teenager when his father died."

"I hear, or find, almost nothing about Maxwell's wife," Rusty said. "What do you know about her?"

"She rarely left their house, from all I've heard," Buddy said. "She was never known to be in the bank. She never acted like the queen of the town, or anything like that. I've heard tales—all passed down, of course—that she was fearful of Maxwell. She'd actually shake and at times get physically sick when he started chastising her in public. I don't even think there's a picture of her anywhere."

"That fits," Rusty said. "Secret vault. Secret well. Secret life. Overbearing brute. Money and power. Well, he didn't take any of it with him. Died young. That's not my kind of life."

"Matilda Wolf did oversee the hotel and this café after Maxwell died," Buddy said. "She didn't deal much with the public, though. She stayed in the kitchen or the little hotel office. I'm told she hired out all the public jobs. After a few years, Frederick took over. That was after he returned from college. I'm told things were still run poorly. When Manny's parents bought this, it was nearly out of business."

Rusty's phone rang. He looked at it. It was Liz. "My office," he said. "I'll call back in a minute." Rusty finished his lunch, then went back over to the other room and called Liz back.

"Rusty, what are you doing out there?" Liz asked. "You're supposed to be solving Jimmy Hanson's murder. Are you sure all this old stuff is relevant? There's that 1897 story. The one in 1955. Now this one too."

"So, what about Pricilla Miller?" Rusty asked.

"She mysteriously disappeared," Liz said. "Just vanished. It's never been solved."

"Disappeared?" Rusty asked. "When?"

"Back in 1930," Liz said. "No trace, ever."

1930... That's when Maxwell Wolf died. Pricilla and Maxine May were to inherit part of Maxwell Wolf's estate—some of the hidden eagle coins too. Pricilla disappeared... Maxine May probably got nothing.

≫— CHAPTER 14 —≪

Rusty sat down on the old broken-back chair he'd been using as he went through the things from the vault. "Didn't they ever solve anything out here?" Rusty asked, more like a statement than a question to Liz. "What about the girl, Maxine May?"

"Oh well, good news, I think," Liz said. "She's still alive. In a senior home in Show Low. She never married or moved away. She was only six years old when her mother disappeared. She was raised in several foster homes. That's about all I could find. I did call that senior home. They said she still has a pretty good mind, but very bad attitude. I don't know what she could possibly tell you that would help find who killed Jimmy Hanson, but I told them you might want to talk to her. They said to come on over."

"The Eagle Well," Rusty said. "Her mother had a map to it, and she was possibly there. Maxine may still have that map."

"This is getting too far out for me to follow," Liz said. "What's the Eagle Well?"

"That's what got Jimmy killed, I think," Rusty said. "Where he was killed too, I believe. I've got to find that well, then I believe everything will fall into place."

"Harland's getting antsy," Liz said. "Come up with something, real soon, or... Well, let me know if you need anything else."

"Thanks, Liz. You're a big help. I owe you."

"Like an evening out with dinner and dancing as payment?"

"Sure," Rusty said. "A juicy horse steak and dancing around a fire out on the reservation. I'll even let you beat on your own drum."

"Rusty Redtail, you're impossible. Forget I ever brought up the thought. Never again. I don't know why, but I'm concerned about you. You know, with you being out there alone... All these side things coming up... A killer of a federal agent lurking around and maybe bad actors still hiding something from these old things you keep turning up. Just be careful."

"I always am," Rusty said. "Don't worry about me. I have a mother who does enough of that. E-mail me the info on that senior home."

"Your mother has to be a saint to put up with you," Liz said. "Oh, gotta go. Here comes Harland."

Rusty sat for some time. Going to see Maxine May Miller would be worth it if she had a map to the Eagle Well or had been there and remembered anything about it. Otherwise, it probably would be a waste of time. Back in 1930—that was when Maxwell Wolf died. If Pricilla and Maxine May were truly in his will... The downtrodden and scorned wife finding out about her... The teenage son having to share with a stranger—maybe several... Lots of possibilities, motives really, to dispose of Pricilla and modify, or dispose of, the will and secret agreements allocating the coins in the well. Still, none of that meant anything to help solve Jimmy Hanson's murder. It surely was intriguing, though.

I'll get up early in the morning and go to Show Low.

Rusty approached the office at the Tall Pines Senior Home late the following morning. The lady behind the desk smiled and greeted him. "Welcome to Tall Pines. How may I help you?"

"I'm Rusty Redtail, FBI. I believe my office contacted you yesterday. You have a Maxine May Miller as a resident here, right?"

"Oh—yes. Maxie has been here for nearly five years, I think."

"I just have a few questions to ask her. Nothing about her directly. Just about some things from way back in her life that may be of help solving a case now. She might not even know that some things she saw, or heard many years ago, could be very important now. Is there a room where I could talk privately with her? Someplace where she'd be comfortable?"

"Well—Maxie's a very quiet person. Doesn't talk much," the lady said. "The dining room is empty now. That would be a good place. I'll have a pot of coffee brought in. Maxie likes her coffee."

"That would be great," Rusty said. "Anything I should know about Maxine?"

"No—just like I said, she's awfully quiet," the lady said. "Follow me. The dining room is back this hallway. I'll have one of the aides get Maxie. I can't remember her ever having a visitor. She's really a forgotten soul."

Rusty sat waiting at a table in the dining room. *Lord, help me to not stir up old, bad memories in her mind. If she can help me, please lead me to get any important information she has. Help me, somehow, to also be a help to her.*

A few moments later, a young woman led in a feeble, aged lady who moved methodically, pushing a walker. She stared at Rusty, who rose and smiled at her. He waited for her to make her way to the table and sit down.

"This is Maxie," the young lady said, then she turned and left.

"Hi, Maxie. I'm Rusty, Rusty Redtail. Thank you for meeting with me."

"Don't know what you want," Maxine said. "Ain't got any money. This place took all of that. You don't look, or act, like a doctor."

"No," Rusty said. "I'm not a doctor, and I don't want any money. You've lived here quite a while now, haven't you?"

"Couldn't stay by myself anymore," she said. "Fell and broke my hip. Had no one to help me. Never did. Just me. Always was that way, ever since mother…"

"Yes, back when you were little, you had your mother," Rusty said after a moment of silence.

A faint smile crossed Maxine's face for a few seconds.

"Your mother was good to you," Rusty said. "She loved you, I know."

"Why'd she go and never come back?" Maxine asked. "I needed her. No one else ever cared for me. I was just a bother to them."

"Your mother was taken away," Rusty said. "She didn't leave you because she wanted to."

"I cried every day for her to come back. For years, I cried," Maxine said. "She never came back."

"She wanted to," Rusty said. "She just couldn't."

"Why didn't I have a father?" Maxine asked. "Everyone should have a father."

Rusty sat silently for a moment. Then he asked Maxine a question. "Do you have anything from your mother? Any papers or anything?"

"Papers? No… not even a picture. I can't even remember what she looked like anymore. It's been so long."

"The day your mother left, do you remember anything?"

"Oh yes. She was happy. She said things were going to change for the better for us. We'd have our own place. I could get new clothes for school. I was all ready to go into the first grade."

"Was your mother usually happy, or was she sad?" asked Rusty.

"She was often sad. She got a letter, I remember. Not many days before she left, I think. She cried for days. She held the letter and cried. Then, there was another letter. That's when she got happy. The sad, it seemed to go away."

"Did she have any other papers that she ever looked at?"

"Papers? Oh—yes. She took some papers with her when she left. I remember that now." Maxine stared out the window in silence for a moment, then softly spoke. "I can't remember her face. I can't see her face anymore. I wish…"

"Do you remember if she told you where she was going that day?" Rusty asked after a moment.

"Going? Well… To meet someone. A young man, she said. Said she'd be back in a day or so. I went to a friend's house. I only had one friend. Most girls wouldn't play with me. They weren't allowed, 'cause I had no father. That's the way it was. I didn't understand that. It wasn't my fault. I couldn't help it."

Rusty sat silently for a moment, looking at Maxine, who looked off into the distance, not seeming to concentrate on anything, just staring blankly.

"Thank you," Maxine said. "I haven't thought of my mother in a long time. We had good times together. We didn't have much, but we had good times. Just mother and me. I'll go back to my room now. I just want to go and think of those good times. Mother and me."

Rusty sat there for a moment and watched Maxine slowly make her way out of the dining room. He poured himself another cup of coffee. Maxine hadn't touched hers. He wasn't sure she'd even seen it sitting there

Such a sad way to close out such a sad life.

≫———≪

On his way back to Magdalena, Rusty stopped in Springerville to see Sheriff Hays. He found the sheriff's truck parked at the White Mountain Diner. When Rusty walked in, the sheriff immediately saw him and motioned for him to come to his table.

"Been thinking about you, Rusty," Sheriff Hays said. "Nothing came of that fella in Oklahoma, I guess."

"He's a bad actor, for sure," Rusty said. "Troubled kid heading for a big-time fall if he doesn't straighten up. He's not our ranger-killer, though."

"Figured that," Sheriff Hays said. "That would have been too easy. How's the investigation coming?"

"I keep chasing off after leads of old things—old things never solved. You know anything about Maxwell Wolf getting a young girl pregnant?"

"Never heard that one," Sheriff Hays said. "Doesn't surprise me, though."

"Girl named Pricilla Miller. Went to Show Low in 1924."

"No, really? Maxwell Wolf was involved in that? You sure?"

"Have it in writing," Rusty said. "She had a daughter."

"Yeah—Yeah. Maxine May Miller. I've heard about that story. Pricilla went missing. Nineteen thirty, oh, right after Maxwell Wolf died. She was seen getting into a fancy black car with a young fella driving it. Out-of-state plates—Utah, it was always said. That's where they looked for her, mostly—what little looking they did. You know back then, unmarried mother... No one really cared that much. Rumors were that she was, well, you know what."

"I doubt all of that," Rusty said. "If I was a betting man, I'd say Pricilla and Maxine May were both in Maxwell's will, sharing with the wife and Frederick—maybe others too. That was probably the first time either of those two knew about Pricilla Miller. Maxwell had sent Pricilla a copy of a map to the Eagle Well and had apparently authorized her to take some of those coins. That may have been their only inheritance—

but it seems that Maxine May was actually in his will. I'd say that young man in that black car was a teenage Frederick Wolf. If the car had Utah plates, they weren't the correct plates. Pricilla's bones are somewhere out in these hills, if anything is left of them."

"You learn something new in this business every day," Sheriff Hays said. "So, did you find that map?"

"No," Rusty said. "I think she took it with her that day when she disappeared. Probably was told to."

"So, Frederick Wolf killed Sheriff Tuttle in 1955 but had killed Pricilla Miller way back in 1930. Cold—that's real cold. Leaving that little girl like that."

"Most likely his father killed Franz Frick in 1897," Rusty said. "Seems to run in the family."

"Pillars of the community," the sheriff said. "Most admired people in San Agustin County for many a year."

"Sometimes all that adoration gets you is a fancy gravestone," Rusty said. "It didn't even get Frederick Wolf that. He ended up buried in a strange town, not even under his own name."

"Not much of a legacy, for what that's worth," Sheriff Hays said. "Speaking of legacies, I'm just stalling around here. I have to go arrest that no-account cousin of mine again."

"What now?" Rusty asked.

"Old Lester punched a fellow, a passerby. Broke his nose. Fella's pressing charges, so he is."

"The guy call Lester a redneck or something?" Rusty asked.

"Fool complained about it being hot. Blamed it on global warming. Old boy was from Iowa. Must not have realized he was in Arizona and we still get hot here in September."

"I've got to get back to Magdalena anyway," Rusty said. "Somehow, I've got to find that Eagle Well."

"Stop back again sometime," Sheriff Hays offered. "When this is over, we'll go fishing or something."

"Sounds good," Rusty said. "Can't even think about something like that now."

When Rusty pulled into the hotel parking lot in Magdalena, he spotted Sheriff Cutter's truck at the café. He parked, walked into the café, and found Buddy and the sheriff sitting at a table.

"What's up, Chief?" Sheriff Cutter asked as Rusty walked their way. "Let me guess, you've been to Colorado now? That's about the only place you haven't been chasing ghosts. Who have you been chasing after now?"

"Maxwell Wolf's daughter," Rusty said as he pulled out a chair and sat down across from the sheriff.

"Maxwell Wolf's daughter?" Sheriff Cutter asked. "He never had a daughter—only kid he had was Frederick."

"Daughter's alive and fairly well, for being over ninety," Rusty said. "I learned a lot."

"I never heard of a daughter," Buddy Bell said. "Must have been a well-kept secret."

"He kept it that way—so did Frederick," Rusty said. "She still doesn't know who her father was. Never used the name 'Wolf' or was any part of the family."

"You're confusing me more with every word," Sheriff Cutter said. "Why don't you just lay it out straight and simple?"

"Oh, I probably said too much already," Rusty said. "It's not important anyway. Well, I've got paperwork to do. See you boys later."

"Just like that? You're going to drop a bomb like that on us, then leave?" the sheriff asked.

"Like I said, it's not important," Rusty said as he got up and started for the door.

"Maxwell Wolf never had a daughter," he heard Sheriff Cutter say to Buddy. "Old Chief's just trying to get into my head."

Later on, Rusty studied one of Maxwell's ledger books. He determined it was a list of Maxwell's gambling debts. Though coded with initials only, it was obvious Maxwell was a big loser in poker. There were deposits to this account marked as "BT." Rusty assumed that stood for bank transfer. If it did, Maxwell had transferred large sums of money each summer during the cattle-shipping season. Rusty figured Maxwell may have welcomed the crash of 1929, which gave him good reason to close the bank without it collapsing on its own from his mismanagement and embezzlement.

From the last pages of this ledger, it appeared that Maxwell Wolf still owed considerable money to several people. Maybe they'd been paid off and it was not recorded here. Maybe he'd used some of the stolen gold eagles from the Eagle Well. *Why did Maxell keep this record? Why not destroy it?* Rusty had no answer. Actually, much of what Maxwell Wolf did made little sense to Rusty.

Tossed into the box along with the journals and ledgers was a tiny brown envelope. Rusty had looked at that before, but was unable to make out the faded writing on it, so he'd paid it little attention. Now, he picked it up again and took it over to a window to get more natural light on it. After a moment, the writing became readable.

Cyanide Tablets!

It was empty. It had been on top of the box, as if it was the last thing put in it. *Had Maxwell Wolf taken his own life? Was the heart attack just a story to save his reputation?*

Rusty thought about this for some time, then determined that it made no difference. Maxwell Wolf was dead, long dead. How he died made no difference in Rusty's solving what happened to Jimmy Hanson. Still, it did say a lot about the character of the man and what he may have passed down to his son.

Rusty left the old saloon, then went over to his hotel room. He started his computer, opened his e-mail, then read through the usual collection of new, boring messages. Some were from his Albuquerque office, others from Washington or various other places. He answered what was required, then opened a blank page to send a note to Liz. He took out his little pad and looked over the list he'd compiled for her to research. It was extensive—twelve things to be exact. He typed her the list, then sent it. He'd wait awhile in the morning to call her, giving her time to overcome any shock, or anger, at such an extensive list.

Rusty shut off his computer, then stretched out across his bed. He couldn't get Maxine May Miller off his mind. Such a sad life. Never knowing her father. Her mother being taken when she was so young. Never marrying and having any family of her own. Never really reaching beyond the confines of that small town. She didn't seem to be at peace with life. She most certainly wasn't at peace with God either.

Should I have told her who her father was? Would that have made her even more bitter than she is now? Knowing her father was wealthy, or at least had access to money, and she and her mother had so little? No, there is no reason to tell her now. All this life of hurt and pain for this poor woman, just for a little pleasure for the greedy old Maxwell Wolf. Such a selfish man. Yet, in the end, in the prime of his life, he apparently ended his own life. So, there had to be pain there too. Was Maxwell as unhappy as Maxine? Was his wealth a curse? It gave him power over others, but that power in the end brought pain to all he touched.

God—may I never be so short-sighted—so selfish. Please, may I never bring such pain and hopelessness to anyone.

Rusty then took out his phone and called his mother.

The next morning at breakfast, Rusty sat sipping coffee, waiting for his food. Buddy came in, saw Rusty and walked over to him.

"Early today, aren't you?" Rusty asked. "Or am I that late?"

"Women's breakfast today," Buddy said. "They'll be coming in real soon now. They like me to say the blessing. Oh, here comes some now."

Three women walked in and started toward the reserved section of tables pushed together. Seeing Buddy sitting with Rusty, they waved. Then one of them, Dee Cutter, broke from the others and came over to Buddy and Rusty.

"Agent Redtail," she said, "how nice to see you again. That husband of mine still trying to get under your skin? I'm sure he is."

"Well, he tries," Rusty said. "He hasn't learned yet that red skin is extremely thick. It takes a lot to get under it."

"Don't let his actions fool you," Dee said. "Wesley likes you. He says he doesn't know how you keep coming up with all the things you do. How are you progressing on your case anyway?"

"One day at a time," Rusty said. "I keep coming up with old cases that were never solved. This can't be another one like that. You know, while I'm working out here, I'd like to see your rodeo stock sometime. I'd enjoy that."

"Well, Wesley's going to be out there all day today. Vet's coming in. You'd get to see them all today," Dee said.

"Well, maybe. If you don't think he'd mind," Rusty said. "I do have a matter to discuss with him that would be best done in private. There's always ears around here, and I never see him in his office, here in town."

"You know how to get to the ranch?" Dee asked.

"Off the road that heads towards the place called Dusty, right?" Rusty said.

"About twelve miles to the south, you'll see a sign pointing back a gravel county road," Dee said. "Trails End Cattle Company—that's us. It's back that road about another dozen miles to the main ranch road. You can't miss it, really."

"Well, I was going out west today anyway," Rusty said. "I'll just swing by there first."

Midmorning, Rusty pulled into the headquarters of the Trails End Cattle Company. A large, old adobe house with a portico running across the entire front sat back a ways from several work and storage buildings. A long barn was farther back the road. Rusty stopped and looked around. He spied a hanging sign that read "Headquarters." He drove up to that building.

Rusty got out and walked up to the door under the extending arm holding the sign. As he reached up to knock, Sheriff Cutter called out through the door. "Come on in, Chief. Dee called me and said you'd be coming."

Rusty opened the door and stepped inside. He glanced around at the extensive taxidermy and old Western memorabilia that adorned the walls and several high shelves. A large oil painting hung behind Sheriff Cutter's desk.

"Great office," Rusty said. "I can see why you like to hang out here."

"In Midland, my oil company office was just an office. Couple of old pictures and such. I said when I came out here I was going to have my dream private space. I didn't care about the house. That's Dee's deal. This is mine. You can see why I don't hang around that sterile, white box of an office the county gives me in town."

Rusty nodded, still admiring some of the things on the wall.

"What's up?" Sheriff Cutter asked. "Dee said you needed to talk to me without any other ears around."

"What's up is a grove of pot growing over on that west edge of your unused pasture land," Rusty said. "Off that old, abandoned east/west road."

"Pot! Growing on my ranch?" Sheriff Cutter leaned forward in his chair. "Someone has the audacity to do that on my land? How much?"

"Not much," Rusty said. "It's for personal use, I'm sure. It's not some commercial enterprise. Whoever it is probably doesn't want to get caught with it on their own land, so they're growing it on yours. What safer place than on the sheriff's ranch, right?"

"Duke Atwood… He's in on this, somehow," Sheriff Cutter said. "Yeah, he would get a kick out of that. Raising pot on the sheriff's land. I'll find it, then he'll pay. I'll pin it on him somehow."

"I wouldn't lose any sleep over it," Rusty said. "It's not enough to get all hyper over."

"Duke Atwood gets me hyper."

"I just thought you should know about this. I know you told me you never go out on that part of your ranch, so you might never find it. If someone else did, it might not look good for you. Enough of that. Let's go look at your bulls, if you have time."

"Always have time to show off my boys," the sheriff said. "Got one ready for his first arena ride. You want to give it a try?"

"You first," Rusty said. "Then maybe."

"That's what I pay young guys for," Sheriff Cutter said. "Guys with lots of muscles and few brains. Wait until you see this bull, though. He's going to be good."

They went to see the bulls, and after an hour looking over them, Rusty was ready to leave. "Gotta get back to work. Need to follow up on some things I spotted from the air."

"Yeah, well, hey," Sheriff Cutter said. "Thanks for not bringing up that pot thing at the café. Those walls have ears, you know? I'll take care of it—with pleasure."

"Actually, most everybody knows I'm nosing around," Rusty said. "I wouldn't be surprised if it's already been destroyed."

"Guess I better keep a better eye on my land. Need to get out of my office and on a horse, well, an ATV, really."

Shortly after noon, Rusty stopped at the Datil Corner Café for lunch. As he sat there, Duke Atwood walked in. He stopped, looked at Rusty, then walked over to his table.

"Have a seat," Rusty said.

"You looking for me?" Duke asked.

"No, not really," Rusty said. "Some reason I should be? You have something to confess?"

"I just thought maybe, well, that deal with Charlie and me, out on the sheriff's ranch," Duke said. "I know you saw who we were."

"You were protecting Charlie. I know that."

"Well, sort of," Duke said.

"I've got bigger things to do than hassle a disturbed old war vet and a mixed-up spoiled guy who hasn't grown up yet and is trying to find life's meaning in all the wrong ways and places," Rusty said.

"You tell the sheriff?" Duke asked.

"Only that I found some pot growing on his land, not whose it was. It was rather entertaining watching his reaction to learning that was growing on his ranch."

"Wish I could have been there and seen that," Duke said with a smile. "He'll blame it on me, for sure."

"Already has. That comes with the reputation you've established for yourself," Rusty said. "I hope you fellas had the sense to get rid of it."

"It's gone. It only needed a few more days to be ready to harvest. It's all gone now."

"But there's a new plot somewhere else now, right?" Duke didn't respond to the question, so Rusty said, "Be careful. Playing games on the sheriff might be entertaining, but he might take it very seriously. He's not one to be mocked."

"Guess you're right," Duke said. "We might want to reconsider some things."

"Maybe reconsider the entire thing? Maybe it's time to mature beyond that?" Rusty asked.

"You sound like Pa now," Duke said.

"I'll take that as a compliment," Rusty answered.

"Hey, you're all right, Agent Redtail. You're sort of a right thinkin' guy."

"Like your pa," Rusty said.

"Maybe… Maybe he kinda is," Duke said, then paused for a few seconds before going on. "He's just never… When Ma died, me and Pa, well, we never even talked about it."

"Maybe he hurt too much that he just couldn't," Rusty said.

"Never thought about how he felt," Duke said. "He was the man—I was just a kid."

"Sometimes, when it comes to things like the death of someone close, there's not much difference," Rusty said.

Later that afternoon, Rusty drove back to where he thought he'd seen the whiskey bottle he believed Travis Evans had lost as he sped from the approaching BLM pickup. He'd seen it from the air. Finding it on the ground though might prove to be different. If nothing else, someone needed to get that bottle out of there as it could act as a magnifier, concentrating the sun's rays and possibly starting a fire—something not needed in this drought-stricken area.

Rusty parked near where he thought he'd seen the bottle. He walked about half an hour in each direction, with no success. He was walking back to his Suburban when he saw something. About twenty feet away, under a small cedar tree, flashed something shiny. He walked over and found a plastic wrapper from a strip of jerky. The contents were gone— probably eaten by ants or other bugs. Maybe even coyotes or wolves. Travis Evans had said he had jerky along with his whiskey. This was probably his. The bottle was most likely close by, but Rusty hadn't seen it. Maybe it was farther back and had fallen off the tailgate before the jerky had.

He took the wrapper and walked back to his Suburban. He debated on going back the road farther and looking more, but it was getting late and he didn't want to have to drive out of there in the dark. He turned around and drove slowly back out to the pavement. A few miles up toward Datil, his phone pinged that he was back in service and had a voice message.

Rusty quickly glanced at the phone. He had three messages. He pulled off the road at the first wide spot and looked at them. All three were from the same person: Sally Hanson. Rusty quickly called her. "Sally, I just got back into service and see you've been calling."

"Oh, Rusty," she said, "I was putting a new picture of Little Jimmy in the computer, and I saw where Jimmy had made a file of photos marked 'E-well.' I opened it and, well, I'm sure you'll want to see them. This might help you a lot."

⤜— CHAPTER 15 —⤛

O n his way to Socorro the next morning to meet with Sally Hanson, Rusty called Chub. "Good morning. Did Sally Hanson call you?"

"Yeah," Chub said. "Pretty exciting, don't you think?"

"I hope this is what I need," Rusty said. "You have time to meet me there? I'll be there in a few minutes."

"You bet," Chub said. "I was hoping you'd call."

"See you there."

When Rusty pulled up to Sally's house not long after he and Chub had ended their conversation, Chub's car was already outside. Rusty walked to the door and knocked. Sally let him in and led him to the kitchen table, where Chub sat with a cup of coffee.

"Coffee?" Sally asked.

"Oh, no thanks," Rusty said. "I was up early. I've had too much already. Guess I was anxious to see what you have."

"Sure," Sally said. "The computer is in the room here that Jimmy called his office. It was sort of his area. I don't go in there much.

I only use the computer to send some e-mails or maybe order an occasional thing I can't find here. Everyone knows that I didn't share his enthusiasm for all that treasure hunting stuff, so he didn't bother me with it. I should have paid more attention. What I'd give to go out there in the dirt and heat or cold or whatever and be with him now."

Rusty and Chub followed Sally to the office room. She had the computer turned on and opened to the e-well photo file. The first photo was of the turnoff from the pavement onto that road on Sheriff Cutter's ranch, back where Rusty was the previous day and where Duke and Charlie had their garden.

The next photo showed a fairly large cedar tree. Looking close, one could see it was right in the middle of where an old, now unused road turned off to the south.

"That tell you anything?" Rusty asked Chub.

"Looks odd, like someone planted it there years ago. Trying to hide the road entrance, maybe?" Chub said.

"Could be," Rusty said. "Probably at least twenty years ago. Maybe twice that long."

The next photo showed some fresh-cut brush piled along this old, southerly heading road. The next one revealed someone sawing off tree limbs, and it wasn't Jimmy.

"Who's that?" Rusty asked.

"That's young Cisco Calderone," Chub said. "So, Cisco was in on this with Jimmy."

"Yeah, and he left the area a few days afterwards," Rusty said. "I think I need to go to Santa Fe and have a talk with Cisco Calderone."

The next photo showed a small section of bare ground under a cedar tree that grew out on top of a wash bank. As Rusty studied it, he spotted something. "Look," he said, pointing to a dark item. "That's an old railroad tie protruding from the ground. Sure, that's a frame buried ground level, made of railroad ties. That's the well. That's it, Chub. We're looking at the Eagle Well."

"Yeah," Chub said. "That's a metal plate over it, hidden mostly by those rocks and that gravel. You really could walk right by this if you weren't looking for it. That tree growing there now really hides it."

"Cisco was there," Rusty said. "He knows where it is. Good bet he knows what happened to Jimmy too. The fact that he hasn't come forward—"

"Yeah," Chub said. "That's not good."

Sally clicked to the next photo. It was in poor light—obviously near dusk. The rocks and gravel were off the plate, and it was lying off to the side.

"That must have been the first time they opened the lid," Rusty said. "It was getting dark. They needed a ladder, rope, and other things. I'd say they left, Jimmy gathered up all that was needed, then went back the next day. That's when—"

"What did they find?" Chub asked. "What's with Cisco? I don't like this."

"That's the last one," Sally said. "I wish there were more. Something to show what they found. He must have downloaded these his last night here."

Rusty thought about things for a few minutes as no one spoke. "Thank you, Sally. I'm sure this will help a bunch. Can you e-mail me copies of these?"

"Sure, I can do that—I think. Why don't you do it now, so it's done right?" she said. Rusty sent himself the photos, then looked at Sally. "How are you getting along?"

"I've had lots of family visit me," Sally replied. "That's helped. It still doesn't seem real, though. This is nothing I ever thought about. We were going to be together forever."

"Little Jimmy? How's he?" Rusty asked.

"He's over playing with a neighbor boy now. He's fine sometimes, then real quiet and grumpy others. He doesn't want to talk. He probably doesn't know what to say, how to express his feelings. He's so young. Then too, being a child, he still has someone doing all he needs for him. In many ways, his life hasn't changed all that much. I still feed him, clothe him, read to him and, well, you see what I mean. Me—my whole world has turned upside down."

Rusty nodded slightly. He had little comfort for Sally. She didn't need a bunch of empty words. Rusty and Chub left shortly thereafter. As they walked outside, Rusty spoke. "I'm going to Santa Fe. Wish you could come with me."

"Boy, do I ever wish I could," Chub said. "I actually have to go out to Datil this afternoon."

"Can you stop by the café and tell Manny that I might be gone overnight?" Rusty asked.

"Sure. Sheriff Cutter too?" Chub asked.

"Oh, just Manny will be OK. He'll worry if I don't show up at the hotel tonight," Rusty said. "Besides, I don't want any rumors to start about Cisco and what we saw. I've got to talk to him first. There could be an element of vigilante thoughts among some of those old boys out there and, well, you know the sheriff."

"A good old-fashioned lynching might get some of them to throw down their canes and dance a jig," Chub said.

"It's not just the old ones I'd worry about," Rusty said.

"Yeah," Chub said. "Cisco might have a logical explanation for everything. He surely doesn't seem like the killer type."

"Nobody I've met out here does," Rusty said.

Once on the road north, Rusty called Liz.

"Rusty, about time you called me."

"Yes, mother."

"I'm not your mother, thankfully. If I was, I'd turn you over my knee and spank you good, for all you put me through."

"My mother loves me, just as I am."

"Twisted minds run in your family," Liz replied.

"I intended to call you yesterday," Rusty said, "but I was out of phone range most of the day."

"Likely excuse. About this e-mail request, all twelve parts…"

"You got it then," Rusty said. "How are you coming on things?"

"You want me to tell you now what I've found so far or just e-mail everything to you?" Liz asked.

"E-mail would be best," Rusty said. "I'm driving. On my way to Santa Fe."

"Santa Fe? Oh, Rusty. Harland's going to go crazy when you stop by."

"Actually, I wasn't planning on stopping by. I'm in a hurry to do an interview. It's important. I have no reason to stop by the office."

"You could say you miss seeing me."

"We're doing just fine arguing by phone," Rusty quipped.

"If Harland finds out you were through here and you didn't stop—"

"I don't intend to tell him," Rusty said.

"If he asks, well…" Liz said.

"Tell him if you have to, of course," Rusty said. "He's too busy to worry about me."

"Right—I worry enough for the whole office. So this important interview, let me guess, is it for the 1897 murder, the 1930 disappearance, the 1955 mystery? Which one, Rusty?"

"Actually, it's a young man who was with Jimmy the day before he went missing, if not that very day."

"What's he doing in Santa Fe?" Liz asked.

"Becoming a priest."

"You're joking, right? You think a priest killed Jimmy Hanson? You have lost your mind."

"Later then," Rusty said.

"Rusty. Please, do be careful."

Shortly after noon, Rusty pulled into the seminary at Santa Fe. He hoped that he might catch Cisco between classes. Rusty approached the reception desk at the main office.

"I'm Sister Tina," the middle-aged lady there greeted him. "How may I help you?"

"I'm Rusty Redtail, FBI," he said, handing her his card. "I'm investigating a case that one of your students might have some very important information on. It's critical that I speak with him today."

"Oh my," Sister Tina said. "This is highly unusual. During the day—on class days—"

"I wouldn't be making this request if it wasn't extremely important."

"I'm sure none of our students here... The FBI... I'll have to get permission. Who is it you need to see?"

"Cisco Calderone."

"Oh—that nice young man. Surely he's not in any trouble."

"I didn't say he was," Rusty said. "Please."

"I'll have to check with Father Steinman. He's really in charge of the students. Right now, this is a prayer and meditation time for the student body. I really shouldn't bother the Father now."

"It's very important," Rusty reiterated.

"How long will this take?" Sister Tina asked.

"I really don't know. As long as necessary."

Sister Tina took a deep breath, then dialed an extension number. "Father Steinman? This is Sister Tina, at the front desk. I'm sorry to bother you, but I have a highly unusual request. There's a man here, an FBI man really, who wants to talk to one of the students, right now. What should I do?" Sister Tina stared at Rusty. "One of the new boys. Yes, Cisco Calderone. Yes. Not until evening?"

"The phone, please," Rusty said, reaching for it.

"Father, he wants to talk to you." Sister Tina handed the phone to Rusty without waiting for a response.

"Father Steinman, my name is Rusty Redtail. I'm an FBI agent working on a very important case. I know this is unusual, but I must talk to Cisco Calderone now. If I have to go back to the federal courthouse in Albuquerque and get a court order, I won't be in a good mood when I return and not nearly as cooperative, so please have Cisco meet me in one of your meeting rooms as soon as possible. Thank you for your cooperation."

Rusty handed the phone back to Sister Tina. Her voice quivered as she again spoke to Father Steinman. "Ahh—yes, the small conference room. Yes. I'll see that he's brought there immediately."

She hung up the phone, took a deep breath, then pointed back a hallway. "You'll see the conference room back there. I'll have Cisco Calderone brought to you."

"Thank you," Rusty said. "Please believe me, this is very important. I'll be as brief as possible."

Rusty entered the room and sat at the end of a large table with twenty chairs around it. He opened his briefcase, took out his computer and turned it on, then opened the e-mail attachments he'd sent from Sally's computer. He waited.

After about ten minutes, the door opened and a very scared looking young man entered. Rusty rose and smiled slightly, trying to relieve some of the tension.

"You want to see me?" the young man asked after closing the door, then stepping slowly toward the table.

"You're Cisco Calderone, right?" Rusty asked.

The young man nodded, then weakly answered, "Yes."

"Come sit down, over here," Rusty said, motioning to a chair around the corner of the table from where he'd been sitting. Cisco slowly walked over, pulled out a chair, then followed Rusty's instruction. His eyes were fixed on the table in front of him, not looking at Rusty.

"I'm Rusty Redtail. FBI agent investigating what happened to your friend, Jimmy Hanson."

Cisco nodded slightly, still not looking at Rusty.

"How is school going for you?" Rusty asked. "This is surely a different life than out on the ranch."

Cisco again nodded slightly, then meekly said, "It's all right."

"I grew up way out in the country, much like you did. Living in the city is vastly different. It takes a while to consider it normal. It did for me anyway. Bet you miss your family."

"Sometimes," Cisco said.

"Your father is very proud of you," Rusty said. "He may not be able to communicate that to you, but believe me, he's very proud."

Finally, Cisco looked at Rusty, but said nothing.

"I was your age once," Rusty said, breaking the silence. "So was your father. Hopefully, someday you'll be our ages and then you'll see things through a different prism of life's experiences. Your dad's older than I am, but I think I understand him."

Rusty paused a minute, then went on. "I wish I could have understood my father better, before he died. But I was about your age, and…"

There was silence again for several seconds, then Rusty leaned back in his chair. "Tell me about you and Jimmy Hanson."

"Nothing to tell," Cisco said.

"Oh? Well, tell me about this picture then," Rusty said as he turned his computer toward Cisco with the picture of Cisco at the road to the well.

Cisco pushed back in his chair but still said nothing.

"Look," Rusty said. "I don't think you killed Jimmy. I'm just trying to figure out who did."

"I don't know who did," Cisco said. "If I knew, I'd tell you."

"Well, tell me about these pictures." Rusty clicked to the picture of the top of the Eagle Well. "Were you there when they were taken?"

"Guess so," Cisco said.

"You were with Jimmy when he found the Eagle Well?"

Cisco stared at the picture, then closed his eyes. "Yeah, I was there. That's the well as we found it. All covered up like that."

"And when you uncovered it?" Rusty clicked to the picture of the well with the rocks and metal cover off.

"Yeah, I was there," Cisco said. "The first day."

"It was you who helped clear the brush and such from the old road, right? Somehow you knew where you were going. You knew the Eagle Well was back that road, right? This wasn't just a fishing trip."

"We knew," Cisco said.

"How? Jimmy had looked for that well for a long time. He'd been all over those ranches."

After a long, silent pause, Cisco started speaking. "One day Jimmy and me, we were sitting in the Datil Café. Jimmy had a map spread out on the table. We were talking about the Eagle Well, I guess. That was one of the most frequent things we talked about. Jimmy was picking places where he'd not yet looked that were in the general area that goofy Charlie fella had told him the well was. Out of nowhere, this old codger was standing at our table. He'd snuck up on us, almost ghostlike. Said he'd heard us talking about the Eagle Well. I don't know where he came from. I never saw him before—neither had Jimmy."

Cisco hesitated for a minute, then continued. "He told us to forget about the Eagle Well. He said it was cursed. Said there wasn't any water there, only blood. He said all the coins would be gone by now. He said several times for us to just forget about it. He said it ruined his life—it might do the same for us. Too many secrets, he said."

Cisco just stared at the table for a minute, then went on. "Jimmy finally got the old man to show him on his map where the well was. He said he'd come out here to see it one last time. Said he couldn't get back into it and that was just as well. He said it was now lost, given back to the earth. He said it would be wrong for us to disturb it anymore."

"Did he say why it ruined his life?" Rusty asked.

Cisco slowly nodded. "He said he was there with Sheriff Tuttle back in 1955 when he fought with Frederick Wolf. Said he helped set up the trap to catch Frederick there. He said he got shot in the leg. He still hobbled after all these years. Had a cane, so he did. He saw the sheriff get shot, Frederick Wolf too. He said he ran, afraid of what Frederick would do to him. He admitted he took a handful of the gold coins that Frederick had dropped, so he was afraid of the law too. He said he'd come back a few times and just sat and stared at the well, remembering what happened. This time was to be the last—but he couldn't get to it. He took that as a sign that was finally all over. It was like he could now let it go. I felt this had haunted him, forever—controlled his life even."

"Did you get his name? Where does he live?"

Cisco shook his head. "No. He said it didn't matter about him. We watched him get into his old pickup. Jimmy just wanted to go find the well."

"Did you believe his story?"

Cisco was silent for a minute, then he looked at Rusty and spoke. "There's no record of anyone else being with the sheriff. He didn't have a deputy. No talk of anything like that anyway, so Jimmy said. Just kinda talking out loud. Jimmy sorta wondered if maybe we hadn't just talked to old Sheriff Tuttle himself. It was sure eerie, I tell you. 'Bout like talking to one of them zombie things you see in the movies or on TV. Gave me the creeps."

"Sheriff Bucky Tuttle would be past ninety now," Rusty said. "You figure that fella could have been that old?"

"Fella don't get any older and decrepit than he was," Cisco said. "I can't believe he drove yet. That truck was about as old as he was. Rough-looking old thing. I tried, but I couldn't read the license plate it was so faded out."

Neither man said anything for a minute, then Rusty got back to the pictures on the computer. "Looking at these pictures, it was getting dark when you got to the well, right?"

"Yeah," Cisco said. "It was a lot darker than it looks in the picture. We didn't have a ladder or any way to go down into the well. We decided to come back the next morning. Jimmy was to bring a ladder and all the other stuff he thought we needed."

"What then?" Rusty asked.

"Jimmy went out the road toward the highway, and I cut over the other way, towards our ranch. I had my ATV. As I was fixin' up the stick-and-wire gate to keep out Sheriff Cutter's bulls, if they came roaming over that way again, someone shot out my front tires."

"Were they shooting at you?"

"No. I was ten feet from those tires," Cisco said. "They just wanted to scare me off."

"And that did?"

"Yeah. Scared me real bad, so it did. I called Jimmy and told him what happened and that the old man was right—we needed to stay away. I begged him not to go back. He didn't listen. He was so excited. To him, this was 'bout the biggest thing of his life."

"You tell anyone about knowing where the Eagle Well was?"

"No—well, that day with the old-timer, after he left and so did Jimmy, well, I was hungry, so I ordered up a burger. Duke Atwood came in and started jazzing me about my going to become a priest. He called me a pansy, bunch of other names. Said I'd never done anything exciting and never would. I told him I was onto something big, bigger than anything he'd ever done. He badgered me into telling him what."

"You tell him where the well was located?"

"Sort of, but not exactly. That was dumb of me, I know, but he made me so mad. What if I helped cause Jimmy's death?"

"You think Duke killed Jimmy?"

Cisco sat silently, staring at the table. Rusty clicked to the picture of the map.

"This dot is where the Eagle Well is located, right?" Rusty asked.

Cisco looked at the picture, then nodded slowly.

"The road you and Jimmy cleared out, is it this trail shown here?" Rusty pointed to a twisted line on the map.

"Yeah, that's it," Cisco said. "It's on the sheriff's side of that backland."

Rusty clicked on the picture of the large cedar tree. "What's this?"

"That's right in the center of the old road, at the intersection. We drove around it. It looked as if many years ago someone planted it there to hide the road that turned off to the well."

"You cut some brush up through here," Rusty said, pointing to the road up to the well.

"You should find that scattered along the road," Cisco said. "It'll be dried up now. It took us all day to get the truck in there. We just should have walked in or just ridden my ATV. That would have saved time, but we'd still had to get a ladder and all in there."

"What else can you tell me that might help find Jimmy's killer?"

Cisco looked back at the table, then slowly shook his head. "Should have gone back there with him. Shouldn't have been afraid. Guess Duke Atwood's right about me. Maybe if I'd been there—"

"Maybe you'd have been killed too," Rusty said.

"Maybe that would have been best," Cisco said, staring at the table.

"Just one more thing. Do you know who shot out your tires?"

Cisco slowly shook his head, still looking down. "Don't know."

"I'll change the question. Who do you think might have shot out your tires?"

Cisco said nothing for a minute. He then looked up at Rusty. "I thought maybe it was my dad."

Rusty drove back toward Albuquerque, planning to spend the night in his apartment. He needed to catch up on paying some bills and other things. As he drove out past the old penitentiary, his mind rolled through what he'd learned from Cisco.

More suspicion toward Duke Atwood... More toward Lonny Calderone too... It's all just as clear as mud. Duke's motive would mostly be the hidden money. He'd want what, if anything, was still in the well. There could be some cover-up, also, if he knew his family had involvement in any of the old things.

Lonny Calderone, his motive would most likely be to cover up old family involvement in unscrupulous things—fraud with Maxwell Wolf, or murder even. Though, with Cisco in school, and having to hire extra help, with the drought and all, money could also be a motive.

Rusty rolled all of this around, trying to apply it to solving Jimmy's murder. Suddenly, his phone rang. He looked at the face—Liz.

"Hello, Liz. What's up?"

"This case of yours just gets weirder all the time. Where are you?"

"Coming out of Santa Fe. I plan to stay in my apartment in Albuquerque tonight."

"Well, we had a phone call from a case worker at the Hot Springs Hospital, down south in Truth or Consequences. She said there's an old man there, Buster Tucker, in very dire shape, who insists on talking to the agent investigating Jimmy Hanson's death. Said he has information about what happened back in 1955 that will help you. You sure you're not setting all this stuff up yourself?"

"Hardly," Rusty said. "I want to solve this more than anyone. Old Truth or Consequences, huh? I'll go down there the first thing in the morning. That gives me a good excuse to not come into the office."

"If you did, you'd have to sign in as a visitor," Liz said. "None of us remembers what you look like."

"Trying to make me feel guilty?" Rusty asked.

"Just concerned about you. Sometimes when someone works a case too long and hard, they need a break."

"I'm not there yet. I'll solve this, soon now."

"Just thinking of your best interests. Maybe you should go out tonight. Nice dinner, good movie. I know just the place. We—"

"I've got bills to pay and mail to catch up on—sleep too."

"OK, Mr. All-Business. Call me after you leave that hospital. I wouldn't be surprised if they took one look at you and kept you there."

"Yeah, whatever. I'll fill you in," Rusty said. "Tomorrow, then."

Midmorning, the next day, Rusty pulled into the parking lot of Hot Springs Hospital. He walked in and approached the receptionist.

"How can I help you?" she asked.

"I'm supposed to see a Mr. Tucker, Buster Tucker," Rusty said.

"Tucker," she said. "That would be Charles Tucker in room twelve. Back the hall to your right, sixth door on the left."

Rusty walked back to room twelve. He looked in the doorway and saw a very elderly man lying elevated in bed with an oxygen tube in his nose. He had his eyes open but didn't look at Rusty, who knocked softly on the doorjamb.

"Mr. Tucker? I'm Rusty Redtail, FBI, Albuquerque office. You wanted to see me about Jimmy Hanson?" The man motioned for him to close the door. Rusty then pulled a chair over to the bedside, sat down, then waited for Mr. Tucker to talk.

"You—working on—ranger murder—yes?"

"Yes," Rusty said. "I'm in charge of that investigation."

"My fault. Told about—about Eagle Well. Got him—killed. Death lives there."

"You met Ranger Hanson and a young man out at the Datil Café, didn't you?" Rusty asked. "You showed them on a map where the Eagle Well was."

The old man weakly nodded. "Ought not—not to have done that." He lay there breathing heavily for a few seconds. Then he again spoke. "Trap—like before— trap—cursed—death—always death."

"Like before?" Rusty asked. "Like back in 1955, right?"

The old man slowly nodded. He lay there, staring up at the ceiling.

"You were there," Rusty said.

After a second, the old man again slowly nodded.

"You're really Sheriff Bucky Tuttle, aren't you?" Rusty asked.

The man didn't respond. He just stared at the ceiling.

"You were injured," Rusty said. "So was Frederick Wolf. You survived."

"Shot—my leg," the old man said after a moment. "Freddie climb—out of well—bag of money—I tried to arrest—he shot me—shot him back—took handful—handful of gold coins—ran—afraid."

Neither man spoke for a while. Then the old man breathed hard and quietly spoke again. "Soak—hot springs—heal up—work Bar B Ranch—still live there—no one knows."

"Why didn't you return after Frederick Wolf left?" Rusty asked.

"Afraid—Wolf powerful—killer—rule town—afraid go jail—took coins—wife—son—couldn't face."

"Your son, he thinks highly of you," Rusty said.

The old man nodded weakly.

"Would you like to see him? I'll bring him to you."

The old man coughed, then shook his head slowly. "No—couldn't explain—he would hate." He paused a moment, then went on. "No—he thinks good—know truth—he'd hate—can't go to my grave—with my son hating me—let him down—too much—too much already—better I hurt—than my son hate."

There was silence again. Then the old man continued. "Mistakes—bad decisions—sorry—too late—now—too late now—don't tell—my son."

"I won't," Rusty said. "He does think highly of you."

The old man again nodded slightly, then spoke softly. "Eagle Well—cursed—wolf—beware the last wolf."

After a moment of silence, the old man coughed several times, then spoke again. "Beware the last wolf—Kill you too." He then closed his eyes and motioned for Rusty to leave.

Rusty left the room, then the hospital. He walked to his Suburban, then stood beside it for a moment. *How much stranger and more complicated can this case get?*

Beware the last wolf… Those words haunted him. What was the old man telling him?

Just before reaching Socorro, Rusty called Liz.

"Tell me," she said, "that old man is the killer, right? You solved the case."

"Not this one," Rusty said. "Pretty well have the 1955 deal wrapped up."

"Rusty—get real," Liz said. "Sixty years ago—solving that doesn't help now. Please, get up to date. Jimmy Hanson—that's what you need to solve."

"It's all tied together," Rusty said. "I get a little closer every day."

"Get real close, or Harland will pull you off the case. Please, don't let that happen."

"Soon, Liz, real soon."

A short time later, Rusty and Chub ate lunch at the Royal Café in Socorro.

"Tell me about Cisco," Chub said. "Where's he fit into this?"

"He was with Jimmy when they found the Eagle Well. It was getting dark, and they didn't have a ladder or any other way of going down into the well. They were supposed to go back the next day. Cisco got scared off when someone shot out the front tires on his ATV on his way home that night. He wouldn't go back. He did have some information that points at some others."

"Like who?" Chub asked.

"Duke Atwood and his own father," Rusty said.

"Duke Atwood and Lonny Calderone? Could Sheriff Cutter be right all along?"

"I think Cisco is letting his teenage animosity towards his father cloud his thinking," Rusty replied. "All he has is a thought. I think he's a very confused kid now, feeling somewhat responsible for what happened to Jimmy. They were friends. I don't think Cisco has many of those. He's in a strange environment, away from home for the first time, big city and all."

"You don't think he's one of those kids who give no warning but one day just go off the deep end and start shooting people and stuff, do you?" asked Chub. "Some of them seem pretty normal most of the time. Then they blow up inside and go nuts."

"Well, I don't think Cisco was at the Eagle Well and killed Jimmy," Rusty said. "I believe he was truly too scared to go back near that well.

Whether it was his father who shot out his tires or someone else. That I don't know."

Back out at Magdalena, Rusty went into the café. Being midafternoon and nearly empty, Manny came over to Rusty.

"Señor Rusty, good to see you," Manny said. "You travel much. To Santa Fe to see Cisco Calderone?"

"Yeah. He was in a picture on Jimmy's computer. Turns out he was with Jimmy when they first found the Eagle Well. It was dusk, so they left. Jimmy in his pickup heading for the highway and Cisco across an old road over to the Calderone ranch. Someone shot out Cisco's front tires on his ATV. That really scared him."

"Who would have done such a thing?" Manny asked.

"Cisco thinks it was his father."

"No—no way," Manny said. "Lonny Calderone would never be so reckless. That is his only son. Scare him to protect him, yes. Shoot so close? Never."

"That's sort of what I thought," Rusty said. "That's what Cisco thinks, though. Anyway, it scared him, all right. He wouldn't go back the next day when Jimmy entered the well. Now, he feels guilty. He thinks that maybe, if he had been there, things would have been different."

"Different, sí. Good chance he'd be dead too," Manny said.

"That's what I told him. Don't think he sees that, though."

"So, Jimmy did find the Eagle Well," Manny said.

"He had pictures on his computer," Rusty said. "Had it plotted on a map, also. I have a copy of all of that."

"So, what do you do now?" Manny asked.

"Tomorrow, I'm going out there. I'm not coming back until I open up that well and see what's in it. I've got to find the actual murder site too, if it's not at the well."

"Such is not good, to go alone," Manny said. "You must see me as soon as you return. Tell me what you find. Pictures too. I so wish I could go with you, but never can I leave here like that."

"As I said, I might not be back tomorrow night. I'm not coming out of there until I'm satisfied I have what I need—all I can find."

"You should not do this alone. Someone should go with you."

"Chub's too busy," Rusty said. "Buddy really doesn't feel comfortable out there now. Sheriff Cutter's not coming back from a rodeo until sometime tomorrow, then he'll have to take care of his stock, vet and all, for several days. I just can't wait. Besides, it's my job."

"Not to get killed," Manny said. "Another FBI agent, no?"

"If I asked for help, I'd be pulled off this case. I'm too close now."

"Sí. I don't like it," Manny said. "I don't like it at all."

Later, about midnight, Rusty's phone rang. He looked at the screen. It was his mother.

"Mother, are you all right?"

"Oh—Rusty. I have some very bad news."

"Are you all right?"

"Pastor Mose… He had a stroke. He's gone, Rusty. Oh, Rusty… Old Mose is gone."

>— CHAPTER 16 —«

R usty left the café early the next morning. After his mother's
call, he'd slept little, only in short, fitful spurts. Somehow, with
all he had going on, he'd have to work in attending Mose's
funeral. His mother promised to let him know once that was scheduled.
She was sure it would not be for at least two days, anyway.

He sipped coffee from his Thermos as he went west to Datil, then
south to the entrance of the Rancho Vaca. He drove in and as he'd
hoped, Lonny Calderone was still there, giving instructions to several of
the ranch hands. Rusty waited until the men mounted their horses and
rode off down the road to the south. He then got out of his Suburban
and walked over to Lonny, who had the engine cover off his ATV and
had obviously been tinkering with the engine.

"This thing's becoming about as contemptible as an old dapple mule
my dad once had," Lonny said as Rusty approached. "Had to shoot the
mule. About ready to do the same with this. Had to have it towed in
yesterday, after I walked about five miles to get help."

"That wasn't any fun," Rusty said. "You the main mechanic
around here?"

223

"Unfortunately so," Lonny said. "Out here you're the main everything. 'Spect it's about time to trade this in for a new one. Those new ones are really nice—price about breaks one, though. It's either break the bank account or keep fixing whatever breaks on this old one. Problem is, I can't find what to fix."

"I talked to Cisco the other day," Rusty said.

"Oh." Lonny straightened up and turned from looking at the engine to looking at Rusty. "Up in Santa Fe?"

"Yeah. I learned that he was with Jimmy Hanson when they discovered the Eagle Well."

"You sure?"

"Have a picture," Rusty said. "He admitted it too. He told me all about it."

"Was he there when Jimmy was killed?"

"Still not sure that's where Jimmy was shot," Rusty said.

"Yeah, sure," Lonny said. "Just assumed that, I guess."

Or do you know that for sure? Rusty wondered.

"Cisco had trouble with his ATV also," Rusty said. "Two shot-out front tires the day he returned from the well, just as he crossed back onto your ranch. Did he tell you about that?"

"I saw the tires," Lonny said. "He never said what happened. Shot out, you say?"

"To scare him from going back to the Eagle Well, most likely," Rusty said. "You didn't have anything to do with that, did you, Lonny?"

"Cisco say I shot out his tires?"

"No, just the possibility," Rusty said. "Not that you'd hurt him, just that you'd do anything to keep him away from that old well."

Lonny shook his head. "I'd never do anything that foolish. Cisco knows that. Why didn't he come talk to me? Does he really think I did that?"

"He's scared," Rusty said. "He doesn't know what to think right now. Maybe after some time at the school in Santa Fe—"

"Had to be that Duke Atwood. He's been trying to corrupt my boy forever. He's finally turned him against me."

"Maybe not," Rusty said. "Don't go off accusing Duke just yet."

"Who then?"

"Someone who has a lot to keep hidden," Rusty said. "I'm going in to that Eagle Well now. I have it plotted on a map—picture too. I expect to find something incriminating there."

"Maybe you can solve those old deals too," Lonny said.

"I've already done most of that. Probably the 1930 one too."

"1930? What's that?"

"That's one murder your family was never accused of—probably didn't even know about. It's all part of the other ones, though."

"You going out there by yourself?" Lonny asked.

"You want to go with me?"

"Too busy. You know how it is," Lonny said. "I can't figure if you're all-out serious or plumb crazy. Those stories of all those gold coins could get control of a fella's mind."

"I believe all those coins are now gone," Rusty said. "There must be some other evidence of something someone wants to keep secret, most likely. Maybe even that's gone from there by now too."

"Now you've got me all confused," Lonny said. "You bring up a murder in 1930 having something to do with this, but no one knows about it. The money's all gone. What's there to kill Jimmy Hanson over?"

"That's what I'm going to find out," Rusty said.

"You're holding out on me. You know where Jimmy was killed? Was it at the well?"

"Probably," Rusty said. "Or on the way to or from there, I 'spect."

"You know who killed him?"

"Got a short list," Rusty said. "Just need a little more proof. I'm hoping something at the well will clinch it for me. What I need is a motive. I see a lot of opportunity, but haven't yet found a motive."

"Am I on your short list?"

"Depends on how short I make the list," Rusty said, then he cracked a smile.

"Sheriff Cutter sure has me on his list," Lonny said. "He had his way, I'd be in a jail cell already."

"Sharing it with Andy and Duke Atwood," Rusty said, then smiled again.

"Now that would be something," Lonny said. "Might be another murder or two on the books by the end of the day."

"Or spending some time together, you just might discover you can get along and become halfway friendly," Rusty said. "That might be worth it all. Maybe you could all forget about what your grandfathers feuded about and just see things as they are today."

"I've been saying for years that the only thing fueling this thing is the sheriff. He seems to get some satisfaction out of stirring us up," Lonny said. "Wish he'd get beat come next election."

"Maybe you should run," Rusty said.

"Who's got the time?"

"I don't think Wesley Cutter is giving the job much time," Rusty said.

"I wish he'd give it less," Lonny said. "Stay home and play with those bulls. Maybe one will gore him."

"Maybe when this is all over, I can get Sheriff Cutter to butcher up one of his bulls and have a barbeque for you and the Atwoods, any other old feuds around here that need fixin' too," Rusty said. "Maybe you can all make nice, as they say."

"Only bull he'd cook up would be so old and tough only a wolf would eat it," Lonny said.

"Might come up with an elk then," Rusty said.

"I'd go for that. The Atwoods could come up with the elk, in season or not."

Rusty shook his head as Lonny grinned broadly.

"I gotta go," Rusty said. "I'll probably spend the night out there, but need to be out tomorrow though."

"You got something besides that little cap gun under your coat?" Lonny asked. "There's coyotes and cougars prowling about out there. Not to mention those wolves the fool government turned loose. Then there's whatever critter that killed Jimmy Hanson."

"I think Jimmy was killed by a sniper from a good distance away," Rusty said. "No gun is going to protect against someone bent on doing that."

>>———<<

As Rusty drove out of the Rancho Vaca entrance road toward the paved highway, his phone rang. It was Buddy Bell.

"Good morning, Buddy," Rusty said, rather surprised to get the call.

"Rusty. I'm so glad I caught you. Where are you?"

"I just left Lonny Calderone. I'm ready to head back towards the Eagle Well."

"Wait for me at the highway when you get there. I'm passing the tracks at the telescopes now. I'm coming out to spend the day with you."

"Oh—well," Rusty said. "I plan to spend the night though."

"I can't stay the night. But I really want to be with you today. I hope we find the well."

"Manny put you up to this?" Rusty asked.

"Oh… We talked."

"I'll wait for you," Rusty said. "I don't need a bodyguard, though. You boys are all worrying too much."

"We should have worried more about Jimmy. Anyway, I've got this old Jeep's pedal to the floor, but she still won't go very fast."

"I'll see you when you get here," Rusty said, then ended the call.

As Rusty waited for Buddy, he studied his map for the umpteenth time. He'd calculated all the distances up each road and converted them to miles and tenths to be able to use his odometer to find the locations. He had that all written on the map as well as embedded in his mind.

After folding the map and finishing his coffee, Rusty looked up the road and saw Buddy's old Jeep coming toward him. Buddy then pulled in beside him.

"Sure glad I caught you," Buddy said. "I didn't know you planned to leave so early."

"You don't have to do this," Rusty said. "I appreciate everyone's concern, but I'm quite all right alone."

"I know, I know. I really want to see this Eagle Well, after all I've heard for years."

"I see you've got your twelve-gauge," Rusty said. "Probably more firepower in the backseat, strapped to your waist too?"

"Well, they won't do us any good in my gun case," Buddy said. "Just being prepared."

"Well, follow me on back that easterly road to the turnoff," Rusty said. "The first thing we need to find is a bottle."

"A bottle?"

"Yeah, a whiskey bottle."

Buddy gave Rusty a funny look.

"Travis Evans, that fella over in Oklahoma that I went to see, when he got chased out of here by the BLM truck, he lost a whiskey bottle off the tailgate of his truck," Rusty said. "I saw it from the air. I need to see how far back this road it is."

"You had me thinking for a minute," Buddy said.

Rusty smiled, then started his Suburban. "Follow me."

Rusty drove south on Highway 12 until he came to the old road that headed back east to the one shown on the map turning south to the Eagle Well. This first road ran somewhat parallel to the east-west fence line dividing Sheriff Cutter's ranch from Lonny Calderone's. Though this road appeared to have been used little for years, at one time it must have been a major entrance as it had a pipe cattle gate straddled by two old railroad ties set in for stretch-posts.

Rusty reset his odometer to zero, then drove over the pipe gate. In the damp sand of the old road's dual tracks, Rusty saw fresh ATV tracks. *Who would be riding up this road on an ATV?* He drove up to where he'd looked for the bottle a few days ago. He then drove on up the road a quarter mile, then pulled off at a flat, wide spot.

I should have picked a good landmark when I spotted the bottle from the air. I thought finding it down here would be easy. It surely looks different down here than from up in the air.

Rusty got out and looked around. Buddy parked behind him. He too got out, then walked up to Rusty. "You see those ATV tracks?" he asked. "You think they're still around?"

"They were a day or two old—maybe more," Rusty said. "No one's here now. Why don't you walk back the way we came in and look for that bottle. It's on the north side of the road, just off the edge as I recall. Travis was planning to camp back in here. This would be a logical place. I'll go on ahead."

Rusty started walking forward along the north track of the old road. Every dozen or so steps he turned and looked at the landscape from the other way. About a quarter mile back the road, there was another flat spot that could accommodate a pickup truck parked off on the north side. There, partially hidden by a large rock and a small start-up cedar, was the bottle.

Rusty walked over and picked it up, turned it upside down, and emptied it. He carried it back to the vehicles. When he came in sight of them, he saw that Buddy was already waiting for him.

"I was getting worried," Buddy said when Rusty got close. "I was about ready to come up that way and look for you."

"I found it," Rusty said. "There's another wide spot up yonder. That's probably where Travis was parked. A bottle like this out here in this sun is a fire just waiting to happen—guess you know that."

"Yeah, that could happen for sure," Buddy said. "You figure it's from that Oklahoma fella?"

"Can't be totally sure, but it makes sense," Rusty said. "He was parked back here somewhere, eating jerky and drinking whiskey. I found this whiskey bottle up there, and back the road a ways the other day I found a wrapper for beef jerky. Both are things Travis said he lost off his truck as he fled the BLM pickup. That adds up as pretty solid to me."

"So, you said he was chased out?" Buddy said.

"He said he was sitting on the tailgate when a BLM pickup pulling a trailer with an ATV on it came out this road. The driver leveled a rifle at him. He took off, losing his jerky and bottle."

"So, Jimmy was probably in that pickup somewhere, already dead? Is that what you think?"

"Yeah," Rusty said, slowly nodding.

"So then the pickup was driven out of here up Highway 12 to the next road, then driven back there, hidden, set on fire, and the perpetrator left on an ATV pulling that trailer?"

"That's about the way I figure it," Rusty said. "The ATV then could have been driven somewhere local, or just as easily to another waiting pickup truck and towed far away."

"So your map shows the Eagle Well is back in here?"

"Yeah," Rusty said. "Quite a ways yet."

"Where'd you get that map?"

"Off Jimmy's computer. He and Cisco got the location from an old-timer who showed up in Datil one day. Cisco verified that and the location of the well."

"There's more to this, right?" Buddy said. "You're not telling me the whole story."

"Only what's best for you to know."

"Jimmy was secretive too," Buddy said. "That might have gotten him in trouble."

"It's more likely he talked too much than too little," Rusty said. "He told the wrong thing to the wrong person, who passed it on to someone else, and, well, that's what I figure."

"Maybe so," Buddy said. "Well, what now?"

"We've come two and two-tenths miles, so far. From here, it looks to be six and two-tenths further to where another old, abandoned road breaks off to the south. There's a large cedar growing right in the center of that other road, as if years ago someone tried to hide the road. I've got a picture of it. That's where Jimmy and Cisco had to cut some brush to get back that southbound road. I haven't figured why Jimmy insisted on getting the pickup in there rather than just taking Cisco's ATV or even walking. He must have seen something that caused him to want his pickup in there."

"Jimmy wasn't one to walk much," Buddy said. "I think his truck was sort of his security blanket."

"Could be," Rusty said. "I guess he needed it anyway when he went back with the ladder and other things."

"Another six-plus miles back here yet?" Buddy asked. "Then how far?"

"We turn southerly on that other road, then go three and eight-tenths miles," Rusty said. "Then we look for the well."

"That's a long way back in there," Buddy said, looking at his watch.

"Just as long back out—by yourself," Rusty said. "You want to do it or head back now?"

"That's over twelve miles, if I added right," Buddy said. "I best start back out by four o'clock or even sooner, really."

"That gives us about five hours to find the well," Rusty said. "All goes well, we'll be in that area in less than two. That leaves three hours or so to explore things. You decide what you want to do."

Rusty opened up the back of his Suburban, took out a plastic grocery bag and put the bottle in it, then tied the top and put it on the backseat floor, then closed the door.

"I'm in," Buddy said. "I came out here to find the Eagle Well and, well, just let me get started out by four."

"Follow me then," Rusty said as he slid into the front seat and started the engine. He drove slowly through the groves of cedar trees and patches of open meadows. He crossed three shallow arroyos and drove around several very large boulders.

Reaching the eight and four-tenths reading on his odometer, Rusty stopped. He opened the picture on his computer of the cedar tree at the road entrance. He looked at it, then looked around. It wasn't here.

Buddy got out of his Jeep and walked up to Rusty's window. "What's up?" he asked.

"I guess my measurements were as the crow flies, not the way we've been winding around in this dirt. The road with its tree in the middle must be farther up. If not, then everything is wrong and I start all over, somewhere."

"How would anyone ever have known Jimmy was way back in here?" Buddy asked.

"I don't think it was an accident," Rusty said. "I just hope no one knows, well, the wrong person, really, that we're back in here now."

Buddy took out his cell phone and looked at it. "Only one bar of service. I'm surprised there's anything."

"Me too," Rusty said. "I wouldn't have thought there'd be any service. I don't know where that tower would be."

"So, once we find that other road, we still have nearly four miles, right?"

"Yeah," Rusty said. "Let's go. It can't be far."

They drove up into a more forested hillside, and as Rusty rounded a sharp curve, he spotted the tree he was looking for. He drove up to it and stopped. If you weren't looking for it and the old road it hid, you'd drive right by. Rusty got out and walked around the tree. He could see where Jimmy and Cisco had driven around it and where they'd cut away some branches to get through.

Buddy walked up to Rusty. "This is it, right? This is what we're looking for?"

"Yeah, this is the road, all right," Rusty said. "I don't understand, though."

"Understand what?"

"See where Jimmy and Cisco cut away some branches to get through, dug out that sapling too?"

"Yeah," Buddy said. "That's easy to see, if you're looking for it."

"Where are those branches?" Rusty said. "Jimmy and Cisco had no reason to remove and hide them, but only to get them out of their way so they could drive through."

"Oh," Buddy said. "That's strange. Why would someone remove them?"

"Because they'd dry up and be easily spotted. They'd make this old road stand out, rather than be hidden."

"So, someone tried to keep anyone else from finding this road," Buddy said.

"I'd say finding the Eagle Well, really," Rusty said. "Three and eight-tenths back this trail, now."

Buddy looked at his watch. "It's nearly noon. I figure we're most of an hour away by the looks of this trail. It's going to be very slow going.

I'm starved. Manny fixed up two burritos and wrapped them in foil. They've been on top of my engine keeping good and warm. What do you say we stop and eat? Once we find the well, we'll most likely not think much about food."

"Hadn't thought much about it now," Rusty said. "But now that you mention it, OK, let's take a break."

Buddy opened the hood of his Jeep, removed the foil-wrapped burritos from atop the hot engine, then handed one to Rusty. They sat on a large deadfall about twenty yards off the newly cleared road. They ate in silence. Buddy finished before Rusty. He balled up his foil, put it in his pocket, then twisted the cap off a bottle of water and took a long drink.

"What do you think about those ATV tracks coming back this road?" Buddy asked.

"Probably hunters," Rusty said. "Early archery season is in. I'd say that's all it is."

"I surely hope so," Buddy said. "That kinda spooks me—someone else back in here."

"Guess I grew up roaming the wilderness," Rusty said. "There's wild game and people all over those mountains back home. Never thought about being scared."

"Before this thing with Jimmy, I never thought about trouble out here, never," Buddy said. "Now—"

"Fear doesn't get you anywhere," Rusty said.

"No, but caution does," Buddy replied. "Maybe I'm just getting old."

"Well, your thoughts are probably wise," Rusty said. "I guess I'm just so concentrated on solving this that maybe I've turned off some of my caution sensors."

"Solving this isn't the end-all," Buddy said. "Jimmy solved his mystery—finding the Eagle Well. Then he got killed. Don't be drawn into the same trap."

Rusty nodded slowly. "I'll remember that. Thanks," he said. He finished his burrito, and then he too opened a bottle of water. He drank half of it, then put the cap back on and set in on the ground beside him.

"Something's been bothering me ever since the first day I came out to this area," Rusty said. "It's not really any of my business—but, in some ways it is."

"Sounds serious," Buddy said. "Something with me?"

"No, not directly," Rusty said. "You know the sheriff well. He's an important part of your church, you've told me."

"Sure is," Buddy said. "Probably couldn't keep the doors open without him."

"His attitude towards, well, just about everyone," Rusty said. "You know it. There's a real cutting-down of almost everyone."

"That's just the way Wesley Cutter is," Buddy said. "He doesn't mean anything by it."

"I'm just a simple Apache boy, real simple," Rusty said. "My relationship with God is just that too—real simple. That's how I see what Jesus taught. He came against the evolved version of Judaism of his time as being all works and no faith. He laid out a simple plan of faith and forgiveness as being the way to God. Good works will naturally follow, a sign of our relationship. Not a bunch of rituals or sacrifices or heroic deeds are needed or really help. Just faith and forgiveness— which we all need. If it's real, a righteous life will follow—like the tracks of an animal. They show what it really is and where it's been and where it's headed.

Rusty paused a moment, then continued. "My people, somehow— it seems almost universally among the so called native tribes—we all worshiped some form of great-spirit. I don't know where that came from, but it's widespread among the native peoples. There was little contact or commonality between most tribes—mostly fighting and stealing. Yet, we had somewhat of a common great-spirit awareness.

"If you look at the simplistic teaching of Jesus in his last days on earth, he said he'd leave and send a supernatural, teaching, comforting spirit to replace himself. Somehow, most of what's called Christianity today relies on buildings, books, money hungry preachers and teachers using doctrines with creeds and good works and laws, on and on. Maybe much of that stuff can be good, used by God's Spirit, but all too often today it's just man trying to add something to us reaching God. Some, many actually, are using all this stuff to elevate themselves, so it seems to me. There's little time or space for the promised, supernatural comforter, the guiding Spirit of God controlling our lives."

Rusty paused for a moment, then continued. "I don't understand all the complexities of Catholicism or Mormonism or Calvinism or even much of today's modern Protestantism—any 'ism,' really. That's all too complicated for a simple guy like me. However, if someone truly finds God through something like that, who am I to judge?"

Rusty paused and looked over at Buddy who stared down at the ground. He then continued, "All those teachings and denominations seem to see God through a narrow perspective—I see God as so big and wonderful, no man-developed teaching can present the fullness of him, only a small part of him. So, someone gets a hold of a part of God and they build their doctrine and teaching around this narrow part of God, thus limiting their followers from the totality of God's greatness.

"It's like the medical field," Rusty went on. "There's few all around, general practitioners today, and a whole lot of specialists. Each of them is an expert in a narrow area and can miss what should be an obvious deficiency in some other part of the body. I see the church today like that. Too many specialists looking at some narrow teaching with few looking at the whole, simple, God-given word and all-present Spirit guidance. Whatever their 'it' is they have to name it, title it, write books on it, sell tapes on it, and what all. I think Jesus sits up in heaven looking down shaking his head saying, 'People, I made it so easy. Why do you have to drag your religious stuff back into my ingenuously simple way?' Sometimes I think that all this man made-up stuff is about as far off the true way as my people's misguided great-spirit worship was."

When Rusty then stayed quiet for several minutes, Buddy responded. "For a simple guy, that's pretty profound. So, you think the sheriff is way too judgmental? That this shows he's not right with God?"

"It's more than judgmental," Rusty said. "He believes he's superior. He seems to have his eternal salvation tied to the good works he credits himself doing. I'm concerned that he doesn't really understand being right with God—only trying to earn his own way to heaven."

Neither man spoke for a moment, then Rusty continued. "Like I said, it's not my business. It's just, well, I like the guy and I'm concerned. He'd never listen to me—not on anything spiritual, for sure. You're his pastor. I just thought, maybe…"

After another moment of silence, Buddy took a deep breath, then spoke. "I had an uncle who was a pastor of a church. I always thought that was a good job. So, I became a pastor. It is a good job, usually. I've been at it for over twenty years now. I've got the church stuff down real good. You know, weddings, funerals, visits, and all of that…"

Buddy stared off into space for a minute, then continued. "As far as someone else's relationship with God… Eternal salvation, and the like… Well, to tell you the truth, Rusty, I'm not all that sure about my own."

≫— CHAPTER 17 —≪

Several times, as he methodically made his way up the old road, Rusty had to back up and rush his way through the mud puddles, sand drifts, and washed-out gullies he encountered going through the various terrains the road traversed. Reaching one particularly deep draw, he stopped and got out. Buddy also got out, then walked up beside Rusty.

"Fella really needs a four-wheel drive to be safe back in here," he said.

"Yeah," Rusty agreed. "That would make things a whole lot easier."

"I could go first, then pull you if I need to," Buddy said.

Rusty shook his head. "Remember, I have to come back out of here by myself."

"Better hope it doesn't rain tonight," Buddy said. "You could be stuck back in here for days."

Rusty just nodded as he figured out the best way to cross this washout.

"How much farther?" Buddy asked.

"We're actually only a little over halfway from that last turn, by the tree," Rusty said.

Buddy looked at the time on his phone. "Maybe things will get easier," he said.

"On the map it looks like it'll climb higher, then drop into a canyon," Rusty said. He climbed back into his Suburban. "Let's go."

They crawled and bounced back the road another mile. Then, lying right in the middle of the road was a small bull elk. Rusty stopped about fifty feet from it. Slowly, laboriously, the elk forced itself to its feet. It stood there, head drooped low, breathing slowly.

Buddy walked up to Rusty's window. "Arrow in his lungs. See the bloody wound?"

"Yeah," Rusty said. "Too bad. I wonder how hard the hunter tried to track it. It's not going to live long. Shameful waste of meat—life too."

"I always preferred a gun myself," Buddy said. "Of course, that's still no guarantee that a poor shot won't be as bad as this."

"This looks like it was a good shot," Rusty said. "I just don't think they tried hard enough to track it down. Just easier to shoot another one."

They watched as the dying elk hobbled very slowly off the road.

"Well, about tomorrow the buzzards will have a feast," Rusty said. "Coyotes too. Guess they have to eat as well."

"Don't forget about those wolves they turned loose out here," Buddy said. "Maybe this will save some rancher a calf or two."

The two men watched the elk labor its way over to a small wash a hundred feet or so off the road, then collapse. Neither man said anything for a minute, then Rusty stepped toward his Suburban. "About half a mile or so to go yet. Let's go."

When they had gone the three and eight-tenths miles on Rusty's odometer, he stopped. He opened his computer and clicked on the picture of the well. He looked around but saw nothing that looked like the picture. He moved forward a little ways, then stopped and studied the landscape again. He did this twice more, then he saw it. Twenty feet off the road, up against a large boulder and underneath an old cedar on the edge of a wash, was a pile of rocks and gravel covering the plate over the Eagle Well.

There was a level spot on the other side of the road. Rusty turned around, then parked there. He turned off the engine. Buddy did the same with his Jeep. Rusty sat there, staring at the covered wellhead. It seemed so anticlimactic. After all he'd heard and anticipated, this pile of rocks was a letdown.

Buddy came up to his window, where he stood silently staring at their quest. After a moment, Rusty opened the door and got out.

"So that's it?" Buddy asked. "What are we going to find down there, Rusty?"

"I 'spect this is where Jimmy was killed," Rusty said, looking around the site. "Doubt if there's any sign of that left. I don't know what I was expecting to find. It was always, find the Eagle Well, find the well, then everything will fall into place. Well, here we are, and I don't know any more now than when I started."

"The thought of this being where Jimmy was killed gives me chills," Buddy said. "Back here, all alone—well, all but the killer. Sad place to die. A fella really has to want to be back in here to be here. It's not someplace you just stumble onto."

The two men silently stared at the wellhead for a moment, then Rusty took a shovel from the back of the Suburban and started walking toward the well. He rolled away the larger rocks, then scraped the small stones and gravel off the iron plate. He then leaned the shovel against the large boulder and looked at Buddy. Reaching down, he took a hold of a handle on the plate and pulled it toward him. The plate slid a few inches. Another tug produced another half-foot of opening.

Buddy reached down and took a hold of a second handle on the plate. Then both men pulled and leaned their weight into sliding the plate off the buried, old railroad ties. "That's got to be why Maxwell Wolf had that boom on the back of his well wagon," Rusty said. "He never intended for a man to move this. How did some of the others who've been here ever do it, I wonder. Jack and tripod, maybe."

Rusty stood there, looking at Buddy for a second, then into the well. Neither man said anything for a moment. Then Rusty spoke. "Well, that's got to be Jimmy's ladder I see. Looks like down in the bottom, if I'm seeing through the darkness right, there's the rope and chain, shovel too."

"Yeah," Buddy said. "Guess he was here, all right. Figure he didn't leave here alive, though. I'd bet on it. He didn't throw that stuff down in there. Whoever killed him did."

"Yeah," Rusty said. "They tried to cover things up. If we hadn't found this, probably no one else ever would have. The stories of the Eagle Well would have just faded away. Guess they hoped no one knew he had a ladder and that other stuff with him. Really, if Chub hadn't seen it in his truck that morning, no one might have known."

"What do we do now?" Buddy asked. "I've only got a short time before I have to head out."

"Figuring I might find things like this, I made a hook and tied it to the end of a rope," Rusty said. "It's in my Suburban. We'll pull the ladder up, extend it, then set it back down."

"You really going down in there?" Buddy asked. "Those bones and all?"

"Those bones can't hurt me," Rusty said.

"Climbing the ladder might, though. I might get stuck down in there."

"You might at that," Rusty said. "Too many burritos."

"I see a metal box," Buddy said. "Think that's where they kept the gold coins?"

"Probably so."

"And you think it's now empty?"

"If what I believe happened here, and who did it, yeah, it's empty," Rusty said.

"Those bones," Buddy said. "Sheriff Bucky Tuttle, you think?"

Rusty said nothing but went to the Suburban and got the rope with the hook. In only a few minutes, he hooked the ladder, then he and Buddy pulled it up out of the hole. They stretched it out, then fed it back down the hole. Rusty was careful not to place the ladder's legs on top of any of the bones.

"How did Maxwell Wolf ever get into this thing?" Buddy asked. "They didn't have extension ladders back then."

"He had that wagon rigged up with a rope ladder dropping from two wooden arms that reached out about two feet," Rusty said. "He'd just back up to the well, winch off the lid, then drop the rope ladder down, and that was it."

Rusty stepped over onto the ladder, looked over at Buddy, then he slowly started down into the approximately three-foot square hole. Step by step, he lowered himself into the well. He stopped and looked at each item resting on the bottom. The bones… He knew they weren't Sheriff Bucky Tuttle's. The skull—it was definitely a woman's. Was it Pricilla Miller? Probably. Had Frederick Wolf lured her out here to retrieve her promised coins, then killed her? He'd have to keep his suspicions about the bones a secret, or Charlie Tuttle and Maxine May Miller would find out and could be devastated.

Being careful not to push against the aged, wooden shoring of the well walls as he climbed down the ladder, Rusty finally reached the bottom. He reached down and took hold of the handle on the lid of the iron box. He lifted it. Only a pile of rotting canvas bags with the stamping that read "San Francisco Mint 1897" lay in the bottom of the chest. Rusty picked each up, but, as he figured, they were all empty.

He once more looked at the other things in the bottom of the well. *What was worth killing Jimmy for? This robbery was nearly one hundred twenty years ago. Unless someone had still been using some coins from here, knowing they were stolen property, and had just now removed the last, after killing Jimmy...*

For now, everything here could stay. Rusty started climbing up the ladder. About halfway up, he stopped and looked at the decaying wood boxes used to shore up the well sides. He was glad he hadn't looked closely at them on the way down as the walls were rotten and crumbling, capable of collapsing the entire well very easily if disturbed much at all.

Once back out, Rusty sat on the large boulder at the side of the well. Buddy stood looking down it. "The great Eagle Well people have been telling tales about for over one hundred years. A rusted iron box, some rotted bank bags, a bunch of old bones, and Jimmy's things. For what was Jimmy killed?"

"For the secret behind all of this," Rusty said. "Apparently the truth coming out will still harm someone."

"After all these years?" Buddy said. "That's hard to figure."

"Daylight's burning. If you're going to make it to the pavement by dark, you best roll out now. You're welcome to stay, if you want."

"You're crazy to stay out here, Rusty. Come back to town with me. We'll come back tomorrow."

"I'm close to figuring this out," Rusty said. "I think with some time here tonight, and with the answers to some things my assistant is getting for me, in a day or so I'll have it."

"Well, at least keep my shotgun with you," Buddy said. "Jimmy was killed here, must I remind you."

"From a distance," Rusty said. "Anyone wanting to do the same to me would never get within shotgun range."

"You have an answer for everything, don't you? I hate to leave you here."

"I appreciate your coming out today," Rusty said. "Remember, I planned to do this all by myself."

"All right then. Let me know as soon as you get back to town, please."

"Sure. Stop worrying. I have to be out of here tomorrow to attend the funeral of an old friend the day after."

"Anybody you want me to tell anything to?" Buddy asked.

"Thank Manny for the burritos," Rusty said.

Buddy took out his phone and looked at it. "You have service?" he asked.

Rusty looked at his phone. "No. I wouldn't expect any."

"No sense me calling you then to tell you I'm out of here," Buddy said.

"Be careful. Take your time going through those bad places. You'll be out of here well before dark, so don't do anything foolish. I'm going to nose around here, looking for anything connected to Jimmy."

As Buddy drove away, Rusty took out a bottle of water from his Suburban, opened it, then sat in the backseat. *Sure has been a lot of bloodshed with things connected with this place, Lord. I guess it all started with Maxwell Wolf killing Franz Frick back in 1897—or did it? Is there something else? Something with the digging of this well way out here? Maybe even some tribal thing that started the bloodshed? Some of my people, maybe? There is an oppression here, I feel it. Something evil lurking in this place. Lord, help me to find the answers to solve Jimmy's murder so I can move on with my life. Oh, and old Mose, Lord. He deserves the best you've got. He never had much down here—he didn't care. Sure thank you for making him a part of my life. You used him to show your ways to a lot of people. He was always seeking guidance from your Spirit, not what was the latest ways of the modern church. He was faithful. Oh, that I could be more like that myself.*

After a moment, Rusty again thought about the well here. What was the origin of it? Why was it ever dug here? Then too, the saddle, concho belt, and knife, all Calderone items—that they were still in the cellar vault made no sense. Why weren't they returned or sold? Was there something between Maxwell Wolf and Fernando Calderone? Some clandestine operation? Did Maxwell Wolf have some secret on the Calderones? Rusty had brought along several boxes of things taken from the old bank cellar vault. He'd skimmed through all of this, but hadn't delved deeply into any of these things.

He now slowly went through the various bundles of papers in the first box. As the sun lowered in the west, and the light grew dim, he unfolded one paper he'd not seen before. It was a map, showing a proposed cattle trail from what was marked "Rancho de Calderone," down in old Mexico, up to an area marked "Holding Pasture." This area included this well and a considerable amount of acreage surrounding it.

This was a ways east of the south branch of the Hoof Highway trail coming up from the Reserve area. Was Maxwell Wolf conspiring with Fernando Calderone to bring in cattle from Mexico? Flooding the market with cheap or even stolen Mexican cattle could have been very advantageous to Maxwell Wolf. Was holding Fernando Calderone's prized possessions done to influence his cooperation? Maybe there was something else held too? Had Fernando Calderone been an accomplice in Franz Frick's death? Was the stolen money to be used to buy the Mexican cattle? Being used out of the country, no one would have traced the origin of the gold coins.

Or maybe it was the other way. This was Fernando Calderone's idea. He needed money and cooperation from Maxwell Wolf.

Whatever the plan, or whose it was, it seems it never materialized. Maybe the valuables were held to cover a debt of some sort, or to buy silence, or were maybe some kind of blackmail.

Rusty thought about what might be the motive behind this Mexican cattle theory. Maxwell Wolf seemed to hold land mortgages or cattle bills on many of those who drove their cattle to the Magdalena railhead. If the cattle value was to crash from the northern cattle buyers' needs being met with cheaper Mexican cattle, Maxwell Wolf could foreclose on many mortgages and call in the collateral on the cattle. Thus, he could break dozens of ranchers and take over thousands or hundreds of thousands of acres of land and head of cattle.

A devious plan for sure. Had it succeeded, Maxwell Wolf would have been one of the West's largest cattle barons. Was this a real plan or some wild dream in Rusty's head? Was this the purpose for digging this well?

Fernando Calderone... A reluctant partner or the mastermind?

If this was the plan, why did it fail to materialize? Someone failed to live up to their end of the deal? Maybe. Or was it something so simple as they found no water in this area that was to be the holding area? They would have needed multiple wells producing thousands of gallons of water each day. Did Maxwell Wolf's empire crash before it materialized for the simple lack of water? Certainly water, and the lack of it, controlled much of what went on in this arid Southwest, as it still does today

Rusty put that map back in the box and put the lid on it. It was getting too dark now to read anymore. He gathered up a few dry branches he'd spied lying near the well. Then he broke these into pieces and started a small fire. He dug out his old camp-style coffee pot and made himself a pot of cowboy coffee. A short time later, he sipped on that while he chewed on a strip of beef jerky.

He started thinking about all that had happened here. The well had been dug by hand. Maybe by Fernando Calderone's men from Mexico? Is that why few around here really knew anything about it? Only what Maxwell Wolf wanted them to know?

When the well, and maybe others around here also, failed to produce water, there most certainly were arguments—maybe right at this spot. Violence? Quite possible. Even bloodshed may have taken place right here back before the events that brought Rusty to it now.

Then Maxwell Wolf converted this into a storage vault. Was there anticipation of what he planned to do to Franz Frick that summer when he came back to town with his usual strongboxes full of gold coins? Strongboxes he refused to put in Maxwell's bank

As Rusty sat there, he pictured Maxwell Wolf pulling that old wagon up to the well, then positioning the hoist and its rope ladder over the hole the night that he had those bags full of freshly minted gold coins. Had he placed that iron box down in the bottom before this? Probably. Surely he did that in daylight, maybe with help.

Sometime later, maybe not until his father's death, Frederick Wolf learned of this well and its contents. It seemed he never learned of the vault in the bank cellar or paid any attention to it if he did. How often had Frederick gone down into this hole to retrieve some of the gold coins? The more Rusty thought about this, the more he figured that it would have been the slender teenage Frederick who made the climb down into the hole rather than the rotund, middle-aged Maxwell Wolf. Then maybe it was Maxwell's wife, Matilda, who went down the hole. It didn't matter now.

The bones... Everyone would believe them to be Sheriff Bucky Tuttle's, but obviously they weren't. Pricilla Miller—they were most likely hers. He'd given the skull a quick look, and it was obvious it was from a small woman. How could he protect Maxine May from learning this? She didn't need to have this dumped on her in her frail late stage of life. Thinking about what her mother went through might be the end of her.

Charlie Tuttle... He believed his father's bones were there, in the bottom of the Eagle Well. Learning the truth about his father could possibly send him into some dark mental place. Even bring on more rejection and confusion than his war experiences had. Like Maxine May, Charlie didn't need his world upset by some new discovery.

Being honest, telling the truth, was always important to Rusty. Sometimes, though, silence and saying nothing were even more right. Far better than hurting fragile minds when nothing was to be gained. Somehow, he had to protect these two people.

Rusty refilled his coffee cup, then tossed another small branch on the fire. As the sunset turned to a black, star-filled sky, Rusty watched the small fire eat up the new branch, then again start to die down. He thought about what Frederick Wolf might have done here.

Suddenly, breaking the stillness of the night, a bull elk bugled from far down the canyon. This calling continued for several minutes. Then, just as the elk quieted, a coyote howled from up the other direction. This was answered by a chorus of several more of the little wild dogs that were scattered in all directions. As abruptly as all of this animal talk had started, the night again turned silent.

Rusty's mind returned to thinking about Frederick Wolf and Pricilla Miller. Frederick was only a teenager when his father died. Could he have devised this devious plan and executed it alone? Maybe. Did he kill Pricilla here, or was it done somewhere else? He couldn't get that fancy car back in here. Did he take Pricilla to their ranch house, then here to the well in that special wagon? Did he lower her body down gently with a rope, or did he just dump her over the edge and let her plummet to the bottom? Surely not while she was still alive. Thinking about that caused Rusty to shudder.

Why am I even thinking about these things? None of this matters.

Yet he couldn't get them out of his mind. If someone else was involved, Matilda Wolf, Frederick's widow, would be the logical one as she too stood to lose money if any was given to Pricilla and Maxine May Miller. Then too, if the situation became known about Maxwell and

Pricilla and their child, there was the embarrassment and loss of prestige of the Wolf name in the community.

Yes, this was probably a mother-and-son plot. This seems to be more than a teenage Frederick would have devised and pulled off by himself.

The elk bugled again, closer this time. After only a few calls, it ceased. Then, eerie, shadowy darkness and silence again prevailed.

So, from 1930 to 1955, Frederick withdrew gold coins as needed. How many were still there in 1955? Matilda was deceased by then. However, after they moved to Fort Davis, Betty Ann returned at least twice, according to old Jeb Hite. He said there were still coins there after her last visit. He tried to find the well, but failed.

It's now empty. Someone else must have known about the well. Who? Did Maxwell Wolf have any other mistresses as Jeb said Betty Ann believed? Maybe even other children? The son of the mystery mistress who Betty Ann feared? Maybe Matilda and Frederick never learned about them. Then too, maybe someone else killed Pricilla Miller. Someone else who stood to have to share money they themselves wanted. How extensive was this web of deceit?

Rusty had no way of knowing how long the well had been emptied of its last coins, but he figured it had been only a short time—maybe even since Jimmy's murder. *Someone, though, still felt they had to keep something else covered up. What could be so important? Not the well itself. Not the empty money bags and box. Not a murder that happened sixty years ago. Maybe someone feared the exposure that they'd been using some of those old stolen coins for their own use now and that they'd still be in trouble for that. That would still be a crime—though probably hard to prosecute. Maybe this was just to cover up who they really were? What could be so important to keep hidden that warranted killing a young man with a wife and son?*

The elk bugled again. Somewhat farther away this time. Rusty watched the last flames of the fire flicker, then disappear. Only a few small coals now glowed in the darkness. Rusty got up, went to the

Suburban, and got out his sleeping bag and another bottle of water. He rolled out the bag, pulled off his boots, then took off his shoulder holster and placed it beside him.

Rusty lay looking up at the stars for a long time as thoughts of things here continued to roll through his mind. After a while, he dozed off to sleep. Sometime later—when, he wasn't sure—he was awakened by a painful sounding bawling from the road behind him. Rusty bolted upright. Loud snarling and growling told him something was attacking that dying elk he'd seen back the road a ways. Then the distinct singing of a pack of wolves pierced the still air.

Wolves! They've found that wounded elk. How many are there? They're not very far away. Rusty reached into his holster and slid out his 40 caliber Glock. *Should I get inside the Suburban? Surely, that fresh elk will satisfy their needs, and even if they pick up my scent, they'll not pursue me. I hope.*

After another weak bleating from the elk, the only sounds were the occasional snarling or howling of the wolves. Rusty lay there and thought of the elk. Its time was over. It was now food for the wolves. That was all there was to the life of an animal—live, die, become sustenance to extend the life of another animal. So simple—so final.

Rusty then thought about old Pastor Mose. How different the human life was from this. Mose was gone—just as dead as this elk. That's where the similarity ended, though. Not only was Mose's soul living on, somewhere in eternity, but he also left a legacy, a part of him in dozens or even hundreds of people who he'd touched while here. Not only did they have a memory of him, he'd been a conduit of real truth to forever influence their lives. This they then could pass on to others creating a never-ending cycle of spiritual truth from person to person that had started with—or at least passed through—this simple old teacher who'd given up much of what most of us too often believe to be important to be a humble servant of the Great Spirit of God that permeates the world in this age.

I'm going to miss old Mose, Lord. Thank you for letting me know him, absorb your truth from him, and to grow in you through his words and life.

In time, Rusty drifted back to sleep. Later, getting toward morning, he was awakened again. He sat up, only to stare through the darkness into the eyes of one of the bloodthirsty wolves standing about ten steps from his feet. Two more of the pack slowly paced back and forth a few yards behind this one. Rusty felt around for his gun. Finding it, he took hold of it in his right hand.

"What do you want?" he asked loudly. "Go eat on that elk. You can't have me. I don't want to kill you—but I will. There's nothing here for you. If you want water, there's none here."

The wolf at his feet, with tongue hanging out, fangs showing, and panting heavily, slowly moved off to its right. It then lurked around with the other two, back and forth. Menacingly, they paced. Then one slipped around behind Rusty, whose mind and eyes raced as he kept watch on all three.

"You familiar with this here?" Rusty asked. "You sense all the death and evilness associated with this place? Your ancestors, you four-legged wolves, were they lurking around here when those two-legged Wolfs frequented this well? They carried your name—maybe some of your ruthlessness too. Yeah, I can see old Maxwell Wolf here and your type lurking around, watching his every move."

The eastern sky started taking on a pale-orange hue. Dawn was coming. Off down in the canyon, the morning was announced by the bugle of an elk—probably the same bull that had called out at sunset. The wolves stopped and turned their noses that way. After a moment of silence, the three wolves resumed their ominous parading around Rusty, trying to intimidate him into doing something foolish.

Rusty pushed himself over toward the remains of the fire. He picked up a stick in his left hand and stirred the ashes, hoping to find some hot coal to restart the fire. Only a hint of ash and smoke rose from the cold fire remains.

He'd taken his eyes off the wolves for only a few seconds, and now when he looked back, they were gone. Not a trace to be seen. They'd silently, yet quickly, slinked away. Why? Surely it wasn't the meager puff of smoke. If there had been a flare-up of flame... Rusty pushed himself back to his sleeping bag. He reached over to his holster, then slid his gun back into it. He rolled over to push himself up to his feet.

He heard the crack of the gun at the same instant he felt the bullet rip through his left shoulder. He tumbled face first onto the rocky ground.

Roll! Get to the Suburban...

Another shot cut the air, and the slug tore through Rusty's left thigh. Blood started oozing out of the hole in his jeans. He stumbled, rolled, and half-crawled to his car. He grabbed the door handle and pulled himself up as the door opened. Another bullet ripped through the door, only inches from the handle and Rusty's hand. He jumped back, losing his hold, and fell flat on his back. He grabbed the doorsill, then with his good arm, he pulled himself upright as he pushed with his right leg. Blood had already soaked his shirtsleeve and upper-left pant leg.

Another bullet shattered the driver's side front-door window, sending chunks of tempered glass all over Rusty and the seat. With all the strength he had, he pulled himself into the Suburban. His left leg hung out through the door. He was unable to get it inside.

Start the engine... Keys... Pocket... Start... Go...

Rusty pushed himself upright enough to see over the dashboard. Another shot blew out the tailgate window. He pressed the accelerator to the floor. The rear wheels spun and the big SUV lurched across the old road and ran over a small cedar on the other side of it. Rusty jerked the wheel with his right arm, causing the Suburban to bounce across the old ruts and up over a half-buried bushel-sized boulder on the other side.

Another shot flew through the blown-out rear window and shattered the windshield. The passenger's side fell out all over the hood, but on his side, Rusty faced only a spider-web of fractured glass.

He jerked the wheel to the left to get back on the road. As he did, he was able to get his leg inside. Another bounce over a rock, and the door slammed closed.

Faster… Turn left… "Oh!" Rusty cried as he rammed into a tree. *Back up… Go…* Another shot slammed through the seat beside him but missed his body. Rusty glanced at his leg, then as best he could, at his shoulder.

Losing blood… Get it stopped… Can't see… Dizzy…

He drove up over another boulder, and when the Suburban bounced back to the road, the rest of the windshield crumbled out. Another bullet whistled by his head.

Gun… My gun… He felt around for it, but realized it wasn't there. *Left back at the well…* He then twisted the wheel again to stay on the old beaten tracks. He glanced into the side mirror. *ATV… Right behind… Stop it…*

It took all his available concentration to stay on the road and to go as fast as he could. He was getting woozy. *Bleeding bad… Shock… Can't see right… Dizzy… Tree…*

Straight ahead of him stood the tree in the center of the road at the intersection. He ran straight into it.

Reverse… He stood on the gas and the Suburban shot backward for about twenty feet, then slammed right into the ATV as it approached from behind.

Forward… He sped back up almost to the tree. *Reverse…* Peddle to the floor, he slammed into the ATV again. He then pulled the shifter into drive and sped around the tree. Another shot cut through the bottom of the Suburban. He took the road west, toward the paved highway. He looked back in the mirror. Nothing. He'd stopped the ATV. A moment later, he sensed something else.

Smell... Gasoline... Shot my tank...

Rusty looked at the fuel gage. *Dropping...* He pushed harder on the accelerator. *Go as far as I can...* He was bouncing from side to side out the mountainous road. Scraping trees and rocks, bouncing across washouts and through mud holes. He looked at the fuel gauge again. *Lower... Almost empty... Can't...*

Rusty's eyes closed, and his head hit the steering wheel. He jerked his head up, then yanked the wheel left to get back on the road. His head again dropped forward, hitting the wheel.

Stay awake... Gotta stay awake... Can't... Lord—I can't make it...

The Suburban sputtered to a stop.

⅍— CHAPTER 18 —⅍

The sun was breaking over the skyline behind him as Chub drove into Magdalena that morning. He hadn't slept well last night. Rusty hadn't called him. Had he stayed out there, alone somewhere? Had he found the Eagle Well? Chub felt compelled to come out here to Manny's Café to see if Rusty was here or if anyone knew anything about him.

He parked in front of the café, then went in. He walked over to the kitchen where Manny was cooking.

"Señor Chub! So early," Manny said. "Something wrong?"

"Did Rusty come back in last night?" Chub asked.

"No. Buddy—he went out to be with Rusty yesterday. They found the well. Buddy—he came back home. It was dark when he got here."

"Rusty stayed out there alone?" Chub asked.

"He is brave—maybe foolish too," Manny said.

"You think Buddy will be in this morning?" Chub asked.

"Not usually, but today? I think he too is worried about Señor Rusty."

"I'd like to go check on him," Chub said. "If Buddy knows where he is—"

"Sí, when I get caught up, just be a minute, I shall call him," Manny said.

"I'll have a cup of coffee and wait," Chub said. He walked away and sat by a window looking out over the parking lot where he could see everyone who drove in. Before Manny could call him, Buddy pulled up and parked beside Chub's truck. When he walked in, Chub motioned for him to join him.

"Tell me," Chub said as Buddy sat down in the booth across from him. "What about Rusty? You found the Eagle Well? Is Rusty OK?"

"We found the well," Buddy said. "Not really much there now. It looks like that's where Jimmy was killed. What for, I still don't know. Unless there might have been some of the old coins still there or something else. There's no money now. Jimmy's ladder and other things are all in the well. Rusty went down to the bottom. The iron money box is empty. Other than that, all that seemed to be there now is just a bunch of old bones."

"Rusty stayed out there alone?" Chub asked.

"Don't know why," Buddy said. "He said he needed to be there to think. Old Rusty does have a bit of a strange side—guess we all do. He'll be in sometime later today. Said he has a funeral to go to tomorrow, back home on the reservation."

"I want to go out there," Chub said. "I just have a bad feeling about all of this. Can you tell me how to get there?"

"Better than that," Buddy said. "I'll go with you. I feel guilty now, leaving him out there alone. Guess I was just too fearful to stay with him. Now I feel more than a little foolish."

"We'll take my truck," Chub said. "It's faster."

"I'll have Manny fix up a couple of burritos for breakfast," Buddy said. "Won't take but a minute."

"I'll fill up my Thermos with coffee, then see you out at the truck," Chub said.

Get out... Hurry... Can't make it... Hide... Go back... High ground... Stop bleeding...

Rusty reached across his body and with his right hand, pulled up the door handle. It swung open and he half-fell and half-crawled out of the Suburban. He fumbled with his belt as he unhooked it, then pulled it out. He got it around his leg, fed the end through the buckle and pulled it tight, then pushed the end back underneath it, trying to stop the bleeding.

Exhausted, he flopped to the ground flat on his back. After a few minutes, he rolled over, pushing himself with his good right arm. As he tried to stand up, he felt his phone in his pocket. He reached in and took it out. No service—then one bar popped up—then it disappeared. A call wouldn't go out, but a text might. He thumbed down through the index. *Chub—text Chub.* He closed his eyes again and rested his head back on the hard ground. Then he pushed himself up again and pushed the message button, then started trying to find the letters. "h"... "e"... "l"... He couldn't find the "p" so he just pushed send, hoping that if Chub got this he'd know what it meant. The phone slid to the ground. He looked at it, tried to pick it up, but couldn't get his hand to reach it. He closed his eyes for a minute, then pushed himself across the road.

Go back... High ground... It wasn't much, but he could see an outcropping of several boulders about twenty feet off the south side of the road and about that far back along the way he'd come. He had the presence of mind to head that way, believing that if the person on the ATV came looking for him, they'd assume he went forward on foot.

He got up on his right knee, then pulled himself along, dragging his left leg. He made it about halfway to the boulders, then had to stop. He rolled over, closed his eyes, then passed out.

Sometime later, Rusty came to. *Water... Gotta have water... In truck...* Should he go back to the water or push on toward the rocks? He pushed on for the cover. After another ten feet, he passed out again, just short of the first boulder.

As Chub and Buddy pulled out of the café parking lot, Sheriff Cutter pulled in. He pulled up beside Chub's truck and lowered his window. "You boys are up mighty early," he said.

"Going out to find Rusty," Chub said. "He spent the night out at the Eagle Well, alone. I've got to find him."

"I'd go with you," Sheriff Cutter said, "but we just got in yesterday from a rodeo. The vet's coming later, and I've got one of my best bulls who seems to have injured itself. I just came in to check the mail and whatnot in my office here. Tell Chief I said howdy."

Chub nodded. "Gotta go," he said, then stepped on the throttle and sped out of the parking lot.

Chub and Buddy sped up through the rising foothills, then broke over the last rise and out into the massive Plains of San Agustin. Chub pushed down on the throttle harder as the road opened up into one straight line for well over ten miles. The speedometer climbed to over eighty-five. In minutes they bounced across the track for the Very Large Array telescope dishes. A few minutes later, Chub's phone pinged a signal that he had a text message. He pulled the phone out of his pocket, then handed it to Buddy.

"Text message," he said. "Who's it from?"

"Oh," Buddy said, looking at the screen. "It's from Rusty."

"Not good," Chub said. "What's he say?"

"Oh... No, no, no! He started to write help," Buddy said. "He's in real trouble, Chub. Oh no... He's in real trouble."

Chub pressed the throttle down to the floorboard. The truck quickly climbed up to the hundred-mile-an-hour mark, then the engine cut in and out on its limiter, refusing to go faster. In minutes, they were in Datil, where Chub turned south on Highway 12. Buddy inched forward a little in the seat.

"I should have stayed with him," Buddy said. "If something has happened—"

"Where do I turn?" Chub asked as he leaned over the wheel as the big pickup truck again sped up to the hundred mark.

"Not until about five miles past the Rancho Vaca entrance road," Buddy said as he clutched the handle on the windshield pillar. "I sure hope he's not all the way back at the well."

"How long did that take after you left this road?" Chub asked.

"It took me almost two hours to come back out," Buddy said. "Even if you go as fast as you can, it'll take nearly an hour, for sure."

Neither man said anything as the pickup sped south, down the road. As they passed the Rancho Vaca entrance, Chub looked at Buddy. "About five miles, you say?"

"Something like that," Buddy said. "It's back to your left. Old two-track road. Doesn't look like anybody's used it much for many years. Nothing much back in there, really."

"So, what was at the well?" Chub asked. "Any clue why Jimmy was killed?"

"Not really," Buddy said. "There had to be something there that would have incriminated someone, but whatever that was, it's gone now."

"So, finding the well really didn't solve anything?" Chub asked.

"Well, I sort of thought that—but now..."

Neither man said anything for another minute.

"Just over that next little rise," Buddy said. "There'll be the road. Old-style, pipe cattle guard with railroad tie stretch-post."

Cresting the rise, Chub backed off the throttle and dragged on the brakes. Reaching the road, he cut across the pavement and bounced over the cattle guard. After putting the transfer case in four-wheel high, he pulled the shifter out of drive and down into second gear, then stepped on the throttle.

Where Rusty and Buddy had cautiously crawled back this road yesterday, not much faster than a quick walk, Chub now bounced across it at speeds well over thirty miles an hour. Water from the mud holes splashed, and sand from the drifts lifted up dusty tails as Chub leaned up on the wheel as he fought to keep the truck centered in the tracks of the old, washed-out road.

"How far back here?" Chub asked.

"I think it was over eight miles on this road," Buddy said. "Then something like four south on another very bad road to the well."

They dropped down into a wide, dry-wash, then up the other side. The truck went airborne for a few seconds, then bounced back down to the road as Chub fought to keep it straight.

Buddy's right hand held the hand grip on the windshield pillar, and he had his left arm over the seatback, holding on as tight as he could. Much of the time he had his eyes closed as tight as his fist.

They slid around a curve to the right, up over the edge on the left, over a protruding boulder, then back to the center of the road, down into another wash. They splashed through the mud, then up the other side. They went nearly airborne again. Then, around a left-hand turn.

There! There, in the middle of the road, its driver's door wide open, was the black Suburban. Chub drove right up to it and slid to a stop. He and Buddy jumped out as soon as the engine shut off.

"Rusty!" Chub called out. "Where are you?"

"Over there," Buddy said, pointing back toward the outcrop of rocks Rusty had started toward. Both men ran that way. Chub was first there and was kneeling over Rusty when the out-of-breath Buddy reached him.

"Rusty, wake up!" Buddy said as Chub checked for a pulse.

"Got a pulse," Chub said. "He's bleeding out badly, though." He took out his knife and cut off a large piece of Rusty's shirt, folded it, then pushed it on the shoulder wound. He tightened the belt Rusty had placed around his leg, then Chub pushed himself up to his feet.

"We can't carry him like this," Chub said. "We'd open up those wounds badly. Hold that bandage tightly on that shoulder. It's probably coming out the back as bad as here, maybe worse. I'll get a tarp out of my truck, and we can roll him on that and use it as a stretcher, somewhat anyway. Got to get him into the backseat."

Chub ran to his truck, opened the rear doors, found a small poly tarp, then he ran back to Rusty. He stretched the tarp out beside Rusty, then knelt down beside his head.

"Careful," he said. "Take his feet, and let's kind of slide him over on the tarp." Little by little, they eased Rusty over onto the tarp. Several times, Rusty opened his eyes and once reached up to Chub, but he couldn't say anything.

"You take the feet end," Chub said to Buddy. "That's the lightest end. Pick him up, real easy."

Once they had Rusty lifted off the ground, they started slowly toward the truck. After having to stop and let Rusty down several times so Buddy could rest, they reached the truck. After a struggle, they got him inside and stretched him across the rear seat.

"Stay back here with him," Chub said. "Keep that compress on that shoulder hole." Chub slammed the rear doors closed, jumped into the front, started the engine, then jammed the shifter into reverse. He cut the wheel to the right lock, then shot backward. He spun the wheel to the left lock as he pulled the shifter into first. He rocked back and forth twice more, smashing into saplings and over rocks, but then he spun around enough to get back onto the old road and head toward the pavement of Highway 12. After straightening the truck out as he sped forward, Chub grabbed his cell phone from the seat where Buddy had dropped it. No service. He dropped it and clung to the wheel with both hands. Another few minutes, he looked at the phone again. No service. Five minutes more, and he looked again. As he did, one bar of service flashed, then disappeared. In another minute, the one bar stayed on steady. Chub braked to a stop. He opened the door and stood on the sill to get as high as he could.

Chub scanned the speed dial down to the Socorro Regional Hospital. He punched the send button. When he was just about to give up, it started ringing. On the second ring it was answered. He didn't wait for the receptionist to finish her greeting, but cut right in.

"Listen, this is Ranger Chub Murry. I've got a serious emergency. I have a man who's been shot at least twice. He's lost a lot of blood and still losing more. He's in shock, I'm sure. I'm way out below Datil. If you get your air ambulance up in the air now, I should be at the viewing pull-off on Highway 60 by the VLA track crossing when you get there. I should be there in about half an hour. Please. He's dying."

"I've got that. The viewing pull-off on Highway 60 by the VLA track crossing. All right. We'll be airborne in a few minutes."

"Good," Chub said, then he tossed the phone to the seat, slipped back into the cab, slammed the truck in gear, then punched the throttle down, spinning all four wheels.

"How's he doing?" Chub asked.

"Same," Buddy said. "Still breathing."

How many more turns? How many of these big washes? Don't bounce too hard. Where's that pavement? Chub asked himself.

Finally, there was the old cattle guard. As he rumbled across it, Chub pulled the transfer case back into two-wheel and pushed the shifter up into drive. Turning north up Highway 12, he stepped on the throttle. Minutes later, he slowed to make the sweeping turn onto Highway 60, then he stood on it again. In a few minutes, he had a view of the straight highway crossing the open plains for many miles. Out ahead was the parking area, the meeting place.

No sign of the helicopter... Maybe I should have picked a place closer to Magdalena...

When they were about five minutes from the rendezvous point, Chub saw a dot in the sky over the road ahead.

It's coming... He'll be there soon after I get there... Please, let it be in time...

Chub pulled off the highway into the parking lot of the viewing area. He jumped out then opened the rear doors. He looked in at Rusty.

"He's bleeding less," Buddy said. "Maybe he doesn't have much left."

Chub looked up into the sky at the approaching chopper. In minutes it set down, only thirty feet from Chub's truck. Two paramedics raced to Rusty. Buddy pushed himself out of the truck to let them in. In seconds they had an IV in his arm and were working to better stop the bleeding. It took a while to get him on a stretcher, but within ten minutes of their landing, they were whisking Rusty toward the hospital in Socorro.

Chub closed one of the rear doors, Buddy closed the other side one, then both got into the front seat. Chub took a deep breath, but both men sat in silence for a moment.

Then Chub spoke. "Who? Who could have done this? What can be so all-fired important to kill Jimmy over and now nearly Rusty too? Maybe they have. He's lost a lot of blood."

"He's tough," Buddy said. "If he wasn't, he'd be dead already, for sure. I never should have let him out there alone."

"Don't blame yourself," Chub said as he started the engine. "Let's go. Maybe he'll be awake by the time we get there."

"We should call his office," Chub said. "You have that number? All I have is his cell phone."

"Manny might," Buddy said. "Or it might be on something in his room. Oh wait. It's got to be on his business card. I have one of those." Buddy looked through his wallet, then found Rusty's card. "Here it is. What's his assistant's name?"

"Liz, I think," Chub said. "Yeah, it's Liz. Don't know her last name."

Buddy called Rusty's Albuquerque FBI office and got ahold of Liz.

"Oh no. Something's wrong," she said when Buddy told her who he was. "What's wrong with Rusty?"

Buddy told her briefly, trying not to be too alarming or gory.

"I knew it," Liz said. "I just knew something bad was going to happen out there. Oh, please, keep me informed, please. Let me give you my personal cell phone number. Call me anytime."

In minutes, they were entering Magdalena. "We should stop and tell Manny," Buddy said. "He too was quite concerned."

"Yeah," Chub said. "That'll only take a minute. He'll get the word out around town. Maybe someone saw something, a stranger or something."

Forty minutes later, Chub and Buddy were in the visitor waiting room at the little Socorro hospital. When they came in, the lady in charge of that area told them that Rusty was in surgery and she wouldn't know anything until the surgeon was finished. Then he'd come out and talk to them.

After waiting for over half an hour, Chub called Liz.

"Oh, Chub, Ranger Murry, right?" Liz said. "How's Rusty?"

"No word yet," Chub said. "He's still in surgery. Can you get in contact with his family? His mother, I guess."

"Oh sure," Liz said. "Guess I wasn't thinking straight, or I'd have already done that. I'll get her number and call her. Then I'll text it to you so you'll have it also."

"Find out if she needs help getting here please," Chub said. "It's quite a ways from Cloudcroft."

"Sure," Liz said. "I'll let you know what she says."

Chub got up and walked to a window. He tried to think about what must have happened out there, but his mind wouldn't stay focused.

Buddy walked over to him. "Don't blame yourself. If anyone could have done anything, it's me. I'm the one who should have stayed with him. I let fear control my actions. That wasn't right."

"What kind of an animal do we have out there? Jimmy... Now Rusty. Over what?" Chub said.

"Maybe Rusty now knows something," Buddy said. "Maybe he'll tell us as soon as he can talk."

"What's taking those doctors so long?" Chub asked. "He can't die. He just can't."

Neither man spoke for quite a few minutes. Then Chub walked over to a chair and sat down. "Think I'll call Sally Hanson."

Buddy nodded, then walked over and also sat in a chair.

Chub took out his phone, and before he could call Sally, it rang. He answered it.

"Chub, it's Liz. I got ahold of Rusty's mother. She said she'll be there in three or four hours. She doesn't have a cell phone. I'll text you her house number. Anything on Rusty?"

"Nothing," Chub said. "Something must be wrong. I'm half-crazy waiting here."

"He's as tough as they come," Liz said. "If anyone will make it, Rusty will."

"Tough or not," Chub said, "he was a lot more dead than alive when I last saw him. I'll let you know as soon as I hear something."

Chub sat silently for a minute, then called Sally Hanson. "Sally, Chub here. I'm at the hospital. Rusty was shot up this morning. Out at the well. Where Jimmy was—"

"Oh no," Sally said. "I never should have given him those pictures. Maybe he'd never have found that place without them. I didn't think of his danger—only getting who killed Jimmy. How is he?"

"In surgery. He lost a lot of blood. He must still be alive, though. Look, Sally, there's a lot of things we all could have done differently," Chub said. "No one expected this. Hopefully if... When Rusty wakes up, he'll know who did this and solve all of this mess once and for all."

"He will be all right, won't he?" Sally asked.

"It seems as if he's been in surgery a long time," Chub said.

"Oh my, let me know, OK?" Sally said.

"Sure, when I know something." Chub put his phone in his pocket. He closed his eyes and leaned back in his chair.

"You fellas with Mr. Redtail?" a voice broke the silence.

Chub jumped to his feet, as did Buddy. They looked at the man dressed in scrubs standing in the archway.

≫— CHAPTER 19 —≪

The disabled ATV had been winched up on the small trailer that was hitched to the pickup. It had been moved from the accident scene and was now back at the Eagle Well site. Rusty's sleeping bag, boots, computer, cell phone, box of notes, and Glock were all now at the bottom of the well. A five-gallon can of gasoline was then run down the old wooden sides of the well, some of it making its way all the way to the bottom. A gas-soaked piece of cloth was then lit and tossed into the well. The fuel erupted with a force that stirred the air even above the ground. The flames rushed up the fragile, old wooden box-shoring that held back the well's walls. The flames lapped out over the old railroad ties holding back the top. The walls started crumbling in.

Next, two one-pound cans of black powder were carefully dumped into a thin paper bag. Then the bag was tossed down the hole. The instant explosion collapsed the well from a depth of twenty feet to now less than ten.

A half-dozen sacks of concrete mix were then slit open and dumped into the hole. Finally, two five-gallon cans of water were dumped on top.

The empty sacks were set on fire and burned at the wellhead with the remnants and ashes pushed in on top of the wet concrete. The empty gas and water cans were tossed in the pickup bed, and after a quick final look around, the truck engine was started, then it was slowly driven out the road, trailer and ATV in tow.

I'm never coming back here again... This is the last time... It's over... No more bloodshed... Let the wolves fight over this from now on.

"How's Rusty?" Chub asked the man standing there as he rapidly stepped toward him.

"I'm Doctor Steinman. I was the lead surgeon working on Mr. Redtail. He's a tough one. Barring complications, he'll recover. It was close, though. Probably another ten or twenty minutes to get him to the paramedics and he'd not have made it. He'd lost more blood than most who survive something like this. He must have a strong will, as well as body. Really, there wasn't that much damage done to his body, he just lost way too much blood. We just need to keep an eye on him to make sure nothing was damaged from that. His actual wounds will heal quickly and almost completely. He's fortunate that way."

"Is he awake?" Chub asked. "Can we see him?"

"In about an hour," Dr. Steinman said. "I'll have someone let you know when that will be all right. I'll be here myself for that long anyway. Just sit tight for a little while longer."

When Dr. Steinman left, Chub called Liz, then Sally, giving each the good news. He put his phone in his pocket, then closed his eyes and tried to rest. Buddy did the same. Neither succeeded. When an hour had passed, Chub got up and walked back over to the window and looked out. He was there for about ten minutes when a female voice spoke.

"Excuse me. Are you men waiting to see Mr. Redtail? I'm the nurse in charge of the recovery wing today. You can talk to him for a few minutes now. Only a few, though. Follow me."

Chub and Buddy followed her back to an elevator, then up to the second floor. "How is he?" Chub asked the nurse.

"Far as I can tell, all signs are good," she said. "He was talking some and seemed to be normal for someone coming out of the effects of anesthesia."

She led them to a room midway back the hall to the right. "Remember, just a few minutes—like five, OK?"

Chub and Buddy walked into Rusty's room. Drain tubes ran into his shoulder and thigh, and monitoring connections ran from the machines to various parts of his body. He turned his head toward them, then smiled slightly.

"Guess you got my message," he said weakly.

"Yeah, but we were already on our way to find you," Chub said. "That was a fool thing you did, staying out there by yourself, knowing that someone else had been killed there only a few weeks ago."

"Had to," Rusty said.

"So you say," Buddy said. "I should have stayed with you. Sorry."

"So you could have gotten shot up too?" Rusty said.

"Your mother is on her way here," Chub said. "She should be here in about a couple of hours or so."

"Oh well, thanks, but it might have been better to have waited until I'm out of here. You know how mothers are."

"You don't know how bad you were," Buddy said. "If I was a priest, I'd have issued last rights."

"That bad, huh?"

"Doctor said another ten or twenty minutes and you might have been too-far bled out," Chub said. "The bleeding seemed to be the worst."

"You know who did this?" Buddy asked.

Rusty slowly nodded. "Almost sure. Just need a couple of answers from Liz on some requests I gave her. Well, a couple of other things, too."

"We talked to Liz," Chub said. "She's quite concerned. I'll call her when we leave here."

"When can I get out of here?" Rusty asked. "The funeral... I've got to get to that funeral tomorrow."

"You'd look mighty funny with all your tubes and wires at a funeral home. They just might keep you," Buddy said.

Chub's phone rang. He looked at it and picked up. It was Liz.

"Chub, you hear anything yet?" she asked.

"I'll let you talk to Rusty for a minute. Hold on." He handed Rusty his phone

"Liz—"

"Rusty Redtail—are you trying to scare me to death?" she asked. "Are you all right?"

"Be good as new. Real soon," Rusty said. "Stop worrying."

"Harland's in Washington," Liz said. "He called. I had to tell him about you."

"Yeah," Rusty said, "and he said he's going to replace me."

"Ahh..." Liz replied. "Yeah, as soon as he returns. That's to be the day after tomorrow."

"All right. I don't have my phone, so you can't get ahold of me directly to tell me I'm fired. Neither can Harland. Call Chub if you need to talk to me. Have you e-mailed me answers on all my stuff?"

"All twelve items," Liz said. "Some of that was way out there."

"Thanks," Rusty said. "You'll see how it all fits. Stall Harland as best as you can. I don't have my computer either. Even so, I'll have this wrapped up as soon as I get out of here. Oh, tell the lab to expect my Suburban to come in on a truck."

"Oh, Rusty," Liz said. "You've lost your phone and computer, and your Suburban is trashed too? Oh my, you are in trouble."

"Well, hopefully it's not burned up," Rusty said. "It might be salvageable. Get all the broken glass and blood out of it. Patch up the bullet holes. Who knows?"

"You're joking, right?" Liz asked. "No, you're not. Oh, Rusty."

"How much is a new Glock?" asked Rusty.

"Your gun too? Rusty, the paperwork connected with losing all this will take weeks," Liz said.

"Just e-mail all those last things to Chub—those answers to the twelve things," Rusty said. "If I need anything else, I'll have him call or e-mail you. Otherwise, I'll talk to you when I get out of here."

"Listen, Rusty Redtail," Liz said, "you do what the doctors tell you—you hear? You can't go out there in the wilds until you're better."

"I am better," Rusty said. "My holes are sewed up. My veins are full of fluid. I'm awake. Be out of here tomorrow."

"Rusty—"

"Goodbye, Liz," Rusty said, then handed the phone back to Chub, who then gave Liz his e-mail address. He then hung up and put the phone in his pocket.

"Nurse said five minutes," Buddy said. "We've been here over ten. We best let you get some rest."

As they turned to leave, Dr. Steinman walked in and looked at all the machines. "Doing well, Redtail. I wasn't sure for a while back there."

"Is there any permanent damage, doctor?" Chub asked.

"A few bone chips off the clavicle. Don't think they'll ever bother him. Bullet just caught the edge. Might need to remove them someday. The worst thing was the artery severed in the leg. Doing that vascular repair work is what took so long. Time will tell, but I think he'll have full blood flow through that. There was no major muscle or bone damage in the leg. We'll get you up and around, very cautiously, probably tomorrow."

"This is enough for now, guys," Dr. Steinman said.

"Yeah, we were just leaving when you came in," Buddy said. "His mother will be here in a while anyway."

"Later then, Rusty," Chub said. "I'll take Buddy back out to Magdalena and go out with Hector to get your Suburban out of there and to your lab. Anything else?"

"Have Manny move my stuff down to a ground-floor room and bring me in a change of clothes, boots too. Must have left mine at the well or somewhere. Oh, take some pictures of the Suburban as it sits now, OK?"

"See you later then," Chub said.

"Probably tomorrow," Buddy said as they walked out the door.

When they were gone, Rusty started on Dr. Steinman.

"I really need to go to a funeral tomorrow. Old Mose was like a second father to me. Besides, I need to get some good old tribal treatment. That'll fix me up quicker than whatever it is you're dripping in my veins now. We've got stuff that'll grow fur on a fish."

"You don't need fur and you're not a fish," Dr. Steinman said. "I'm giving you the best treatment I know how."

"I believe you, doctor," Rusty said. "The trouble is, you've been to medical school—I need to be treated by someone who's been to healing school."

"Get some rest," Dr. Steinman said, shaking his head. "I'll check on you later."

Early that evening, Chub came back to the hospital. Rusty had been moved to a regular room.

"How are you feeling?" Chub asked.

"The truth? Pretty punk. I think it's all this junk they're pumping into me."

"More like all the blood your heart pumped out of you," Chub said. "It just might take some time for your body to adapt to all that new blood, you know? Your own blood was healthy and unpolluted. Who knows what they put in you—junk from some wino who sold his booze-diluted fluid for another bottle."

"How long until my body replaces that with all new stuff?" Rusty asked.

"Ask the doctor or nurse, I guess," Chub said. "I didn't mean to bring up this much detail. By the way, did your mother make it?"

"Oh yeah," Rusty said. "Her sister came with her. They're off getting a room and something to eat. They'll be back a little later."

"Here's a copy of all that stuff from Liz," Chub said. "I couldn't help but read some of it as I made copies. Does all of that have anything to do with Jimmy? Now you?"

"Maybe," Rusty said. "Some of it anyway."

"Buddy and I went out with Hector" Chub said. "It looks like someone rummaged through your stuff. Buddy said a box of files was gone. There was no computer or phone there either."

"They're both locked," Rusty said. "They won't do anyone any good. They can't get any information off either one. I think I left my gun back at the well."

"We didn't see that either," Chub said as he put Rusty's fresh clothes into the tiny closet area of the room. "I gotta run," he said. "I guess your mother will be leaving in the morning to go to that funeral."

"It's not until the afternoon," Rusty said. "Guess she'll leave midmorning."

"I'll see you tomorrow," Chub said. "If you need anything, have someone call me."

Now alone and his mind clearing some, Rusty started thinking about what had happened to him. Had he really been that close to death? He remembered that he did have some strange things go through his mind for quite some time.

There must be things I'm still to do here, yet. Wrap up this case, first of all. Then, well, I'm not too sure about this FBI thing. Maybe there's something else for me.

The medication was wearing off, and Rusty's leg started burning as if a hot coal were pressed against it. His shoulder ached, and his arm was numb with tingling clear to his fingertips. Pushing his physical problems out of his mind, Rusty opened the folder Chub had brought him. Liz had found answers to everything he'd requested. Slowly, he read through each page. When he finished, he closed the file. It was all as he'd suspected.

Couple of more things. I should have them tomorrow. Then...

Rusty got little sleep that night, as the pain and discomfort woke him often. Then too, every hour a nurse came in to check on him. That didn't help. Soon after daylight, Dr. Steinman came in. "Fever's up," he said. "Almost 101, but that's not unexpected. You look good. Get any sleep?"

"A little," Rusty said.

"Don't expect to get a lot," the doctor said. "Nobody ever gets much sleep in here. I'll have your dressings changed. I don't see signs of much seepage, though. Need any pain meds?"

"I'm all right."

"Yeah, you'd probably rather bite on a stick than take a pill. They're approved on your chart. You want something, just let a nurse know."

Rusty nodded.

"Be back later," Dr. Steinman said as he turned and left.

About eight o'clock, Rusty's mother and aunt came in. "Oh, son, how are you?"

Rusty nodded, then answered. "Sure want to go with you. Mose meant so much to me."

"He knew that. He'd be the first to tell you to stay right where you are and get better. Don't be foolish."

Rusty didn't respond. His mother leaned down and put the back of her hand on his forehead. "Got you a fever. I could see it in your eyes," she said. "Let it burn out the infection. I'll be back tonight. Bring you what you need to fix you up right. Don't you worry none. By tomorrow we'll have you back on track, heading toward full recovery."

"Be careful," Rusty said. "It's a long way home."

"Got angels on the hood, you know that, Son," she said. "You had them with you too, or you'd be dead. You just get better so's you can go find who did this. We'll be back tonight."

A short time later, Chub came in. "I don't think I got anymore sleep last night than I figure you did. All I can think of is you in here, how everything yesterday was terrifying, and how you have to wrap this case up. How can I help you? What can I do?"

"You want to help?" Rusty asked. "Good. Hand me that pad in your pocket, your pen too."

Chub took out his pad and pen, then handed them to Rusty. "I'll see if Buddy can help me," Chub said.

"That would be best," Rusty said. "Someone else, anyone, but you shouldn't be out there alone." Rusty wrote a list of things for Chub to do, then handed the pad and pen back to him. Chub read the list.

"Let me get this straight," Chub said. "You want me to look around the intersection with this tree in it to try and find a bullet? It'll just be laying on the ground?"

"I believe that's where my gas tank was shot through," Rusty said. "The tank is poly, so it wouldn't distort the bullet much, then going through all that fuel in a flat tank, it would really slow the bullet down to where it might have come out with very little energy and just dropped to the ground somewhere."

"I'll have to say, your body might be damaged, but your imagination isn't," Chub said. "I'll look, but—"

"Actually, it still might be in the tank," Rusty said. "If you don't find it, have Liz check with the lab to see if they found it."

"Yeah, OK," Chub said. "So, next is to look back the trail from there to the well for a fired shell casing. A 44 Magnum? I thought we were looking for a 45-70, or maybe a 444 Marlin."

"That's what I thought at first," Rusty said. "Now I'm sure it was a 44 Magnum, fired from a rifle, that was shooting at me yesterday. That's a distinctive sound that I'm familiar with."

"If you say so," Chub said, then again looked at Rusty's list. "Then I'm to go see Shorty Walker in Pie Town. Yeah, I know him. He does reload for a bunch of guys out there. Putting this together, finding what you want, all these pieces, you're looking for a miracle."

"I believe in miracles," Rusty said. "Sometimes we don't see them because we're not looking for them or fail to facilitate their happening. We step right over them, too busy doing the traditionally accepted thing to receive the supernatural."

Chub had no response, but kept looking at the list. "Then see Toby Wilson. OK, I can do all of this. Anything else?"

"If you find a shell casing, and Shorty has any empties, someone will have to get them to our lab," Rusty said.

"I guess that would be me too," Chub said.

"That's what I figure," Rusty said. "Probably not until tomorrow, though."

Chub looked over the list again, then put it in his pocket. "Better get going."

"Find someone to go with you," Rusty said. "Keep your eyes and ears tuned for trouble. The first hint of anything, get out of there, understand?"

"You bet. Later then," Chub said as he turned for the door.

An aide carrying a tray knocked on Rusty's doorjamb. "Breakfast, Mr. Redtail," she said as she walked in and put the tray on the stand, then rolled it over to Rusty. "Want to sit up a little straighter?"

"Yeah, a little," Rusty said. "I'm not really very hungry."

"Good," she said. "Then you won't be too disappointed with what they call food around here."

Chub and Buddy drove back to where they'd found Rusty yesterday. They stopped for a minute, but didn't get out. Hector had removed the Suburban, and there was nothing left but a bunch of tire tracks and mangled brush to indicate that anything had happened here.

They went on back to the intersection with the tree growing in it, where the road took off southerly towards the well. Chub parked his pickup, then got out. "This is where Rusty thinks his tank was shot," he said. "He thinks there's a possibility the slug went through the tank and the fuel slowed it down enough that it came out and just dropped to the ground."

"Possibility, I guess," Buddy said. "He was shot from behind—from back this road toward the well. So, any slug like that would be down around the tree or in front of it."

Both men looked for quite a while, but found nothing. "Let's walk back up here and look for a shell casing," Chub said. "A 44 Magnum, Rusty says. Fired from a rifle, no less."

"I think he was dreaming," Buddy said. "That's so odd for anyone to use something like that. There's only been a couple of rifles ever chambered for the 44 Magnum and very few of them sold."

Fifty yards from the tree, they found a piece of a broken mirror mostly buried in the sand. "This must be where Rusty had rammed into the ATV," Chub said. "I'll take this to the lab if I go there in the morning. I'll bet there's paint from that ATV on the bumper of Rusty's Suburban. The lab should be able to identify what type it is from that and this mirror too."

"Somebody's shaking in their boots, I'd say," Buddy said. "There's got to be some evidence here implicating someone. Especially if we can find a casing."

"Let's drive back this road, looking for glass or some other sign of where Rusty was shot at," Chub said. "We'll look for casings around there."

At the third place they stopped, Buddy walked up ahead for quite a ways. There it was: an empty shell casing, partially buried in the sand. "Hey, Chub," he yelled. "I've got one." He bent over and picked it up. "Know what? It's a 44 Magnum."

Chub put it into a baggy, then started the truck. "How far from here is it back to that Eagle Well?"

"Probably twenty minutes," Buddy said.

"I'm this close—I'm going to see that thing," Chub said. He drove on back to the well and parked where Rusty had. They then both got out and walked over to the now-uncovered wellhead.

"Wow," Buddy said. "What has someone done? That's concrete down there. Look, it's all collapsed, burned too."

"This gets weirder all the time," Chub said. "There's nothing left here." They stood silently for a minute, then Chub spoke. "Let's get out of here. This is creepy. I feel like someone's watching us, right now."

Later that afternoon they met up with Shorty Walker out at the Pie Town Café.

"Heard about that FBI fella gettin' all shot up," Shorty said. "How's he doing?"

"He'll make it," Chub answered. "Mostly flesh wounds. He lost a lot of blood. That was the worst of it."

"Seemed like a right nice fella when I met him," Shorty said.

"They don't come much better," Chub said.

"I brought you an empty case from all the 44 Magnums that I load. Had to pull out one of the bullets, but this is one for everybody—all three," Shorty said. "Their names are on the bags. Don't do much of them these days. Nobody uses them anymore over at the club. All I ever load for these now are either 240-grain hollow points or a few half-jacketed. Did some bigger bullets, once, for a fella. Ain't seen him for years. Moved, I 'spect." Shorty handed Chub a small paper bag that had three casings in individual baggies with names on them. "Paper in there too, where I wrote down everyone I know hereabouts who has a 44 Magnum. Some fellas load their own or just buy them factory loads from the store or Internet now."

"I'll take all this to the lab in Albuquerque," Chub said. "We'll see what they come up with. They'll look at firing pin and ejector marks or anything else that matches up with the one we found."

"Hope this helps," Shorty said. "Gotta go be with Mary Jane. She was afraid of things before. Now with this second shooting…"

"Thanks, Shorty," Buddy said. Chub nodded, but said nothing as his mouth was full of apple pie.

About an hour later, Chub and Buddy met with Toby Wilson at the café in Magdalena.

"How's that young fella doing?" Toby asked. "He gonna get back out here and solve this before anyone else gets themselves shot up or killed? This kind of craziness always gives us gun owners a bad name. Gotta get this nut before anything more happens, I tell you."

"Rusty will be fine, in time," Chub said. "It's just going to take time."

"You fellas go back out in that area?" Toby asked.

"Yeah," Buddy said. "No more, though. Not until the killer is locked up."

"Don't blame you," Toby said. "Here's that list you asked for—all the gun types and aliases used since the club started. I marked the ones who are still active and the ones who've died or moved. The others are still around, but not active. Hope this helps."

"So do I," Chub said. "Rusty wants it. I don't know what for. He's working some angle. We're just being his legs out here."

"You see him, you tell him we're all pullin' for him," Toby said.

Later that evening, Chub walked back the hall to Rusty's room. He stepped to the doorway and looked in. Rusty looked over at him, then gave a half-smile.

"Thought maybe you'd be sleeping," Chub said.

"Too much on my mind to let it slow down," Rusty said.

"You're in a hospital," Chub said. "You're to be resting. Sleep helps restore the body."

"But it doesn't solve crimes," Rusty said. "You come up with anything?"

"Couldn't find a bullet by the tree," Chub said. "Like you said, it might still be in the gas tank. We did find an empty shell casing. You were right—it's a 44 Magnum. We met Shorty and got three empty shell-casing samples that I'll take to the lab tomorrow morning. He gave me a list of everyone he knows who has a 44 Magnum out there. Here's your alias list from Toby," he said, handing Rusty the list. "Both of them wish you well, as does everyone else I talk to."

"Thanks a lot," Rusty said. "When you take this to the lab in the morning, call Liz and have her lean on them for the results, immediately. Since it involves one of our own, they'll do it. Oh, have her get my phone numbers down from the cloud onto some phone or her computer, anything. She'll know what to do. Have her e-mail you a copy of my numbers for me."

Rusty opened the list from Toby and ran his finger down it. Halfway down, he stopped. "Just what I thought," he said.

"But you're still not going to tell me, right?" Chub said.

"Day after tomorrow—I think," Rusty said. "Yeah, I think so. Get me that casing comparison data, then set up a coming-out party for me at the café. Ten in the morning—the day after tomorrow."

"What if the doctor says no?" Chub asked.

"Then I'll arrest him for obstruction of justice," Rusty said. "Throw him in jail. Who's to stop me then?"

"You'd do that too," Chub said. "Who do I invite?"

"Everyone. Anyone who's had anything to do with this. Tell them it's important. Oh, my wallet is in that dresser drawer over there," Rusty said, pointing to a drawer by the bathroom. "I have some business cards in it of people I personally want to invite. Oh, take my credit card and go over to Walmart and get me a prepaid disposable phone. Just a couple of hours, whatever the minimum is. I'll make some calls too."

"You won't tell me who you're going to call, right?" Chub asked.

"Oh, just say the wolf among us," Rusty said, then he smiled at Chub. "Those too, who'll want to see who, what, and why."

"I won't sleep for another night now," Chub said.

"Just get me those lab results tomorrow, please," Rusty said. "Or maybe…"

"You still don't really have proof, do you?"

"Tell Liz that I need the results by the time you get back here. Then come here, and we'll call her."

The next morning when Dr. Steinman made his rounds, Rusty told him he planned to check out early the morning. "Wish you'd stay another day or two," he said. "Let those wounds heal up a little more. But your fever's down. No signs of infection. I know your mother brought you some potion, or who knows what, from over on the reservation. Maybe that's helping—in your mind anyway. Be careful, please. Don't put any strain on that leg, like driving or climbing stairs. Don't twist that shoulder either. Any signs of internal bleeding or anything, you get right back in here, understand?"

"I'll be careful," Rusty said.

"Well, rest up today then," the doctor said. "I'll see you later."

Chub came into Rusty's room right after lunch. "I'm to call Liz and let her talk to you. She said you're officially off the case, but she'll not tell you that—for another day."

Chub called Liz, then handed the phone to Rusty.

"Liz," Rusty said.

"Rusty, you all right?" she asked. "Hurting badly?"

"Getting out tomorrow," Rusty said.

"Your idea or the doctor's?" she asked.

"Oh—we agreed on it," Rusty said.

"You talked him into it," Liz said. "Oh, Rusty. Be careful."

"The lab report on the shell casings?" he asked.

"They found a match," she said. "It was very distinctive."

"Not just pin and extractor marks, but action marks too," Rusty said. "They'd been run through a lever-action rifle."

"How'd you know?" Liz asked.

"It had to be. I just needed to have official confirmation."

"Oh, and they did find a fired bullet in your fuel tank," Liz said.

"I'll have this wrapped up tomorrow," Rusty said. "I need two agents to be in the rear parking lot of the Trails End Café in Magdalena at ten tomorrow morning. Oh, a new phone and computer would be nice too."

"You think I can pull that off, now?" Liz asked.

"You've done bigger and braver things that that," Rusty said. "I didn't even ask for a new gun or car."

"Rusty Redtail, you're impossible."

"Difficult, maybe, but not impossible," Rusty said. "Later, Liz."

"Wait!" Liz said. "I didn't even tell you who the match on the casings was."

"You don't have to," Rusty said.

"I used up all my favors at the lab for a year probably, to get you the results, and you don't even want to know who the match is? If I could get my hands on you, hospital bed or not, I'd... I'd... Oh, you're impossible."

"I already know now. There can only be one match," Rusty said.

Rusty ended the call, then handed the phone back to Chub. "You know who?" Chub asked.

"We have all the pieces now. Enough anyway," Rusty said.

"Anything I can do?" Chub asked.

"Just work with Manny and whoever to get all the players there in the morning," Rusty said. "Then go home and get some sleep. Pick me up at nine in the morning. Oh, and thanks for all your help. There's no way I could have gotten all this set up without everything you've done."

"For Jimmy," Chub said. "I'm doing it mostly for Jimmy."

➤— CHAPTER 20 —≪

The next morning, Chub drove his truck into the parking lot of the café in Magdalena. The lot was mostly full of pickups, with a few cars also. Manny had saved a space by the door for Chub and Rusty. He stood at the doorway, waiting for them.

"You ready for this?" Chub asked Rusty, who sat staring down at the floor.

"Gotta get it over with," Rusty said out loud, but in his heart he silently pleaded, *God… This is hard. Why did any of this have to happen? All this killing… Franz Frick in 1897… Maxwell Wolf's apparent suicide in 1930… Pricilla Miller in 1930… Frederick Wolf in 1955, with the ruining of Sheriff Bucky Tuttle's life then, his son's too… And now, Jimmy Hanson… So much blood and destruction. Over what? Greed, power, lust, self-centeredness, pride… Nothing of real importance.*

Rusty opened his door and with Chub's help, slid his good right leg to the ground. He held onto Chub's shoulder and hobbled over to Manny, who held the door open.

"Señor Rusty, we are so happy to see you," Manny said. "We worry so much." His mother, Yolanda, stood inside the door, tears on her cheeks.

"Thank you, Manny," Rusty said. "This has become like a home to me out here. You've been very kind and helpful." Manny had a chair set only a few steps inside the door for Rusty to sit on. He sat down slowly, then looked around

"Hey, Chief," Sheriff Cutter said. "You're looking a mite pale. Must be that paleface blood they filled you up with, no doubt."

Rusty didn't respond but continued to look around the room. It seemed as if most everyone he'd met out here was in the little dining room. Many stood up against the walls. Even Sally Hanson had come up from Socorro. There were no reporters from Albuquerque, not even the one from Channel 12, Wally Whiteside, who'd talked to Rusty in Socorro, though Rusty had called him. They all knew they'd get briefed at a news conference in Albuquerque later.

He took a sip of the coffee Manny had given him, then set the cup down. "You don't know how good it is to be here and see all of you," Rusty said. "This is a place I'll never forget. All things considered, these last few weeks here have been rewarding. You've made me feel like one of you. I came out here to find out what happened to Jimmy Hanson. I know he too felt at home here. What happened to him was a major blow to your community. It was something that shouldn't have happened. Fear, distrust, and anger upset the tranquility you usually enjoy here."

Rusty paused a moment. He looked across the room again, then continued. "It's important to solve things like this. If not, it goes on and on—as was the case here. You all know something about the events of 1897 here. Well, I've pretty well solved that, finally. But that led to events in 1930. Few of you even know that another unsolved murder most likely happened here back then. The unsolved events of 1955 with Frederick Wolf and Sheriff Bucky Tuttle, yeah, I've also solved most of that, too. All of this laid the foundation for what happened to Jimmy

Hanson. He was turning over rocks and finding things. Actually, he was opening old things that contained old family secrets—haunting, embarrassing secrets, incriminating even. So he was stopped from learning the truth that would bring embarrassment, and maybe even legal action.

"So too, it was with me," Rusty continued. "I also entered into the area that some considered forbidden truths. Truths about things that never should have happened, or once they had, should have been solved and justice served. If the 1897 murder and robbery would have been solved and justice done, none of the others would have happened, because they were all a follow-up to it—even now, nearly a hundred twenty years later."

Rusty paused again. He took another deep breath, then went on. "Two things are common in all of this. There's the Eagle Well and the Wolf family. The Eagle Well is truly legend-like, almost mystical, in local lore. Many don't believe it's real. It is. I've been there. I almost didn't leave there alive, but I've been there. It's nothing now—empty, almost, of those old things. All the money and family secrets are gone.

"Family secrets," Rusty continued. "The Wolf family secrets. They also are no more—so most believe. Frederick left here mysteriously in 1955 with his wife, Betty Ann, and little daughter, Debby. Frederick died shortly afterward from a gunshot fired by Sheriff Tuttle at the Eagle Well. Betty Ann died fifteen years later from a bad heart. Debby developed terminal cancer while at Baylor University and died shortly after her mother—so everyone thought. But the records at Baylor show that two years after she dropped out, she reenrolled and finished her studies. She used a different name then. Oh, she never was registered by the name of Wolf. No, the family had taken on the name of Weston when they moved to Fort Davis, Texas. But by the time she'd returned to Baylor, Debby had married and so used an even different last name, first name then also.

"The old property out here, the Wolf ranch, it was sold, sort of, from Wolf to Weston. A straw transaction only. That little girl who left here as a preschooler with tears in her eyes and her puppy on her lap in the backseat of the family car, she secretly returned several times. She wanted to keep the family secrets hidden and, of course, there was that cache of eagle coins in the Eagle Well. Added to the stash of stolen money in the well were incriminating documents. Documents that had meaning to only the family, but could cause them dire consequences and extreme embarrassment. Exposure would rewrite local history.

"I only investigated this from the angle of solving Jimmy Hanson's murder," Rusty said. "I do believe, though, that there are other crimes, probably numerous and serious, that the Eagle Well held clues to or proof of. Those will probably now be forever history, forever unsolved—some even unknown."

Rusty paused. He looked across the room at the confused and inquisitive expressions on most of the faces staring at him.

"I've said enough." Rusty paused, then took a deep breath. "Dee Cutter, you're that little girl, Debby Wolf. You're under arrest for the murder of Ranger Jimmy Hanson and the attempted murder of an FBI agent, me."

Sheriff Cutter jumped up. "You're crazy. You have no proof. This is insane, all made up. Who are you to come in here and make up a story like this?"

"Proof, Sheriff?" Rusty said. "I have tons of proof. It took me a long time to put all of this together. I didn't want this to be true, so I chased after a dozen other suspects. Things always ended up pointing back here."

"Conjecture," Dee Cutter said. "All you've spewed out is conjecture."

"It started the first night I met you, Dee," Rusty said. "Right here in this café. You had on a very distinctive perfume—expensive, no doubt. I left here and went to my room. Someone had been there and gone through my things. There, lingering in the room, was a hint of your perfume. Right then I knew there was something not forthcoming about you.

"In Fort Davis," Rusty continued, "I talked to your old friend, Hazel Dodds. She goes by McCoy now. You remember her? You confided in her. You told her everything. Even about going to New Mexico and having to climb down into a well and retrieve gold coins. Jeb Hite, your mother's friend, he will tell the same story. He was with you, twice, remember?"

Rusty paused for a minute, then continued. "Your grandmother was Margareta Houser. Yolanda Rodriguez will tell how she had several prized paintings she wouldn't sell. One was of the stockyards here with cattle being loaded onto a train. She wouldn't sell it, but she did will it to her granddaughter. It now hangs on the wall in your husband's office.

"You did a good job of cleaning up after trying to kill me," Rusty continued. "I'm told you really did a good job of destroying the old well. However, you missed one empty shell casing. When I met Shorty Walker in Pie Town, he gave your husband a box containing reloaded ammunition. The large bag in that box was marked '38 Cowboy.' Those were for your husband's cowboy action shooting. However, there was a small bag of 44 Magnum hollow-point bullets. The box of empty shell cases your husband gave Shorty to load also had a baggy of empty 44 Magnum cases.

"I had the two cases compared, the one found where you shot at me and one of the ones your husband gave to Shorty to be reloaded," Rusty continued. "The firing pin, chamber, and action marks are a match. They were used in the same gun—a Marlin lever-action rifle. When you were active in the cowboy shooting, you shot a 44 Magnum Ruger handgun and that Marlin rifle, which you nicknamed 'Miss Maggie' and the fact is, your official, registered alias with the group is 'Madam Maggie.' Our lab has a bullet recovered from my fuel tank, a 44-caliber

240-grain hollow point of the same manufacturer that Shorty loads for you. I'm sure it will match up to the rifling grooves of your rifle.

"At the scene of Jimmy's truck fire, Hector found a piece of paper with a list of dates and abbreviations on it," Rusty went on. "Those were rodeo cities and dates. We checked those cities and found five where you have gone for the last several years. In each we found a coin dealer who will testify that a lady fitting your description has sold them 1897 gold eagle coins each year when the rodeo is in town. I contacted the dealer you've sold coins to in Las Vegas, and he told me you called him recently to see if he would be interested in twenty more of those same coins. I assume that is the last of them. We'll find them somewhere hidden out at your ranch, probably in your husband's floor safe, when we search for them.

"The paint chips on the rear of my Suburban where I smashed into an ATV match the make and model of yours, and when we find it, I'm sure the piece of broken mirror we have from the scene will match too. That bandage around your wrist is surely for an injury from being slammed into by my Suburban. A medical exam will probably show other bruises and abrasions from that also," Rusty said, then paused a second. "Should I go on?"

"I had nothing to do with shooting you or Jimmy Hanson," Sheriff Cutter blurted out.

"Shut up, Wesley," Dee Cutter said, poking her husband with her elbow.

"Maybe you didn't pull the trigger," Rusty said, "but you did cover all of this up. You tried to steer me to accuse either the Calderone or Atwood families. You certainly lied to a federal officer. For that, you're being charged with obstruction of justice, for starters. More to come later."

"This will never hold up in court," Dee Cutter said. "My attorney will make a fool out of you."

Rusty looked up at two men who'd quietly come in the back door and now stood in the kitchen. He nodded to them.

"Dee, Wesley, stand up, please," Rusty said. "Sheriff, please slowly place your weapon on the table in front of you. The two men behind you are my fellow agents. Those bulges under the left side of their coats aren't from big hearts, just large handguns. Don't try anything stupid."

"This is all stupid," Sheriff Cutter said. "I'm the sheriff here. I have been for twelve years. Nobody believes this. Look around. No one believes you. You come out here and spew out a wild story—"

"Just put your hands behind you. You know the drill," Rusty said. "Agents Martin and Hooks will read you your rights on the way to Albuquerque."

"My bulls," Sheriff Cutter said. "I have to take care of my bulls."

"We'll have your hired hands take good care of them," Rusty said. "They'll be fine. They'll probably sleep better than you will tonight."

The two agents handcuffed Wesley and Dee Cutter, then led them toward the back door of the café.

"Don't believe this," Sheriff Cutter yelled over his shoulder, back into the crowded room. "I'm your sheriff. This is all a big story."

Dee walked silently, her head lowered, making no eye contact. When they were gone, the room was silent. It seemed no one wanted to be the first to speak, so Rusty did. "I'm sorry if I treated any of you as a suspect or something like that. I didn't want this to be anyone out here. I know this is a total shock that will rock your little community, maybe even more than what happened to Jimmy. You're a strong bunch of people. Maybe now that these old mysteries are put to bed, old feuds can be also. Forget what someone's grandfather may have done. Rise above that."

Rusty looked across the room, then slowly nodded. "That's all I have to say, but I'll answer any questions."

"Thank you, Rusty Redtail. Thank you so much." It was Sally Hanson, sitting way in the back. "You put your life on the line, almost lost it, to get to the bottom of this. Now I can go on."

"I'll call you and come see you, Sally," Rusty said. "I want to talk to little Jimmy."

"That will be important to him," she said.

"I can't get my head around this," Chub said. "How did you ever put all of this together?"

"Things just kept pointing back here, but made no sense until I went to Fort Davis. Then once my hunch of Debby Wolf being alive proved true, it all started falling into place. Still, other suspects kept popping up, but always fizzled. The Eagle Well was always associated with the Wolfs—right to its end. Debby will spend the rest of her life in prison. She survived her cancer, but it left her unable to have children, so she's the last Wolf. Unfortunately, she's paying for the deeds of her father and grandfather who started, and perpetuated, this dynasty of corruption."

"Are you going to tell everything you learned?" Buddy Bell asked.

"No," Rusty said. "Some things would really hurt some people now. There'd be nothing gained by that. No, buried with the Eagle Well are a lot of old secrets. That's good. It's time to forget all of that and move forward."

Rusty looked up and noticed Charlie Tuttle staring at him. He figured Charlie wanted to talk.

"Excuse me a minute," Rusty said. "I'd like to talk to Charlie privately, please." He motioned for Charlie to come to him as the others stepped away a few feet and started talking amongst each other.

"Charlie," Rusty said quietly once he'd reached him. "I have your shirt. I'll bring it out to you, once I recover some."

Charlie nodded. "OK, thanks. That's not real important. I knew you'd figure all this out. I just couldn't tell you."

"I know. Hey, I was wondering, this might be important," Rusty said. "Would you like to go over to the Eagle Well and put up some kind of a monument for your father there?"

Charlie's eyes lit up. "Yeah, I'd like that. Me and you, Duke maybe too, OK? We could do that?"

"When I get healed up some," Rusty said.

"Yeah," Charlie said. "Me and you could talk some too. Gotta go now. Too many people in here. Came in with Duke. He's waiting for me."

Charlie left, and Manny came over to Rusty. "Señor Rusty, what are you going to do now?"

"Hide out here for a few days," Rusty said. "Let my boss get over my destroying a new Suburban, losing my laptop, phone, and gun. He might never get over all of that, really. I'll probably spend the rest of my FBI life on desk duty."

"Whatever you need," Manny said. "Someone here will help you. We feel safe now for the first time since what happened to Jimmy."

Rusty nodded. Most of the people had now left the café. Some had mumbled "Thanks" or something similar as they walked by.

"Tell you what," Rusty said. "I'm really exhausted. A cup of coffee to go and someone to help me find my new room would be great. We can talk more later. Besides, those guys left me a new cell phone and computer in your kitchen—compliments of my assistant, Liz, for sure. I have a report to file on this. There's a one o'clock news conference scheduled by my boss. All the Albuquerque stations should carry it. I need to get my office all this information right now."

"A news conference without you?" Buddy asked. "How can they do that?"

"Watch it and see," Rusty said. "The bureau can do wonders with the press."

≫———≪

Shortly before the news conference time, a handful of people gathered in the hotel lobby to watch the TV there. When the conference started, there at the microphone stood Special Agent Carter. Behind him stood a line of six black-suited, stiff-looking men—obviously FBI agents.

"Good afternoon. I'm Special Agent Harland Carter, in charge of this Albuquerque office. Today I'm here to announce that my office has made two arrests in the brutal murder last month of BLM Ranger James Hanson, down in San Agustin County. This was a very difficult case. We pursued leads and suspects from Arizona to Oklahoma to Texas. But in the end, by delving into several old, unsolved murders and other well-kept secrets of the past down there, we were able to build a rock-solid case against the local county sheriff, Wesley Cutter, and his wife, Dee Cutter, as the guilty parties. They are also charged with attempted murder for the wounding of one of my agents in an altercation, destruction of federal property, and various other charges including obstruction.

"Mrs. Cutter is a member of the old family there who are now implicated in many of the previously unsolved events as far back as 1897. This is a major breakthrough for this remote area. The Cutters are well known in the professional rodeo circuit, raising some of the country's best bucking bulls, I've been told.

"Bail has been set at one million dollars each. This case is one of the most complicated and difficult that I have ever solved. I thank my agents and staff for the help they gave me. As I develop more on this story, my staff will keep you informed. I thank you for your attendance."

Harland then turned and walked off the stage, the other agents following him. The TV reporter started in on his analysis.

"That's it?" Chub said. "Not even a mention of Rusty's name? Wounded in an altercation? Who is this guy?

"It's called being the boss," Rusty said. "If he lauded me now, he'd have a tougher time reprimanding and disciplining me later."

"That stinks," Buddy said. "He fought you every step of the way."

Twenty minutes later, back in his room, Rusty stretched out on the bed. His phone rang. "Liz, hi," Rusty said. "Thanks for getting me the phone and computer. I'm sure that was your doing."

"Did you see it?" she asked, ignoring Rusty's last comment. "How could he get up there and do that?"

"That's why he's the boss," Rusty said. "Give the press what they want. Besides, I'm down here. He wasn't coming down here. No one would have covered it. He couldn't tell them that one lone rookie agent who was nearly killed over this solved this by himself—with your help, of course—all while he sat in his office pushing paper."

"How can you be so nonchalant?" Liz asked. "You deserve more."

"These people here appreciate me," Rusty said. "That means a whole lot more than a bunch of reporters. I'm going to see Sally Hanson, little Jimmy too. That they now have some peace and satisfaction makes this all worthwhile."

"So, when are you coming in to Albuquerque?" asked Liz.

"Probably not for a few days. Not in any hurry to get in the office. I'm at the mercy of someone to transport me. Chub will do that, I'm sure. However, he's been out working for me a lot, and I'm sure he's backed up on his work. If Harland wants me in his office, I guess he can send someone to get me."

"You going out to celebrate?" Liz asked.

"Hadn't thought about that," Rusty said. "Maybe I'll go to Pie Town and have a piece of strawberry-rhubarb pie."

"Maybe even splurge and have ice cream on it?" Liz said. "Really, Rusty. Is that the best you can think of? You have to tell me all about everything. How all that crazy stuff you had me do fits into solving this. I've kept a list."

"Yeah, all right, you deserve to know, I guess," Rusty said. "I couldn't have solved this without you getting me all that information you did. Tell you what—I'll kill two birds with one stone. I'll celebrate and tell you all about things at the same time. I'll take you to dinner. We can cover all of this then."

"Dinner? You and me? I remember the last time you mentioned dinner."

"No, really," Rusty said. "You pick it. Any restaurant in Albuquerque. Someplace quiet, where we can talk about the case."

"Am I hearing you right?" Liz asked.

"Well, don't make it more than it is," Rusty said. "Two employees discussing business and celebrating."

"Of course," Liz said. "Dinner and a briefing."

"Something like that. Unless you don't want to."

"Rusty Redtail, you're impossible," Liz said. "For a moment I thought maybe all that new blood they gave you changed your calloused heart. All business, all the time. Well, call me when you get to town. We'll have our briefing, but it'll cost you."

"OK," Rusty said. "I've gotta go now. I have to call a couple of sheriffs, an attorney, my mother, and some others, after I take a nap."

That night as Rusty ate dinner in the café, Buddy came in and sat at his table.

"What are you going to do now?" Rusty asked.

"Been thinking a lot ever since we had that talk out there. I called an old friend. He's got a big church over by Tucson. He needs a staff member to help with the seniors. That's right up my alley. Before I make any career decisions, though, I think I'll just go off alone, me and God. Get all of that worked out first. Then I think things will be clearer. Your coming here just might have been the most important thing to ever happen to me."

Rusty slowly nodded. "Stay in touch, all right? I want to know where things take you. I think you're going to be surprised."

Manny brought out a big bowl of posole and set it in front of Rusty. "From Mother," he said. "She says it will help you heal quicker."

"She's right, I'm sure," Rusty said. "Tell her thanks. I'll never forget her posole. You've been awfully good to me, Manny. I appreciate everything very much."

"Only you could have solved this awful thing," Manny said. "None of us would ever have figured it out. Now, it is so clear. We owe you much."

"Some good will come of this, I'm sure," Rusty said.

"That I hope," Manny said. "Maybe so. I did see Andy Atwood and Lonny Calderone talking in the parking lot when they left here. Now, that would be a good thing."

»———«

Two days later, Chub dropped Rusty off at Sally Hanson's while he went to his office for a few minutes. Rusty knocked on the front door.

"Come in, Rusty," Sally said. "I'm so glad you came."

"It's the least I can do. Solving this hasn't given you much peace, I'm sure."

"It still seems so meaningless," Sally said. "Jimmy was killed for what? To keep hidden some old family secrets?"

"Pride," Rusty said. "She wasn't even using the family name, no one knew who she was, yet there was that pride in the Wolf heritage, tainted though it was. That's all I see. There could be more, but I'm no shrink."

"I guess I'll let this go in time," Sally said. "I still look at little Jimmy and—"

At that, little Jimmy came out of his playroom and ran to his mother. He then slowly walked over and looked up at Rusty. "You found the bad people who hurt my daddy, Mommy told me."

"Yes," Rusty said. "They won't hurt anyone else, not anymore."

"My daddy's not coming back now, is he?"

"No… That can't happen. Don't ever forget about your daddy. Remember going places with him, all the things you did together. He loved you very much."

"That's what Mommy says. She misses him a big bunch."

"I'm sure," Rusty said.

"When I grow up, I wanna be like you, Mr. Rusty. I wanna catch bad people who hurt little kids' mommies. Gonna put all the bad people in jail. You should be on TV, Mr. Rusty. You'd be a real-good superhero. Yup, when I grow up, I wanna be a superhero, just like you."

CPSIA information can be obtained
at www.ICGtesting.com
Printed in the USA
BVOW11s2226190217
476598BV00002B/103/P